Silver Rogue

EBONY OLSON

EBANDMUSE
PUBLICATIONS

EBANDMUSE
PUBLICATIONS

Published 2020

Published by

EbandMuse Publications

Sydney, Australia

Cover by Strange Angel Designs

http://ebonyolson.com/

alking into the wedding chapel, my was stride purposeful, knowing I was cutting it fine. My name was murmured in greeting, heads bowing in respect like a Mexican wave through the renovated seating. No wooden pews in this upmarket venue. Marching straight to the front, I met the eyes of the groom and his brother as they turned to acknowledge me. "Alpha, thank you for coming." Dante, my beta, and the groom today, smiled and pulled me into a hug.

"Drop the Alpha crap, there are humans present," I muttered. "Sorry, I'm late. Business as usual."

Dante smiled. "There's a reason you're not in the wedding party."

"That and the groom is meant to be the star of the show. That's why Milton's ugly mug was perfect for the best man," I teased, smacking his brother's shoulder in jest.

Milton was one of my deltas, and anything but ugly if his conquests were anything to go by. Rolling his eyes, Milton grinned. "The best man gets the pick of the best tail, Knox, and you should see the bride's younger sister. You are so going to regret missing the rehearsal dinner last night."

"I was busy being an alpha. Plus, I don't go in for all this hoopla. When I wanted our pack to move with the times, and to become educated, I didn't intend on church weddings," I grumbled, looking around the renovated church.

"Evaline and I both made friends at college. This is how the humans recognize our union," Dante defended for the fifth time.

"All this expense for a man to take his mate. This is where the old way of marking them and mounting them makes more sense."

"Our modern alpha, sprucing the old ways as best?" Dante jested. "Next, you'll tell my wife her place is in the kitchen, bare pawed and heavy with cub."

The image made me smirk. "Evaline is the daughter of an alpha. She already knows her place."

Both Dante and Milton's mouths fell open, then they burst out laughing. When Dante met Evaline, I'd been told that Alpha Stirling had three headstrong daughters, one of whom left the packhouse to make something of herself in the human world, without a man. The scandal that must have caused in an old-style pack like the Beachrunners, I could only imagine. Even in the Valleymorgans pack, I'd only enabled the women so much independence. In a race where women were in high demand, running off to pursue a career was just not allowed. Especially, fertile women who came from a line of alphas, like Evaline and her sisters.

Sobering, Dante lowered his voice. "I heard our stray she-wolves appeared again?"

The reason I was late. If it wasn't for Dante's wedding, he'd have been investigating it all night with me. "A body was found not far from the base. We're not sure if he was just unlucky enough to cross them on a run, or if they hunted him down. Either way, I'd say there are three of them that tore him apart."

"Three?" Milton's eyes went wide. "We've only seen evidence of two before now."

My concern exactly. Each kill, there was a new female's scent on the body. They were gathering numbers, which made them more deadly. "It's been three years since the first stray turned up with the she-wolf's scent on him. They've only killed a handful of times. I'm starting to think we have a wolf recruiting stray she-wolves. He could be offering them protection and letting them deal with strays that enter his new territory."

Milton lifted a brow. "Creating himself a new pack and harem at the same time."

"Either way, they are killing in our territory on occasion," I grumbled. "I don't care if they are taking out stray wolves, but what if they go after one of ours? And why haven't we found them yet?"

"Good morning," a man's voice interrupted to my left. We all turned to see the middle-aged wolf and bowed our heads in respect. "Knox," he greeted, offering his hand.

The alpha of the Beachrunners was a solid man, in his fifties, the silver at his temples spreading further into his short red hair than the last time we met. Taking his hand, I gave it a firm shake. "Stirling. I apologize for not making dinner last night."

"And so you should. If I had to sit through this youthful nonsense, you, as an advocate of modernism, should too." A smile tempted the side of his mouth. "At least, I managed to escape walking Evaline down the aisle."

"How did you manage to escape that?" I liked Alpha Stirling. We'd only met a handful of times, but he was a sincere man. "I was under the understanding that you were wrapped around your daughters' fingers?"

Stirling chuckled. "Since the day they were born. I remember being so proud of their fierce determination, then Evaline turned fourteen, and I realized how mistaken I'd been. I tried to remedy the error of my ways with the younger two. Rhiannon likes tradition, but she wants freedom too. Anique..." Stirling shook his head. "She is worse than the other two combined." Stirling looked around, then to Dante. "Have you seen Anique? Her mother is fretting."

Dante frowned. "She isn't with Evaline?"

Stirling shook his head. "She is not in the bridal party, so no one bothered to worry until now. Rhiannon called her an hour ago and she was nearly here. I know she worked last night, but she should have been here hours ago."

"Maybe she got stuck in traffic getting here from work," Dante reassured.

Stirling shook his head. "That was one child I should not have permitted to leave the packhouse."

"A bit wild, is she?" I asked, amused this was not a problem I suffered in my pack.

Stirling gave me an exasperated look. "I didn't start going grey until Anique became a teenager. Wild isn't the right word. Fiercely independent would be apter. Had she been a boy, she would have made an amazing Alpha." Turning, Stirling went to sit in an empty chair on the bride's side.

Dante chuckled. "What he fails to mention is that Anique is his baby and his favorite. At least that's how Evaline tells it."

"Siblings are always jealous of each other. Wait until you have a few cubs hanging from your tail, then tell me about parental favoritism."

"This from an only child and perpetual bachelor," Milton teased.

"I'm waiting for the woman who can handle me. I'm happy to sniff around until I find her," I winked. While the brothers laughed, I moved to the front row, greeting Dante's mother before I took the seat left free for me.

The Beachrunner Luna walked down the aisle quickly, looking

at every face as she did. When she reached her mate, she complained about something, glaring pointedly at the empty seat on her other side. Taking her hand, Alpha Stirling whispered to her. Loud murmurs by the door made me expect to see the bride preparing to walk down the aisle. Instead, Stirling's son and eldest child, Edward, was manhandling a young woman. Gripping her upper arm, Edward scolded her while another of their pack moved forward to take the girl.

On spotting the other man approaching, the she-wolf gritted her teeth and slammed the heel of her stiletto into Edward's ankle. The move forced Edward to release her, and she stepped out of reach. The Beachrunners gasped. Understandably. That was their future alpha, and he was just assaulted by one of their girls.

"I said, no!" The she-wolf growled in defiance as she marched towards Dante. Despite her determined step, she looked terrific, walking down the aisle. She wore a long flowing dress in emerald green that highlighted her tiny waist and made her breasts appear generous. Her cherry hair was hanging the length of her back, in a feminine but straightforward style, and her green eyes were ablaze as she closed on her prey. She could have been walking a catwalk, the way she managed to move with purposeful grace.

"You left this behind last night," the she-wolf announced to Milton, holding out a ring box for him. "Rhiannon called me when I was nearly here, and I had to get the taxi to drive all the way back to the hotel and get it. You owe me fifty for the taxi."

Taking the ring box with wide eyes, Milton patted his breast pocket in surprise. "Shit, I didn't even realize I'd lost them. You're a lifesaver, Anique." When Milton tried to pull the girl into him to kiss her, she pulled away, looking disgusted.

"Gross! I know where your mouth has been."

Laughing, Milton stopped his attempt. Grimacing as Dante kissed her cheek, Anique made her way to Alpha Stirling, where she was scolded anew by the Luna. When Anique explained her lateness, the Luna quieted. Kissing her cheek in greeting, Stirling directed her to sit. Glancing over her shoulder, Anique snapped her teeth at the man who tried to help her brother. Adjusting her seat, she looked poised to escape as soon as the opportunity arrived.

Her green gaze flitted towards Milton, who winked at her. Glaring at him, Anique slid her gaze passed him to meet mine. The instant our gazes met, stars exploded in my vision. The full moon shined down upon her pale face, moonlight radiated out of her, and the need to kneel and howl, forcing her to shift and submit to me, was almost overwhelming.

The bridesmaid walked between us, breaking our eye contact, and snapping me back to the present. "Shit!" Dropping my gaze to the floor for a moment, I then dared another look. Anique was staring at the floor, her eyes wide, chest heaving, fingers griping her chair as if her life depended on staying in that seat.

Blinking, I realized everyone was standing, and the music was playing. Quickly rising up, I turned my eyes down the aisle to watch Evaline make her way towards the groom. She looked beautiful, her auburn hair cut in a short but feminine style, as was the norm for our women. Long hair in human form, meant mangy hair in wolf form. That dragged my eyes back to Evaline's baby sister.

Still sitting in the chair, eyes seeking out the closest exits, Anique kept her focus everywhere but in my direction. It was as if, by avoiding looking at me again, she could pretend it never happened. It also meant she wasn't standing watching the bride come down the aisle, something the bridesmaid, her middle sister, Rhiannon, noticed also.

Taking a step back, Rhiannon whacked her little sister with her bouquet, giving her a meaningful look. Shooting out of her seat, Anique kept her eyes on the ground. Frowning, Rhiannon turned her attention, and smile, back to their older sister. Reaching the front, Edward handed Evaline off to Dante, before taking his seat next to Anique. Edward glaring at his sister, seemed to break Anique out of her thoughts. Lifting her eyes to the front of the church, Anique watched the ceremony, her attention not budging from Evaline.

The celebrant was quick and concise, thankfully, so it was only fifteen minutes later when Dante and Evaline were pronounced man and wife. After waiting for Alpha Stirling and his Luna to congratulate the couple, I stepped forward and did the same. Intending to introduce myself to Anique straight after, I found her chair empty.

"Knox." Sterling approached. "Take care of my eldest and good luck with her."

"She has Dante to keep her in line."

Stirling nodded. "The bonus of a true mating; once a she-wolf submits to her mate, she tends to become more placid." My eyes went to the empty chair where his youngest had sat. Stirling followed my gaze. "Where has that girl gone now? She's acting even more bizarrely than usual today. She didn't even stand for her sister's entrance." Stirling's eyes returned to me with a glint in them. "She seemed very distracted, don't you think?" Realizing he'd witnessed our first glance, I felt unsettled for the first time in my life. "Maybe I should check on her, see if something happened at work."

"She works in the human world?"

"Yes. Once I let Evaline go to university, I had to let the others." Stirling was searching the church with his eyes.

"Is it normal for Anique to assault her brother?"

Stirling gritted his teeth. "No, but when he tries to assert dominance over her, she does fight back." Stirling met my eyes. "They used to be quite close, but when Anique went away to college, something bitter grew between them."

"Did Edward not get to go to college?"

"Yes, of course. All our males are given the opportunity. We need to earn a living after all. No, the issue is that one of our pack, wanted Anique to be his. Anique has aspirations, ones that required years of dedication, so she refused him. He didn't take the rejection well. Edward thought it was a good match, and his persistent harassment for her to submit to the other wolf drove a wedge between them."

Hissing beneath my breath as if something bit me, I clenched my jaw. Jealousy has sharp teeth. "If Anique is like I've heard, that would not have gone down well."

"They've been at each other ever since. Edward is nearly ten years older than Anique. She was a surprise pregnancy, nearly three years after we'd stopped." Stirling shook his head. "Edward, as the eldest basically took her under his wing. She followed him around, hunting him down when he tried to get away from her. She's never forgiven him for turning on her."

"Alpha Stirling." The man who tried to take Anique from her brother earlier approached confidently. "I was looking for Anique? She was meant to be my date tonight."

Narrowing his eyes, Stirling glared at his pack member. "You and everyone else, Dan. Unfortunately for you, I know you are not Anique's date this evening. You know better than to lie to your alpha."

Instantly, my hackles raised. This was the man who thought to tame my she-wolf.

Stirling indicated to me. "This is Alpha Knox, of the Valleymorgan pack. Knox, this is Dan Strum, my son's best friend. Would you abide one of your pack lying to you?"

"They know better than to try," I growled, not liking the disrespect this wolf was showing.

"But you have a modern pack," Stirling raised a brow to bait me.

"Modern does not mean soft. Modern means being open-minded to new ways of doing things."

"Well, good luck with Evaline, she'll be right at home with your open-minded ways," Dan smiled through the finely veiled insult.

Taking the hand he offered, I squeezed until his smile vanished. "Thank you, we are delighted to gain a she-wolf with such a good lineage. Having heard about Evaline's sisters, I'm thinking perhaps the Valleymorgans should take them off your hands also."

Tilting his head to appraise me, Stirling eyed the power challenge occurring in front of him. Stiffening, Dan tried to crush my hand back, but while not a weak wolf, he didn't possess my strength or training. Wincing, he relaxed his grip. Only then did I release his hand. "Good luck getting the girls to go along with that," Dan grumbled and left.

Watching him walk away, I couldn't resist my smile.

"Are you serious about taking on my daughters, Knox? I didn't think you allowed new wolves unless they were mates?"

"I don't, but how are we to meet potential mates if we don't allow single she-wolves to visit? It might also benefit Evaline if her sisters visited for a few weeks, to help her settle in." Looking over to where Rhiannon was flirting with Milton, I chuckled. "I think at least one of your daughters might be happy to visit."

Stirling smirked. "Don't read into that too much, Knox. Rhiannon is not saving herself for her true-mate. She quite enjoys having her tail chased."

"And, Anique?" I couldn't help but ask.

"This conversation is very reminiscent of one I had with Shona's father, the day before I marked her." When I hesitated, Stirling nodded. "Be careful, Knox. The one you have your eye on will rip a wolf's throat out before she submits to him."

The challenge warmed my insides, my wolf grinning in anticipation. "She would be the first to refuse me."

"I don't doubt that for a second, Knox," Stirling smirked.

"Excuse me, Alphas, it's time for the family photos," Rhiannon interrupted politely.

Stirling groaned. "Have you seen Anique?"

"She's outside, hiding from Dan and Edward," Rhiannon informed her father. "She texted me where to find her when she was needed."

Nodding, Stirling pursed his lips at me. "Knox, could you find Anique and keep her free from being harassed for the rest of the wedding? If you can do that, I'll consider your request regarding my girls visiting with their sister." Eyebrows jumping, Rhiannon opened her mouth to talk. "No!" Stirling cut in, "He has to find her, Rhiannon. We can delay the full family photos by ten minutes." Stirling smirked as he walked off. Studying me with curiosity, Rhiannon gave a quick bow of her head and followed her father.

Stirling was testing me, or he was providing privacy for his daughter to reject me, I wasn't sure. Either way, a challenge had been issued. Taking a deep breath to clear my nose, I exhaled it away. Going to the chair Anique had been sitting on, I breathed in deep. Her scent was a mixture of herbs, almost free of the usual she-wolf scent, but also free of the perfumes human women liked to wear. It puzzled me for a moment, then I remembered that this girl was trying to avoid being found.

"How clever. She used an anise base." Taking another deep breath, I tried to catch the combination. The anise hid her wolf scent, the other herbs hid the aroma of the anise, but not quite. Waiting a moment to cement the smell, I moved towards the side door. Following the herbal trail, I wandered through the gardens where people were smiling and chatting, and down a path that seemed to lead into a paddock. Turning just before the fence, I almost doubled back around the back of the building, until I found a willow tree hanging over a pond.

Sweeping back the fronds, I found Anique sitting by the edge of the pond, watching the fish swim. She almost appeared cat-like, the way her head tilted as she watched the fish.

"I don't want a mate. I don't care what the Goddess says, I won't submit to you." Keeping her eyes on the fish, Anique snapped her arm out quickly, then back, water falling from it. Gently, she unfolded her hand to reveal the suffocating fish. She plopped it back in the pond just as quickly.

Impressed by her reflexes, I smiled as I edged closer. "A mate was not on my agenda either," I informed her, coming to stand by her. "At least, not yet. I have plans that being mated would get in the way of." Becoming qualified as a trainer would take months away from home to study and to clock up the teaching hours. Before I could do that, I had to train up Dante to fill in for me at work. With he and Evaline about to embark on their honeymoon, taking a mate of my own would put my ambitions on hold permanently.

Rising up, Anique brushed the grass and leaves from her dress. "Then we are agreed. We will ignore the first phase and go back to our lives unaffected."

Removing a leaf from her hair, I lifted a brow. "I didn't agree with that."

Anique frowned. "But-"

"I agreed I don't want a mate right now. However, we are true-mates, and we have already seen the first phase of the moon. It would be impossible to forget each other. My proposal is that we get to know each other; become friends. That way, when we are ready, it's is just a matter of completing the other three phases."

Clasping her hands together, Anique looked at me through her brows, refusing to meet my eyes again. "And how would the Valleymorgan Alpha, and a rogue she-wolf of the Beachrunners, account for spending time together?"

A what?! When I rocked back like she'd elbowed me in the chest, Anique's eyes sparkled. "Oh, no one told you I'm rogue?" She stepped away from the pond. "I turned human. I live with and date humans. I've never returned to the packhouse since I left for college. It's why I'm going to have to spend this entire farce avoiding my brother and his friends, or they are going to drag me home, tie me up, and force me to shift," Anique growled. "And that would kill me."

Assessing her, I saw the ferocity her father described in her forest eyes. "Because Dan would mark you and force you to submit."

"He'd try," Anique frowned.

Now, I understood why she stayed away. If Dan marked her, she'd have to rip his throat out to avoid submitting to him. It's what Stirling was warning me about. That didn't explain why she was rogue, but I'd find that out soon enough. "Well, avoid no more." I offered her my arm. "Your Alpha has asked me to be your escort tonight, to keep the wolves at bay," I winked.

Studying me, the side of Anique's mouth twitched, giving an edge of a smile to her lips. "Really?"

"Really," I acknowledged the real question. Has my father asked you, an outsider, to protect me? "Really," I assured. Stepping closer, I was tempted to put my nose to her neck and breathe her scent. "Now, it's time for the family photos."

Placing her arm in mine tentatively, Anique allowed me to walk her to the makeshift photoshoot. Dan was there waiting with Edward, but we ignored them and walked up to the wedding party. "Stirling, your daughter, as requested." Grinning, I delivered her to her father.

Taking his daughter's hand, Stirling pulled her into his nook protectively, his eyes lighting up. There was no hiding that this wolf adored his daughter, and wanted her to be happy. Starting to suspect he'd been protecting her all these years, I puzzled out what I knew. Anique was the first to be allowed to move out of the packhouse. What happened that forced an Alpha to take such drastic action to protect a she-wolf?

*A*fter the photos, I walked towards the car park with my family. Alpha Knox walked with Milton, just in front of me. His hands were in his pockets, straining his suit pants tight across his gorgeous rear. Goddess, did he have to be so good looking? Why couldn't my true-mate be an ugly bastard, so the moon couldn't even tempt me? He was a head taller than me and twice as broad. His dark hair was cut short, almost military, just like Dante and his brother; like all the men from their pack, I'd seen at the church or met at Evaline's engagement party.

"How does it work?" I asked my father quietly. "The true-mate thing?"

Lifting his brows at me, my father then studied Knox's back; and a knowing gleam entered his grey eyes. "The first phase is called 'the seeing.' You see the light in each other's souls, but the darkness too. The second phase is called 'the knowing.' You sniff each other out, learning each other's scents, learning each other's deepest secrets. You will see your mate's, and he yours. After this phase, you will always be able to find each other again."

"What if you mask your scent?" I asked hopeful, shivering a

little at anyone knowing my secrets. Knox had already sniffed me out. If I ever did it to him, that was phase two ticked off.

"You can't truly mask your scent. If he managed to find you masked, then he will have taken your scent into them, and that connection is formed," he lectured, smirking at my pout. "The third phase is 'the marking.' I don't think I need to explain that one. And the fourth phase is 'the mating.' You're a grown woman, I'm sure you know about that too."

Taking it all in, I walked in silence by his side. "Does it have to happen?"

"It will, no matter what, from the moment the first phase takes hold. The stronger the alpha, the faster it will steal you both," Stirling assured. "Not necessarily in that order. Modern times have changed the way women conduct themselves. For sure, Rhiannon will probably complete the second, third, and fourth phases before she gets the first."

"That's because the first phase requires meeting his eyes. That's not the body part she's interested in."

"Too much information," Stirling grumbled.

Chuckling, I moved my focus to Knox's broad shoulders and sobered. "I'm not ready for this, dad. I'm enjoying my life."

Patting my hand, my father sighed. "Knox is very modern. Take the time to get to know him, see if your mind changes. Either way, if the first phase has taken you, it's only a matter of weeks until the Goddess will have her way."

We reached the cars. The bridal party was climbing into the limousine, leaving my parents, Edward, Dan, and Knox standing with me. Moving alongside me, Edward grabbed my wrist.

"Alpha Knox, is that your car?" I asked, pointing to the Aston Martin, swallowing the fear in my throat.

Smiling, Knox nodded. "Yes, Anique, it is." His eyes flashed down to where my brother held my wrist. "Have you ever been in one?"

"No."

"Would you like to travel to the feast with me?" Knox asked, offering me his hand.

"She doesn't," Edward replied sternly.

"Actually, I do," I defied my brother and stepped towards Knox, offering my other hand. When Knox took my palm in his, I glanced down at my restrained wrist, then up to my brother's eyes. "You're hurting me, Edward."

Edward didn't release me. "Alpha Stirling, surely you don't approve?"

"I don't see an issue with it. Alpha Knox is single, and I've asked Anique to be his date for the evening. Let her go, Edward. You don't own her."

Releasing my wrist angrily, Edward looked to Dan, who looked ready to shift and bite Knox's hindquarters.

Escorting me to his car, Knox opened the passenger seat door, holding my hand as I lowered myself into the seat. Closing the door, he moved round to the driver's seat. Dan was fuming to Edward across the other side of the car park, and I felt my stomach drop when Edward calmed him, reassuring him. Growing up, I never thought Edward would be the one who betrayed me.

"I will drive you home after the feast," Knox informed me as he pressed the button to start the ignition. Knox glared through the windscreen at Edward.

"I'm don't live locally. I'm only going to the feast long enough for the bride and groom to arrive, then I'm heading back to Campus."

"You attend the local college?" Knox asked, swinging out onto the road.

Here was a risk. "No. I'm at Dempsey. Campus is the name of the suburb I live in." It was bordered on three sides by the research hospital to the east, the Defense Academy on the west, and the special forces training base to the south. Campus was full of defense students, medical professionals, and military personnel.

Knox's jaw fell open. "Dempsey hospital?"

"Yes. I want to be able to help our kind in both our forms."

"You're a nurse like Evaline?"

Snickering at the sexist assumption, I shook my head, though, I understood why he thought it. The she-wolves usually trained in wound dressing and first aid to patch up the men. Evaline was the first I knew to get a professional qualification to do it. She stopped at the enrolled level and took an admin position in a GP center. She never saw the inside of a hospital.

"Doctor. I'm two weeks out from finishing my residency," I corrected him.

Knox tapped the steering wheel. "My packhouse is only thirty minutes from there." Frowning, Knox considered me with his pale green eyes. I adored his eyes. They were so different from anything I'd ever seen. "You went to the reception dinner last night, drove two hours south, and worked all night, then drove two hours here for the wedding?"

"I love my sisters. We aren't the best of friends, but they've looked out for me on occasion, supported my independence." I stifled a yawn. "But I didn't attend the dinner. I finished a seventy-two-hour shift at seven this morning. I caught the train up and slept on the way. Hence, I don't want to stay too long at the feast. I still have to get the train home."

Knox smiled. "As it happens, I have pack business to get back to. I would happily give you a lift back to Campus. I have to pass by there anyway."

Meeting his smiling eyes, I blushed under the naked look he gave me. "I guess I could suffer to be in this car for another two hours." Without thinking, I leaned into him, put my nose to his neck, and breathed in his scent. Warm amber, damp earth, and eucalypt stimulated my olfactory, embedding the smell into my psyche. My eyes fluttered as the warm amber flooded my system, heated me inside, made my body react to him.

Swerving off the road, Knox stopped the car a few meters up a fire track. My eyes went wide as Knox shifted, his hands capturing my face, and then he was kissing me, heatedly. This wasn't first base kissing, or second, or third. This was a desperate, lust-driven, crazy passion. His lips moved over mine fast and hard, his tongue searching my mouth, his hands all over me. He hit the button for his seat belt, quickly followed by mine, then he pulled me tight against him.

His scent was everywhere around me, filling me, infusing into me. I couldn't breathe. Grabbing at his shirt, whether to push him away, or to try and breathe, I wasn't sure, but I needed...something. I whimpered, in need, with desire, in... pain pierced the lust fog in my brain.

Over and over, there was pain, and darkness, claws ripping across my back, arms, chest. The smell of fire, of gun powder, of worse things I couldn't put a name to. Then there was blood, human blood, the scent and taste of it, drowning me.

Opening my eyes terrified and, like with the first phase, that smokey light, like moonlight barely breaking through the heaviest of fogs, surrounded Knox's face. Staring at him awed, I floated, lost in time as the fog light held me captive. When I drew in a jagged breath, the fog moved, and a big dark wolf was snarling at me. Whimpering, this time in fear, I screamed when the wolf lunged for my throat.

In a blink, I was out of the car and running. "Anique!" Knox called behind me. Despite my speed as a runner, the stupid strappy heels I wore slowed me down. Heavy footfalls thundered the earth behind me, and I screamed when strong arms encircled my waist and pulled me back against the front of him.

When I moved to free myself, Knox pinned my arms and body against him in one smooth movement and lifted me a few inches off the ground so my legs couldn't find purchase. "Anique, it's okay. I saw it too," he murmured.

This surprised me. "You saw the wolf go for my throat, smelt the fire, the blood?"

Knox stiffened. "No. I didn't-" Placing me down gently, Knox turned me to face him. "I saw what he did to you, why you ran."

It took me a moment to understand, to comprehend that while I'd seen his greatest secrets, he saw mine. My eyes widened as I recognized what he'd seen in me. Tears fell unbidden, and I cringed out of his hold.

"Your father doesn't know, does he?" Knox asked.

Shaking my head, I huddled against the cold of my biggest secret being revealed to someone. It was a warm spring evening, but I was freezing. "You kill people. You enjoy what you do, torturing, and killing." Shivering, I backed up another step. Lifting my eyes to the sky, I cried harder. "What did I do to offend her so badly? First, him, and now you."

Knox's face was shut down, but his eyes were wide, and pupils pinpoint despite the night. Fear? Maybe anger? Possibly both. He took two giant steps, and though I tried to back away, he imprisoned me in his arms, pinned my head to his chest, and buried his nose in my hair.

"It's my job. That's all I can tell you. You should never have known this much." He breathed the last as if pained. "There are women born into my pack, who still don't know what you now do."

"Does Evaline?" I sobbed.

"No." Knox's arms tightened a little harder. "She won't ever know." Taking another deep breath, he slowly released me, stepping back, forcing my hands to uncurl from his suit jacket as he stepped out of reach. My fingers ached to hold him, to touch him. Knox made sure he had my full attention. "I will keep your secret if you keep mine?"

Sucking in a painful breath, I slowly nodded. Returning my acknowledgment, Knox turned towards the car, and I followed. I wasn't exactly going to be left out here in the middle of nowhere. I'd left my purse in his car. He held my door, and I took my seat, pulling down the mirror and trying to hide the evidence of my tears. Getting in the car, Knox started the engine again.

"So, that was the second phase," he murmured to himself. "I thought the phases took weeks?"

"The stronger the wolf, the faster the Goddess has her way with him," I muttered, trying not to cry again. When Knox glanced at me, I kept my eyes forward. "I felt your strength, so I know the truth of you now."

"Ditto." Putting the car in gear, Knox turned to assess me. "If the kissing was anything to go by, the mating should be interesting."

Body jolting at just the memory of the kiss, I bit my lip. The rest of the car trip, an entire ten minutes, I spent staring out the window.

As soon as we stopped in the car park for the reception, I got myself out of the car before Knox had a chance to come open the door. My father was standing talking to the manager of the function center, paying the bill. "I thought you were ahead of us. How did you fall behind?" Stirling asked me. When my eyes filled with tears, my father's face softened. He blew out a deep breath. "That second phase can really pack a punch." His eyes went to Knox. "It needs to be announced."

Knox nodded in my peripheral vision. "With humans present, you will need to use their terminology."

"No, I don't want this." Shaking my head, I stepped away from both of them. "I still have to finish my residency and to specialize. I have years until I'll be ready. Even then, not with you." Meeting Knox's eyes, I hesitated, tears brimming mine at the cold look on his face, in his eyes, as if I betrayed him. "It would be going against everything I stand for. I won't be another slave to wolves. I won't closet myself away in the packhouse birthing pups and raise them to treat women as second best. I won't give up my life for a wolf."

Utter silence.

My father cleared his throat. "I'll let you two discuss this. Let me know what you decide."

"Daddy?" I begged as he turned to walk away.

Stirling paused. "I've given you all the freedom I can, Annie. Once the first phase took place, you were as good as his. By tradition, he is your alpha now."

"Screw tradition!" I growled, my wolf snarling along with me, sending a sharp pain to my womb. "Screw anything that doesn't let me have a say in what's going to happen with my life."

My father wouldn't look at me. "I'm sorry, Annie. That's just not how life works for a she-wolf." Opening the door, Stirling walked inside.

Knox offered me his hand. "Let's find somewhere private to talk this through?"

"I don't want to be anywhere private with you. I'll probably come away with teeth marks."

To give Knox credit, he winced at the idea. It's probably the only reason I took the hand he still held out for me. That, and the innate sense of trust I had in him from the moment I laid eyes on him. "I promise not to mark you until you ask it of me," Knox assured me.

Leading me inside, Knox turned down the hall that led to the bathrooms, instead of into the banquet hall. Taking us passed the toilets, he pushed open the door into the parent's room. Closing the door, he turned to look at me. "I meant what I said, I'm not ready to take a mate, not yet. However, with the Goddess moving quickly with this, we may not have the luxury of being formal about it. Despite your situation being what it is..."

He meant being rogue.

"...Your father is still recognized as your alpha. If he announces us, formally, to both our packs, it benefits you, not me, Anique," Knox explained. "Your brother and his friend instantly are unable to touch you. If they do, I get to deal with them. It also frees you of any obligation to the Beachrunners."

"But my obligations turn to your pack, and to you," I argued. "It would be expected I go home with you tonight, that your pack welcomes me."

Knox took a quick deep breath. "Traditionally, yes. We aren't traditional. When Evaline and Dante met, it took two weeks for the second phase to take them. Still, because they chose to have this wedding, Evaline won't move into our packhouse until they leave here tonight. Tomorrow, we will welcome her into our pack, and then they will go..." Knox sort of choked on the last.

"On the mating purge?" I finished for him. New mates were uncontrollable with when and where the urges took them. Some packhouses had a cabin they could go to until they could control themselves around others. Other packs sent them on a kind of honeymoon.

"Yes," Knox confirmed.

Calming my breath, I studied him. "You are suggesting we announce tonight to free me from my pack, but hold off on completing the last two phases as long as possible so that we both have time to do what we need?"

"Yes. I fly out of the country on Sunday night for work. I'll be gone for two weeks. If we can get through tonight without biting or-" Knox's eyes traveled over me, his body reacting to what he saw. When I raised a brow, Knox cleared his throat. "We won't be near each other for the Goddess to have her way."

"The Goddess always has her way," I mumbled.

Knox smirked. "She can try."

I couldn't help but smile at his cockiness. "So, after tonight, I won't see you again?"

"Until I'm ready," Knox agreed. As I opened my mouth to argue,

Knox shook his head, causing me to remain silent. "I know you are disgusted by what you think you know about me, but we are fated. You can run and hide from me, but the Goddess will eventually stop letting us play cat and mouse, and force us to do her bidding," he reminded me. "All I can do is assure you that you will be the first female in my pack to work away from the packhouse."

When I lifted my widened eyes to him, Knox stepped forward and brushed his knuckles down my cheek. "You have worked very hard to get your qualifications. If you wish to work as a doctor, I'm not going to stop you, Anique. Perhaps, you can convince me to allow our she-wolves the same freedom."

"Convince you?" I breathed, fire burning my skin where he touched me. My body was reacting to him.

Knox took another step forward. "I've been more open-minded than other alphas. All our females can study, but they do it via distance education, and their learning benefits the pack. Some even have successful businesses, but they do it all from home. We have so few she-wolves, I won't risk them to strays and rival packs also desperate for a she-wolf."

"How can they meet their true-mates if they never leave?"

"Events like today. All our mature females are here. They will spend the feast circulating, making eye contact with all the males of the Beachrunners, seeing if more than one match can be made with that pack," Knox enlightened. He moved closer still. "Will you allow your father to announce?"

Knox's lips were just above mine. Fiercely attracted to him as I was, the idea of waiting to be with him was near painful. Stepping back, I blinked myself clear of the need inside me.

Straightening, Knox double blinked, then ran his hand over his short hair. "Damn, she's keen for this to happen, isn't she?"

"Apparently, so." Clearing my throat, I put a little more distance between us. "I want to have a say in when it happens, Knox. I don't want you turning up unannounced, demanding I give up my life. I want it to be discussed and negotiated."

Knox chewed his cheek. "As much as I would like to guarantee that, Anique. I don't think I can. Once we complete all four phases, I will take you home with me and make it formal. That might not work for your plans. It most definitely, based on tonight alone, will not work to mine. But, once you are truly mine, I want you where you belong."

We stared at each other for a moment, both of us fiercely determined to hold out on the Goddess as long as we could. My body swam with heat, I felt pulled towards him, as if he were my center of gravity. Blowing out a breath, I moved to the door. "Do it, but we need to get out of here, or we'll have finished phase four before the night is through," I grumbled.

Despite avoiding his eyes, I saw the smirk and heard the chuckle to mask his relief as I opened the door and walked out.

I'd always thought, if I met my true-mate, I'd be burdened with some needy, placid she-wolf, or a demanding lunar. Anique was nothing like I expected. For the first time, I could see this working. Anique could live her life, work at the hospital, and home in bed with me when we could both be there.

Shaking my head as we walked, I wanted to take her so badly in my car before her secrets were revealed to me. The ring was hard enough to see, and I wondered if she was going to admit it to me eventually. Then, there was the reason she left the packhouse, still barely able to walk, in so much pain, and covered in bruises. Gritting my teeth, I resisted clenching my fists while Anique's hand was in mine.

The Goddess had shown me every damn detail. The secret played in black and white like Anique had tried to wash all the color from her memory. Or maybe, color brought her joy, and she didn't want it marred by that secret. She should have told her Alpha, but I know why she didn't.

When we walked into the banquet hall, the concierge was there to show us to the table set aside for family. While I wasn't family, I was the pack Alpha, so I'd been seated at the same table as Dante's parents, and Alpha Sterling. The bonus was that Anique was already sitting at the same table. When we arrived at the table, Anique had been placed between her brother and father. When Stirling raised a brow from his seat, I nodded. Smiling, Stirling picked up his son's name card and moved it to the other side of his wife, where I had been placed. After he swapped our name cards, Anique and I took our seats.

Despite how calmly she had walked across the room like she owned the place, Anique was trembling. Placing my hand into her lower back, I kissed her exposed shoulder. "Relax. You're mine now, remember? No one can touch you." Lingering a moment to breathe her scent into me, Anique's hand gripped my thigh, her trembling increasing.

"I am more scared of you right now, than them," she murmured, keeping her face forward, head down. "The Goddess is not playing this slow."

Realizing how close I was to her, and how intimate our positioning was, I composed myself. Sitting back, I put a little distance between us. "Better?"

Anique shook her head, caught herself, and nodded. Chuckling at the blush creeping along her cheek, I lifted my gaze, ready to talk with the others, only to see Dante's parents staring open-mouthed at me. To that matter, so was Anique's mother. Lifting my eyes further, I estimated half my pack had seen that little display of intimacy. Though most of it would see it as me being inappropriate with another Alpha's daughter, the gossip was quickly spreading. By the dark looks I was getting from the Beachrunners, they hadn't missed it either.

Two tables over, Dan stood talking to a few other Beachrunners. The sheer hatred on their faces told me they'd seen it. By the way, they were huddled together, I really wanted to know what was happening. At the table next to them was another of my deltas, Rion, and his sister, Raven. Rion had his head turned to his sister as if watching her, but I knew better. He was listening to what was said. Raven suddenly tensed beside him. Putting a hand on her shoulder to calm her, Rion stopped her from giving away she was listening, then his eyes slid to Anique, and from her to meet mine.

Keeping his gaze for a moment, I then turned it to Anique. She was drinking her water like she was hoping to drown herself. "Want me to get you something from the bar?"

"No. I don't drink alcohol." She was growing more nervous by the minute.

Taking her hand in mine under the table, I gave it a gentle squeeze. When my phone buzzed, I pulled it out of my pocket to answer it. "Alpha, get your mangy paws off my pretty sister-in-law," Dante's voice came through.

Peering towards the bridal party entrance, I could see the wedding party gathered just beyond the curtain. Dante made a gesture to tell me he was watching me and laughed. "Get stuffed," I teased.

"See you have it all wrong, Alpha. As the male, I do the stuffing. The bitches get stuffed," Dante joked.

"What did you just say?" Evaline's voice was cutting in the background.

"Just pulling our alphas chain," he assured hurriedly. "Can you tell the MC to get his act together. We've been trying to catch his eye for five minutes."

"Get stuffed," I replied and hung up the phone, putting it back in my pocket. Waiting a full minute, I snickered at the rude gestures Dante was making at me. By the time he was giving me the finger and Milton was pretending to suck on it, I burst out laughing and stood. Anique looked up panicked. "I'll be back in a moment."

Finding the MC was too busy trying to chat up one of the human female guests, I tapped him on the shoulder. "Hish, the groom is ready to come." Hish burst out laughing at the grin on my face. His female companion's eyes went wide before she blushed, her eyes drinking me in, but I ignored her. "Let's get this banquet started. I want to get out of here," I directed. Nodding, Hish went to the microphone waiting on the podium.

Returning to my seat to find Edward about to sit down in it, I gritted my teeth in annoyance. Thankfully, Stirling was on top of this one. "Edward, that is Alpha Knox's seat. You are over beside your mother," Stirling directed in a no-nonsense voice.

Frowning, Edward checked the name card and grumbled. "Why are you encouraging this?"

Stirling met his son's eyes. "Because I prefer an honest man to sit by my daughter, then to lump her with a two-faced," Stirling replied angrily.

Edward's eyebrows reached his hairline, and his jaw dropped. "I've never lied to you."

"But the man you think your sister is poor enough to deserve lied to my face several times, and I know he's lied to you," Stirling all but hissed the last. His eyes were narrowed and angry.

Sitting there, motionless, Anique kept her head down, her chest rising and falling, to the point I could almost hear her heart pounding in her chest.

"While I am the Alpha, I make the decisions. You go behind my back again with a stunt like you tried this morning, I'll throw you out of my pack, and you can make your home with the strays."

Jaw still hanging open, Edward swallowed, moved to his mother's side, and glanced at Anique. A frown crossed his face before he looked back to where Dan was sitting, smiling as he glared at Anique. The doubt of his friend's motives flickered across Edward's face for the first time as he sat down.

Taking my seat, I popped open the button on my suit jacket as I did, so I would be comfortable. When Hish announced the wedding party, I retook Anique's hand, rubbed that spot between her thumb and index finger, and watched her shoulders drop as she relaxed.

Lifting her gaze from her lap, Anique met my eyes. Emotions passed through her eyes like a hurricane. I knew how strong Anique was because I'd seen what she'd been through. I also knew she was dead tired and barely able to cope with anything more tonight.

The bridal party walked onto the floor, and for the first time all day, they held to tradition. Serving carts were brought out by the caterers, and they followed the bride and groom from table to table, serving their guests the entree personally.

In the past, it would be an animal that the couple hunted and cooked on a spit. But with fire bans and the lack of trust between packs now, most had moved over to the banquet.

"Has your pack married into many other packs, Alpha Knox?" Edward asked civilly.

"Yes. We've lost more females than we gain. Though, this is the first we've included a civil ceremony."

"This is the first time we've lost a female. Since our females stay home, we've always mated them within. Evaline going to the local college allowed her to meet an outsider," Edward didn't sound happy with that.

Aware of how Stirling had changed things for them, I nodded. "It was a good move on your father's part. The inbreeding of she-wolves has been linked to the decline in our female population." Edward and Stirling were now very interested.

"And you believe this is true?" Edward asked.

"I do. Two generations ago, we bred one she-wolf to every ten wolves. Like you, our women never left. A stray female entered our territory when my father was young. Instead of chasing her on, my grandfather gave her food and a bath. Then he introduced her to every wolf in our pack, even the mated ones that weren't true-mates." The Beachrunners looked shocked by this.

"She found her mate, joined our pack, and after the first wolf was born, provided our pack with four she-wolves." I took a sip of my drink. "My grandfather found this interesting. As an experiment, he arranged a meet and greet with a southern pack on neutral territory. We gained two true-mates from that meet, and they each provided our pack with an even mix of cubs. After that, my grandfather started arranging to meet with a new pack every year. My mother came from a pack on the west coast. Gilda," I indicated Dante's mother, and she blushed, "came from a pack in the north."

"Our two daughters found their true-mates in the same pack last year," Gilda smiled happily. "One is already heavy with cub. It's a girl."

When I smiled at Gilda, her blush deepened, and she lowered her face. Her mate kissed her bright cheek. "My grandfather outlawed forced mating in our pack," I advised. "We now only take a mate if it is blessed by the goddess." Squeezing Anique's hand in my lap, I saw her mouth turn up slightly at the side.

"I've heard you hunt down stray she-wolves and sell them to other packs," Edward flicked his eye to Anique before glaring at me again. "A practice that has made your pack very wealthy."

Anique tried to take her hand from mine, but I held onto it firmly. "If we find a stray, we take her in, give her a home, and the opportunity to find her true-mate in our pack," I defended. "If her mate is not ours, I take her to meet our trade partners, to see if her mate is there." I met Edward's glare with one much more deadly. "We are paid the dowry if a mate is found, nothing more. Don't you agree it is better to find the she-wolves a loving home, then force a bitch to mate against her will?" I bit off the end, the memory of Anique's pain still fresh in my mind.

"I have to agree," Stirling nodded. "My lunar was from a pack five hours west. We met at a heavy metal concert that she'd sneaked out to see. She gave me a strong wolf and three headstrong she-wolves. The most we'd seen in our pack in quite a while." Stirling patted his mate's hand. "It's why I agreed to allow our daughters to attend college. It's well known the wolves of different packs go to college. We thought if they meet their true-mate, perhaps, things might change for our pack."

"I highly recommend arranging yearly sniffs, as we call it. Perhaps, your wolves will find their true-mates to add more females to your pack." I looked to Rhiannon, who was flirting badly with Milton. "It's not like you have many females to lose currently."

Stirling looked at his middle daughter and chuckled. "Aye, if Rhiannon finds her mate this night, we will have none to lose by morning."

Eyes widening, Edward looked to Anique and I. "There is still Anique."

To her credit, Anique didn't flinch as she lifted her eyes to her brother and smiled. "No, there isn't." She held her brother's gaze and raised our joined hands to the top of the table for her brother to see.

Edward looked between us, then to his father, who smiled at his son. "The Valleymorgan's are favored by the Goddess when it comes to your sisters."

Anique's mother smiled. "An alpha from such a strong line and our daughter. Their cubs will be strong, indeed."

Dante's parents were grinning at a hidden joke across the table, but I knew it, even before Zeld lifted his glass to me. "Here's to many cubs, Alpha, and all the fun of making them."

Gilda elbowed her mate but chuckled just the same. "Congratulations, Alpha. Will you announce it tonight, or wait for the second phase like is tradition?"

Swallowing, I forced my smile to stay in place. "Alpha Stirling will announce it tonight since both our packs are present."

Edward was the only one not smiling. He looked worried and anxious. "Congratulations to both of you. Now I really wish you luck, with both Evaline and Anique under your roof."

"Better outspoken she-wolves than a wolf who would dare to lie to my face." I turned to Stirling. "Have you decided how to deal with that wolf yet, Alpha Stirling?"

Stirling looked pensive. "It's been a while since we've done anything more than expelling a wolf. What would you suggest, Alpha Knox?"

He was letting me have a say in how he punished Dan. Personally, I wanted to disembowel the wolf. "Cut his lying tongue out would be a good start," Anique grumbled quietly, but not so quiet that her father and brother didn't hear it. "Then cut off his-"

"Ear," I cut in. "A slice to his ear with silver will disfigure him in human form too. Then every time he looks in the mirror, he will remember the price for disloyalty."

"Hope you guys enjoy this food," Evaline announced as she approached with plates, setting them in front of her father and myself first. "My feet are killing me from serving everyone. I don't know how you did waitressing all those years through college, Annie."

"Grubs here," Dante grinned, serving his parents. His eyes flicked to me, then to my hand in Anique's. He frowned, then his eyes went wide. He opened his mouth to say something sarcastic - it was all over his face - but I shook my head at him in a warning. Removed our hands from the table before Evaline noticed, I kept Anique's warm palm in mine.

Shutting his mouth, Dante gave me a look demanding to be read in, sooner than later, then plastered on his smile and got back to serving. Purposefully, Dante made sure he served Anique and sniffed her head subtly when he placed her plate down. Anique stiffened, but when Dante moved away, with nothing more than a curious look, Anique relaxed again. Well, as relaxed as she was going to get tonight.

The bridal party took their seats and ate. Milton did his speech while the main course was served, and Rhiannon hers. After mains, Hish asked me to talk. Striding to the microphone, I buttoned my jacket. "Traditionally, the groom's father welcomes the bride, I believe. However, that's not the case for the groom's family tradition. Dante's parents have asked me to speak on their behalf, as someone who Dante looks up to. Quite literally." Everyone chuckled. "I'm not one for flowery speeches, so I'll keep this brief. I've known Dante and Milton for a long time. All our lives basically. I can quite honestly say, no woman before Evaline has ever affected him the way she does. I knew the moment Dante knew she was the one. One. Because he told me. Secondly, because I was forced to stand there and watch them make out like horny teenagers for a good twenty minutes. If you think that wasn't so embarrassing, you should probably know that they met while shopping for condoms."

"Knox!" Dante laughed while Evaline went bright red and hid her face.

"So, while those two dry humped each other in the middle of the shopping market, I read a lot of interesting information on prophylactics and lubricants." Again, everyone laughed, and a few of the guests made a few catcalls about coming to me for advice. "Okay, now that I've embarrassed the couple... Evaline," she looked up at me, still embarrassed. "I know you must be someone special because no other woman would be able to put up with my best friend as you do. I wish you all the happiness one can for a successful marriage, and many healthy cu...ddly babies," I cringed over my near stuff up. "Welcome to the family, Evaline."

All of our pack stood, raising their glasses and repeated the welcome. I returned to my seat. "I am so ixnaying any more human weddings," I grumbled.

Anique chuckled. "Well, we've already agreed on one thing, Alpha."

"You wouldn't want to invite college friends or work colleagues?"

"Can't we just send them postcards of us with matching rings and leave it at that?"

"You want matching rings?"

"Goddess, no. I was just going to try them on in a jewelry store and take a photo, so everyone thinks we have them."

Looking at her, I couldn't help the smile on my face. Without thinking, I took her face in my hands and kissed her. Our tongues volleyed, I pulled her close and was about three seconds from pulling her into my lap and taking her when we were drenched in cold water.

Anique pulled away, shock clear on her face, probably as much as it was mine. "Cool it," Edward scowled quietly. None of the other tables had really noticed, thankfully. "Our father is sitting right beside you. Not to mention the other hundred guests."

Looking to where Edward was putting his empty water glass back on the table, and everyone at our table was sitting surprised. A little irritated, I glared at Edward, despite him being right. Edward rubbed his face in his hands, distressed. Muttering under his breath.

"What phase are you two up to already?" Zeld asked. "Because if that was the second hitting, it's moving you two fast."

"I'm going to go fix myself up." Excusing herself from the table, Anique walked out to the bathroom.

Dante took her place a moment later. "A word, Alpha?" Standing, he walked off.

Excusing myself, I apologized to Stirling, who merely sat with a crooked grin on his face, murmuring to his happy lunar. Following Dante out through the entrance where the bridal party came in, Dante made sure we were clear of eavesdroppers before he faced me. "What the fuck is happening out there?" Dante growled. "You nearly banged an Alpha's daughter in front of him, on a banquet table. Have you lost your mind?"

Running my hand over my head, I huffed. "Very possibly." Taking a deep breath, I shrugged. "You're going to hear it tonight anyway. Anique is my true-mate. The first phase hit at the church."

"So, we are taking two girls home tonight?" Dante checked.

"No."

"Not until the fourth phase rule?"

"That, and I'm about to leave for two weeks, and you will be gone with Evaline for a few weeks. It would leave Anique in a strange house with a strange pack. I don't want to do that to her."

Dante hesitated. "I'm concerned. I don't think you should let Anique go, she may not be there when you go back for her."

"What did Evaline tell you about her sister?"

"Nothing...really," Dante shrugged. "It's more what the second phase showed me, which isn't for you to hear from me, but there is a reason Anique left her pack, and I can't see her hanging around to see if we are any different."

Pinching the bridge of my nose, I breathed through those black and white images. "The second phase hit on the way here, I know what you are talking about."

Dante stared at me, mouth hanging open. "Two phases within a matter of hours?"

"The Goddess is keen," I huffed.

"Possibly because she knows your mate will take off the moment she gets clear of you."

"I know her now. I'll be able to hunt her down when I'm ready," I grumbled. Sensing someone loitering, I turned. "What is it?"

Rion stepped out of the shadows. "I thought you may like to know that conversation I overheard. Those wolves were planning to kidnap a she-wolf tonight."

I shook my head. "Not going to happen. Anique will be leaving with me."

Rion raised a brow. "Good to know. But do you realize that the bitch is missing, and so are the men planning to take her?"

"What?" Moving closer to Rion, I surveyed the banquet hall. Rion was right. Looking passed Dante to where the bridal party had entered, I started forward. "Follow me."

Rion filled us in as we made our way around to the bathrooms from this direction. Dan and his mates planned to take Anique and force her to mate and submit with Dan this evening. I growled at just the thought. Not only because she was my mate, but because of what I know they'd already done once to her when she was only a cub.

"Let go of me!" Anique's silent growl reached us as we headed for the last turn.

"You think you can talk to me like that?" Dan snapped. "You better learn to hold your tongue quick, Anique, cause now you're mine, and I won't put up with this feminist shit."

"Get your hands off her!" I roared as I rounded the corner.

Holding Anique just above her elbow, Dan was trying to drag her outside. He turned feral eyes my way. "Get lost, Alpha. This bitch is ours to deal with."

"Wrong! That is my mate that you are trying to drag out of here. Let. Her. Go. Now!"

Dan's eyes went wide, and his hand automatically released Anique. Taking a moment to compose herself, Anique turned to face me. "Don't you turn your back on me," Dan fumed and grabbed a handful of Anique's hair.

Anique reacted faster than me. Stepping back into Dan quickly, Anique jammed her elbow into his sternum, winding him and forcing him to release her hair. Stabbing the heel of her shoe into his ankle, Anique turned and stuck her thumbs in the inside of

Dan's eyes. Jolting with the viciousness of seeing a she-wolf get violent, and yet, I was proud of her.

When Dan tried to pull back from her, Anique got a grip on his face and pushed her thumbs in harder, blood rivulets painting either side of his nose. "Don't you ever touch me again. You have never been wolf enough to be my mate, and you never will be." Jerking her knee up into his groin, Anique let him fall to his knees with a howl of pain, but she jabbed her thumbs further in when he tried to curl over himself. The girl knew how to torture a guy.

"See, Dan. It's you who belongs on their knees in front of me," Anique spat. Yanking her thumbs free, Anique threw a palm to his face, breaking his nose. The nose was to distract, I realized too late. Pulling something shiny from her purse, Anique jammed it into Dan's chest.

Dan howled in anguish. I didn't need to see it. I could hear the sizzling and smell the burning flesh of a wolf exposed to silver. Anique stood there, twisting the knife back and forth. "This won't even the score, but it will make me smile every time I think of it." Twisting the blade one more time, Anique pulled it out. Dan's eyes rolled back in his head and fainted. "Weak," Anique muttered.

Dan's friends, who had stood speechless while Anique took out a wolf, rushed forward and quickly removed their unconscious packmate from the premises.

"That was-" Rion whispered.

"Impressive," Dante finished.

Blinking down at her hands, Anique frowned, then her face contracted in disgust. Her eyes came to us, vivid green irises and stardust glowing pupils. Anique's wolf was watching us, assessing us for a threat. She blinked, and the wolf was gone. Moving her eyes to me, Anique held up a hand.

"I'll just clean up and be right with you." Confident as can be, she sauntered, model like into the bathroom.

"Wow!" I whispered, absolutely besotted.

4
ANIQUE

"...*A*ll the happiness in the world." Stirling raised his glass and everyone toasted the couple. "Before I let you all start the partying," Stirling continued, "I have another announcement. I have been told that my youngest, Anique, has been blessed to find the love of her life, the groom's best friend, Knox Morgan."

Shocked silence went through the banquet hall.

"It seems we will have another marriage to celebrate very soon. Please join me in congratulating Anique and Knox on their engagement," Stirling finished. The Valleymorgans cheered and catcalled. The Beachrunners were very sedate.

Stirling returned to his seat. "It's done. You have two of my daughters in your care now, Alpha Knox. Treat them well."

Taking my hand, Knox stood. "Anique came straight from the night shift, and I have work to get back to. We'll bid you farewell."

"You're leaving together?" Gilda asked, with her brows lifted high.

Knox met his pack mate's surprised eyes. "We are." His pack

mates didn't question him any further. His eyes must have communicated what he needed to.

Making our farewells, we walked out to his car. No one tried to stop him taking me, no one would ever object now. As far as every wolf in that room was concerned, I was Knox's.

Slipping off my heels the moment I sat in the car, I sighed. Removing his jacket, Knox threw it in the back, discarding his tie also, before he dropped into his seat. Starting the engine, he brought up his navigation system while unbuttoning his top two buttons. "Type in your address. You can sleep on the drive home." When I hesitated, Knox noticed. "While I agree you should never trust a strange wolf, I assure you, I'm not planning to abduct you, Anique. Whatever address you give me is where I will take you and leave you."

Typing in an address, I relaxed back into my seat. "What do you do for work, Knox?" I asked, wanting to know what took him back on a Friday night.

"I work for the government. Go to sleep." Putting the car in gear, Knox pulled out of the car park. Planning to stay awake, I resisted at first, but with how fast Knox was driving, I laid my seat back, shut my eyes, and didn't have the energy to reopen them.

"Anique." A hand touched my thigh.

Startling awake, I blinked into the dark car and saw Knox looking back at me. Only the light of the dashboard to see with.

"We're here," Knox informed me gently.

Glancing out the window at the suburban house in Campus, I cringed. Brett was home and sitting out on his porch, watching the car in front of his place. "Thanks for the lift," I yawned, righting the seat. Opening my clutch, I removed the diamond ring from inside, slipping it back onto my ring finger.

"That's going to be a problem, Anique," Knox grumbled, only the smallest tendril of possessiveness lacing his words.

"I told you, I date human," I replied, not meeting his eyes.

"Dating is not engaged. Dating is not marrying. We all date humans, experiment with them, but we can't breed with them."

Staring at the ring, I tried to smother the sadness I felt at having to end what I had with Brett. "I never intended to breed." I never intended to meet someone I'd come to care for like I do, especially a human. Opening the door, I stepped out, grabbing my shoes from the floor of the car. "Thanks again for the lift."

"Anique," Knox grabbed my hand. "You know we can't control this. He will be a problem."

Pressing my lips together, I nodded before I stepped back, closing the door. Walking towards Brett's front porch, my heart broke. Like Knox, Brett was older than me, thirty-two to my twenty-three. He was special forces, so his hair, while not as dark as Knox's, was cut the same, and Brett's eyes were a pale brown that wasn't quite hazel. Their builds were similar. Though Brett was nowhere near as tall as Knox, he was still taller than me.

Rising out of his chair, Brett came to the porch steps, his hands in his pockets. He was still in uniform, so he hadn't been home long. "How was the wedding?" He asked, his mood calm, but I could smell suspicion building under the surface.

"Beautiful."

"Your family?"

"It was uncomfortable, but I was glad to see my parents and sisters again," I admitted, stopping a step down from him.

"That guy dropping you off, was that your brother?"

"No. It was the groom's best friend. He lives another thirty minutes south of here and offered me a lift. I slept all the way home."

Brett took that step down. "Why'd you get him to drop you here, Annie? You knew I was meant to be away until tomorrow?"

Inhaling, I met his suspicious gaze. "I didn't want him knowing where I live. I was going to wait for him to drive off and walk to my place."

Brett's eyes flicked down to where his ring was on my finger. "You explained who I was?"

"Yes. He already knew I was engaged." Knox hadn't been surprised by the ring, so more than one secret was revealed during the second phase. Now, I was wondering how many.

Brett put out his hand. "Well, since you're here?"

Frowning, I wondered how I was going to end this when I didn't want to. "You don't need to decompress?"

Brett and I had sex once after he'd been gone with work for a few weeks. He'd been rough and aggressive. Freaking out, I told him to stop and ran out of his place in hysterics. It took him days to get me to talk to him again. After that, he'd decided him taking time to decompress after going dark was best for our relationship, and that I needed to learn self-defense. What happened with Dan tonight, that was four years of personal defense lessons with Brett.

Pulling me closer, Brett huffed. "Yes, but I don't like a strange guy dropping you off either. I want you to stay the night." When I opened my mouth to say goodbye, Brett put a finger to my lips. "Don't say it yet, Annie. You warned me going home might change things between us. I saw it on your face the moment you got out of the car. I would ask what happened, but I worked out five years ago there is a part of your life that is like work for me. You can't or won't talk about it. So, I'm just going to ask you to spend this last night with me, say goodbye in the morning like normal, and I'll wait for you to tell me if we can work past this."

He was so composed, so gentle, and understanding. Swiping at the tears leaking down my face, I squeezed his hand. Leading me inside, Brett locked the door after us, then took me back to his room.

Spinning me under his arm as we entered his room, Brett pulled me in to dance with him. "Did you dance at the wedding?"

"No, we left as soon as the speeches were made," I sighed at the press of his hand into my shoulder blade.

"The groom's best mate didn't stick around?"

Smirking at the jealousy, I could swear Brett was a wolf, just lacking the ability to shift. "He had to get back for work."

"He works night shift? Is he a doctor too?"

"Actually, I don't know. I was so tired and worried I'd miss my stop on the train home, so when he offered the lift, I went with it. Plus, two hours in that car or on public transport..."

Brett smirked. "Didn't need much persuading then?" I shook my head, then leaned it on his muscular chest. "You are normally very wary of men, Annie. Why so carefree with this one?"

How do you explain to a human how finding your true-mate works? Knox wasn't my be-and-end-all. If that was how it worked, being in Brett's arms now would be unbearable for me. Knox would probably still take other lovers until the four phases completed our union. After that, it would be loyalty to each other that would keep us faithful.

Yawning, I put my cheek on Brett's chest. "I'm so dead on my feet. If you want sex tonight, you need to get there sooner, or I'll be doing a different type of heavy breathing." Brett chuckled. I'd come back to him plenty of nights after working three days straight, with only cat naps to sustain me. Those nights I'd fallen into his bed with only a kiss and his arms around me.

Dragging down the zip on the back of my dress, Brett stepped us in the dance while I leaned against him. With only a little encouragement from Brett, the thin material floated gently to the ground. Smoothing his hands over my bare back, Brett sighed at the feel of me naked against him.

Dropping his head to my shoulder, Brett kissed along it as he walked me back to his bed. Unbuttoning his top, I kissed across his chest. He moaned when I traced the scar tissue of a bullet wound near his shoulder, my fingers tickling across the mark along his left ribs from shrapnel. I loved his scars. I didn't want some pretentious wolf who hadn't known any pain other than his first shift. Brett's injuries told me he understood physical pain. The stories behind them, the lost mates or close calls, meant he understood the emotional pain too.

Pushing me back on the bed, Brett bent over me to remove my underwear. His eyes went to the tattoo of the crying wolf low on my abdomen. "Was he there?" He asked gently. I cringed as he traced the scar the tattoo covered. Initials carved into my flesh with a silver blade, so I couldn't heal it, and so I couldn't forget.

"Yes!" I growled.

"Did he try and talk to you?"

"He tried to force me to go home with him. I left him bleeding on the floor. The man who drove me home interceded and got me out of there." I'd been terrified, not sure if I'd been strong enough, but once Knox was standing there, once I'd seen how confident and sure he was, I'd felt like there was an army there to back me up.

Sucking in a breath, I pushed Brett away. His eyes were angry, his jaw tense. "I can't. I'm sorry." Standing up, I grabbed my clothes from the floor and started dressing.

"Just let me hold you," Brett asked. "Whatever you need, Annie?"

Blinking away the tears, I wished he could understand. "I'm trying to do the right thing," I pleaded. "I never thought it would happen. I'd left that world behind, so I thought I was free of its binds." Staring at my hand, I slid off the beautiful ring he'd put on my finger two months earlier and held it out for him. "I was wrong, and I hate that I'm losing you because I can't escape what I am."

Taking my hand holding out the ring, Brett moved closer to me. "Are you sure this isn't just a reaction to seeing him again?" He asked, his hand lifting to my cheek, his thumb caressing. Closing my eyes, I nodded, the tears falling faster. "Something else happened, didn't it?" I nodded again. "And you're not going to tell me, are you?" I shook my head. Sighing, Brett pulled me closer to him, pressing my face to his chest. "Whatever you need, Annie. I will hate losing you, but if you can't be with me, for whatever reason, I won't make it worse for you."

"Thank you," I whispered against the bare skin of his chest. Stepping back, I zipped my dress.

"If you need me for anything, even just a hug, you call me," Brett insisted with sincerity.

As I reached the bedroom door, I placed the ring that was still in my hand on the chest of drawers and walked out.

"Of course," Brett called to me, and I turned to see a devilish grin across his face, "if you just need to be fuck friends, I'm good with that too."

Despite the sadness in my heart, I smiled. Opening his door, I walked the four blocks home. When I walked in the door, two of my three housemates were curled up on the lounge, eating popcorn and watching Werewolf in London, their favorite movie. They both looked up at me and instantly turned off the television.

"What happened?" Mandy asked jumping up and walking over to me. Her shoulder-length, dark hair in hot rollers to give her a curled bob. "Did something happen?"

"I just broke up with Brett," I answered glumly.

"Why? Did he cheat on you? Hurt you?" Danielle asked surprised, pushing her pixie cut blonde hair off her face. "I thought he was one of the good guys?"

"He is." Throwing my shoes and bag to the side, I collapsed on the lounge. "I met my true-mate tonight. We are already halfway through the moons' blessing. I had to give Brett up."

"Oh, crap!" Mandy sat down taking my ringless hand. "Please tell me it's a stray?" I shook my head. "Is he from your family pack?"

"No, thank god! He's the alpha of the Valleymorgans . He's gorgeous and strong and just as put out about this as I am."

"Is he old?" Mandy winced.

"Maybe thirty. Hard to tell the way we age and all."

"When will he be back for you?" Danielle asked.

"Not for two weeks, at least. He doesn't want this. We've agreed to avoid each other if we can."

"If you can't?" Mandy chewed her bottom lip.

Closing my eyes, I exhaled the weighted air of that outcome.

"We could get rid of him for you if you like?" Danielle offered. "The girls and I could take him out of the picture, allow you and Brett to be happy?"

Mandy smacked Danielle. "Don't be stupid. We'd only do that if he hurt her."

"I don't get that vibe from him. He's very progressive and has told me he'll allow me to keep working after we mate."

Danielle huffed. "Sure, up until he gets you with cub, and then you'll never be allowed out of the packhouse again."

Shoving her, Mandy glared at her with large eyes. A clear 'I can't believe you just said that' in neon lights.

"What?" Danielle asked confused. Mandy flicked her eyes to me, and Danielle's face paled, realizing what she'd said. "Goddess, Annie, I'm so sorry. I totally forgot."

"Don't fret." I stood up. "I got over that years ago. I'm knackered and need to crash. Good night."

Moving towards my room, I turned off the light. Standing there, in the dark, the memory of Knox's secret played in my head. My brain caught details I'd missed the first time, like the khaki uniform. Before I could dwell on the puzzle, I stripped naked, throwing my clothes to the side messily, and crashed onto my bed. Today had given me much more than I'd bargained for.

KNOX

The Lockheed commando landed with a jolt. Groaning beside me, Milton lifted his head suddenly aware of the change in engine noise. "Please tell me that was home?"

"Home," I confirmed.

"You itching to go find your bitch?" Milton smirked.

"Yes." My fists clenched. Every time I closed my eyes, I was dreaming of her. "But it'll have to wait."

"Why? We have nothing else lined up. You can take a few weeks off, claim and mount your bitch and get the mating purge out of the way. That way, when we get called up again, you won't be distracted by long red hair or her pale tail." Milton nudged my shoulder with his.

Taking out my phone, I woke the screen, showing Milton the message I'd received as soon as we entered our own airspace again and didn't need to be stealth. "This came in two hours ago," I muttered.

Milton read the email. "So, he wasn't stray? He belonged to the Burrows pack? What the hell was he doing seven hours south in our territory?"

"That's what I've told Rion to find out. He should be waiting for us at the base and have our answer." Putting my phone away as the aircraft came to a stop, we unlatched our restraints, grabbed up our bags, and headed out into the late evening.

"Morgan." Captain Franks was waiting for us when we entered the debrief room. "Report."

"The target was tracked by my team, taken hostage, and questioned."

"Determination?"

"He gave us the name of their leader." Taking a piece of paper from my pocket, I handed it to the Captain.

The Captain read the name, then handed it off to his signals person to run it. "Threat status of the target?"

"We determined that releasing the target would endanger our mission and invalidate any information collected."

"Target was terminated?" Captain asked. When I nodded, Franks smiled. "Good job, as usual. Shower and report to Lieutenant Hamilton of the MP's. He has questions about that man found mauled outside our fence two weeks ago."

"Yes, Sir."

"Morgan?" I turned back. "Are you sure it's not one of yours?"

Franks was the only person on base aware we were different species. He was our handler when it came to all things military. Our pack became the hunt dogs of our government so long ago, I don't even know how it started. All my father told me when it was my time to go to the defense academy, was this was how our pack built their strength and money. While I wasn't a traditionalist, I saw the business sense in our pack's agreement with the military.

Not all of us went abroad. Those who couldn't pass special forces training became our experts in other fields. Rion, while strong, turned out to have an irrational fear of planes. He'd become our communications expert. "It's not one of our pack.

However, when we find them, we want to be the ones to deal with them."

Franks nodded. "I don't want to know what you do to them. I just want to stop finding naked males mauled in the woods around my base," Franks grimaced. I knew which part of the autopsy report caused that.

Turning to my team, I motioned my head to the barracks and the showers. We filed out, Milton staying by my shoulder. "You want to go sniff out these she-wolves tonight?"

"Might be worth a try. If they are running, it will be late night, or early morning. Let's wait until we speak to Rion. I'd like to know what that wolf was doing in my territory without permission." First, we all needed to shower the dust of the desert from us.

Two hours later, we were all seated in the dining section of our favorite local burger place. It stayed open until two in the morning catering for late-night hospital staff and the base. I was still eating, having to deal with Lieutenant Hamilton before coming to meet my team. Some of the wolves were having seconds.

"I spoke to the Alpha of Burrows. Our dead wolf is one of his enforcers and was hunting a she-wolf named Monique. She ran away from their pack three years ago, and they've been hunting her since," Rion explained.

"Why? No one hunts a she-wolf that long."

"They do when she's your last, and she ripped a wolf's throat out when he marked her as his." Rion picked up his Coke. "Monique is the Alpha's daughter. She was promised to the Alpha's son when she turned eighteen and failed to find her true-mate within the pack. They not only lost their last bitch, but she killed their future Alpha. Now, whoever brings her back and gets her with cub, gets to be Alpha."

"They're desperate," I shook my head.

"Have to be to mate your own cubs," Milton looked disgusted.

"This pack is old school. They've effectively been force mating their she-wolves for four generations now. They've bred themselves out," Rion educated.

With a sigh, I sat back. "Let's arrange a meet under the pretense of seeing if that new she-wolf we found last month will be a match for them," I decided.

The boys smiled. "You think they are weak enough to take?" Rion smirked.

"Their enforcer got taken by three she-wolves. They're as weak as they come," I answered. "Not to mention stupid, if they actually admitted they were out of bitches to breed."

"Cleaning out the weak and stupid from the gene pools," Milton chuckled. "Because we don't get enough action at work."

"Humans are nothing," Edgar grumbled. He was a short but bulky wolf. Ugly as anything, but a damn strong fighter. One of the few still working from my father's team. "Taking out a weak pack is our duty. Especially a pack that would force a she-wolf to mate against her will, let alone with her own brother," Edgar growled. "Our women are our future, we should treat them with respect and adoration, not as pieces of meat."

"Well said, Edgar," I acknowledged. His mother had been a stray we'd taken in and found her mate in our pack. She'd been poorly treated by her own pack, so she ensured Edgar knew better.

Edgar huffed. "From a man who mounts every bitch who lifts her tail to him."

"Every bitch lifts their tail to me, Edgar. Trust me, I don't mount them all. Sniffing around isn't a crime."

Edgar's eyes grew humored. "Your mate hasn't lifted her tail to you. She'd be waiting at home for you if she did, not running around like a stray."

The team went quiet. My smile dropped. No one, other than Milton, had brought up Anique since Dante's wedding. They definitely hadn't mentioned the fact I hadn't seen my way to completing the mating.

Edgar sobered. "Apologies, Alpha, I meant no critique. I was just teasing. Everyone knows this can't be easy for you."

Looking around the group who were nodding, I frowned. Milton was shaking his head, and Rion cringed. "Why?"

Edgar licked his lips in nervousness. "We heard, after you left, that her own pack thought her rogue. They think she went human."

Rion frowned. "Hang on, you said she lived here, at Campus, right?"

"If she hasn't run from me, yes." When everyone looked at me bewildered, I realized I'd said that out loud. I cleared my throat. "The rumor was true. Anique went human when she left her pack. She was hurt badly by a wolf there and didn't trust wolves anymore. I believe she is also scared of giving up the life she's made for herself here if she's forced to join our pack."

Everyone stared at the tabletop. They knew what happened to she-wolves in other packs, how badly they could be treated, so they understood why a she-wolf would fear that life.

Rion made a choking sound. "Don't kill me for what I'm about to suggest," he murmured. "I saw Anique fight off that wolf at the wedding."

"What?"

"What'd we miss?"

"There was a fight?"

The others all sat forward. I glared at Rion, but Rion ignored us all. "Do you think it's possible if one rogue has managed to hide out here this long, that she may have crossed paths with other stray she-wolves?"

"Or is one?" Edgar added. When I gave Edgar a dark look, he held up his hands. "She fought off a wolf in human form.

Depending on how she did it, she could be one of the she-wolves we are looking for."

"She used human self-defense. It only worked because no one would have suspected it," Rion cleared up, throwing me a meaningful look.

"I know her scent. She isn't one of them, and Rion is right. She fights human. I've already easily restrained her because of it."

The memory of holding Anique restrained against the front of me, or the heated kissing that led to that in my car, caused me to groan. A few eyebrows raised around the table, but no one commented. They'd seen wolves in the midst of going through the mating phases before. We held sympathy for them. Well, until it was complete and they started the purge, then we were all jealous as hell.

"But, Anique may know of them," Milton pressed. "Rion is right. If she's lived here this long, and they've been here a few years, the potential is that she's crossed paths with them. You should go see her and ask." There was a light in Milton's eyes. Doing a double-take, I realized he was hoping the next phase would hit.

"Let's try searching ourselves first. We'll spread out, park at all the forest access points, shift, and go for a run. We are staying out until morning, so keep away from the running tracks," I instructed. "Sniff them out, or look for paw prints to give us an idea of their entry point." I started to walk out. "If we can't find anything this week, I'll see if my mate knows anything."

We left Big Al's and headed to the parks, which gave access to the forest surrounding Campus. Sending Milton with the others, I told them to split up in pairs. Rion came with me, and I drove to the park closest to Anique's place.

Rion frowned. "I didn't even know there was an entry point here."

"Neither did I. I found it two weeks ago when I dropped

Anique home." I looked back over my shoulder. "She lives a few blocks back towards the base. Or she did."

' "Are you sure she'll give up her life here to run?" Rion asked.

While I hoped that wasn't the case, there was one aspect of her life here she needed to quit, and if she was living with him, she probably had to move when she ended it. If she ended it. The one thing Anique allowed me to see willingly that night, was that she loved the man she'd agreed to marry.

Locking my car, I walked into the park, passing through until we reached the running track that disappeared into the forest. We walked a kilometer along the trail, found a fallen tree, grown over that we could hide behind, and strip before shifting.

Shifting for me was a blink and smooth. I'd been doing it for fifteen years already, and my shifting was almost fluid now, flowing from human to wolf and back again seamlessly, and without pain. Rion took a little longer, but still, it wasn't the popping and yelping of a weaker wolf, he just had to concentrate on the shift a little harder.

My pack was strong. Two generations of mating only with the Goddess's blessing had produced the strongest and healthiest cubs our pack had ever seen.

Once Rion was ready, we set out in opposite directions, searching for tracks, sniffing out any indication of the she-wolves, listening for them. After several hours of searching and no one finding anything through the forest, we all retreated to waiting positions.

Sending Rion further into the woods, I hunkered down under the fallen log by our clothes. Putting my head between my paws, I closed my eyes to rest.

A bird flying off startled, woke me to see it was early dawn. Lifting my head, I heard a runner coming up the track, paws hitting the dirt beside her. The runner was human, and female, I could tell that by the sound of her gait and breathing. She had dogs with her, the number of paws hitting the ground, and the panting told me there were at least two.

'Rion, there is a runner with dogs coming up the track.' I used our wolf talk.

'I hear her, Alpha.'

Waiting as the runner approached, I watched the forest around me, in case the wolves came by. When the woman came into view, I froze. Anique was running with two dogs, laughing at something as she set a reasonable pace along the track.

Her running clothes revealed a lot more than her flowing dress did at the wedding. Yet, the outfit was still conservative compared to other workout gear I'd seen women wearing. Automatically, the need to force her to shift and submit rose. I fought it off by moving my focus from her.

Anique's dogs weren't on leashes, and we're running off in between trees, before coming back to join Anique. That's when I realized how big the dogs were. Alerting my pack to my location and the presence of the she-wolves, I told them to surround but watch. I didn't want Anique getting hurt.

'Wait, they're with the human?' Rion sent back astounded.

'She's not human,' I answered withholding a growl. Anique was with the she-wolves we were hunting. Was she one of the ones who attacked the enforcer?

Anique suddenly stopped running, her eyes searching the forest around her. The wolves were still playing behind her, not paying attention. Turning to the right, Anique spotted two of my team sneaking into position. A human wouldn't have seen it, hell the she-wolves hadn't noticed either. Anique stepped backward, once, twice. That's when the she-wolves with her paid attention. Sniffing the air, they snarled.

"It's their territory," Anique murmured, eyes searching around her for a clear path out. "They were bound to patrol it one day." Patting the pale-colored she-wolf behind the ear, Anique turned the wolves back the way they came. "Let's go. We have no qualm with the Valleymorgans unless they start one with us." Anique's eyes fell on where I was hiding, watching before she started jogging back the way she came. The she-wolves were running alongside her now as if protecting her.

'Are we pursuing?' Milton asked from nearby.

'No. They didn't try to fight us. We need to learn more about them,' I decided. *'Let's go home.'*

After shifting and dressing, Rion watched me, but he kept quiet until we were halfway home. "What's the plan?"

"You are going to dig into Anique's life since she moved to Campus. Actually, go back to when she left her pack. I'm going to organize a date with my mate and see if I can find out who her friends were."

"Why do you think she stayed in human form to run?"

I gripped the steering wheel a little harder. "She went human, remember?"

Rion chewed his lip. "That may be so, but I got the distinct impression that they deferred to her. That would make her the Alpha of that pack."

"Could we be so lucky?"

"What do you mean?"

"If she is their alpha, and I'm her true-mate…"

I watched the smile bloom on Rion's face. "Then, when she submits to you, they become ours by default." Rion looked out the window. "I wonder how much they'll be worth?"

I couldn't help my smile growing. "We already know one of them is an alpha's daughter."

"Yes, we do. If only Anique wasn't your mate, her bloodline would fetch us a fortune." Rion hesitated. "Should I ask how much her dowry cost us since I know Evaline wasn't cheap."

"Not as much as she's worth. Anique is priceless." Rion appraised me. "Her bloodline is one thing," I educated him. "To be strong enough to lead a pack of she-wolves and keep them hidden in another pack's territory for years..."

"Your cubs will be very strong, Alpha. Probably the strongest born in centuries," Rion considered.

Glancing at him, I turned my focus back to the road. I'd been dreaming about Anique for weeks now. Very intimate dreams that fulfilled the final two phases. Never, in any of those dreams, had I seen Anique heavy with cub. Knowing that dreaming of getting your mate with cub was one of the indicators to concluding the phases, I wondered if that meant we weren't close to that yet.

"Considering her family doesn't know her worth, did they charge us the same as Evaline?" Rion pushed.

"No," I answered shortly, but couldn't help the smirk trying to pull up the side of my mouth. "She was rogue, Rion." Meeting his eyes, I watched him smile. "They couldn't charge us a cent for her."

In truth, when I called Stirling the next day to negotiate her dowry, Stirling told me he couldn't conscionably charge for a rogue she-wolf. Still, he'd like to be kept in contact with his daughters, and for his pack to have the first opportunity with their daughters when they came of age. I didn't have an issue with that, and so the price of his second daughter would be allowing two she-wolves to keep contact with their former Alpha. Unheard of, but doable.

When my phone rang through the car system, I pressed the button to answer.

"Alpha."

I smiled. "Dante, you've resurfaced?"

"Yes, we got home an hour ago."

"Did you enjoy the purge?"

Dante's grin was audible. "It's so much better than you think, Alpha. I have to admit, the only reason we are home already is that my mate is already with cub," Dante yawned. "I'm so damn tired.

Barely got any sleep while away. You are going to love it. All you do is eat, sleep, and-"

"I'm very happy for you. We'll keep you local until after your first cub is born," I assured. Mates tended to prefer to keep close through the first litter. At least I could start my date with Anique by telling her she would be an aunt soon.

I frowned at the phone. "Dante, is your wife still awake?"

Dante chuckled. "She's very energized right now. She's unpacking her belongings in my room and talking all things nursery."

"Good, I need to talk to her about her sister when I get back in fifteen," I decided.

I heard Dante take a deep breath. "Bad or good, Alpha."

"Just some background about her childhood, what she was like, and all that. I'd like to get to know her."

"Is there a reason you can't ask your mate about her own childhood?" Dante asked cautiously. He warned me of her past, that she might run.

"I've been away for two weeks and haven't caught her yet."

Rion laughed at my choice of words.

"Okay, I've missed something here, haven't I?" Dante asked.

"I'll fill you in after I talk to Evaline," I informed.

"We'll meet you in the lounge when you get back."

"Make it the kitchen," I decided as my stomach growled, "we haven't eaten breakfast yet."

The call disconnected, and Rion looked at me. "You hoping to find something in her childhood to indicate what you're up against here?" I nodded. Rion focused his eyes on the road. "You are going to have to mark her as soon as you can, Alpha. The sooner she submits, the sooner we get those bitches."

Gathering my thoughts, I chewed my cheek. "I promised her I'd give her a say in when I marked her." Rion raised a brow at me. "If I could," I finished. "I have to do this right with her. If I hurt her or try to force her will, she might turn on me." I didn't want my mate to hate me, to feel forced to be with me.

"She's not strong enough to take you on, Alpha."

"An hour ago, none of you would have thought her strong enough to run a pack."

"True."

"I've seen her strength and determination, Rion. The second phase shows you all you need to know about your mate."

Rion chewed his lip as we turned down the driveway to our property. "What did the Goddess show you about your mate that makes you worry?"

"Her secrets are mine to keep," I reminded Rion. "Some things were shown clearly, and in great detail, others were fleeting flashes. Those flashes are like puzzle pieces being connected as I get to know her."

"And those puzzle pieces worry you?"

Shaking my head, I pulled up in front of our packhouse, though country estate or chateaux may have been a more apt word for the size of it.

"No, it's the stuff I was shown in detail that worries me," I admitted. "The Goddess needed me to know that was important. But other than how it affected Anique psychologically, I don't understand why she made sure I saw every detail." The silver blade flashed in my mind, I flinched at Anique's screams muted by a gag.

"It was bad, wasn't it?" Rion observed my reaction to that memory.

Blinking back to the present, I met Rion's eyes. "If I found out anyone in this pack did even half that to a she-wolf, I'd rip his throat out for the sick psycho he was. I ever catch that fucking wolf away from his own territory, I'll make sure he never hurts another female cub."

I could see the whites in Rion's eyes as I started to get out of the car. "Alpha?" I turned to look at Rion, he dropped his gaze. "How old was she when she ran away?" There was a gleam in his eye, which told me he had an idea.

"I don't actually know, I just know that she was young." Grabbing my bag from the boot while Rion got out of the car, I headed for the door. "Let's go speak to our newest she-wolf about her rogue sister."

6

ANIQUE

"Holy shit!" Danielle cursed as her fist slammed the lockers in the staff change room at Dempsey hospital.

"Calm down," Mandy groused under her breath, checking to make sure we were alone. "They didn't chase after us, so we're fine."

"Fine?" Danielle sounded hysterical. "They saw us. They may have been patrolling this time, but next time they'll be there for us."

"That wasn't a patrol." Shaking my head. I stared at the floor beneath my feet. "There were too many. They were moving in to surround us, to cut off our retreat." Lifting my eyes to my housemates, I glared at them. "They came looking for us. What have you done to bring them looking for us?"

Swallowing Mandy backed up a step. "It was to protect Monique," she whimpered.

"We had no choice," Danielle argued. "An enforcer tracked her here, he found her down the shopping center and followed her home. She lured him out to the woods, and then we jumped him."

You could have frozen ice with how angry I was. Both the girls cowered. "You killed him in the woods behind my house?" Both girls nodded. "Are you stupid?! Our lives are here. We've hidden inside another pack's territory for years, and never even come close to being found. But if you dump a wolf in their backyard, they are bound to pay attention."

"It all happened too quickly, and it never brought them looking any other time…" Danielle trailed off. "Shit!"

Tilting my head at her, I was angrier than ever. "Any other time?"

Danielle looked to Mandy for help. "They've been sending guys after Monique since she left. This is the third who found her."

"And no one thought to tell me?"

The girls winced. "We could handle this, so we did. You've always been studying or working on getting your degree and sacrificed so much time to help us become self-sufficient as is. We didn't want to stress you," Mandy trembled.

Huffing, I opened my locker as I changed into my scrubs. "No, much better to bring the Valleymorgans down on us." Slamming my locker shut, I leaned on it as I took a deep breath.

"We're sorry, Anique. We did the best we could." Danielle wasn't anywhere near as remorseful as she should, but that's why she was a stray in the first place. It's why we were all strays. We didn't submit to male wolves weaker than us.

Taking a deep breath, I turned to look at them. "I need to get ready for rounds. Tell Monique it's beer and pizza night. We need to find a way clear of the Valleymorgans ."

"You're mated to the Alpha," Mandy reminded me.

"I meant for you," I grumbled as I walked out. Knox had my scent now, I couldn't escape him, but the girls could still avoid them if I could help it. That's why I'd accepted a permanent position at Dempsey when my residency completed last week. I'd been invited into a few specializations and had two months of the roster left to choose. I know what I wanted to go into, but I was waiting to see what happened with Knox before I decided.

Basically, I was choosing between what benefitted me or what benefitted a pack.

Two hours from finishing my shift in the emergency department, one of the nurses called me over. "Annie, there's a phone call for you," she explained, handing me the receiver and pressing the connect button before I could object.

"Dr. Burns speaking," I sighed, wondering if I was meant to be observing something today.

"Needless to say, I'm back from my work trip," Knox's voice purred down the line. My knees turned to jelly, both for how sexy that voice was, and the fear that he was contacting me.

"How'd you find me here?"

"You told me where you work, and Evaline gave me the name you exist under."

What else had she given him?

" I think we should go on our first date," Knox continued, "tonight."

"I'm busy. Beer and pizza night with friends," I quickly excused.

"The friends you were running with this morning?" He asked cheerfully. Clenching my jaw, I stayed quiet. "I'll take that as a yes. I'd love to meet them."

"Not going to happen."

"Come on, Anique. Two she-wolves in my territory? They're unmated, I'm guessing. Fate brought them here for a reason. Possibly because their true-mates are in my pack also," Knox reasoned.

"They'll pass. We all left our homes for a reason. None of us are jumping at the chance to be in that situation again." The nurse at the station lifting her eyes to me briefly. "Can we discuss this later? I'm at work."

"Want to give me your personal phone number?" Knox requested.

"Evaline didn't give it to you?"

"She said she didn't have your contact details, that she always went through your father," Knox replied like that bothered him.

"I have to go."

"Phone number, or I turn up at the hospital and follow you home," Knox threatened.

"Meet me in the emergency waiting room tomorrow night at six," I directed and hung up the phone.

"Date?" The nurse asked with a sly smile. "What happened to that gorgeous soldier you were engaged to?"

"Fate had other plans," I muttered unhappily.

She rubbed her lips together. "Sorry. That's the shit about relationships. I don't think any of them are meant to be long term."

I gave her a small smile. "Only Death does long term."

She chuckled. "Yeah, well, he'd want to be packing, if you know what I mean, or I'll be hanging out for reincarnation." We both laughed.

Grabbing up the file for my next patient, I went off to deal with the defense academy student who hurt his ankle abseiling.

"You're overreacting," Mandy scolded between slices of pizza. "We all work here, so leaving town and finding somewhere new to live is insane."

"I think Anique's right. We've existed here under their noses now for years. We don't have to give up our jobs or lives, just move town and travel a bit further to work."

"With Knox wanting to pursue our mating, it's not safe for us to still live together anymore," I reinforced. "I've been going over this all day. They don't know where you guys work or live yet, but Knox is going to come after you, there isn't a packhouse that couldn't use more she-wolves. Any alpha worth his damn would try to procure you."

"You said his pack has the highest she-wolf population in our country?" Mandy fussed.

"It does, by breeding. That pack is made up of three genetic lines, it'd be like mating with your cousin if they interbred. Most of their girls have been mated into other packs. They still need she-wolves for their young wolves," I explained. "Any stray bitch they find, who doesn't find her true-mate in their pack, is then paraded around their trade partners until she finds a mate, and they collect that dowry too."

"That's why they want us?" Danielle shivered. "They can sell us off to another desperate pack. We get sentenced to submission; they make a fortune from our suffering."

"We can guarantee they know who that wolf was by now," I groaned. "Knox has enough contacts in other packs to find out, which means they'll know about Monique. An Alpha's progeny has the biggest price tag. They are going to come after her, and they'll want the two of you too."

All three girls sat staring down at the pizza box. Eventually, Mandy lifted glassy eyes to me and nodded her head. "We'll find a new place, but we'll still do pizza night, right? Still, hang out on occasion?"

"Up until I move to the packhouse, then we'll have to see what freedoms I'm permitted."

Monique picked up her beer. "Here's to our Alphia. May her Alpha be as progressive as they say, or may she rip out his throat as he bays."

"To our Alphia," the other two saluted.

Overcome with emotion, I lowered my face. "Annie, are you crying?" Monique asked gently.

On the verge of tears, I shook my head. "I'm proud of you. When you found me, you were scared strays with your tails between your legs. Now, you are all independent bitches, and I love you."

Dannielle swiped at a tear. "We wouldn't be where we are now if it wasn't for you, Annie. You taught us to hide our scent and encouraged us to go to college and get qualifications. All of us are working and able to support ourselves."

"And you arranged the women's self-defense classes with Brett so that we could protect ourselves," Mandy added.

"I can't be your Alphia anymore; you know that, right?" I lifted my glassy eyes to them. "If he takes me, he gets you, and I can't be responsible for that. I have to disconnect."

All three girls were tearing up. I was only managing to hold the tears back myself. Mandy and I first while I was studying. We moved in together, and she started her nursing degree. Danielle came the following year and entered the hospital administration. Monique came with Danielle, and she just finished her radiology degree.

They didn't have to follow me to Campus and take jobs at Dempsey, but they did. Somewhere along the line, we'd become a pack, and they all decided I was their Alphia. From the day we met, we'd been sisters. "We still have the issue of Monique's pack to deal with," I muttered, taking a drink of my Coke. I didn't drink alcohol, no matter what.

"What do you suggest?" Danielle asked with mischief in her eyes.

Turning my focus to Monique, I lifted a brow. She smiled. "The packhouse is remote, so they rely on tank water."

We all smiled at each other. "Tomorrow night would be a good time to be out of town. I have a date with my mate, and I don't want him distracting me while his pack takes you."

"We'll make ourselves scarce," Monique assured with a glimmer in her eyes. I'd seen that look before in Danielle's eyes; revenge suited these girls.

"So," Mandy gave me a cheeky look, "is Alpha Knox well hung?"

Blinking, I bit my lip. "We haven't-"

"But you dream of him, right?" Danielle pressed. "We've heard you moaning in your sleep. So, what's he like?"

Cheeks filling with heat, I smiled at my chest. The girls started laughing and teasing me. We finished dinner like that, Monique and Danielle stumbling to bed after a few too many beers.

"Does he know?" Mandy asked as we played cards. "About your disability?" I shook my head. "Will you tell him?"

"Yes. I want to tell him before he marks me."

"If he's your true-mate, it shouldn't matter, right?"

"I'd like to say it wouldn't, but I've met enough alpha males to know how prideful they are. Knox won't take being mated to a rogue well, especially one who can't..." Swallowing my fear, I looked away ashamed. "I'll tell him tomorrow night and see where he wants to go from there."

Mandy watched me. "He could kill you."

"He wouldn't be my true-mate then, would he?"

"Still, as progressive as he claims to be, no wolf, especially an alpha, is going to want a mate who can't-"

"The goddess matched us, Mandy. She has her reasons. It's not for us to question." I was already anxious enough about it, I didn't need Mandy adding her fears to mine.

Mandy chewed her bottom lip. "I don't know if I could take the risk. I would have run to the other side of the country if it were me." She swiped at the tears falling down her face. "I don't know if I could have done half of what you've done, Annie. To have even continued on with your life, limited as it is. I think I would have killed myself if I'd been in your place."

Sighing, I threw my cards on the table as I stood. "What happened made me determined, Mandy. Determined to live life to the fullest, to work hard and prove she-wolves are more than cleaners and mothers. It made me determined to help others." Bending down, I kissed her forehead. "I chose the research hospital for my residency for a reason."

"It's in the middle of nowhere, and no one wants to come here?" Mandy raised both her brows.

When I smiled, she returned it. "I'm going to beat this, Mandy. I'm going to save others, and I'm going to save myself," I assured her. "Just wait and see." Before she could add to my worries, I went to my bedroom door. "Stay safe tomorrow." Stepping into my room, I closed the door.

Pulling off my shirt and pants, I threw them on the ground and walked the path free of textbooks and clothes to my bed. It was a hot night, so I only pulled the sheet over me as I lay down to sleep.

His hot lips across my breasts startled me as his large hand encircled my waist and pulled me against his broad, muscular chest. My heart accelerated as his lips nipped at my nipples. My breath rushed out of me, and back arched as he pulled my thigh over his hip, his erection springing straight to my opening.

Growling as he pushed into me, I moaned. I'd dreamed of this every night since we'd met. He took me in different ways, sometimes in my bed, other times in a bed I didn't recognize, but he was always gentle, always getting to it quickly.

There was no foreplay, there never was with wolves. Their idea of foreplay consisted of chasing you around the woods and sniffing your tail, or in human form, kissing and getting naked.

Knox kissed me deeply, passionately, as he moved inside of me, the sweet feeling I was used to with intimacy built. Gripping his shoulders, I sank my fingers into thick silky fur. Lifting his head, Knox howled, shifting into a wolf while he took me. Every part of him changed to wolf except the part still deep inside of me, that stayed very human.

He was a giant wolf, big and dark, and yet his pale green eyes stayed his. My eyes went wide with fear. "Knox, stop!" His weight was pinning me down, making it hard to breathe. Lifting his head, Knox howled again, his thrusts growing faster. Tears stung my eyes, the weight of the wolf on me too heavy, I couldn't draw breath. "Knox…" I gasped.

His wolf looked down at me, sniffed at my neck, at my fear, and he growled. All my excitement and pleasure of what was happening washed away with the appearance of his wolf. Knox's wolf didn't like that I was scared that he was here.

Snapping at my neck in warning, he told me I should like him, that we were mates and I should be happy we were lucky enough to find each other. In my mind's eye, I saw my pale-tawny wolf cower in her dark corner, refusing to come out and acknowledge him, to be with him.

Snapping again, he demanded I shift for him. Snarling, my wolf snapped at him. Howling, the wolf insisted she shows herself. Angry and scared, she rushed out of the darkness and bit him on the neck. Knox moaned above me; his wolf's tongue hung out.

The wolf went to nudge my wolf happily, but she swiped at him and retreated back to her dark den, trembling. Knox snarled unhappily. Sniffing my neck again, he demanded she come back, insisted we submit. The she-wolf wasn't having it. She was terrified of being hurt, of being damaged. Sticking his nuzzle into the soft part of my throat, Knox gave a last warning. When it didn't work, he took my throat in his jaws and squeezed. I screamed, or I tried to. With no air and his jaws tight around my throat, no sound came out.

Blood trickled from where his jaws punctured my throat. Pleading to both of them in wolf, I asked for him to understand, and for her to be brave and trust him, but it was no good. Hurt badly as a cub as she was, my wolf didn't trust other wolves. Knox warned one last time, the growl of his throat vibrating through our entire bodies.

Giving up, I closed my eyes. "No."

When Knox's eyes flicked to me, anger flashed through his smothering disappointment, and then his jaws closed.

Waking suddenly, I sat up, drenched in sweat, and my hand checking my throat was still intact. When I realized it'd just been a nightmare, I hunched over my legs and cried. My subconscious had really taken Mandy's concerns on board last night, or maybe it just took someone else voicing my own fears.

Looking at the clock, I decided not to try sleeping again. It was easier just to get my day started. The Valleymorgans were looking for she-wolves, I was safe to go about my regular morning run routine. Well, for now, I was.

KNOX

"So, there was nothing different about Anique growing up?"

"No," Evaline answered with a smile. Evaline had been quite happy to chat about their childhoods, what the Beachrunners were like growing up, how it used to be a pleasant house, and everyone felt safe and friendly.

"What changed?" Rion asked.

"What do you mean?" Still a bright smile on her face.

"You said the packhouse used to be happy and friendly. That would indicate that something changed."

The smile vanished from Evaline's face, she swallowed and quickly replaced it with a fake smile. She wiped the air away as if deleting those words. "Just a turn of phrase, you know."

Frowning, Dante sniffed his wife's neck, allowing his tongue to taste her just the slightest. He looked unhappy. "Knox is your Alpha now, Evaline. Don't lie to him. We don't allow disloyalty to go unpunished in our pack."

Flinching, Evaline turned her gaze to me. When I stared her down, Evaline dropped her shoulders. "I changed it, I guess. I nagged my Alpha to let me attend face to face classes at college, like Edward. He let me. Rhiannon went the following year. We lived at home, but were gone most of the day."

"The wolves in the pack didn't like it?" Dante asked.

Evaline's brows creased. "I don't think college was really the problem. They didn't like us being out of the packhouse, but we were home every night. Then Rhiannon and I started working in the human world too. We didn't choose mates, and our Alpha didn't force us to, even though he was under a lot of pressure from the wolves to do so.

"The change was subtle, I guess. I hadn't even noticed the looks we were getting off the wolves. Then Annie finished her homeschooling studies ahead of time, and father allowed her to apply for college." Evaline shook her head. "She was so young; she hadn't even shifted for the first time yet."

Rion sat up straighter, his face full of worry.

"Rhiannon and I were so busy with our lives, our dad busy running the pack and his business, mum keeping everyone fed and clean. No one noticed she was missing for days. It wasn't until Rhiannon went missing for two days that anyone noticed Anique wasn't there. Then dad got the phone call. He ran out of there so quickly, that's the first I even knew something bad happened."

Evaline's words came out breathy, her eyes unfocused for a moment as she remembered the events around that day. After a minute, she refocused, took a breath, and rolled her shoulders back to sit straight.

"The packhouse wasn't the same after that. The wolves our age, they were uncomfortable to be around, the way they looked at us, whispered to each other. Rhiannon stopped coming home as often, she'd stay out and started drinking and sleeping around. Our Alpha really pissed off the pack when he didn't bring Anique home."

Evaline swallowed. "The wolves got in Edward's ear. He wanted to send out hunting parties to bring Anique home, and he wanted Rhiannon disciplined and forced to mate. Dad refused. He told them that Anique was gone, that while she was family to us, she was no longer part of our pack, and that Rhiannon was free to live her life as she chose."

"No one challenged your father?" Dante asked.

"A few," Evaline nodded. "After he killed the third easily, they stopped and let it go."

"What happened to Anique?" While I knew what happened, I wanted to hear what Evaline and the pack were told.

Tears edged Evaline's eyes. "I don't know. When dad came back, he brought Rhiannon home. She was like an angry cat for days, hissing and starting fights with some of the wolves, scratching at them if they came near her." Evaline shook her head. "Anique never came home. Rhiannon told me she was in the hospital, that's all she would say. I went to visit her with dad, about two weeks after it happened. She was a small broken child in that bed. The doctors told dad she wouldn't survive, and seeing her, I didn't believe she could."

Dante put a strong arm around his mate's shoulders. "She did, and she's made a good life for herself."

Evaline nodded but pushed to standing. "She did." She gave me another false smile. "And she's found her true-mate. I know she'll be happy here, when you complete the phases, she'll remember how to be one of us again and be happy. I'm exhausted. I'm going to bed. Goodnight."

"Evaline?" I called before she walked out. "How long was Anique actually missing for?"

Evaline looked ready to scream, that's how much she hated discussing this. "It was five days from the last time mum saw her until dad was called to the hospital."

We all watched Evaline push through the kitchen swing door,

her sadness and guilt radiating from her. It was Dante who broke the silence. "What's going on?"

"Anique has formed her own pack of stray she-wolves, and she's kept them hidden from us within our own territory," I informed him. "Rion believes Anique is the alpha of the pack."

Dante's eyes widened. "Why?"

"The other she-wolves deferred to her, and she could communicate with them while they were in wolf form, and she remained human," Rion explained.

Dante lifted his brows. "Goddess! I wouldn't have expected that from Anique. I mean, she is obviously pretty strong, based on what she survived and that she fought that wolf off without breaking a sweat. But to be an Alphia? Has anyone met an Alphia in the last century?"

"It had happened before when there wasn't a strong male to take the place of alpha," I reminded them. "As it is a she-wolf pack, it's quite expected they have a female alpha."

Dante grinned. "So, when Anique submits to you, we get a pack of she-wolves for free?"

This is where my smile disappeared. "These bitches have killed wolves for trying to force them to submit and join a pack, Dante. They will not come easily to us. Anique may not be easy to dominate."

Dante shook his head. "Anique warmed to you by the time you left together. That she went home with you showed that you had already developed a trusting bond, Knox. She will submit to you if you show her you can be trusted."

Rion frowned. "I'm concerned about some of the things in Evaline's story."

"She didn't lie," Dante sneered.

Rion sat back a little. "I didn't say she did. It's not her version of the story, but what happened to Anique." Rion looked at me. "You said what happened to her was pretty horrific, right?" I nodded.

Rion looked at Dante. "You saw Anique through Evaline's eyes at the hospital?"

"Not that you should know that, Mr. Eavesdropping, but yes," Dante muttered angrily.

"What did you hear the doctors say to her father at the hospital?" Rion asked. He had his phone out and was googling something.

Dante frowned as he concentrated. "He said Anique was badly injured, they were having trouble stopping the internal bleeding, the rest was said very quietly. Evaline only picked up a few words after that, something to do with transfusions, and she freaked out when they started talking about a silver blade."

Rion showed me his phone. "Anique didn't do her medical degree near here, but she constantly chose to do her placements and then her residency at Dempsey. Guess what one of the studies they are doing is?"

Taking his phone, I read the information on a study on blood transfusions and whether the receivers can have adverse effects. I looked at Rion, confused.

"Consider that they couldn't stop her bleeding. A human hospital would have given her human blood to keep her alive," Rion explained. "What if that affected her in some way, a way that made her unacceptable for her pack?"

"That's not why Stirling never brought her home. If he saw her immediately after the attack, he knew what happened. No Alpha would bring her home after that."

"That's what I don't get," Rion shook his head astounded. "If that happened to your daughter, you would have killed the wolf who attacked her and brought her home."

"That's the thing, I understand why Stirling didn't do that. I understand why he chose to let his favorite daughter go, to risk her in the human world than to punish those responsible."

"Stirling said he should never have let her leave the packhouse, out of all of his daughters," Dante reminded me.

"He meant, he should never have agreed to let her go to college, then she would never have been attacked."

"Or he knows his daughter has created her own pack, and he realized that of all the daughters, she was the most dangerous to let go," Rion suggested.

"He spoke proudly of Anique," Dante debated. "He is proud of what she's accomplished on her own, that she found the strength and courage to not only survive but to move on."

"I think we are missing something from the story, and I think Evaline gave us a hint where to find it," I brought them back on topic.

"Rhiannon," Dante nodded, understanding. "She went missing as well, but she wasn't injured, just angry."

"Rhiannon found Anique and helped her escape, taking her to the hospital when she realized how injured she was," I admitted.

"So, she realized Anique was missing and hunted her down without telling anyone," Rion decided. "You want to get her side of things?"

"I do. More so, I want Rhiannon in our packhouse." Both men looked at me, warily. "I invited both Stirling's daughters to come to stay when I realized Anique was my mate. Stirling wasn't opposed to it. I'll call Stirling and make the arrangements."

"If her mate was here, she would have met him at the wedding," Dante protested.

"No," Rion objected. "Rhiannon is very careful not to make true eye contact with any wolf. I tried, so trust me, she's good at avoiding. I doubt she even looked Milton in the eye."

"She doesn't want a mate?" Dante asked, astounded. He looked at me. "What is wrong with these girls? It's like Evaline was the only she-wolf raised properly in the family."

"Perhaps," I answered evenly, "Rhiannon's issues with wolves, is the same as her sister's? After all, she was the one to notice Anique missing, and knew where she would find her."

"Evaline did say it was that incident that sent Rhiannon off the rails," Rion agreed. "Perhaps, after Evaline left, the wolves created a new hazing ritual for she-wolves who planned to go to college?"

"We can speculate, or we can ask Rhiannon," I decided.

"Why don't you just ask Anique?" Dante queried.

"If I bring it up, if I make her remember, she will resist me because of the remembered pain. I need her focused on our future together, not on our pasts." I stood up. "I'll call Stirling now with the good news about his first grandchild and arrange Rhiannon to visit. Rion, call the Burrows pack and arrange to take Clarise for them to meet, next week at the earliest."

"Wait, why are we suddenly trading with the Burrows pack?" Dante asked, confused.

Remembering that we hadn't filled Dante in on that development, I sat back down and explained what Rion had uncovered.

"So, we are taking them out. What if Clarise meets her mate there?" Dante asked.

"Then, we'll take out the rest of the inbred bastards and let Clarise and her mate create their own pack." I shrugged. "I'm not opposed to another pack, but we all know what happens when a pack runs out of she-wolves."

Rion and Dante nodded. "They raid and steal from other packs," Dante scowled. "They don't care about age, they kidnap Cubs, already mated women, and kill anyone who tries to stop them."

"We have the highest she-wolf population of any pack. That becomes known, with our work taking half the pack away for long periods, we'd be the first target," I reminded them.

Sometimes it was necessary to remind your pack that their wives, sisters, and daughters were at stake. It's what my father taught me when he took me out the first time to annihilate another pack. Of course, that pack had already murdered half another pack, kidnaped, and raped the two she-wolves of age. We'd caught one of their wolves sniffing around our territory, heard what had happened, and decided to be proactive.

"Rion, make the arrangements. I have to go make a date with my mate." I started to leave.

"Should I allow time for the mating purge?" Rion asked, hopeful.

Pausing mid-stride, I chewed on the inside of my cheek. Half turning to face them, I nodded. "Give me two weeks. If she is not with cub or exhausted by then, she'll just have to do without me for a few hours."

"Alpha?" Dante called. I turned to see a smirk on his face. "Did Anique give you her number?"

"No. I was just going to call the hospital and ask for Anique Beach."

Dante shook his head. "Burns. Anique dropped her pack name when she went rogue. She goes by the name Annie Burns."

"Why, Burns?" I asked, confused as to why anyone would drop their pack name.

Dante shrugged. "No idea. Ask her."

8

ANIQUE

"Wow, you look spiffy," Eric complimented as I slipped into my shoes in the change room. "Date night?" I nodded. "Enjoy it. The academy starts running maneuvers tomorrow."

Looking heavenward, I groaned. "So, I can expect forty-eight hours straight minimum?"

"Sure can. Not going to miss emergency when you specialize, are you?" Doctor Eric Solomon was an orthopedic surgeon. One of the specializations I was considering. He was also my doctor, and my mentor.

"I haven't chosen where to specialize yet."

Eric laughed. "As if you're not going to choose orthopedics, Annie. You've jumped at every chance to sit in on my surgeries and research, especially the shrapnel operations. You've already clocked the hours; it'd be a waste not to specialize with me now."

Nodding, I looked at the clock. "I'm late," I excused, grabbing my bag and heading out towards the emergency waiting room.

"Have a good night, Annie." A few of the nurses and wards

people called as I left. Pressing the button to unlock the doors, I found Knox immediately; his presence dominating the waiting room, smiling and flirting with two nurses.

Spying me, Knox instantly stood straight as we made eye contact. "Excuse me, ladies, but my date has arrived." Farewelling them politely, he walked towards me. Every eye watched him walk towards me and lean down to kiss my cheek. "Evening," he murmured in my ear.

The sparks of his lips on my skin fired throughout my body, causing me to shiver. Waiting until he'd pulled back to a respectable distance, I bit my lip. "Sorry I'm late, I was assisting in surgery," I explained when Knox looked at his watch. Usually, being forty-five minutes late was never a good first impression.

"I was told." Knox nodded to the reception, where two nurses were staring at him dreamily. "I pushed back our reservation till seven."

"Thank you for understanding," I frowned, not expecting him to be happy about being kept waiting. Not that I'd done it on purpose, but it was my job, so he'd need to get used to it.

"Shall we go?" Knox indicated the door. Nodding, I walked out with him. "It will take some getting used to," Knox decided once we were outside.

"What will?"

"The potential of you being late home," Knox explained. "I'm used to punctuality."

"Well, either of the specialties I take will give me a rotating roster and lead to short notice call outs," I counseled. "If anything happens at the base or academy, I may not make it home for three days at a time."

Knox frowned. "You're entitled to maternity leave, correct?"

I laughed. "We haven't even gone on our first date, and you've already brought up babies."

"Cubs," Knox corrected. "We have cubs, humans have babies." Pressing my lips together to prevent responding, I held my tongue. "And it's normal for our kind to be interested in progeny from the moment we meet our mate."

Sucking in a breath as we reached Knox's car, I met his eyes. "Knox, I haven't. I have no interest in becoming a mother."

Knox opened the car door. "That will change, Anique. It's your nature to want to provide your mate with-"

"No, it's not," I interrupted. "That's always been the case because we've never been given the option of anything else. I'm not restricted, Knox, and I won't be forced to that way of life again."

"Annie?" a man's voice called. Stiffening, I turned to see Brett walking towards us from where he parked his car.

My heart became stone in my chest. "Brett." We hadn't seen each other since the night Knox drove me home. "What are you doing here?"

Brett indicated the hospital. "One of my guys got injured."

"Oh, I'm sorry to hear that." I met his eyes, ignoring Knox.

Brett looked at the car I was about to get into and then at Knox. "Well, now I know who drove you home from the wedding. Morgan." Brett nodded his head at Knox in acknowledgment, his face entirely unhappy.

"White," Knox returned.

Brett looked between us. "Well, if you were going to dump me for anyone, I guess it had to be a hound," he grumbled.

"Brett..." My chest hurt at the anger in his eyes.

"Guess I don't need to ask what happened that night now, do I?"

"It's not like that." Stepping towards him, I grabbed his forearm. "I've not seen Knox since the wedding."

"She's telling the truth," Knox confirmed. "I called Annie yesterday and asked her to have dinner with me. I had some news about her sister and thought we could celebrate it together."

Brett looked at Knox untrustingly. "Really? So, you two haven't slept together?"

"No," I cringed. Guilt suffocating me as I thought about what happened in Knox's car before the reception.

"Not yet," Knox answered simultaneously. Brett and I glared at Knox, but he just shrugged. "As far as I knew, Annie was engaged. You just let me know that's not the case anymore." Collecting my shoulder in his hand, Knox moved me away from Brett and to the car. "I guess that changes things."

"Knox," I scowled at him quietly.

Brett watched me, his eyes begging me to walk away from Knox and back to him. Lowering my eyes in shame, I dropped into the car. "Goodbye, Brett."

"Bye, Annie." Brett shook his head, disappointment evident on his face. He continued walking into the hospital.

Shutting the door, Knox walked around to drop into the driver's seat. "Well, that saves me asking if you'd fixed that situation."

"Can you not sound so casual about it," I barked. "I had to break his heart because the Goddess chose you."

Knox watched me quietly. Exhaling with effort, he pushed the ignition button. "Try not to sound so disgusted with the mate the Goddess chose for you, Anique. Many other bitches would love to be in your place."

"Those bitches don't know you torture and kill people," I sneered.

Moving quickly, Knox grabbed me around the throat, pinning me back in the seat. "Don't judge what you don't understand, Anique," he growled into my ear. "A rogue bitch who runs with a pack of murderous she-wolves shouldn't be throwing stones, after all."

Throwing my hand out, I punched into the bend of his elbow,

forcing his arm to release where it held me. He'd moved to stop my response, but because of the position he was sitting in the car, he couldn't get his other arm up. Not bothering to try to get out of the car, I just glared at Knox as I checked my throat. Huffing, Knox put the car in gear and started driving. We spent several minutes in silence.

"I didn't know about the wolves, okay?" I fumed. "They only admitted it to me yesterday when I asked why you would be hunting them." Sucking in a deep breath, I found my throat hurt a little. "If you only came tonight to gain access to them, it won't work."

Knox looked annoyed, or maybe it was frustration. I don't know what he expected our date to be like tonight, but I'm sure he wasn't expecting this. He would have been used to submissive she-wolves who bowed to his will, flattered him repeatedly, and didn't dare to talk back. I wasn't that sort of woman, and I wasn't about to let him believe I could ever be like that.

"I came to see my mate," Knox objected to my accusation. He pulled the car into the car park of a restaurant.

"Your pathetic rogue of a mate? I find it hard to believe an Alpha of your standing would truly want to be mated to a bitch like me?"

"Me too," Knox muttered. Catching himself, Knox turned to me wide-eyed. "Anique-"

"Save it!" Getting out of the car, I shook my head. "Let's just keep away from each other. With any luck, the Goddess will change her mind and give you someone else in a few years."

Slamming the door, I took one step before Knox appeared in front of me. Cuffing his palm around the back of my neck, he pulled me into him. "I don't want anyone else."

He didn't kiss me. Moving the wide strap of my dress out of the way roughly, Knox pressed his teeth into the soft flesh of my shoulder.

"No!" I screeched, trying to push him away.

Holding my body to his, Knox covered my mouth to mute my screaming. Pressing me back against his car, he released his canines, sinking them deep and injecting me with his saliva, completing the marking. Pain pierced my shoulder, then immediately faded as the enzymes of his saliva acted like an anesthetic.

Moaning in discomfort, I held tight to Knox's shirt as my body's natural defense system moved to attack the foreign cells. I'd studied the mating process with a medical perspective. It was the equivalent of injecting a virus into the human body and the body's immune system choosing whether to fight it off.

As Knox pinned me there, his fangs buried in my shoulder, his body pumped the bond virus into me. Instead of my cells attacking, they supplicated and replicated the virus. It was changing my body chemistry and ensuring my immune system would recognize his DNA from now on. It would make me pliable to his will and loyal to him.

My body would only accept his seed and kill any other man's sperm instantly. In his absence, I would miss his presence and crave his touch and affection. Worst of all, if he gave me a direct order, I would instantly obey or fight very hard to resist.

In truth, this was the pure form of submission. Knox didn't need to stand over me and make me kneel to him, or to dominate me. That was all to satisfy the male ego, and to make sure the female knew her place. The Goddess's version of submission occurred at a microscopic level, and it felt incredible.

When Dan marked me against my will when I was sixteen, I'd fought it off. I didn't relax and let the pleasure drown my senses. Gritting my teeth, I yelled and screamed and refused to be owned by him. My body rejected his claim and killed the bond virus he'd injected into me. He'd never owned me. It's why he carved his initials into my womb. Punishment for rejecting his claim.

This time, as my body went limp in Knox's arms, I moaned and hung my head back, and I didn't stand a chance at fighting him. The Goddess had chosen Knox for me because Knox was strong enough to be my Alpha. Withdrawing his fangs, Knox licked over the wound, then slowly lifted his head. His green eyes were lust glazed.

"Please, tell me you didn't do that by choice?" I panted.

"The Goddess wants this, Anique." He kissed my jaw. "I want this."

Groaning, I clung to his shirt. "I didn't want this." Knox's fingers dug into my back. "Not until we had a chance to talk. I need to explain my situation before we finish this."

Stepping back, Knox made sure I had my feet beneath me before he let me go. "We can talk over dinner."

Keeping hold of his shirt, I shook my head. "Despite the fact I'm now bleeding, this isn't a conversation for the public domain."

Taking out a handkerchief, Knox applied pressure over the two punctures from his teeth. "Okay, let's eat, talk about stuff that isn't so bad, and then we can go for a walk afterward, and I can hear what you need to say." Knox lifted the hankie to show me the clean material. "It just feels like it's bleeding."

Taking my hand, he led me into the restaurant. "I'll start," Knox decided after we were sat at our table. "Your sister, Evaline, is with cub and very happy in her new home."

Swallowing, I bowed my head." She would have fit in easily." I wasn't excited about the baby, but I expected that was the news he meant when he'd spoken to Brett.

Knox inhaled deeply. "Your sister, Rhiannon, is coming to stay two weeks with us. To be there for Evaline while she settles in."

This, I was instantly suspicious of. "Really?"

"I organized it with your father yesterday. She jumped at the chance to see Milton again. I don't know if I'll bother making up a room for her."

"Don't, she'll spend every night with Milton," I sighed, shaking my head.

Knox tilted his head. "What do you know that I don't?"

"I have a medical degree, so I dare say a hell of a lot of anatomy," I answered vaguely.

"I meant about your sister?"

"Again, she's my sister, so a lot." I kept my eyes focused on the menu.

Grabbing the menu, Knox set it aside. "You chose what you wanted as soon as you sat down. Spill."

Lifting a brow at his presumptiveness, I chewed my bottom lip. "Rhiannon is my sister; I'm not going to betray her to you."

"You are my mate. You will be honest with me."

"I haven't been dishonest," I debated.

Pinching the top of his nose, Knox closed his eyes and counted, to fifty. "Let's try this. Your sister is renowned for being promiscuous, but she hooks up with Milton on every occasion. Why is he special?"

Leaning forward, I smiled, my eyebrow jutting higher. "You really want to know?"

Knox gritted his teeth. He was kind of cute frustrated. "Yes."

"He's got a huge-"

"I've seen it," Knox cut me off with a growl. "Mine's bigger."

Snickering, I shook my head." You've measured it, haven't you?"

"We were young wolves together. You do those sorts of things." Impressed, I smiled at Knox. "What?" He grumbled.

"You couldn't bear for me to talk about another man's package in a positive manner, could you?"

Knox didn't look happy. "No, it grated on my nerves. Why Burns?"

My eyes jumped to his. When determined curiosity stared back at me, I exhaled. "Have you ever been cut with a silver blade?"

"Yes, it's excruciating." Lowering his voice, Knox took a deep breath. "I know it was excruciating for you."

"Excruciating doesn't cover it," I whispered. "It burned for months while my body slowly healed. You see, we can't heal silver until we shift, and they gave me a human blood transfusion at the hospital."

Knox's eyes went wide. "You couldn't shift till the human blood left your system?"

Clenching my jaw, I wanted to fill out that knowledge for him, but it wasn't the time and place for that. "You know Brett?" I queried. "Do you do work at the base?"

Knox hesitated, which, in itself, answered the question. "Yes."

Fidgeting with my water glass, I studied my mate. "Brett's spoken about the hound platoon. They are a special unit within the special forces."

"He told you that, did he?" Knox sat forward, intrigued.

"He tried out for the platoon. It's the only one he's ever been knocked back from." Keeping eye contact, I took a drink. "My guess is that his humanity instantly got him rejected."

Knox took a large gulp of his water. "He shouldn't have told you that."

"It was a trade of secrets," I admitted. "The story behind my scars for his biggest disappointment."

"Scars?" Knox's eyes drifted down to where the table hid my pelvis. "From the silver?" We can heal anything, but we need to shift to do it. Even then, silver leaves its mark. "I hadn't considered his initials would still be there," Knox frowned.

"I covered it with a tattoo."

Knox frowned harder. "To keep a tattoo after shifting, you'd have to have used silver-based inks." Swallowing, I nodded. "Jesus, Anique, you must have some pain threshold."

"Exposure builds resistance. It stopped hurting years ago now and was better than seeing his initials every time I looked in the mirror."

"I can't argue with that."

When our meals arrived, we ate in relative silence. Eventually, Knox asked his next question. "How did you support yourself away from the pack?"

"My father paid for my tuition and rent. A compensation of kind, I guess. I worked to pay for everything else."

"You were living with Brett. Where are you living now?"

"I own my own place. A graduation gift from my father."

Knox's eyes went wide. "So, you left the pack, but the Alpha still supported you?"

"No, I couldn't return to the pack for my own safety. My father, not my Alpha, set me up with a trust fund that I could access for educational needs and to purchase a house when I graduated," I shrugged. "You'll probably pay twice as much for my dowry, considering my genetic line. He won't be out of pocket in the end."

Quiet for a moment, Knox watched me as his Adam's apple bobbed. There was a sense of hesitation flashing in his eyes before anger followed through. When the bill came, I stood up. "Do you want me to go Dutch?"

"Don't insult me," Knox grumbled.

"Then, I'll use the ladies before we leave." Going to the bathroom, I checked my phone on the way there and sent a message to Mandy.

Me: *You girls clear?*

Examining the puncture marks, I cringed poking the heated red lump that had developed from the inflammation response. Soon, I'd be running the usual bonding fever, something most couples were too busy finishing the fourth phase to really notice.

Goddess, I needed to get out ahead of this. My phone buzzed, stealing my focus.

> **Mandy**: *House is clean, scents covered. Finished our visit to Monique's family and heading to our new place. How is the date?*
> **Me**: *Has been intense. About to have that talk.*
> **Mandy**: *Hugs. Good luck.*

KNOX

$\mathcal{T}$aking Anique's hand, we left the car at the park near her house. The other she-wolves were here somewhere, I could feel it. "Those she-wolves you were running with the other day, are they just friends of yours, or your pack?"

Anique gave me a half-smile. "We run together on occasion, nothing exciting." Her eyes stayed with me. "I'm not giving them to you, Knox. They've been betrayed by their packs, they deserve their freedom and happiness."

"What makes you think I'd take that away from them?" I asked, surprised by her bluntness.

"You're a wolf, aren't you?" Anique grumbled as if that's all that was needed to mistreat a bitch.

"I'd like them to have the opportunity to find their true-mate, Anique, to find what we have together."

Anique sniffed in disbelief, and I was insulted by her attitude. "I've disconnected myself from them, Knox. I won't put them at risk. I told them to leave town, find a new place to live and be free."

Her words were honest, but there was something in them misleading, something I couldn't put my finger on. Walking into the park, Anique paused to sit on a bench, but I squeezed her hand and led her to the running track that led into the forest. What I wanted to do couldn't be done here in the open.

"Where are we going?" Anique hesitated as we crossed into the forest.

"I want to be alone with you amongst nature," I eased her worry, coating it with my will to have her come along. Feet slowing only a touch, Anique allowed me to lead her back to that fallen tree I'd stripped behind only a few days ago.

At the tree, I turned her under my arm, caught her waist in my hands, and kissed her. Anique stiffened, then melted into the kiss. This wasn't the burning passion of our first kiss, where the Goddess meant to smother our common sense. This was tentative, lips pinching gently, tongues tasting with wariness.

Tugging Anique closer to me, I stepped her back against the fallen tree. When I deepened the kiss, Anique moaned and rubbed her body against mine. That's all the encouragement I needed. Cuffing the back of her neck, I kissed her harder, with more need. In the back of my mind, I kept expecting the Goddess to take over and to force this to move into the last phase, but she let me control this. Skimming my hand up Anique's thigh, I lifted her dress to touch her naked flesh.

Anique's body flinched a little from my touch, her fingers grabbing hold of my shirt as if she might sink into the ground if she let go. "Wait," Anique breathed between kisses, "we need to talk."

"No, I want you now." I wanted her on all four paws, for her to make me chase her, catch her, for my teeth to grab her ruff and hold her until she lowered herself in submission. For Anique to lift her tail to me, let me have her in wolf form, for our bodies to fuse with our mating and not to pull out of her until she acknowledged I owned her wolf.

That did it. The thought of having Anique over and over until I put my cub in her, triggered the last phase. Just as Anique opened her mouth to insist we talk first, the moon washed over us, and we were lost to the needs of a Goddess.

Kissing Anique hard, I was determined that I wasn't leaving here until she was mine in every way. Anique's fingers gripped my shirt, but it wasn't enough. I wanted her hands on my bare skin, her nails dragging over my muscles as I took her. Afterward, I would take her home and purge ourselves on each other until we had no energy to continue, or she found herself with cub. That's how it worked. How it had always been done.

Tugging my shirt off, Anique gasped for the few seconds I freed her luscious mouth. Pulling her back to me, I tossed the shirt away as I pressed her harder into the tree. Anique's fingers were expertly removing my belt, and from there, she unzipped me and took me in hand.

Cursing at the spectacular feeling of her holding me, I lifted my face to the moon in thanks. Dropping her mouth to my neck, Anique kissed along my jugular. Shoving her knickers down her legs, I lifted her out of them as I sat her bare ass on the rough tree and stepped between her thighs.

Just as the head of me touched the silk of her, Anique sank her canines into my shoulder. Blinking wide-eyes at the pain and pleasure her marking me as hers caused, I moaned, despite me knowing she wasn't meant to do that. Only the men marked their women, but the Goddess had taken Anique and demanded I be marked hers as much as she was mine.

Fisting her beautiful russet locks in my fist, I used her hair to pull her mouth free, and lifted her face so I could access her mouth. Blinking rapidly, Anique stared at me for a moment, her eyes clear of the lust glaze. "Knox, wait-" anguish choking her pleasure.

There was no time to analyze the fear that suddenly radiated from her. Shoving my hips forward, I surged into her, thrusting my tongue into her mouth, penetrating her doubly. Her nails scraped at my biceps, my body pushing further into hers with every strangled breath she took.

As our bodies merged fully, I kissed her. Gently, lovingly, and with all the adoration I felt for her. Kissing her as I moved within her, I knew Dante spoke the truth. It felt amazing being with her, my senses heightened beyond anything I'd ever felt before. It wasn't just our bodies, but our souls were merging with every push of my body into hers. Every touch, every kiss, I felt her all the way to my bones and deeper.

When Anique moaned, I thought the sound alone would bring me to climax. Murmuring her name as I rocked into her, I told her how much I loved her, how I was going to protect her, that she'd never be hurt again. Told her she was mine, and I was hers.

As I rocked into her, Anique tightened her grip around me, with her fingers, and her body. It was more than I could bear, sensitive as I was with her. Thrusting into her deeply, I groaned as I claimed her fully. Holding her tight to me for several minutes, I breathed in the scent of her. Expecting her to smell of the happiness I felt, I frowned to find her fear was growing with every passing second.

"What happens now?" she whispered after the quiet went on too long.

"You come home with me, and we spend the next couple of weeks away together, mating, till we can't bear another moment of sex," I chuckled. Anique's body tightened around my softening erection. Instantly, I was ready for her again, but the Goddess had her way now, and my head was mine. I needed to make her submit to me. "Shift." Stepping back from her, I kicked my boots off before dropping my pants altogether. "We need to finish this."

Freezing like a deer in the headlights, Anique shook her head. "No, Knox, we need to talk, I need to explain-"

"Shift now, explain later," I growled as I let my own shift wash over me. Stamping my paws for a second, I waited for her. Anique's fear was spiking as she backed away from me. Grabbing at the bottom of her dress, I tugged.

"Knox, please, we need to talk. I wanted to discuss this before any of this happened, please-"

Tugging at her dress harder, I ripped it a little. Gasping, Anique picked up her shoed foot and shoved me away from her. Growling, I positioned my paws ready to pounce, giving her warning that she needed to shift now.

Turning on her heels, Anique bolted. She was fast, very fast in human form. Lifting my head, I howled. Unable to resist her mate's call, Anique tripped over. She cursed as she tried to find her feet again. Howling a second time, I called her to shift. Crying out, Anique fell back to the ground, curling her fingers into the soil, she gritted her teeth on a scream of anguish.

Padding closer to Anique, I circled her. She still wasn't shifting as I'd demanded. She was strong-willed for a female, but to resist the call of her mate...? Again, I howled for her to change.

Crumpling to the ground, Anique screamed. Flashes of lights behind my eyes blinking in the night, but I couldn't understand what she was trying to tell me. "Stop!" Anique begged as I raised my head again. "I can't, Knox. I can't shift."

Her words reeked of honesty and pain. So, much agony. Confused, I nuzzled her, breathing her scent deep, and as I did, that horrible secret of hers ran through my head again.

Stepping back from her with a whimper, I paced the forest litter. This couldn't be right. My mate, my true-mate, couldn't change her form. Anique had never shifted. In pure anger and frustration, I snarled at her. The Goddess betrayed me. Stretching back to human form in a snap, I glared down on the crumpled mess the Goddess tricked me into thinking was my mate. "You can't shift?! That's why your father waived your dowry. He knew you were worthless, nothing more than a pathetic wolf-born human."

Lifting her distressed green eyes to meet mine, Anique blinked a flood of tears free. Her breathing was harsh and strained from the pain. "I'm sorry, Knox," a sob racking her chest. "I'm so sorry."

The fury of hell burned in my veins as I struck my fist into the closest tree. The tree creaked and cracked while Anique whimpered at my feet. "This is a joke. I can't mate with a bitch so weak she can't even shift. This is done! The Goddess can go to hell. I don't want to see you ever again."

Meeting my eyes, Anique sucked in a breath as all apology for her weakness vanished. "You free me of my obligation as your mate?"

"Yes! I free myself from a pathetic whelp like you."

The forest in her eyes became hard, unyielding, and filled with complete hatred for me. With utter determination, Anique gritted her teeth and struggled to her feet. With one last glare in my direction, she left. She was in agony, I could feel it and smell it on her, but Anique forced herself to stand and run.

Staring after her, feeling betrayed by the Goddess, I wanted to kill every wolf in her pack that helped desecrate her. Beneath my rage, I wanted to go after her and soothe her pain, but it wasn't strong enough to breach the surface yet. Only after Anique disappeared from sight did I let the reality of what just happened, of the words I'd just yelled to my mate, set in.

"Anique!" What had I done? "Anique, wait!" Nothing. She'd vanished into the night as fast as I'd destroyed the Goddesses gift. "Fuck!"

Dropping into a crouch, I covered my face in my hands. The Goddess had her way, we'd completed the mating phases. It didn't have to be done in wolf form, but if we didn't, she didn't have to submit to me either. Then I'd released her from any commitment to me in my fit of anger. Now, we'd be mated without loyalty.

Anique's inability to shift wasn't her fault. The Goddess showed me that with those more delicate details of her torture, and yet, I'd blamed her.

Returning to the fallen tree to find my clothes, I dressed. As I turned to leave, I spied Anique's little panties on the ground. Collecting them, I wrapped them around my bleeding knuckles. Absently, I touched her bite mark as I walked back to my car. She'd marked me as hers, infected me with the bond virus, already the heat of inflammation was flaring. My mark would protect her. Any stray that sniffed around her would know she was mated to a strong Alpha and leave her alone.

Her mark meant that any bitch I got naked with now would know me for a disloyal bastard who abandoned his mate. If that got around the packs, I'd be seen as weak and would find wolves challenging me. That would put my pack in danger, and I couldn't have that.

Arriving home in the late evening, I slammed the front door behind me. Rion rushed out to greet me, smile as big as they come. "Did you do it? Do we have them?"

Standing there, glaring at Rion, I growled. His smile fading, Rion backed up a step. His eyes drifted down to find my knuckles bloodied from punching the tree, and his brow creased in confusion. Dante entered the room, took the scene in quickly, and yanked Rion back just as he opened his mouth. "Did you kill her?" Rion whispered.

Dante quickly shoved Rion back towards the hallway. "Don't answer that," he warned me, moving with Rion into the back of the house. "You take the time you need, do what you need and if you want to tell us later, when you are calm, do it then."

Glaring at them as they left, I snarled at Dante for having the perfect she-wolf for a mate. His mate could shift, she was of a good bloodline, and she got with cub during the mating purge. Evaline, despite her pigheadedness, had done everything a she-wolf was expected to do. The Goddess gave me a bitch who was stray, rogue, and so damaged she couldn't even release her wolf.

Clenching my fists, I had to try not to tear the place apart at the unfairness of it. Storming out of the packhouse, I shifted mid-stride and ran off into the forest to hunt. I needed to rip something apart with my teeth, to taste blood, and pain, and fear. I needed to kill.

Waking up hot with fever and desiring my mate, I looked at the clock beside my bed. Anique would be halfway through her day already. Picking up the phone, I dialed the hospital. "Dr. Annie Burns, please?"

The operator placed me on hold as I kicked off the quilt and shivered with the fever.

"Dr. Burns speaking," Anique's tired voice came on the line. Then and there, I knew she was suffering the bond fever too, the sound of her voice increasing the intensity of mine instantly.

"I want you out of my territory," I told her civilly. "I find you and your pack in my territory, I'll sell you all off to-"

The phone line went dead. Unsure if we'd been cut off or she'd hung up on me, I called back. "Dempsey Military Hospital. How may I direct your call?"

" Dr. Annie Burns, please?"

"Please hold." After waiting for fifteen minutes, the operator came back. "I'm sorry, but Dr. Annie Burns can't be located in the hospital right now, she must have finished for the day."

Satisfied that Anique took my threat seriously, and was currently at home packing to run again, I threw my phone aside and went back to sleep. Or, at least, I tried to. The reason we send couples away for the mating purge is so they could burn off the bond fever and get it out of their system. Anique and I weren't going to be getting anything but frustration. So, I ended up tossing and turning in feverish dreams of Anique naked beneath me, her red locks strewn across my pillow, and the sound of her moans as I filled her with my climax.

As the next few days came and went, I realized the biggest downfall of letting Anique go. Not only the constant desire for her, or even dreaming about how amazing sex with her had been. No, it was that my wolf longed for her.

Every time I shifted, I sat baying for her for a good twenty minutes. Exhausted, frustrated, and throat howled raw by the time day four came around, everyone in the packhorse was steering clear of me. It was Dante who eventually broached the subject. "Are you ready to talk about it?"

"No." I focused back on the screen of my computer.

Sitting in the chair opposite my desk, Dante waited patiently. "Evaline checked in with her father last night. He's been unable to get a hold of Anique. Should Evaline be grieving her sister?"

Slamming my laptop shut, I growled before I caught myself. "I said I don't want to talk about it." Standing up, I went to stand at the window. "Where's Rhiannon? She was meant to arrive two days ago."

"We don't know."

Turning to face him, I assessed Dante's discomfort. "What do you mean, we don't know?"

"She was put on the bus to Campus. Milton went to meet the bus, but she never got off it. Stirling says she hasn't contacted her Alpha, but he doesn't seem overly concerned either, if anything, he seemed angry." Dante shook his head. "Evaline just rolled her eyes and grumbled about Rhiannon going off the rails again."

Thinking of how Stirling had continued to support Anique, how Anique had differentiated between him being her father and Alpha, I pursed my lips. "Rhiannon hasn't contacted her Alpha, but I bet she contacted her father," I murmured as I considered the timing. "Anique!" Rhiannon was more than likely looking for or running with her sister.

"Did her pack attack you?" Dante pressed once I said her name. "You are within your rights to protect yourself, even from your mate, Alpha."

"She didn't attack me, neither did the pack. They'd already taken off by the time I went back."

Dante nodded as if he'd expected that. "But, Anique stayed, and you marked her?"

Huffing in annoyance, I avoided looking at Dante. "What makes you say that?"

"The set of fang marks she left in your shoulder." Dante nodded his head towards my left shoulder. "I saw them the night you came back, so did Rion. It's why he thought you'd killed her."

"I didn't kill her. I should have. Would have put us both out of our misery."

"Do you really think killing your true-mate after completing the mating, would make you any less miserable?" When I met Dante's sad eyes, he sat forward. "What happened?"

"She's gone. Her and the pack of she-wolves are out of our territory, and out of our reach. That's all that's important. Tell Milton to take the team to the hospital and see if they can pick up Rhiannon's scent there. I don't want to have to pay a dowry for a bitch we didn't even get." Storming out, I headed for the gym. I needed to lay into the bag and sweat my annoyance out.

ANIQUE

*A*lready looking like a corpse the next day at work, I'd dismissed everyone's concerns about my failing health. No one died of the bond virus that I'd ever heard. But when Knox called me, his voice ramped the fever into overdrive. Hanging up, I'd passed out on the floor. When I came to, I had my own bed in the emergency ward, and Brett was sitting by my side.

Hands pressed together, refusing to touch me, Brett watched me wake with wariness. "I'm still down as your next as kin."

"I'm so sorry, Brett," I sobbed. I'd given him up for a fate that would turn against me.

Staring down at his hands, Brett rubbed his lips together. "I called your sister. She jumped on the train an hour ago. I'll pick her up from the station and bring her over to you."

Holding in tears, I nodded. The fever was still burning in me. Noting the cannula in my hand, I tried to read the drip bag above my head.

"They couldn't identify the virus, so they are just hitting you with the good stuff," Brett informed me. When he stood up to leave, I grabbed his hand. Still refusing to meet my eyes, Brett shook his head. "You said you had years yet, did you leave me because that wasn't the case?"

"No. I left you because I needed to sort some shit out."

"And how does Morgan fit into that?" Brett asked, angrily.

"He got what he wanted from me last night. I won't be seeing him again." I wouldn't lie to Brett.

Frowning, Brett hesitated, and for the first time since I woke, he met my eyes. "Wait, are you sick because of something he did to you?"

Oh boy, how did I answer that one? "I think you'll find he's just as sick. He was coming down ill when we parted ways last night." Closing my eyes for a moment, I shrugged one shoulder. "Maybe we were allergic to each other."

Brett shook his head. "I'm sorry the bastard used you."

"Maybe that needed to happen for me to find my way forward? I'd felt trapped again since going home to see my family. Don't get me wrong, I feel like shit now, but something has shifted too."

Brett gave me the ghost of a smile. "You trying to tell me something, Annie?"

"Not yet, I'm not. I'm going to take a little bit to recover from this, but I will recover."

Sighing, Brett nodded. "I'll go get Rhiannon. When you're ready, you know where to find me."

My tears fell a little faster. "Fate will bring us back together when it's time."

Lips twitching in a smile, Brett dropped a peck on my forehead and left.

By the time Rhiannon arrived, I was sitting up, ready to be discharged. "What happened?" She asked worriedly.

Eyeing the staff who were my work colleagues, I shook my head. "When we get home."

Holding her tongue until she got me in the door of my house and sitting up in my bed, Rhiannon sat down beside me. "So?"

"It's the bond fever."

"Well, no wonder you are sick. You are meant to be with your mate. The fever is barely noticeable during the purge."

Tears streaming faster, I nodded. "He couldn't get me to shift, Rhi. I had to tell him that I couldn't, that I'd never shifted."

Rhiannon frowned in confusion. "But, you explained it's because of what happened, that they took you during your first heat, so you hadn't shifted yet, that the silver poisoned you and that-"

Through her reasoning, I was shaking my head. The blood drained from Rhi's face. "He wouldn't hear it," I bawled. "He's removed himself from me."

Rhiannon stood up, shocked. "Just physically, right? I mean, you completed the phases."

"He released me of my obligations as his mate."

"No, loyalty!" Rhiannon gasped. Mouth hanging open, she sat hard. "But a bond with no loyalty, forever tied together, neither of you can breed with another, and you'll always yearn for each other."

Sagging down in my bed, I started blubbering. Knox's absence was already a hole in my chest.

Swiping tears from her own eyes, Rhiannon stood up. "I'm ducking down the shops. We need junk food, alcohol, and horror movies."

Six days later, we'd watched nearly every horror movie in the movie store, eaten gallons of ice cream, and cried, screamed, and laughed together. The doctor who treated me gave me the week off work sick - passing out in emergency with a high scale fever will do that - and this morning, I was due back.

"Are you sure you're going to be okay?" Rhiannon asked.

"I always am."

"Lies. You just fake it better than the rest of us."

Taking my sister's shoulders in my hands, I stared into her eyes.

"You need to stop punishing yourself, Rhi. You aren't to blame for what happened to me."

Hiccuping once, Rhiannon started crying. "No, but I'm the reason you're dying."

"God, no, Rhi. You're the reason I'm living." Pulling her into a hug, we cried on each other's shoulders until the taxi blew its horn outside.

Wiping the tears from her cheeks, Rhiannon stepped away. "I have to go. Milton will arrive at the station soon. If I want him to believe I just got off the train, I need to be there before him."

"Enjoy the Valleymorgans' hospitality."

Rhiannon gritted her teeth. "I'm going to knee Knox in the balls for you, Annie. I promise. I may not do it till the day I'm leaving again, but I will do it."

Not discouraging my sister from giving Knox his dues, I smirked, ignoring the void itching beneath my sternum at the mention of his name. Grabbing her bags, Rhiannon headed out. She promised she'd come to see me before she went home if she could. Keeping my lips pressed tight, I didn't call her on her delusion.

Rhiannon was never going home from the Valleymorgans'. I'd known that the moment Knox told me she was going. But I wouldn't stop her. I knew why she kept going back to Milton, even if no one else did, and the Valleymorgans would be better for her than the Beachrunners.

Stepping out of the shower, I stood in front of the mirror. The redness in my mark had died down; the lump was gone, so only the nearly healed puncture wounds remained. Knox's would have recovered the first time he shifted. After six days, it'd just be my scent mixed with his. Caressing the mark, I wondered how bad the fever had been for him?

The next month passed by quickly. Throwing myself headlong into work, I picked up extra shifts and committed myself to the orthopedics specialization. By the time I finished my last shift for a few days, my girls were running an intervention.

"Okay, let's see," Danielle surveyed the nightclub, "looks like the guys from the base are all here, and the academy graduates are ready to party."

Mandy grinned. "Lots of fruit on the tree tonight, girls. What's the play?"

Danielle smiled. "No one goes home alone tonight. Each and every one of us picks up, and Annie is up first."

"What? No. I haven't picked up in ages, not since Brett. I need to watch the masters at work."

"I'll go first," Monique offered. "I'm going academy." We all laughed. Most of the girls preferred the special forces' men. They were like fully charged vibrators with arms and legs who could go all night. "What?" Monique blushed. "I'm still walking funny after that communications officer last Friday."

"If he's here, I'm so calling dibs," Danielle cut in.

"Well, I'm going base," Mandy decided. "Annie?"

"Considering my body is still wanting to relieve the purge, I'm definitely hitting base."

"Will it feel weird?" Monique asked.

"Yeah, but if the guy is good, it shouldn't matter, unless he wants to cuddle after." The sucky thing for a she-wolf was that we couldn't orgasm until we are mated, and only for our mate.

Don't get me wrong, sex is good. We get everything else out of it, and we can scream and moan for how fantastic it feels. We just don't have the climax. Which is sort of good when you are on sex marathons because your body doesn't get that shut off. So, once he's right to go again, you are pretty much already in full throttle.

"So, the order is, Monique, Danielle, Annie, then myself," Mandy decided. "No restrictions other than he, or she," Danielle sometimes played both sides of the fence, and occasionally at the same time, "must be from the chosen campus."

Monique grinned. "Let's get me my giggle juice and start surveying the menu then."

At the bar, the girls did shots with chasers while I had water. We had an audience already. All of us dressed to impress, which meant a lot of leg and cleavage. Taking our drinks, we moved around the room, hunting out our night's fun, sniffing out our prey.

On our first round, I spotted Brett. He was standing with some of his friends in a dark corner, hunting out their own prey. One of the guys nudged Brett's arm then pointed to us. Brett met my eyes and held it as I walked by. I didn't flinch, and as I moved to where I'd have to turn my head, I smirked.

When I looked over my shoulder, Brett reflected my smirk. His mate, Nathan, was laughing at us. But I waited like a good girl. Monique and Danielle picked their prey and stalked them until the right moment to pounce. Studying their different techniques, I laughed at how predatory they were.

Monique was all about stealth. She stayed hidden from her prey, eyes peeled and ready. Then, when her victim turned around, she was just there and on him.

Danielle, however, was about the suspense. She'd move around her prey, catching his eye for a moment, then disappearing, before making herself visible again. The victim stood helpless after a moment, looking around anxiously for its predator, paralyzed by the hunt, his heart rate racing as every sighting brought her closer. She always let the last sighting be the longest and allow her prey to wonder if she'd lost interest. He'd turn his head astounded, only to find her there. Grabbing his neck, Danielle went for the throat.

Watching this, Mandy and I laughed when Danielle licked up the guy's throat, watching his eyes roll back, his hands encircling her tiny waist. "Danielle is such a drama queen," Mandy giggled.

Mandy and I both hunted in a similar way. We lured our prey to us. While Mandy chose to play shy and coy, I preferred just to be still and available. Mandy and I tended to go for the dominant men, who usually fancied themselves predators, so it was best to let them feel that way.

"You good to go?" Mandy asked. When I nodded, Mandy smiled, "Have a good night."

She moved away, knowing I'd found my prey and would stand and wait now. Turning my eyes to my right, I made eye contact with him ten meters away, smiled, and focused back on the writhing bodies on the floor. When I felt his body press up next to mine, his large hands smoothing around my waist as he lowered his face to my ear, I bit my lip. "Let's get out of here, Annie."

Gazing up into Brett's gorgeous eyes, I took his hand, and he led me out to his car. The drive to his place was quiet; we'd always been happy in silence together. The moment we got inside his door, that all changed. After locking his door, Brett turned, and I was on him. Shoving him against the door, I kissed him like I'd been suffocating without him.

Helping me out of my dress and underwear, Brett turned us and put my back to his wall. Naked and ready for him, I relieved him of his clothing while Brett kicked his shoes off." God, Annie, what took you so long?" Brett asked as he lifted my body so I could wrap my thighs around his waist.

"I needed time to accept things. Time to be sure."

Carrying me into his bedroom, Brett laid me beneath him. "Tell me you're mine again, Annie. Tell me that you'll marry me?" Brett begged as his mouth made a wet path to my breast.

"Till death do us part," I promised with a gasp.

I meant it. We both knew that I was dying. I'd been dying since the day Rhiannon helped me escape from Dan. Until earlier this year, Rhiannon and my father were the only ones who knew, apart from my doctor. But when Brett proposed, I'd told him why kids weren't an option for me, why I needed to live for the moment, and why I'd chosen Dempsey to do my residency.

Breaking away, Brett opened his bedside table, grabbed out my engagement ring, and gently put it back on my ring finger. "Don't you dare take that off again."

Grinning down at him as he kissed down my stomach, I ran my fingers through his hair. The ring sparkled as my breath rushed out of me when his tongue probed my core. Despite the niggle under my skin that it wasn't my mate, it felt so good. It could have been worse. If Knox hadn't released me of loyalty to him, it would sting to have another man touch me like this.

"Fuck!" Why was I still thinking about Knox? The bastard mated with me, then ditched me. He didn't deserve me. How the Goddess ever thought he did, was beyond me.

"Annie, what's wrong?"

I knew what was wrong and what I needed. I didn't know if I could handle it, but I needed it. "No foreplay, don't be gentle, just take me," I breathed against his lips.

Biting his neck, I scratched down his back. The bite was with my human teeth, the fang thing only happened for your mate, and only the initial claiming. I couldn't even fathom what would happen to a human injected with the bond virus. "Please, Brett. I'm ready," I pleaded.

Groaning like he'd been waiting for those words for five years, Brett lowered his hips between my open thighs. As he slid himself between my folds and found my entrance, I bit my lip. Kissing me passionately, Brett drove into me as hard as he could.

Nails biting into his back as he pounded his body into mine, I cried out. Psychologically, it was tough for me, but probably long overdue to be done. I trusted Brett, loved him, and knew he wouldn't hurt me like that. As soon as I remembered that, I relaxed and enjoyed the rougher way he was taking me. Physically, it was a welcome relief. I hadn't fed the purge, and now my body was crying out for Brett never to stop doing this to me.

Spurred on by my vocalization, Brett raised himself up so he could reach between us and play with my clit. Closing my eyes, I hung my head back as my body climbed straight to the pinnacle of ecstasy. All I needed was that last push to send me tumbling over, an experience only one person could give me.

It didn't matter, I cried out, my body tight and ready to go. Since I'd never climaxed to know what I was missing, I loved this feeling. Pulling away, Brett flipped me over and shoved back into me lying down - not on all fours, never in doggy style. Rough sex or no, he knew doggy was a big no.

Racing towards his big finish, Brett sucked in ragged breaths, his heavy cock throbbing where I held him tightly. Withdrawing suddenly, Brett groaned. "I need that condom if we want to be sure about kids, Annie."

Rolling to face him, I knelt up and moved to him, forcing him to sit cross-legged as I straddled him. "You can't get me pregnant, Brett," I assured him. Loyalty or not, my body was programmed to my mate's now. Impaling myself on him slowly, both of us moaned at the sensation.

"You're sure?" Brett checked as his hands firmed around me. Brett wouldn't have cared. He'd have me pregnant in a heartbeat if I'd agreed. It's why it'd taken five years for him to propose. He'd been waiting for me to change my mind, thinking it was just while I was studying that I didn't want kids. When he proposed, and I'd told him my life expectancy, he'd finally understood why I didn't want a family.

"I want you to cum in me and make me yours," I whispered in his ear.

Groaning long and hard as I started riding him, Brett was throbbing already. Holding me tight, he moaned my name as I cried out how good it felt to have him inside me. Cursing loudly, Brett pulsed inside me. Every spurt of his seed was a fire to the inside of my uterus. Clinging to Brett, I cried out, not having expected pain for letting him do that, but the pleasure...

Collapsing limp in his arms as my body finished burning off the foreign seed, I whimpered. Brett chuckled, wrapping me tighter. "You've never screamed like that for me before, Annie."

Biting my lip, I would never tell Brett I hadn't climaxed. "It's never felt like that before," I replied honestly, kissing his shoulder.

Falling quiet a moment, Brett held me tight. "I don't want to wait, Annie. I've waited long enough."

I snuggled tighter to him. "Okay."

Mouth falling open, Brett leaned back, taking my face in his hands to ensure eye contact. "Really?"

Laughing at him, I lifted a brow in challenge. "Do that to me three more times before sunrise, and I'll go with you tomorrow."

A grin spreading across his face, Brett threw me back on the bed and started round two. There was foreplay this time, humans needed recovery time, even sex machines like Brett. As the sun rose, I cried out as my body burnt off his seed for the fourth time that night because Brett was an overachiever.

KNOX

The floor was littered with the bodies of wolves. Some were dressed, others were in their pajamas, in other rooms, some were still in bed, not having got out of bed for breakfast.

"They're all dead," Dante frowned. "Maybe another pack got to them first?"

"And left their throats intact? Didn't even wake half of the pack? Unlikely."

When the Barrow pack hadn't turned up to the meet, we hunted them back to their packhouse. Now, we were counting the dead. Frowning as Rion was checking the bodies, I worried it was viral, and should I be getting my men out of here and burning the place to the ground.

"Poisoned," Rion finally decided as he stood. "By the looks of it, I'd say they were given the poison for dinner. It was fast-acting, some just asphyxiated, others also suffered gastrointestinal upset. Hence the mess where they lined up for the toilet."

Moving into the kitchen properly, I used my nose to try and find the poison. Very few toxins that were lethal to humans were dangerous to wolves, at least, it needed to be in a stronger dose. Edgar stood by the sink. "It's here, I can smell it faintly."

Joining him, I sniffed. Sure enough, there was a slight odor, one I didn't recognize. "What is that?"

Edgar's grey brows pinched. "You're all too young to have come across it." He turned on the tap, and the smell got stronger, but only because I was sniffing for it. I'd have missed it otherwise. "Wolfsbane," Edgar snarled then turned off the tap.

Mouth falling open, Rion looked over the bodies. "Well, that fits. Those who ingested it would have got the gastro before it affected their respiratory system. It's readily absorbed by the skin, just picking the leaves can give you a fatal dose, so showering in water laced with wolfsbane would be fatal, maybe one to three hours after."

"Am I right in thinking they've been dead nearly two weeks now?" I asked.

"Easily. I'd say a day or two after we contacted them." Rion shook his head. "This will be the third pack wiped out in a matter of years."

"That's right, there was a pack in the west that got taken out a few years back, and another probably three years ago."

Rion nodded. "The Carrington Mountain pack was poisoned at a banquet to mate the last of their she-wolves. The bitch was the Alpha's daughter and was the only one not killed, and couldn't be found afterward."

Tilting my head, I stared at Rion, so I saw the lightbulb go off in his head as it did with the rest of the team. Clenching my fists, I looked at Edgar. "Where's the water supply?"

Edgar moved instantly. Most packs relied on tank water. They liked to be self-sufficient from the humans. The older the packhouse, the more likely that was the case. Following Edgar out as he located the tanks that fed the house, I already knew what we would find. Lifting the cap, I didn't even have to try and smell it. In fact, the smell was so strong, I had to recoil.

"Check the perimeter, you're looking for the scent of a she-wolf," I ordered.

"From two weeks ago?" Dante asked. "It's summer, but we've had rain."

"Yes, but we should all recognize this scent as one of our killers from Campus."

Suddenly excited, they spread out sniffing for bitches. Dante stayed with me. "You think one of those bitches Anique knew in Campus is our killer?"

"Three packs are gone, and three she-wolves killed the last enforcer who came from here." I didn't believe in coincidence. "I think if you checked, all the packs taken out would have lost their last she-wolf after forcing her to mate against her will." I thought about it. "And every one of those bitches is an Alpha's progeny." Cursing, I started storming back to the car.

"Alpha?" Dante marched beside me.

"Call Alpha Stirling and tell him to check their water supply daily," I directed.

Dante frowned. "You think they will take out the Beachrunners next?"

"Yes. The only reason they weren't taken out years ago is that Anique's sisters were still at home. Not only have we taken both her sisters, but I've made one of the strongest she-wolves I've ever met, very, very angry."

"They did this after we came after them after they had to run again," Dante decided as we reached the cars where Clarise was waiting. "Anique wasn't with them, Alpha. She stayed behind for you, remember?"

"They needed a new territory." Dante watched me. "What if they took out this pack for the territory."

"They wouldn't do that," Clarise interjected passionately, then sat back covering her mouth as she'd spoken out of turn.

We both looked at her. "You know them?" I asked, stalking towards her.

Backing up a little, Clarise shook her head. But when I growled at her, she trembled like a rabbit about to have its throat ripped out. "I met one of them, the one you mentioned, Anique," Clarise admitted. "I was starving, hiding out in the woods when she found me. She brought me a meal and put me up in a hotel for the night. She was really nice, strong, but she doesn't have it in her to be a killer."

"Why didn't you stay with them?"

"I left my pack because my father was abusive, not because they tried to force-mate me. I still want to find my mate. When I told Anique my story, she gave me a map with directions on how to find your pack. She said you would give me a home until I found my true-mate."

Blinking at her, I wasn't sure how to respond. Anique knew I would introduce Clarise around and keep her safe, so she sent her to us. Clarise still looked worried. "I wasn't the first she sent your way, Alpha. It's a choice she lets us make. The Lunas don't want to find their mates, that's why they formed their own pack and stay away from wolves. They only hurt a wolf if he threatens them."

"The Lunas?" Dante asked, frowning.

"Daughters of the moon."

"Think very carefully, Clarise, was it Luners or Lune-as?" Dante prodded.

Clarise frowned. "Actually, she pronounced it Lune-as. Why? Is it different?"

Closing my eyes, I massaged the bridge of my nose, a headache starting to form. "The Lunas was the first silver blade created which killed the King of wolves centuries ago. Mythology says the King went mad and started killing any maiden who refused him.

The King killed every she-wolf in his territory. All but one. The story says that the blade was forged by the Goddess's hand and given to the maiden whom the King had chosen to devour last. She waited until the King filled her body, then thrust the Lunas through her own chest and into the King's."

Dante nodded. "Their mingled blood seeded in the earth and bore a she-wolf like no other. History doesn't tell us how she was different, other than she was immune to silver."

Clarise frowned, obviously her pack hadn't been big on any mythology which had a female overpowering a male. Shaking my head, I sighed. "All totally irrelevant to the fact that this pack has been wiped out, and the prime suspects are The Lunas pack."

Clarise chuckled.

"What?" I pinched the bridge of my nose, counting in my head. Clarise was quite immature despite her twenty-two years.

"Nothing," Clarise sobered. "Sorry, Alpha."

The rest of my team arrived. "Anything?"

"I found three sets of footprints heading away from the tank. They led to an isolated and overgrown track that headed to the road on the other side of the estate. Size of shoe and depression would indicate three females," Edgar offered.

When I raised a brow at Clarise, she dropped her eyes. "I maintain that this pack must have posed a threat to them for them to attack."

Coming out of the house, Rion handed me some papers. "I found this inside."

Reading them, I scowled. "You're right, Clarise, this pack was a threat. It seems before the Lunas could dispatch the enforcer, he managed to inform his pack he'd found three stray she-wolves living with the one he was sent to find." Scanning the photos he'd sent back, I paused on one of my mate. My heart raced at the idea of her being taken. "They were making plans to take them all."

Thrusting the papers back at Rion, I stormed to the car. There was nothing to be done here, but now I needed to go purge myself before the frustration of giving up my mate got the better of me. "Clarise, go in the other car," I directed as I climbed into the pack SUV with Dante, Milton, and Rion.

"I maintain Anique wasn't involved in this," Dante repeated once we were on the road. "You know her scent, you'd know if she had been here."

Sighing, I stared out the window. "Milton, Rhiannon's been with us a week now, in your bed every chance she gets. Is there any chance she'd betray her sister to you?"

Milton chuckled. "None. She still maintains she was at a horror movie festival before she came to us."

Grunting, I clenched my fist. "Rhi should have showered before coming, so she didn't stink of Anique to pull that off." I'd gone with Milton to pick Rhiannon up this time. The smell of her younger sister on her was a beautiful perfume I'd never get sick of smelling. The moment they saw each other, Milton and Rhiannon had been all over each other, nearly going for it in the car.

"It's time you two made eye contact; let's see if the goddess designed the sisters for brothers," I ordered.

"She's good at avoiding. I'm better at getting what I want."

"Good. I'm going out when we get back. Have the first phase done by the time I get home."

Dante looked over from the driver's seat. "You want Rhiannon's secrets."

"I want those Alpha bitches begging me not to end them."

Pulling on my pants, I gazed at the redhead sprawled face down on the bed. Sex hadn't been the same since Anique. It wasn't horrible, but once you've known the Goddess's touch, it's hard to want a simple human again, no matter how pretty they are.

Growing hard just remembering her hair wrapped in my fist as I took her from behind, I cursed my actions three weeks ago. Taking her from behind meant I didn't see this woman's face. That way, I could believe it was Anique. Of course, touching her wasn't the same. There was an itch that I couldn't quite scratch, no matter how hard I pounded her tight little body. She just wasn't my mate.

Slipping into my shirt, I grabbed my car keys. The girl was out to it. I'd ridden her harder than a human could probably bear, the purge needing an outlet. She'd need to sleep off the last four hours of fucking, and she'd be feeling me for a few days after.

Driving the hour and a half home, feeling somewhat relieved, I walked into the quiet packhouse and moved towards the kitchen, wanting a nightcap before bed. Opening the door to the back hall, I heard the yelling instantly.

"...is such a problem?" Milton argued. "We've obviously got a connection, so let's see if it's a lifetime thing or not already."

"I said, no! I'll sleep in my own room tonight."

"Rhi, be sensible," Milton ordered, exerting his will, instigating some sort of physical struggle.

Striding forward into the doorway of the kitchen, I stayed in the shadows. Milton was preventing Rhiannon from walking out of the room and trying to get her to make eye contact.

"Why are you so set against us mating?" Milton growled releasing her. He'd seen me but wasn't looking at me, so Rhiannon didn't know I was there.

"I am not against us mating, Milton, I just don't want to go through the phases," Rhiannon argued, tears in her voice. "You want to mark me, make me yours? We can do that."

"We only do Goddess blessed mating's in this pack, Rhi. The phases are important."

"Why? Your Alpha doesn't think so? He had the woman the Goddess chose for him, and he threw her away," Rhiannon hissed bitterly. "Annie's past was too much for him, and he rejected their bond, destroying what the Goddess blessed. So, why, Milton, are the phases so important?"

Staring at Rhiannon, Milton glanced at me angrily but moved back to the woman with who he was besotted. "This is about your secrets?" Milton asked carefully. "You don't want to go through the phases, and have anyone learn what you keep hidden?"

Rhiannon hiccuped as her crying grew louder. "No one could want me, Milton. I wouldn't want me for what I've done. If he could do that to her for something that wasn't even her fault, you could never love me for the part I played in it all. I can't forgive myself."

A bonfire burst to life in my heart. I needed to know what Rhiannon had done. From what the Goddess showed me, I thought she saved Anique, but maybe there was another reason she knew where to find her sister. Moving forward quickly, I used one arm to hold Rhiannon, the other to cover her mouth and nose. The natural reaction to suddenly being restrained from behind and suffocated would give Milton what he needed.

When Rhiannon tried to scream, Milton stepped forward and met her wide-eyed stare. When the first phase hit, Rhiannon jolted in my hold. Releasing her gently, I shifted her into Milton's arms and went to the fridge to get that drink. By the time I sat down with the scotch over ice, it was over. Blinking, Rhiannon looked down at her feet a moment, then turned and glared at me.

Standing up, I didn't smile. What I'd done was underhanded, and Rhiannon knew it. "Welcome to the family, Rhi." I bowed formally.

Striding towards me, her body language told me I was about to get slapped, Rhiannon snarled at me. "You selfish bastard!" she screeched. At the last minute, she stepped into me and lifted her knee hard.

Groaning, I dropped my drink as I bent over myself. "Bitch!"

"That's right," Rhiannon snarled. "But that was for putting

Annie in the hospital." Rhiannon turned on Milton. "You better think long and hard about this before you finish the phases. If you abandon me like your disloyal Alpha did my sister, I'll tear you apart." Rhiannon turned to walk out.

"What happened to Anique?" I hissed, snatching her wrist so she couldn't storm out. Milton growled at me for touching his mate. He didn't mean it, it was just an automatic reaction. In all honesty, I think he was still shell shocked by the first phase. Still, out of respect, I released Rhiannon.

Rhiannon shook her head at me. "You don't deserve to know anything about Annie. Not anymore." She stormed out.

When I looked at Milton, he sighed. "This is going to be bad, you know that, right?"

"You just found your true-mate, how can that be bad?" I tried to tease.

Milton shook his head. "I meant her involvement in what happened to her sister. She went off the rails, has avoided finding a mate, just so no one would ever know the part she played."

I met Milton's eyes. "Well, that's about to change."

"What if I can't handle her secret, Alpha? What if she helped them do that to her own sister?" Milton asked, sounding desperate.

Putting a reassuring hand on his shoulder, I shook my head. "Firstly, you don't know half of what happened. Secondly, she's your mate. You will give her a fresh slab and start your new life together with your sins where they belong, in the past."

Milton shrugged my hand away. I was surprised by the anger suddenly coming from him. "Tell that to Anique."

12

ANIQUE

"Annie, there's a phone call for you."

Looking up from the X-ray's I was assessing, I eyed Rachel, one of the E.R. Nurses, suspiciously. It had been two months since Knox last tried calling the hospital for me, but that didn't mean it wouldn't happen again. I'd made it clear that any callers for Doctor Burns were to be refused. "Who is it?"

Rachel smiled. "Your husband."

The disappointment and relief hit me in equal measures. My body heated a little as I walked to the desk. While I still wasn't used to people calling me Dr. White or the word husband, I liked the meaning behind it.

Brett and I eloped a month ago, the day after we got engaged again. Yet, it felt like we'd been married years already. Picking up the phone, I could barely suppress my happiness. The Goddess may have chosen Knox, but my heart had chosen Brett.

"This better be from the base," I teased.

"I wish," Brett groaned.

My smile dropped. "I know it sounded like I was joking, but I wasn't. You better be back."

"Our flight back got redirected to pick up another team, and then we had to put wheels down and deal with an incident. For six hours, we've been stuck in the middle of nowhere with a bunch of hounds. I had to wait till the communications were cleared to call, I'm sorry."

"Wait, are you there with-?"

"Yep," Brett cut off.

My heart raced, knowing Knox was out of the country, partly because my body responded to the knowledge my mate was so far away. Telling that part to shut the hell up, I focused on being more concerned with my husband.

"It's always great to be stuck on a plane with a guy who used your girl for sex and then gave her a virus which hospitalized her. Best ten hours of my life, I tell you." Biting my lip, I stayed quiet. Brett blew out a breath. "Annie, it's fine. My guys trade girls like they're candy, so I'm used to hearing the guys talk about each other's girls. It's no difference between our teams."

"Knox talked about me?" I asked, fearfully, while telling the bond to stop getting excited. In all likelihood, it wouldn't be complimentary.

Brett laughed. "Hey, relax. He hasn't said a word to me other than hello."

Sagging in relief, I took a deep breath. "So, you won't make it back for our week-long sex marathon on the beach?"

"I'm still twenty to thirty hours out from the base, then I need to debrief. I'm sorry, can you call the resort and get them to move our reservation back till Monday?"

Sighing, I nodded. Pointless on the phone, but a habit. "Brett, I'm so friggin horny. I need you inside me." The fact I was on heat hadn't escaped my attention, but thanks to Knox, Brett couldn't get me pregnant anyway now. 'Would you stop thinking about that bastard!' I growled to myself.

Brett chuckled. "I'll buy you a toy for when I'm away from now on."

"Not the same."

"I know," Brett sighed. "Call the girls to stay with you the weekend; just hide my good bourbon from Danielle. I promise I'll make up for it Monday." I groaned. "How was your last shift in the emergency department?"

This week was my last before I took leave. When I came back, I'd be starting my specialization. "Can't answer that in case I curse us, and everything goes to hell."

Chuckling, Brett lowered his voice. "I've got to go, Annie. Signals about to drop. I love you."

"I love you too," I murmured, just before the line cut out.

Sighing, I hung up the phone and looked at Rachel, who'd been eavesdropping. She was married to one of the base guys as well. She smiled. "Worried?"

"Ever known the man you were meant to marry, and the one you did, were stuck in a remote location together with live ammunition?" Rachel grimaced. "Worried doesn't begin to cover it. I've got to run down to radiology."

She nodded as I headed for the door. Walking into radiology, I stuck my head in the staff room. "Hi, Annie, Monique's in one if you need her," one of the techs called.

"Thanks." Waving, I moved down to the MRI room. Opening the control room door, I stepped in. Monique was up against the wall, legs around the waist of a man with his pants around his ankles.

"Shit, sorry," I cringed, closing the door. "I'm never unseeing that."

Monique started laughing. A second later, she stuck her head out the door. "Important?"

"Uh, no. I just wanted to see if you girls wanted to crash with me the weekend? We could go clubbing and for a run."

Monique frowned. "Brett on a mission?" I nodded. "What about the Valleymorgans ?"

"Also, on a mission, and not due back for twenty hours." Grinning broadly, Monique sobered a second as her eyes flicked back inside the door. "Couldn't you use the supply room like everyone else?" I whined, still trying to get the man's hairy bum crack out of my memory. Wolves didn't have that much body hair in human form.

Monique feigned innocence. "Just a regular heart check-up with my cardiologist. You know how it is." Monique wiggled her eyebrows. "I'll let the girls know and head to yours after work."

"Great, bring pizza." Turning back down the hall, I smirked, while Monique returned to getting her blood pressure checked.

Four hours later, I was dancing my heart out at the nightclub. The girls, well, did similar things to what I'd sprung Monique doing earlier, except in the bathroom, hallways, and car park of the nightclub. Once they'd all got their rocks off, we headed back to Brett's place. We were snuggled in the living room watching season one of Teen Wolf again. Mandy loved it.

"So, how's married life?" Monique asked, squeezing onto the lounge with a big bowl of freshly popped popcorn. "Lots of sex?"

My cheeks and chest flamed. The girls laughed at me.

"Is it weird?" Mandy asked. "You know, desiring one guy, but being with another?"

"It's not like that. It might have been if I'd met Brett afterward, but I was in love with him before I met Knox, so, I don't know, it's just-" Licking my lips, I tried to find the right word for it. "It's like getting pins and needles in your foot and trying to walk on it. You know it's there; you can feel it because it hurts to walk on, but you can't control it, or feel it properly."

The girls sat there quietly, watching me. They all looked a little sad by my description.

"Did I mention the sex is mind-blowing? I love sex with Brett, it's always been amazing. With Knox, my body reacted with such intensity, and that was with me terrified out of my wits. If I'd actually relaxed enough to enjoy it-" I shook my head. "It would have been so much harder to move on again."

The girls all looked ready to cry. "Hey, enough of that. I am truly over the moon to be married to the man I chose, who I love, and who loves me despite my issues."

"Who makes you scream and writhe all night, so you turn up at work looking like you haven't slept for weeks. Happy, but tired," Mandy teased. We all laughed. After watching teen wolf, we curled into Brett's queen size bed together. Yes, it was crowded, but we always found comfort with physical closeness to our packs.

In the early morning, before daylight, I went for my usual run. Unlike the last few months, when I'd started to run the track at the defense academy to avoid the Valleymorgans patrols, we ran the forest. The girls shifted and ran with me for the first time since the Valleymorgans tried to trap us.

Afterward, we curled up on the lounge and spent the day watching Buffy reruns. "Anything further about the Burrows issue?" Danielle asked, casually.

"Knox forced Rhi to enter the first phase with one of his pack; she's theirs now."

"Does that leave the Beachrunners bitchless?"

Eyeing Danielle, I shook my head. "Leave it be, Danielle. While my father is Alpha, no one touches the Beachrunners."

"I wasn't suggesting anything, just asking."

"Yes, well, considering Knox already suspects us for the Burrows pack, we can take a respite on any more mass revenge plans." I leveled Danielle with a steely gaze. "Especially any that would harm my family."

Danielle bristled a little. "You're not our Alphia anymore, Annie. You can't tell us what to do."

The other girls shrunk back. "What are you doing?" Monique

whispered, trembling.

Intrigued that Danielle was ready to challenge me, I raised a brow. "You think you could take me?"

"I can shift," Danielle snarled. "You are restricted to human form, Annie. You'll lose."

Smiling, I stood. "Let's find out, shall we?"

Mandy jumped up. "Stop, this is insane."

Danielle rose to her feet. "Butt out, Mandy. Annie gave us up. It's time a new Alphia stepped up."

Gesturing for her to lead the way, I waved a placating hand at Mandy. This was always going to happen one day. Following Danielle into the backyard, I was confident this would end in my favor. As soon as I was clear from the house, Danielle shifted and launched at me. She was a quick shift, and in all honesty, had she not been threatening my family, I might have agreed she was strong enough to be Alphia, but she was also verging on being a sociopath

Ducking, I spun as Danielle flew at me. Grabbing her hindquarters, I swung her with me. The jolt of her stopping mid-flight and being yanked back the opposite direction elicited a yelp. That was quickly followed by another when I threw her across the yard, and she hit the fence.

Shaking her head, Danielle hunched into an attack position and snarled at me. Before she could launch again, I focused my will over hers. "Shift!"

Growling, Danielle snapped her jaws at me. Drawing harder on my strength, I smothered her will with mine. "Shift!" Danielle's body shivered all over. Tilting my head, I stopped playing nice and let her have a taste of my real strength. Focusing my energy, my wolf trotted out and stood over Danielle in my mind's eye. "Shift!" I whispered.

My will smashed into Danielle's and ripped her back into human form. Yelping, Danielle crumbled. Trembling on the ground naked, Danielle sobbed in pain as I walked up to her. Lifting fearful eyes to meet mine, Danielle opened her mouth to say something, but I cut her off.

"No more killing, Danielle. Not unless it's necessary." Not bothering to ask her if she understood or agreed, I punched her in the face, and she fell to the ground, unconscious. Wincing, I shook out my hand. Punching people's faces hurt. Turning on my heel, I stormed back inside. Mandy nodding approval while Monique clutched Mandy's arm and cowered as I approached.

Meeting my eyes, Mandy let her jaw fall open. "Your eyes?"

Glancing in the glass of the backdoor, I witnessed my vivid green eyes with a ring of wolf gold around the pupil. A partial shift. To be expected since my wolf got in on the action, but something none of us had seen happen with me before. I guess I'd just never been angry enough.

Gazing back at Danielle, I sighed. While it was tempting to leave her outside to sleep it off, it was autumn, and in the valley of a high-altitude mountain range, that meant freezing when you're naked. Glancing at Mandy, I sighed, and she nodded understanding. "Come on, Monique. Let's get Danielle inside," Mandy instructed. Prying Monique's death grip from her arm, Mandy examined it for a bruise.

Nodding, Monique rushed out the back. Mandy patted my shoulder gently. "It needed to be done, Annie. Go put the kettle on. I think we could all use a hot chocolate."

Scrubbing my face, I sighed. "Yeah, definitely."

Danielle was only out for a short time. She shifted to heal her black eye once she came around, then showered before coming back into the lounge. Avoiding my eyes, she seemed humbled, but I was suspicious of her tendency to violence since I'd found out about the killings. "I'm sorry. I'm on heat, you're on heat; us bitches are slaves to our hormones."

Smirking, I shook my head. Sitting down, Danielle snuggled in next to Monique at the far end of the lounge from me.

"How come when wolves fight, they are being men. When she-wolves do it, we're hormonal crazy bitches?" Mandy grumbled.

"Because they have gonads and willies, they can measure to show how manly they are. Us she-wolves have a uterus and are smaller. Therefore, we are not meant to be aggressive but protective and compassionate," Monique grimaced. "We are baby makers and should leave the running of a pack where it belongs."

"To the wolves!" we all chorused.

"Different packs, same bullshit," Mandy shook her head. "Even the progressive Valleymorgans think that way."

Sobering, I turned my head away. Knox was the very definition of a modern alpha, and yet, not so contemporary with his sexist thinking. He was my mate, the only Alpha strong enough to rule me. Nevertheless, he couldn't force me to change.

Knox, Knox, fucking Knox. Always in my head, even when I was wrapped in Brett's arms. Right now, I couldn't miss Brett without thinking of Knox because I knew they were stuck somewhere together. A growl slipped through my teeth before I could hold it. "Fucking asshole." The girls all paused. Mandy raised a brow. "Knox." I shrugged.

"He needs a good dressing down, that one," Danielle snickered.

"Rhiannon kneed him in the balls for me."

Danielle nodded. "Perfect starting point." She looked at me, sadness creeping into her eyes. "Do you think he'll feel it when you go?"

Swallowing, I nodded. I know I'd feel it, almost like a corset being taken off if Knox died. It would be painful, and I'd feel like I was missing half my soul, but at the same time, I'd be released from our bond. Even as I considered how wonderful it would be to be free of him, I knew I'd hate it for the rest of my life.

Thinking about Knox having to live with that pain and emptiness for the rest of his years, I smiled. "Will serve him right."

13

KNOX

"**R**eady to go?" I asked Milton walking into the lounge room. When I saw Milton standing white as a ghost, I paused.

Rhiannon was in tears, her eyes pleading with Milton. "I warned you," she cried and ran from the room.

Milton stared at me. "After everything Annie went through, you abandoned her because she couldn't shift."

The wind rushed out of my chest cavity like I'd been punched. Stepping back, I leaned against the wall. My secret. Rhiannon not only carried Anique's horror, but my disloyalty, and now it had been revealed.

Milton shook his head. "I can't even fathom what I just saw."

"The second phase packs a wallop."

Milton frowned at me. "Was it all scattered for you? Like pieces of the puzzle, but not the entire picture?"

"Most of it, yes. The Goddess only shows you the important parts. The revelations you need to see to know your mate's truth," I explained. "Some things, you can work out immediately. Others will become clearer as you get to know your mate better, and things are revealed."

Dante walked in, his smile fading as he looked between us. He observed his brother a moment. "Second phase?" Swallowing hard, Milton nodded. "Do we want to know?"

Milton grabbed up his bag. "I don't understand enough yet. Let me process it. I don't want to cause misunderstanding."

Hanging my head, I collected my rucksack. "Your mate's past is meant for you alone, Milton. If you think it would cause disharmony in the house for others to know, don't reveal it to anyone." Meeting my glare, Milton tilted his head. After a moment, he nodded and stormed out of the room, understanding I didn't want what he knew about why I left Anique to be common knowledge.

When I turned to leave, Dante put his hand on my shoulder to stop me. "Why did you give up something that you were seeking for weeks?" Glaring at Dante's restraining hand pointedly, he removed it." You've been bugging Milton to complete the second phase and tell you what Rhi saw or did, but now you are willing to drop it?"

If I could breathe fire, it would have come out my nose right then. "We need to respect the bond. Rhi needs to trust her mate, to trust us, if her being here is going to work. I need to respect my pack and their privacy, and that they would tell me anything important that I would need to know," I answered clearly.

Nodding, Dante followed me out the door.

"I'm over this desert," Milton grumbled. "I miss Dante, but if you ever tell him that."

Watching Milton, I smirked. It was our second mission without Dante. The first because he was on his honeymoon, and now because I'd promised him base duties until his cub was born. "Flip, call in and see where our ride home is," I ordered Sasha, our signals man when we were abroad.

Nodding, Sasha got on the satellite phone. "Twenty minutes, Alpha. We are catching a ride with another team for the plane trip." Acknowledging the information, I signaled my men to get ready. It would be a touch down and pull out with a black hawk, then we would fly to another base to get the plane home.

The black hawk arrived on time and flew us to the closest base where we were loaded onto the waiting plane. As we walked on, I stopped when I saw whose team was on board. "Fuck!" I murmured to Milton.

Noticing White, Milton cursed similarly. Nothing had ever been said to me, but he and his team had been giving me the stink eye for four months. I'm guessing I'd been wholly blamed for Anique leaving him -which, I should be - but also for Anique leaving town.

Milton met my eyes. "Well, the next twelve hours are going to be cheery," he scowled, then went to take his seat.

"Morgan," White greeted almost growling my name. He could practically mimic a wolf at times with his vocals.

"White," I acknowledged back. I wasn't going to posture. White was human and not worth my time proving I was the stronger wolf. It was frustrating to have this thinly veiled aggression between the teams. White and I used to get along. Our teams would joke and laugh together, but from the moment he saw me taking Anique on that date, we'd done no more than greet each other civilly. His team had turned equally hostile towards mine.

We were in the air an hour, most of us snoozing when I woke to the plane descending. White was already up at the cockpit being informed, so I waited. Walking back, he belted in again. "Emergency stop. You boys got tagged," he grouched.

"What?" Henderson, White's second, whined. "We've already

been delayed seven hours for them, and now we have to scan all our shit?"

White held up his hand in peace. "It could happen to any of us. Let's just get on the ground and fix the problem so we can get home sometime before Monday." White then said a few choice words under his breath, a lot of it swearing, but I did catch something about some girl killing him.

Milton startled awake. "Home already?"

"Wake the others. Someone got tagged. We'll have to do a scrub."

"Oh..."

Tuning out Milton's cursing and that of the rest of my team, I made a mental inventory. "Tell Sasha to start with the phone."

Everyone was pissed. It wasn't just the case of finding the item. There was that, which could take hours, but then once that was done, we had to make sure we were clean before we were even allowed to ask permission to take off again. We could end up stuck in some backyard airport of a barely-there village for the entire weekend. I wanted a hot shower to get the sand out of places it shouldn't be, and my bed.

We were nine hours testing everything and ensuring we were clean before we got communications reopened. As I was walking onto the plane, I heard White on the line. "...gonna drop. I love you." He was smiling at the reply as he hung up. Turning to the pilot, Brett gave him the biggest smile I'd seen in months. "Get us out of here, Reynolds, some of us have a beautiful woman to get back to." Coming back out of comms, White saw me. His smile vanished, and he didn't say anything, but his eyes said it all.

"Just say it, White," I dared. Our teams, who were repackaging everything, stopped.

White shook his head. "You know already."

"Look, I'm a dog, you said it yourself. Annie's family commitments made her break up with you, and my being an ass made her leave town. I get your issues with me, but my team doesn't deserve that hostility; they weren't involved. We all do the same job for the same country."

White looked like I'd told him the President was a woman masquerading as a male. Confused and doubtful. "Family commitments? Really? Did you bother to learn anything about her, or was she just a conquest?" White hissed.

"I'm engaged to Rhiannon, and my brother is married to her eldest sister," Milton butted in. "They gave us a lot of insight into Annie."

White tilted his head. "So, you'd understand why I can't believe Annie dumped me because of family commitments."

"The communities our families come from believe in arranged marriages."

White's left eye flickered. There was an angry awareness in his eyes and I got the feeling this went beyond my sleeping with Anique. "And you were the husband they chose for my precious Annie?" White looked from me to Milton. Milton and I didn't answer, just stood watching. White shook his head. "Do you also gang rape sixteen-year-old girls and torture them for days on end as a hazing ritual?"

"No," I barked angrily. "I would kill any bastard who I caught doing that shit to a girl or a grown woman." My team went rigid behind me. They hadn't known. Only Milton and Dante knew more than Anique was hurt or possibly force-mated, but they didn't know the details.

Catching it, White rolled his shoulders back before he lifted his eyes to mine again. "Your team didn't know?" He asked quietly. I shook my head angrily. White nodded. "Well, the situation as it is, it's good she lost the baby. God knows how she would have handled that."

My blood ran cold. "Baby?" Goddess, did abandoning Anique during the mating purge cost me my cub? I wanted to vomit. I needed to find her and beg forgiveness and promise never to be a jerk again. I wanted to...

Groaning beside me, Milton covered his face in fear. White saw it too. "You knew?"

Milton nodded. "Rhi told me just before we left."

Nodding, White looked to me. "You didn't, though?"

"They were done, it wasn't worth dredging up," Milton answered for me. When we got home, I was going to kill him.

"You may want to." White jerked his head towards me. "Morgan looks ready to pull a man apart barehanded." White walked off before I could retort.

"She lost a cub?"

Milton blew out a breath. "Come for a walk, I'll fill you in." We walked away from the plane, far enough so none of our guys could hear. "They took Anique during her first heat. She should have shifted immediately after, like normal. Instead, they took her and when the others finished their fun, Dan kept her. He made sure he got her pregnant, then he marked her and tried to force her to shift."

Milton shuffled his feet, fear, anger, hatred, utter sadness; he reeked of it all. "I know what happened to Anique because they did it to Rhi on her eighteenth birthday."

"That's what broke her?"

Milton shook his head. "No, it wasn't as physically traumatic. They got her drunk and raped her for the night. She was too intoxicated to fight them off. She wasn't injured, and she had already shifted the first time, so she healed the physical damage immediately. The psychological damage made her promiscuous and hateful towards her pack, but not all wolves." I watched Milton chew his cheek. "I'm revealing my mate's biggest secrets here, Alpha. I need your word, that what I tell you will go no further?"

This must be extremely bad if Milton was going to extract a promise from me. Blowing out a breath, I removed my knife, slicing my hand. "You have my oath, as Alpha, and blood kin, that Rhiannon's secrets shan't pass my lips to another than yourself," I swore on my own blood.

Milton still looked hesitant. "I don't know if I can finish the mating." He admitted in a harsh rush of breath. Squatting, he held his head as if he was in pain, as if the weight of his emotions crumbled him. "What she did... I... I have to carry that, forgive it, in order to love her. I... I don't know if I can."

Watching warily, I stayed quiet. I'd never seen a wolf be like this about his mate.

"Rhi killed the wolf who force-mated her, but she was smart about it. She waited until he went to college, and he just disappeared, and never came home again," Milton admitted. "He got her pregnant, so he got to mark her." Milton lifted his tear-filled eyes. "Rhi had an abortion." Milton shook his head in agony. "It was horrible, and really disturbing for her. The guilt of doing it made her hate herself even more. She wanted to save Anique going through that."

I frowned, not understanding.

Milton cursed. "I wasn't going to tell you. You may hurt her. That's why I needed the promise first. This is already eating Rhi alive. It's why she went off the rails, why she adores Anique, why she carries all this guilt for what happened."

Despite seeing the train wreck coming, I couldn't look away.

"When Rhi found Anique, the silver blade was right there," Milton started a lot quieter now. He was running his hands through his hair anxiously. "Anique was barely conscious. She'd fought so hard against them, and when that bastard marked her, she fought it and won." Milton shook his head. "She's a strong-willed bitch, Alpha. Rhi wanted to save her little sister any more pain. So, before she released her from the binds, she listened for the heartbeat of the cub growing in her baby sister, and she killed it."

Rocking back like I'd been hit with the force of a tsunami, I gaped at Milton. The Goddess had shown me the pain, but not who wielded the blade or why.

"She helped Anique escape and tried to get her to shift to heal," Milton was crying. "That's when she saw the blade, saw the tip broken off, and she realized Anique wasn't getting better. Discovering the silver was still in Anique, Rhi knew it would kill her, and that she would be the one who killed her sister.

"Rhi took Anique to the hospital and told them she'd found her. It was Rhi who called her father," Milton finished. "The silver was in Anique too long. She couldn't heal or shift, so she nearly bled out. They gave her human blood, and with the silver poisoning-"

"She couldn't shift, and now it hurts too much to try," I finished, guilt suffocating me.

"Rhi blames herself. Anique doesn't, she's told her a million times, but Rhi has never been able to tell her that it was her, not Dan, who stabbed her and sentenced her to a human existence."

Glaring at Milton, I wanted to howl my anguish for my mate, but I couldn't. Shoving my knife back in my boot, I walked away. I couldn't be near anyone right now. How could I ever face Rhiannon again without strangling her? She stole my mate from me.

14

ANIQUE

"Where are we going?"

Glancing over his shoulder at me with his trademark smile, Dan winked at me. "It's a surprise."

Since I was a cub, I'd had a crush on Dan, but he was nearly ten years older than me, and my brother's best friend. Like many of the other wolves, he was waiting for Rhiannon or Evaline to be ready to take a mate. He'd rocked up to my bedroom door fifteen minutes ago and asked me to go for a walk with him. Of course, I said yes, he was a trusted friend of my brother.

Taking my hand, he walked me out of the packhouse heading deep into the forest. Further than I'd ever been allowed to go. That would change next week. Once my first heat was finished, I would shift for the first time, and I'd be free to roam the limits of our property.

My stomach filled with the weight of knowing I was leaving for college in a month. Grateful that my acceptance was to the closest medical school, but I struggled with the idea that it was still an hour away. Rhiannon and Evaline both helped convince our father to let me live on campus.

"Are you looking forward to college?" Dan asked cheerily.

"Yes and no. I'll miss my family, miss my home, but I'm really looking forward to learning how to heal us in our human form. When I finish college, I can come home as the pack doctor, and that makes it worth it." Entering a small clearing as the sky grew darker, we stood before a small stone cabin. "What is this place?"

"Come on, I'll show you." Dan smiled, pulling me towards the cabin.

Suddenly, I felt uncomfortable and didn't want to go inside. "No, Dan, we should get back. It will be dinner time soon."

Ignoring my protests, Dan opened the door pulling me after him into the cabin before he released me.

"Ow!" I gritted, rubbing my hand where he'd gripped it hard. "Why did you do that? You know you're way stronger than me."

He was bigger than me in every way. Chuckling, Dan turned to shut the door. In the small light the door allowed into the cabin, I could see the kitchenette and the bed. The rest of the cabin was too dark.

When the door shut encompassing me in darkness, and the lock clicked into place, I jumped, trembling a little. "Dan? What's going on?"

There was a click as the small lamp beside the bed switched on, only illuminating that area. Grabbing my shoulders gently, Dan walked me backwards to the bed. "I wanted to show you where I would make you my mate, Anique."

Confused by his words, I frowned. "What are you on about? We aren't mates?" Over the last year, I'd made eye contact with all the wolves in our pack, as per tradition. None of them was my future mate.

"Well, we aren't true-mates, no, but you will be my mate, Anique."

The back of my calves hit the bed. Shoving me onto it, Dan yanked my arm a little to have me lay along it properly.

Whimpering, I tried to pull away, but Dan was on me before I could get off the bed. "Dan, I don't want to do this. I'm not ready. I haven't shifted yet." Females always waited until they shifted the first time before engaging in mating. It was an unspoken rule of our traditions.

Placing his body over mine, Dan made soothing noises as my breath hitched. "But you have your first heat, Anique. You're a woman now. I can put my cub inside you, mark you, and force you to obey me."

Breath coming in short, I shook my head. "No, not yet. When I've finished college."

"I know, but I want you mine before you go away, Anique. I want to be your first and your last."

Running his hands along my body, Dan tried to put his hands beneath my skirt. Shoving him away, I slapped his face. "No!"

Growling, Dan punched me in the stomach. Pain roared through my abdomen, air rushing out of me as I curled in on myself. Crying, I tried to run for the door, but Dan grabbed me by the throat and held me. "We can do this one of two ways, Anique. You can be a good little bitch and let us send you off to college with good memories of us all." Five other young wolves from the pack materialized out of the darkness. They were all the same age as my sisters, and every one of them were smiling as they pulled their shirts off. "Or, your first shift is going to be even more painful then you could imagine."

Shaking my head, I clawed at his hand, holding me. Dan shook his head. "Anique, always the disappointment." Throwing me on the bed, Dan punched me hard in the stomach again. "Hold her down."

One of the guys pinned me down before he licked up my face. "Fight, baby girl, I'll enjoy it all the more." When his hand grabbed between my legs, I screamed, trying to throw him off me.

"This cabin was located and designed, so the rest of the pack don't have to listen to the mating purge, Anique," Dan lectured me as he undressed. "No one is going to hear you, so scream all you like."

"Dan, please, please don't do this. My father will kill you."

Grinning as he knelt on the bed, Dan started ripping my clothes from my body, exposing me to the hungry wolves who stood watching. "Rhiannon never told, Anique, do you know why?"

Crying harder than I ever had in my life, I shook my head. God, they did this to Rhiannon, no wonder she avoided the place.

"Because we are just the first round." Dan motioned for the wolf that was holding me to flip me over, so I was on my hands and knees.

Struggling, I tried to kick Dan and clawed the bastard holding me. The wolf restraining me pulled back with a hiss, but another took his place, as Dan slammed his elbow into my kidney. Dropping my chest to the bed, I coughed hard between whimpers.

Grabbing my hips hard enough to bruise, Dan got comfortable between my thighs and readied himself. In too much pain to fight him now, I sobbed into the blanket.

"See, Anique, tonight, every unmated wolf in the pack is going to take turns coming down here and congratulating you on getting into college. So, if your father kills us all, he'll have killed his entire pack. Do you really think your father is strong enough to take on the entire pack?"

Gripping the sheets, I knew my father wasn't. I wasn't strong enough to fight them, and our Alpha couldn't punish them all.

"I get her first and last," Dan growled.

I screamed.

Strong arms wrapped around me as I fought to get free. "Annie, it's me! It's Brett!"

Hesitating, I breathed in his scent, holding myself back from attacking him, but by the Goddess, it took every ounce of control. Slowly, Brett let me go, and I crawled from the bed and into the corner. "You dreamed of that night again?"

"You don't normally try and hold me."

"That was more restraint and self-defense, Annie." Hissing a little, Brett gently rubbed his chest where there were fresh claw marks.

My eyes went wide. "Oh, my god! I'm so sorry." Only Brett brought me free of my past. It's one of the reasons I loved him. Climbing back onto the bed, I switched on the light on the nightstand to examine him. "I've never attacked you before."

Side of his mouth pulling up in a grimace, Brett gave me a guilty look. "You've tried a few times, but I normally wake before you and get away from you. I was dead to the world and missed the cue that it was that nightmare you were having." Brett was exhausted. He'd arrived home early Monday morning and driven us three hours to the resort. We spent the first twelve hours giving rabbits a run for their money.

It wasn't until I'd gone to molest him again that he'd taken me in a bear hug and confessed he hadn't slept for forty-eight hours and could he have four hours reprieve. Feeling guilty as hell, I'd agreed and curled into his arms to sleep. Now, feeling doubly guilty, I went to the bathroom and wet a face washer. Following me in, Brett let me wash his chest.

"It's just superficial grazing."

Brett cupped my face in his hands. "Annie, don't." Lifting my gaze, I tried to read him. "I've known you five years, Annie, since your first placement at Dempsey, I know that look on your face." He ensured my eyes were on his. "Most women couldn't recover from what happened to you, let alone enter a physical relationship with another man just a few years later. I can handle a few scratches on occasion."

The floodgates opened, filling my eyes. "How could you forgive me?"

Forehead furrowing, Brett's lips turned down. "For a few scratches on my chest?"

"For leaving you. I don't deserve you, Brett."

Shaking his head, Brett pulled me into a hug. "I know about you and Knox, Annie. It must have been a shock, and of course, you would react-"

"What?" I asked, pushing Brett away.

Studying my eyes, Brett hesitated. "Knox told me your families do arranged marriages, that they picked him for you." Closing my eyes, I leaned back on the sink. "I get it."

Shivering with anger, I gritted my teeth. "Stop saying that! Stop telling me you understand because you don't. You can't possibly." Brett swallowed, and I watched his eyes flare with the emotions he'd been trying to hide from me, but I could smell them.

"Okay, I don't understand. You haven't had anything to do with your family in years. They tell you to marry some man and you dump me instantly," Brett thundered. "You have a one-night stand with the manwhore who is meant to be your husband, and then you are suddenly ready to settle down, to have rough sex, to... Jesus, Annie, I want to know why the huge turnaround? You seem so much more at ease about things now, happier, and at the same time, not."

Hanging my head, I bit my lip as I thought of how to explain this to a human. "I was raised in a strict community that teethes on traditions and family values. I may have left for college, but I never intended to leave permanently until that night. That sense of honor to our ways is still at the heart of me."

"They raped you, Annie! You owe them nothing!"

"That is not one of our traditions." Glaring at him, I swallowed the anger burbling inside of me. "Women don't work, and they don't go away to college, they stay home, keep house, and have babies. That's the tradition. Evaline was the first to challenge that by going to college, then she further insulted the men by refusing to pick one of them as her husband."

Listening intently, Brett sat on the edge of the bathtub. I'd never told him about my family other than my sibling's names.

"When Rhi got accepted to college, the men in our community saw a pattern starting to emerge. The weekend before she left, they got her drunk and spent the night-" I couldn't say it. Over the years, I had seen men riddled with shrapnel, open wounds where you could see all the way to the marrow, bones protruding from bodies like shards of glass. However, I still cringe just thinking about Rhiannon being raped.

Taking a breath, I cleared my throat. "It was punishment, for going against our traditions, for daring to say any of them were not suitable for us." Swiping at the tears falling down my cheeks, I stood straight. "There is one person who my sisters and I will listen to when it comes to marriage. She serves all our communities and she matches couples from other communities with each other. That is who introduced Evaline and Dante. At the wedding, she matched Knox and me."

"Did she pick you two because you were the most commitment-phobic people in the room?" He asked sarcastically. Shame crawled up my neck, and I dropped my head. Brett sobered. "What happened, Annie? If this is such a big deal for you, why didn't it happen?"

Turning side on, I swiped a tear away. "The groom must pay a dowry. I'm an elder's daughter - my father is a high-profile figure. Evaline's dowry could have paid for a house." The pain of Knox's rejection burned as I took a breath. "When Knox enquired about my dowry price, my father declined it."

"I'm guessing that's a bad thing?"

"He may as well have offered to pay Knox to take me. It made Knox suspicious, and he soon realized I'm what our community consider a ruined woman. So, Knox had his fun with me and rejected the match."

"Does that free you from being matched again?" Brett asked, standing with his face turned away, as if he couldn't meet my eyes.

That's when I realized his concern. I'd dumped him for an arranged marriage once, I could do it again. "It's a once in a lifetime offer. To our people, Knox and I are meant for each other and no other. It is as much a black mark on him to reject me after sleeping with me, so he won't be telling anyone that he did. He will be a bit more covert in the women he sees."

"Because seeing other women when he's meant to be with you is worse than you being ruined?" Brett narrowed his eyes, a fierce distaste burning in them.

Considering the implications, I laughed sorrowfully. "You know, I suddenly understand why she thinks we were perfectly matched."

Exhaling hard, Brett wrapped his arms around me. "So, it wouldn't be good for him and his team to discover we are married, would it?"

Cringing, I ignored the itch between my shoulder blades I'd come to recognize with missing my mate. "He can't do anything about it. It will hurt him, more than me. Having said that, I may have led Knox to believe I'd left town after he rejected me. He doesn't want his family knowing he's a disloyal dog."

Nodding as if that wasn't news, Brett sighed. "Rhiannon is engaged to Milton."

"I know."

"Was that a replacement arrangement?"

Shaking my head, I took a breath. "Knox's family and mine are both considered very high ranking in our community. The matchmaker felt my father's three daughters belonged with the Morgan's. My perfect older sister has taken well to her new family and is already in the family way."

"Don't be jealous, Annie; it's unbecoming." Smirking, I kissed him, but Brett pulled back. "I've only had three hours of sleep, Annie. I need more. Then we can get back to satisfying that sex drive of yours."

Smiling, I hugged him tight. "It broke my heart to leave you. I was mortified when he rejected me, but when I saw you at the hospital, I realized I couldn't have prayed for a better outcome. It meant I could be with the man I love."

"Damn it, Annie. How can I not make love to you when you say stuff like that?" Grumbling, Brett picked me up and carried me back to bed.

KNOX

"What's going on?" Milton asked, entering the kitchen.

"We've been called up. Finally got some solid intel on the leader we've been looking for."

"Should I go and get my stuff together?" Milton pointed over his shoulder. He was way too keen to go on a mission.

"In a minute," I murmured, lowering my voice. "Milton, don't make my mistake."

Milton's jaw tensed. "I haven't run her out of town."

Gritting my teeth, I gripped my coffee mug harder. "You have been avoiding her and haven't completed the bonding. Rhiannon is miserable here, but if we send her home, it will look bad for you."

"So, we keep her here."

Exhaling, I shook my head at him. "Last night, Rhiannon asked to be allowed to visit her sister for a few weeks. She wants to make sure Anique is doing well."

Frowning, Milton took a step closer. "They call each other all the time."

"Milt, Anique is a rogue who managed to not only hide within our territory for years, she also hid a pack of strays. If Rhiannon leaves to see her sister, she will not go home, nor will she return here. Since Rhiannon believes you have decided not to complete the binding, she will try to leave and join her sister as a stray."

Sinking into the chair opposite me at the table, Milton studied the surface. "Maybe we should let her. You completed the mating and still let Anique go. You are still seeing other women..." When I tried to object to that, Milton dismissed before I could defend myself. "Don't, Alpha, we've all smelt Louise on you. My point is, the Goddess was determined to bind the two of you, and you managed to reject it. Surely, I can do it if we haven't even finished the four phases."

Staring at the black coffee in my cup, I sighed. "Milton, you will miss Rhiannon with every breath you take, and you will hate yourself for turning your back on what the Goddess ordained. Make it right with her for your sake."

"Do you regret letting Anique go?"

'Every morning that I wake up, every night before I go to sleep, and every minute in between.' "We aren't talking about me."

"Have you thought about going to find her?" Watching me closely, Milton tried to determine if I was lying to him.

"Anique is very good at covering her tracks and scent."

Eyebrows lifting, Milton cocked his head. "When did you try and find her?"

"A month ago, after you told me Rhiannon's secret. Anique looked at me with such loathing the night I rejected her, Milton. You don't want your last memory of Rhiannon to be the hatred in her eyes when you let her go because trust me, if she goes to Anique, you'll never find her again unless she wants to be found."

Staring at his clasped hands on the table in front of him quietly, Milton was thinking hard about his options, so I didn't disturb him. The door opened to the kitchen as Rhiannon walked in with

Evaline, happy, and chuckling about something. Rhiannon's smile fell away when she saw the two of us.

"You two look pensive, what's happening?" Evaline observed as she made her way to the fridge.

"Just got called into work." Gulping down my coffee, I stood up, ready to go pack.

Evaline's shoulders tensed. "How long will you be gone this time?"

"Miss me, will you?"

Dismissing my tease with a wave, Evaline huffed. "No, but Dante gets all anxious and fidgety when you are away without him."

Reaching out, I rubbed her already bulging tummy. Our females only had a six-month gestation. The fetuses were fast-growing, and when they birthed, they were nearly equivalent to a full-term human, if not slightly more developed.

"It's a quick trip this time. By the time another comes up, your cub will be in your arms," I reassured her.

Evaline smiled sadly at where her cub kicked my hand. "Will you find another to give you cubs, Knox?"

Slamming her coffee mug down on the bench, Rhiannon glared at me. Apparently, Evaline didn't know I'd completed the bond with her sister. Frowning, I took my hand away. "I don't know."

"If you are going away, it would be a good time for me to visit my other sister," Rhiannon suggested.

"I'd prefer you to stay here with Evaline."

Rhiannon's glare intensified. "Dante will be here, and, if the last time you were away was anything to go by, they would be too busy to notice I am here. I want to go and check on my baby sister."

"Why?"

Gritting her teeth, Rhiannon looked ready to rip my throat out. "Because it's what good sisters do! But if that isn't enough... there is the fact that the wolf our Goddess chose for my sister rejected her, broke her, and then forced her to leave the home she loved."

"Rhi!" Evaline whispered in a warning.

My anger flaring at her words, I shoved my hands in my pockets as I approached her, so I wouldn't accidentally hurt her. "I wasn't the one to break your sister, Rhi. I didn't rape her, and I damn well didn't carve my initials into her with a silver blade." Rhiannon's eyes filled with tears, Evaline sobbed behind me. Stepping closer to Rhiannon, I lowered my voice into a snarl, so only she could hear. "I sure as hell didn't stab her with silver before she'd even shifted for the first time, trapping her in human form for the rest of her life."

Rhiannon's watering eyes met mine, full of fear that I knew her worst secret. As she backed up, I advanced on her. "My mate was broken when I found her. She was worthless when I took possession."

There was a split second where Rhiannon's eyes hardened, and I registered I'd gone a step too far. Now I was being driven backward, Rhiannon's nails raking across my chest, slicing my shirt and flesh open under the partial shift of her wolf claws.

"You heartless bastard!" Rhiannon yelled as she tried to take another swipe. "She is not worthless."

Grabbing Rhiannon's wrists, I spun her, forcing her down to face plant the kitchen bench, so I could restrain her easily. Evaline was screeching at the top of her lungs, which brought several of the pack running, especially Dante.

Holding Rhiannon down, I waited while Dante comforted his wife and got her to stop sounding like a parrot getting its tail feathers yanked. Once Evaline was quiet, I spoke. "This is your only warning, Rhiannon. I am the Alpha here: you are not even an official pack member. You attack me again: you won't like what happens to you."

Laughing through her tears, Rhiannon jerked against me. "Do you really think you could do worse than my own pack, Alpha?"

Releasing her, I stepped back to give her space. "Do you want to find out?"

Standing straight, Rhiannon moved back from me. "You're right, I'm not a member of this pack. I'm leaving."

"Milton is your mate," I replied, baiting her to reject him.

Eyeing the growing audience, Rhiannon composed herself. "I think it's obvious your wolf is just like you, Alpha, and has no intention of honoring the Goddess' blessing. I wish to leave now."

"Milton is still getting to know you. Not all bindings happen overnight, Rhi," I defended Milton from the glares he was getting.

The side of her lip turning up in a snarl, Rhiannon took another step back, anger darkening her eyes. "No. I will not let him do to me what you did to your true-mate!"

"Rhi, don't!" Milton stepped forward in warning.

"What? Doesn't the pack know what a dog they have for an Alpha? Don't they know you completed the phases before you rejected my sister?" Rhiannon smiled sinisterly as gasps went through the room. "That you left her in agony, crying on the ground, and freed her of any obligation to you."

"Enough!" I snapped, the pain of that memory like a brand on my soul.

"No! Did you know you nearly killed her? Did you know that without the mating purge, the bonding virus landed her in hospital, her body cooking her alive trying to fight your claim on her."

When I stepped menacingly towards Rhiannon, she backed away. "Let's not forget that because you did finish the phases, she will never be able to have children with another. So, no, I won't stay here to be condemned like my sister because you and your wolves lack honor."

Questioning our honor crossed the line. In a blink, I moved,

Rhiannon's eyes went wide. A second later, Milton was between us, stopping me from reaching his mate.

"Alpha!" Drawing my attention, Milton bowed his head in supplication. "I beg forgiveness for my mate. She is upset and emotional, and I am the cause."

"No, your dog of an alpha assisted."

"Rhi! Look at his eyes, then shut the fuck up!"

At Milton's scolding, Rhiannon's eyes lifted to mine, her pupils dilating, her throat swallowing with difficulty, and the scent from her was pure fear. Letting out a small whimper, Rhiannon huddled behind Milton a little.

"Either complete the phases or get her out of my house, Milton." Growling, I stormed out of the room. Shifting as I moved, I let my wolf, who was already in control, have his body. Running into the forest, we hunted the largest and most dangerous thing we could find. Bear sounded good.

Several hours later, I arrived back at the packhouse. Dante was waiting in the foyer for me, all our stuff packed. "Milton is talking to Rhi, sorting it out between them." Standing, Dante moved a step closer. "A dishonorable wolf rarely stays Alpha long. You need to fix this."

"I tried to find her, but her scent has changed, and I can't track her."

Dante thought about it. "Her scent is now merged with yours. Have you tried searching out yourself?"

Honestly, I hadn't thought about that. "I'll try when we get back. I need a shower." Going off to my room to clean up, I then changed into my uniform. When I came back out, Milton was there with the rest of my team. "And?"

"I've assured her once we get back, I'll finish the phases and be honorable, or Dante will take her to Campus, and she can leave permanently. She wanted it done now. I explained, with Dante out, I needed to go on this mission, and I couldn't do that if the mating purge needed to be handled. After seeing what Anique went through when-" Milton licked his lips nervously. "Rhi understands it's best to wait."

My team stood listening quietly. Looks of judgment over what I'd done passing between them. "You all know my mate was horribly attacked when she was sixteen?" They all nodded. "It was her first heat, and she hadn't shifted yet. During the attack, a silver blade was used on her."

Shock and revulsion flooded the foyer.

"Part of the silver blade was left in my mate. She couldn't heal and escaped to seek treatment in a human hospital. They gave her a multitude of human blood transfusions. As a result, my mate has never been able to shift."

Pity filled their eyes.

"I didn't discover this until after the phases were completed. Hyped on taking my mate, I tried to force her to shift. When she revealed she couldn't, I was angry, I felt duped by the Goddess. I took it out on my mate and rejected her." Shame gnawing at my insides for my behavior, I shook my head. "It's no excuse for what I did, but that's what happened. I tried to find Anique a month ago. She has vanished, and because I didn't catch her scent after the binding virus did its job, I have no way to track her."

Stepping forward, Rion raised a brow in question. "Will you correct the errors of your ego if you find her?" My jaw tensed at his words, but Rion held up a hand in peace. "Alpha, I respect you. We all respect you. We accept you are not infallible. But to reject what the Goddess blessed you because of scars she has born seven years now, you would be lying to deny your ego caused that." Hands down, Rion was the smartest wolf here. Not always when it came to knowing when he crossed a line, but he read people well, and puzzled out situations better than I ever would.

Bowing my head, I wouldn't deny his judgment. "Yes, I would correct my arrogance."

Appeased, Rion nodded. "Dante and I will try and get you a lead while you are away."

"How are we going to do that, Brainiac?" Dante sniffed.

"Forwarding address at her last employers would be a good start. She lives human, so stop thinking wolf to find her and follow the human trail."

Dante picked up his bag. "Smartass. Let's load up."

Smiling at the playfulness in Dante's voice, I relaxed. "You heard your Beta. Load up," I ordered, patting Milton on the shoulder as he walked out. "She'll make you happy, Milton. She's a worthy bitch."

Eyes distant, Milton looked at my chest. "I knew the moment I stepped between you two to protect her that I wanted her. I think I just needed to realize what losing her would be like." Milton waited for the others to leave, then he licked his lips. "What's it like, to have lost her?"

Sighing, I stared at my boots. "Like a permanent itch between my shoulder blades that I can't reach to relieve. Even with other women, it's like half an orgasm. Like your body holds onto half of your load because that other bitch you're in isn't worthy of your seed," I admitted crudely. "It leaves you only a little less frustrated."

"So, basically, it sucks."

"Yeah, it sucks." Grabbing my stuff, I followed the others out to the car, spying Rhiannon standing eavesdropping in the shadow of the stairs. Milton saw her, too, but said nothing until we were outside.

"If Rion can't find Anique, we could use Rhiannon to get to her."

"There is something you are all forgetting. I hurt Anique

deeply. Turning up and telling her I want her now is not going to win her over any more than being a rich alpha did." Throwing my bag in the car, I met Milton's eyes. "I'm going to have to repent big time. Anique is a strong Alphia, so she's going to make me beg."

Milton smirked a little. "And rightfully so." He threw his bag in the boot. "Can I watch?"

ANIQUE

"*I* told dad everything." My legs fell from under me and I winced when my ass smacked the floor. "Annie? Are you okay?" Rhiannon heard the thump through the phone.

"Why?" I choked. "Why now?"

"I called to tell him Milton, and I finished the final phase last night, that we'd set a date. He wanted to organize the banquet. So, I told him I wasn't inviting the Beachrunners."

"Bet that went down well?" I bit my lip.

"Which is why I had to tell him what happened to you and me. I don't want those bastards at my banquet. I just want my parents and my siblings." Rhiannon took a breath. "Which leads me to the next problem."

"No!"

"Annie, I want you there."

"I can't, Rhi. Knox told me to leave and that he never wanted to see me again, or he'd sell me on."

"He's looking for you," Rhiannon confessed quietly.

My mouth dropped open. "Wh… what? Wh… why?"

"He wants you, Annie. He realized he was a dick and wants what the Goddess offered him."

"No, he was adamant, Rhi. What happened to change his mind?" Rhiannon was quiet for a moment. "Oh, Rhi, you didn't?" My stomach fell through the floor. A snarl ripped from my lips before I could stop it. "Why in the Goddess' name would you do that? Forgetting about how that affects me because no one cares about a rogue, he is your soon to be Alpha, and you called him out?"

"We got in a fight, and he said something mean, something that he only knows about me because of the second phase," she blubbered. "I was angry he knew, angry Milton revealed my secret, furious he dared to use that to make me fall in line."

"He's an Alpha; of course, he used your weakness."

"I lashed out and called him and his pack disloyal bastards."

Shaking my head, I growled. Rhiannon always had a loose tongue when she was angry. "It doesn't explain why he's decided to go through-"

"We weren't alone when I revealed his secret."

Balking at the phone, I blinked several times. "How many?" Rhiannon cleared her throat. "The entire pack? Rhiannon, are you...?" I gritted my teeth. "Well, of course, he has no choice but to follow through. He'd be challenged if he didn't. Goddess, Rhi, did you even consider how this would affect me? I'm married!"

"I know."

"To a human, Rhi. I'm rogue, mated, and married to a human. I'm the Goddess' poster girl for she-wolf rebellion." Rhiannon started chuckling, or maybe she was crying. It was hard to tell the difference over the phone. Sighing, I chewed the quick of my fingernail. "It doesn't matter. He lost his right to me the moment he removed my obligation to him."

"I'm sorry, Annie."

"I'm sorry too, Rhi. I'm not coming to your banquet." Rhiannon sobbed on the other end of the line. "I hope he treats you well, Rhi. You deserve to be loved."

"No, Annie, I don't deserve this happiness if you can't have it." Rhiannon whined.

"Don't be ridiculous, I'm with the man I love."

"You can't have children."

"I gave that dream up long ago, Rhi. You know my forecast. I wouldn't bring children into the world that I couldn't raise and keep safe." We were both silent for a minute, so I decided to change the subject. "What date did you set?"

We talked for a little bit longer until Rhiannon announced Milton was home from work, and we hung up. Sitting at the kitchen bench, I stared out into the backyard at the place I'd beaten Dannielle. I was dialing my phone before I even realized what I was doing. "Mandy, I changed my mind."

\\\

"...not good enough," I muttered frustrated.

"What's not good enough?" Walking into the kitchen, Brett observed us girls clustered around the kitchen bench.

"Goddess! How did you sneak up on us?" Mandy jumped, nearly knocking her wine glass over.

"Rare as it is, I believe you were all were rather intent on something." Brett's eyes watched Danielle packing the papers on the counter into her handbag. Stepping in behind me, Brett wrapped me in his arms as he kissed my neck. "Should I ask what mischief you are up to?"

"No, mischief," Monique chirped, "just talking about this guy Danielle is seeing."

"Danielle is seeing a guy? More than once?" Brett asked, disbelieving. "Sure..."

"I have, on occasion, slept with the same guy twice," Danielle argued.

"In a different twenty-four-hour timeframe?" Brett challenged. Danielle thought hard about it, too hard. "That's what I thought." Shaking his head, Brett went to the fridge to get himself a Gatorade. "You know I'm trained in interrogation, right? I can tell when you girls are bullshitting a mile away. You don't want me to know what you are up to, just tell me to mind my beeswax."

Mandy cleared her throat. "We were here to cheer Annie up."

That made Brett move back to me. "Why, what's happened?"

Blowing out a breath, I dropped my face to stare at my toes. "Rhi called. Her and Milton have set a date."

"She doesn't want you to come?"

"She does, but I can't."

"Knox Morgan will be at the wedding, along with both their families," Mandy filled in. I'd told her the impression Brett had on our 'arranged marriages.' "Annie can't go because then our communities would know he's rejected her. That would make Knox look bad."

"And because Knox is a high-ranking member of our community, it could spark dissent between our families," I finished.

"Oh, Annie," Brett pulled me into his arms for a hug. Over his shoulder, I mouthed thank you to Mandy.

Nodding her head, Mandy downed the rest of her wine. "So, we might take off," Mandy excused grabbing her stuff.

Showing everyone out, I organized to meet up again when our rosters allowed it. When I came back in, Brett was leaning on the kitchen bench watching me. "Want to tell me the rest of it?" Brett raised a brow at me.

"What do you mean?"

Brett gave me an admonishing look. "Don't even, Annie. Besides the fact that I've planned enough missions to know what I walked in on; I saw your panicked look when I entered the room. You look like I busted you guys smoking pot."

Exhaling, I deflated into a barstool. "The girls are planning to steal me away for the weekend of Rhi's wedding for a girls-only vacation. I wanted to run it passed you before I agreed. Then, I have to see if I can get the weekend off work."

Brett chewed his cheek. "Is this vacation going to take you anywhere near your sister's wedding?"

"No, why?"

Turning, Brett leaned over the bench, so we were eye level. "Because Knox hurt you. It's hurting you not to be permitted at your sister's wedding. It would cause him a lot of embarrassment if you were to show up unannounced and reveal what he did to you."

My eyes were wide. "I would never do that. Goddess, the amount of trouble that would cause, not to mention it could totally backfire, and Knox might try to-" I swallowed.

Brett's eyes narrowed in suspicion. "He might what, Annie?"

"He might force me to pretend that we are a couple," I elucidated, quietly as I met Brett's unhappy eyes. "Knox has a lot of power in our community, and he's physically overpowering. I'm not stupid enough to go up against him, Brett."

Brett stood to his full height. "I've known Knox a long time, Annie. He's a manwhore, his entire team are, but they've never struck me as the kind to force women to do anything unwillingly."

"This isn't about sex, Brett."

Brett moved around the bench to be next to me. "You wouldn't tell me if it was, would you?"

Lifting my eyes to meet his where he rested back against the bench, I bit my lip. "If Knox changed his mind and decided he wanted me after all, he could throw me over his shoulder, lock me away in his house, and I'd never be heard from again. No one in my community would even think twice about it. It's a man's right to control his woman. Raping of a woman is not accepted, but raping the woman everyone considers to be your wife-"

Brett's jaw was grinding.

Standing up, I placed my hand on his chest. "Knox wouldn't do that. He's one of the more progressive leaders in our community. My sisters are lucky to be married into his family." Leaning into Brett, I rested my head on his chest. "There is a reason, Mandy, Danielle, and Monique left their families. Some still have no issue treating their women like fifties housewives."

There was tension in Brett's body, anger in every restrained breath he took. "I can't believe that bullshit even still exists in this day and age. Anyone would think your families were raised by wolves." Lifting my head slowly, I observed Brett's face. He met my eyes evenly for several seconds, then Brett shrugged. "That alpha male bullshit. The female will submit crap. I grew up in a family with a similar mindset."

The way he dismissed alpha males made me smirk. "Because you're not an Alpha male?"

Brett growled. "Only for you, Annie." Pulling my face up to his, he kissed my lips slowly. A tiny growl escaped his throat when I rubbed my body against his. Brett was sensitive and caring, he listened to his team, listened to me, but I could see him as the pack Alpha. My attraction to him wasn't there for no reason.

"I like it when you get all-dominating," I breathed.

Smiling, Brett turned us and started relieving me of my clothing, then he lifted me to the kitchen counter. Managing to get his top unbuttoned, I shoved it off his shoulders before Brett pushed me back on the bench. Kissing his way south, Brett ascended each of the mountains to lay claim to their peaks, before leaving a trail of saliva across the abdominal plain. He delved deep into the valley of pleasure, licking and sucking the gates to nirvana, ensuring the threshold was more than ready.

Only after I yielded surrender, did he drop his pants to the floor. Then, stepping between the pass, Brett plowed headlong into the dark delicate tunnel of man's deliverance.

Circling his hips, Brett drew out the pinnacle of our pleasures. He took his time to extract every whimper, moan, and cry for release he could from me before delving into my depths and flooding my body with his claim. Resisting clawing him, I cursed, the pleasure only just holding out the pain of my body's rejection of his seed.

Falling upon me, Brett kissed me possessively. "I love you, Annie. If anyone ever tried to take you away from me, I'd never rest until I found you and brought you back. I meant every word of our vows. Till death do us part."

Misery falling to the side of my cheeks as my mortality pained me, I sobbed. Brett wiped the tears. "Don't think of that, Annie. When death comes looking for you, I'm going to fight him too. I won't accept that we only have a few more years together. I'm going to demand longer because you deserve the time it's going to take for me to show you all the ways I can love you."

Wrapping my arms around Brett, I held myself tight to him. "I love you. I don't care what my family says, what the Goddess herself says, you are the man I was meant to find and fall in love with."

Sighing, Brett kissed my neck. "I knew it was you the moment we met, Annie. You were so young, your eyes so absolutely haunted with betrayal. Yet, you smiled and stitched up my brow, as if treating an idiot who got punched in the face during a sparring lesson was the highlight of your day."

Meeting Brett's eyes, I smirked. "You were the highlight of my day. You were the first live person I ever got to stitch up, and you were gorgeous to boot."

Smirking, Brett touched the brow in question. "You did a superb job for the first time."

I assessed the barely visible scar. "I've improved a lot since then."

"In more ways than one," Brett chuckled, moving his hands to my hips. "I remember you stepping between my open thighs to stitch me up, and how you jumped a little when I placed my hands on your hips. I told you it was to keep you steady, but I just wanted to touch you."

"I know. I liked it though."

Wrapping my legs around him, Brett lifted me to him. "The guys started lining up to punch me so I could have an excuse to come back and see you. Eventually, the captain just told me to ask you out already."

Laughing as he carried me into the bedroom, I clung to him. "I thought you were a really terrible fighter with all the times you got hurt. I only said yes to the date because I felt sorry for you."

Chuckling, Brett buried his nose between my boobs. "I missed you every damn day you were away at uni. I swore when you got your residency, I'd never let you go again. It killed me to let you walk out the door that night, but nowhere near as bad as it did to see you lying sick in that hospital bed. I knew then, I'd be here waiting when you came to your senses."

Finding it difficult to breathe over the lump of guilt in my throat, I forced it down and held tighter to the man I loved. "Never again, Brett. I'll never leave you again."

KNOX

My hips slammed into her pale body, making her cry out. Reaching forward, I grasped her red hair in my fist as I pounded her from behind. Running my other hand over her sweat-drenched back, I landed a hard smack on her ass. She cried out to her God and came. Clenching my teeth, I went with her, letting her body milk mine, taking the half orgasm my body allowed in the absence of my mate.

As if on cue, my mobile rang. Pulling out, I picked it up to see the number belonged to Alpha Stirling, Anique's father. Pressing receive, I put it to my ear and went to the bathroom to dispose of the condom. "Stirling, what can I do for you?"

"Evening, Knox, I was phoning to see how the banquet plans are coming along?" Stirling's voice sounded steady, but not happy. Telling me that's not what this call was for, considering he could have called Rhiannon to get that information.

"I've only just returned today from an overseas trip and haven't made it home yet. I've given Rhiannon a budget and free reign. It's her day after all."

"It shouldn't be too overdone; Rhiannon was never as flamboyant as Evaline."

"My understanding is that it will be traditional, none of the hoopla that Evaline required."

"Thank God. It will be nice to see my three daughters again. How is Anique? I believe we had an agreement for me to keep in contact, and yet, I haven't heard from her in months."

My gut wrenched at the sound of her name. There was a knowing undertone in Stirling's voice, which made me wary. How much had he heard from his daughters? Rhiannon admitted a few weeks ago that Anique hadn't contacted her father since we'd completed the moon's blessing.

"Is she with cub? Have you allowed her to continue working?"

Taking a deep breath, I chose honesty. "I don't know where Anique is. She is very adept at hiding."

"I see. I worried that was the case. I warned you when the first phase took you, Anique would not submit willingly. Have you given her up?"

That was a loaded question. "No," I answered deceptively. I'd looked for her, but I had given her up too. "I've been searching for her, but I still have my responsibilities. I was hoping Rhi might help bring Anique around, but it appears that won't be the case."

"Rhi has confessed to me what happened to her and Anique." The sorrow in Stirling's voice was hard to hear. "I knew there was more than one behind what happened, I never knew to what extent, and I never knew they did it to Rhi. I'm at a loss of what to do. To punish one, I need to punish them all."

"Did you cut the ring leader's ear as I suggested?" The girl on the bed raised a brow over her closed eyes. She was still awake.

"I did."

"That's a start. Why don't we talk about this in person at the banquet?" I walked over to gather my clothing.

"I will see if I can lure Anique out for you," Stirling offered in return.

"Thank you." Hanging up the phone, I started dressing.

"You told a man to cut another's ear?" Louise asked, opening her brown eyes.

"He raped two women, one of them was my wife."

"Not the one currently at home planning your wedding?" Louise pushed.

"That is my sister's wedding."

"So, the one who is hiding is your wife?"

Gritting my teeth, I glared at her. "Don't eavesdrop, Louise, you may hear things that lead you to trouble." Opening my wallet, I pulled out the fifteen hundred dollars, dropping it on the bed next to her. "Thanks for being available on short notice."

"Always for you, Knox." Taking her payment, she stashed it away. "I'm sorry about your wife. She must be something to have won your heart."

"She's one of the strongest women I've met. To have survived what she did and still build her life…" I let my thoughts continue silently. I'd blamed her for her disability, I'd thrown her away when she was vulnerable and hurting. Grabbing up my keys, I left.

Arriving at the packhouse, I let myself into the kitchen. Sinking into a chair at the table, I closed my eyes while I waited for the kettle to boil. Anique's face flashed before me, her scent filled my nose, the feel of her body itched across my skin, her heavy breathing and moans of pleasure filled my ears.

Growling, I opened my eyes and glared at the wall. It took me ages to figure out why these visions came to me. They didn't start until just over a month after we completed the moon's blessing. It had taken nearly the three months that passed since to realize I was hearing and feeling my mate fucking someone else.

Initially, I'd assumed it was just longing, but that only hit me when I was alone in my bed. This, it came and went at all manners of the day and night, sometimes several times a night. Two weeks ago, I realized I was feeling my mate's infidelity. I'd been so angry, I'd nearly torn the place up. In my anger, I'd cornered Rhiannon, since she was the closest link I had to Anique. Rhiannon reminded me I'd released Anique from any loyalty to me, and just as I purged my need with someone else, Anique had the right to move on with her life.

The moans in my ears grew and turned into a restrained scream of pain mixed with pleasure. My growl died in my throat. A few days after I realized what I was feeling, I understood that it always ended painfully for Anique. All I'd lost was the ability to father a child and to reach a fully satisfying orgasm. To be with someone else meant pain for Anique, and yet it didn't stop her. Some nights, it went for hours.

Groaning, I remembered the night when we'd first got back from that extended mission a month ago. As if being stuck with Brett White and his team for over a day hadn't been agony enough, by the time we debriefed and got home, I'd been exhausted. After I'd shifted and gone for a run, I came back intending to sleep for a day straight. Instead, I'd been woken up within an hour to this. I lost count of how many times I was woken that day and night. By dinner time, I realized Anique was in heat, so I couldn't be angry with her. She needed to find her release as much as I did.

"Anique?" Dante's voice inquired quietly.

"Yeah," I admitted, scrubbing my hands down my face.

"Finished?" Dante winced.

"Yeah." Getting up, I went to fix myself a coffee.

"Has Rhiannon been willing to-"

"No. Anique refused to attend the banquet. Rhiannon claims she tried to talk her into it."

"Evaline told me Rhiannon was in tears when Anique refused to come," Dante confessed. "If you weren't Alpha-"

They would have refused to let me attend in place of

Rhiannon's sister. In my pack's eyes, I was dishonorable for what I'd done to Anique. I needed to fix that before there were more repercussions. My phone rang. "Morgan," I answered.

"It's Franks," the Captain announced, urgency in his voice. "Get your team and get back here now." He hung up.

"Get the team together," I grumbled, putting my phone away.

"We just got back four hours ago," Dante looked surprised. "Evaline is due any day now."

"I just got in, but Captain wants us there now. You won't be leaving base, so if Evaline goes into labor, you'll be close by. I'll meet you out front," I told him before going to quickly repack my bag, in case we needed to fly out.

We were in the cars fifteen minutes later and arriving at the base twenty minutes after that, thanks to the lack of traffic this time of night. "Morgan, the Captain wants you in the comms room immediately," the gate guard directed.

We parked the cars and started marching across the base. A scent hit my nose, and I halted, sniffing the air. "What is it?" Milton asked, watching my face.

"Anique. I can feel her, and I thought I caught her scent."

The others frowned. "Here on base?" Dante looked around, confused.

"Yeah, it doesn't make sense," I shook my head, my wolf responding to her proximity, wanting me to sniff her out. My head turned towards the barracks.

"Morgan," Franks yelled from the door to the comms building. "Get your ass in here."

"Rion, go check out what's going on in the barracks, then come meet us in the comms room. You see Anique, you keep her with you, understood?" Nodding, Rion marched towards the barracks. With no more time to consider why Anique would be here on the base, we rushed forward. I'd come back to Anique after I'd spoken to the Captain.

The comms room was a hive of activity, more so than usual. "Right, so the man you brought in turned out to be the real deal. He has a lot of information we've been trying to gather," Franks filled us in as we came through the door.

"Did he talk?"

"Not yet, I think he's been delaying, and we think we know why." Franks showed us a baggie with what looked like the remains of a tracking device in it.

"No, we stripped him clean and scanned the bastard twice," I shook my head angrily.

"It was surgically implanted in his upper right thigh, right near his dirty bits," Franks scowled, "and I do mean dirty bits. The ugly bastard hadn't washed in years by the smell of him. They didn't activate the tracker until twelve hours ago. You would have been in the air already. We picked up the signal on a routine scan. The base has been locked down. Anyone already here is staying until we can ensure the base is safe. You and your team are going to transport the prisoner to Quantum, just in case."

Nodding to Franks as Rion stepped into the room, I noted his eyes were unhappy and a little fearful. "When do we leave?"

"Now," Franks ordered. "The bird is already waiting for you, the prisoner is in the holding bay. Get the prisoner to Quantum and interrogate him."

"Yes, sir." Pivoting, I marched out, my team right behind me. "Dante, stay in comms, get a direct line to me and keep me in the loop of what's happening here."

"Yes, Alpha," Dante turned back and entered the building.

"Rion?"

"She's here, with the base on lockdown she can't leave. She's just finished working, so she's crashing out in the barrack."

"Good enough, for now, go with Sasha and meet us at the chopper. Establish a direct line of contact with you for me, not on the same channel as comms, just in case there is trouble." Rion and Sasha changed direction.

We collected the prisoner and had him on the helicopter in under ten minutes. Milton was just running up with our stuff from the car when the first explosion shook the ground. I looked up in time to see a second projectile rocket into the guard's booth at the gate.

My eyes went wide. "Fuck, get us up," I ordered the pilot. "Rion, tell Milton to get to Anique and keep her safe," I yelled to Rion through the direct line as the chopper started to lift forward, the same time I signaled Milton to find her. Dropping the bags, Milton ran as a rocket zoomed straight for the comms building. "Dante, get out!"

The bird was in the air as the rocket hit the far end of the building. From above, I was helpless to do anything. The building my best mate was standing in fell under an explosion of rubble. My eyes tracked to the barracks where ant-sized people were streaming out, ready to defend. Somewhere, down there was my mate. As gunfire lit the ground below us, I waited for the unique pain which would tell me my mate was injured. Nothing. Even as we flew into the darkness away from the chaos, there was nothing.

ANIQUE

"*T*hanks for dropping my stuff off, Annie," Brett murmured, his voice rough.

"What are wives for?" I half laughed. Removing my arms from around his neck as he helped me place my feet back to the wet tiled floor, I stepped away. "How long until you fly out?"

"A few hours. We're waiting on the information to be confirmed before we go," Brett revealed as he finished off the shower I'd interrupted. He'd been at the base for training when he'd received word he'd be flying out tonight. Calling me at the hospital, Brett asked me to bring up some stuff he'd need. Since Brett was still in the middle of training, and I was finishing my shift, it was easier for me to drop it off.

"I'll miss you," I kissed his shoulder. Stepping away from him, I stole his towel to dry. Moving to the bench where I'd left my clothes when I saw Brett naked, I redressed.

Brett chuckled as he dried himself. "You're damn lucky no one else needed a shower."

"Nathan said he'd give me ten minutes," I winked.

"It's been twenty," Nathan cut in cheekily as he stepped into the room, "but you might as well go for another. We are on lockdown, effective ten minutes ago. No going out or in without express orders."

"Suck's for you. I'm exhausted after a thirty-two-hour shift and heading home."

"Annie," Brett shook his head, unhappy. "Lockdown means you can't leave either." Chewing his lip, Brett looked at Nathan. "What's happening?" Brett was getting dressed, listening as Nathan explained what was wrong. All I got from it was that the Hounds had brought someone to the base, something happened, I wasn't going home to my comfortable bed until it was sorted.

Taking my hand, Brett kissed my temple. "Come on, Annie. You can sleep on my bunk until this gets sorted. Should only be a few hours."

"Will you be sleeping with me?" I batted my lashes.

"I'll check in to see if I'm needed, then I'll come back and snuggle if I can."

"A-huh," Nathan stirred. "Snuggling, that's what you'll be doing."

Showing me his bunk, Brett left me with his team while he went to do what he does. I couldn't sleep with the noise, which was odd because I was used to catching Z's at the hospital when I could, and it was never quiet. Giving more consideration to the feeling of unease, I realized my wolf was excited, getting all worked up about something.

"Hey, Rion, you boys here to clean up your mess?" Nathan called jokingly.

"Yeah, just got to base. Looks like I'll be here overnight, so I thought I'd stash my stuff here in case I'm able to get some sleep later," the voice answered.

Taking a breath, I opened my eyes, lifted my head, and focused on the far end of the barracks where one of Knox's pack was throwing a bag in his locker. His eyes were watching me. "Don't get any ideas, Rion," Nathan warned, seeing where his attention was.

"What's she doing here?"

Nathan turned to look at me, a flare of knowledge in his eyes. Brett had told his team the Hounds weren't to know about us. "She was dropping off something for the boss, got caught here by the lockdown."

"Thought her and White broke up?"

Nathan just shrugged. "None of anyone's business now, is it?"

Rion gritted his jaw. "I best go see what's going on."

"Argh, he's so running to tell Knox you've been riding the boss' cock," Nathan shook his head as soon as Rion left. When I raised a humored brow, Nathan shrugged again. "It's true. Get some sleep, little red, I'll keep the big bad wolf away."

Laughing at just how close Nathan was to the reality of that comment, I curled up on the bunk and drifted into that half-sleep phase I reach when I'm trying to sleep at work. That state of mind that lets you get some much-needed rest but know what is happening in your surroundings. The helicopter's engines roared to life, and not long after that, I heard a sharp piercing whistle growing closer. Sitting up suddenly alert, I tried to identify the noise. "What's that whistling sound?"

Glancing at me, Nathan cocked his head. A moment later, everyone was diving for cover, Nathan throwing me off the bed and covering me with his body as a loud explosion shook the building. "What the fuck?!" Nathan looked around.

"Here comes another one," I warned, already hearing the projectile moving through the air at speed. My hearing had always been better than the other wolves. Pushing my head down, Nathan covered us with a mattress. Again, the building shook, the explosion was loud, but nothing hit us.

"They took out the gates and transport shed," someone yelled from the door. "We need to get out of the buildings."

Hauling me to my feet, Nathan moved me to the back door of the barracks, some of his team coming with us, everyone else through the front door.

"Again," I yelled as we escaped the confines of the building.

When Nathan looked up, I followed. Spotting it with my wolf sight first, I pointed. Nathan and I tracked the rocket to the main building. "That's the comms!" Grabbing my hand, Nathan started running with me.

"Where's Brett?"

"I don't know, he'll find us," Nathan assured, dragging me further into the base. Turning, he pointed to three of his team. "Head to the armory."

"Where are we going?" I asked.

"The bunker, the boss would kill me if I didn't get you to safety."

Stopping, Nathan turned to the loud popping sound. His eyes were wide, and ears keen as he pinpointed where it was coming from. Watching the helicopter disappearing into the night, I didn't have to wonder who was on it. I could feel his presence retreating by the second. Turning ahead, Nathan ran holding my hand until he reached a hutch. Pulling it up, he helped me down the narrow stairs. "Stay there until the shooting stops, or someone comes to get you."

Nodding, I huddled into the far corner of the bunker. I was a doctor, not a soldier. The best I could do was wait until it was safe, and then get out of there and help the injured. The entire time I was down there, I was worrying about Brett. So, I felt like I'd been down there hours when the hutch opened, and someone basically jumped down the steps.

"Anique?" The strange voice called. While I could smell he was wolf, I didn't know him, so I stayed still. "It's Milton, Rhi's mate."

Exhaling in relief, I stepped forward. "I'm here."

Rushing forward, Milton started to check on me. "Are you okay?"

Shoving him away, I growled. "I'm fine, stop touching me. I'm not good with dark places and men's hands on me."

Milton backed up instantly. "Sorry, I needed to be sure."

"Did you see Brett?"

Milton gnashed his teeth together. "Yeah, he's defending with his team."

"Why aren't you up there?"

"Because I was ordered to secure you, and keep you safe," Milton bit back. Doing something with his gun, he huffed. "That and I used my ammo up just getting to you."

"All of it?"

"Most of it." Milton pressed something at his ear. "Flip, you there?" He waited a minute, then Milton growled. "Buzz, you still out there?" He nodded getting a reply this time. "Let Alpha know I've secured the package and that it's not damaged." He waited listening to whatever was being said in his ear. "Is Seeker with you?" I watched Milton stiffen. "I watched the building go down; did he get out?" Milton turned to look at the hatch.

"What's happened?" I asked, understanding he wanted to be out there.

"Dante was in the comms building when it got hit. Rion says no one got out, but there's been a few who have crawled out of the wreckage."

"You want to go look for your brother?" Milton nodded. "Then let's go." I moved forward to the hutch.

"Wait..."

"No, the gunfire has died down now, and it's nowhere near us."

"You can hear that?" Milton looked surprised.

"I can hear the opening and closing of someone's mitral valve in their chest, so trust me, I can tell you that what was happening up there is nearly over, and we shouldn't be at risk going up there."

Milton studied me. After a second, he launched forward and slowly lifted the hatch. "Stay here while I clear the area." Climbing out, Milton moved around. Seconds later, he put his hand down and waved me up. I ran up the stairs carefully and to Milton's side. "Stay behind me, keep your eyes and ears open."

We moved quickly, staying away from the distant random gunshots and moving to the comms building. People were lying on the ground as we approached. Progressing to each of them, I checked their pulse and shook my head when there was nothing to feel. Milton's anxiety was growing by the minute, his gun pointing around us, watching for any threat.

"Brett and another are about to come around that corner," I pointed to where I recognized Brett's footsteps approaching. Spinning around, Milton held up his hand to let them know we were friendlies.

"Anique, what the hell?" Brett called as he came around the corner, gun pointed at us until he recognized us. Rushing forward, he knelt by my side. "What are you doing out here?"

"My brother was in comms, Anique's a doctor, do the math," Milton grumbled.

His eyes lancing towards Milton, Brett snarled. "You put her in danger..."

"Hey! I'm safe. We knew it was you. You do your job, I'll do mine."

Shaking his head at me, Brett gritted his teeth before focusing on Milton. "They've fought through to the holding cells; we've got them pinned down there. We were backtracking to make sure there were no others before we head down there."

"Go, I'll keep her safe," Milton advised.

Reaching forward, Brett touched my cheek, forcing me to meet his eyes. "I'm okay."

"Stay that way." He pulled me in for a quick but emotional kiss.

Gripping his shirt, I didn't let him go. "I love you, come back safe."

"I wouldn't dare disobey you." After kissing me again, Brett signaled his buddy to move forward.

Moving closer, Milton brushed the wedding band on my left hand. "You're married?"

"I'm pretty sure that rocket didn't cause these bullet wounds," I muttered, ignoring his question and pointing to the hole in the head of the body I stood over.

"Executed while they tried to escape the building," Milton growled. Letting his panic take over, Milton scanned the bodies. "Dante! Dante!"

When he opened his mouth to yell another time, I whacked his leg. "Shh." My eyes were searching for the whimpering I could hear.

Frowning, Milton watched me as I slowly moved half bent over towards the burning building. "Anique!" Milton scolded in a whisper.

Ignoring him, I kept moving towards the noise of a wounded animal. Getting down on my hands and knees, I peeked under a door thrown from the building and found the source. "Milton!" I pointed to the door.

Lifting the door, Milton threw it away, dropping to his brother's side. "Dante," he murmured.

Assessing all the blood covering the giant wolf, I sucked in a breath and caught the scent of hell. "We need to get him to the hospital."

"He's in wolf form," Milton grouched.

"Which he can't stay in. He shifted to try and heal, but that's silver in him. If we get him to a hospital, we can get that out of him, and he can heal. We stay here, he'll be dead in the hour."

Milton looked at me with wide blinking eyes. "How do you know that's silver?"

"Trust me, I know the smell." Eyes scanning around us, I gnawed at my lip. "You need to go find a car..."

"I'm not leaving you undefended."

"Go get a car!" I raged, my wolf coming through on my voice. Falling back, mouth open and eyes wide, Milton turned and ran. Looking down at Dante, I patted his head until I reached his scruff. His eyes watched me fearfully. "Your turn, Dante. I need you to shift to human for me."

He tried, but the pain was too much, and he backed away.

"Come on, Dante. You shifted to wolf to try and heal, you can shift back," I coaxed. Whimpering, Dante looked away. "I so don't have the patience for this tonight."

As I allowed my wolf to come forward, Dante's eyes flashed to me, he hesitated and tried to back up, but I held his scruff as I waited for my wolf to be front and center. I couldn't shift, and it was painful to come this far into my wolf, the silver burning me in my pelvis as soon as I let her forward, but I needed her at full strength. Waiting until she was steady and able to cope with the pain, I bit my lip against the agony of it. My wolf took control, my eyes flashed up to meet Dante's. "Shift!"

My will washed over Dante, he whimpered, unable to resist, and his body melted back to human form. My wolf backed out as quick as she could, and I keeled over in agony at the burning in my womb.

"Anique?" A gentle hand stroked my head.

Gritting my teeth, I lifted myself a little, letting Dante see the tears in my eyes. "I'm okay." Pushing past the pain, I started to assess his wounds in human form. "None of these are fatal if we can get the silver out," I assured, my voice weaker than it was.

A black ranger pulled up just behind me, and Milton jumped out, opening the back door. "Let's go," Milton ordered. Jumping out of the passenger seat, Rion came to help lift Dante into the ranger. "How did he shift?"

"I asked him too." As we pulled away, a loud explosion covered over the chaotic static around the base. Flames danced into the air toward the back of the base, the ground beneath us shaking like a massive earthquake. Staring into the burning night, I clenched my fist as my heart dropped into the pit of my stomach. I sent up a prayer to the Goddess that Brett was safe. He would be. He always came home.

"Shit!" Rion put his hand to his ear as if to say something. Milton grabbed his arm, and when Rion looked at him, he shook his head, eyes flicking to Dante and me in the back seat. Rion let his hand drop, throat swallowing hard. A moment later, we were racing through the ruined gate.

Pulling out my phone, I pressed the speed dial. "Monique, get the MRI ready to go."

"What's going on?"

"I'm on my way in from the base with a silver ridden wolf. I need the MRI to be ready when we get there," I gritted, trying to push through the burning agony in my abdomen.

"It could damage the machine, Annie."

"It will save his life. Have it ready."

"It will be," Monique assured and hung up.

"You're in pain?" Rion observed.

"Really? I hadn't noticed."

"Milton said you weren't hurt," Rion snapped back.

"Rion," Dante whispered, getting his attention. "Leave her be." Rion turned his eyes to Milton and let it drop. Five minutes later, we arrived at the hospital.

"Get me a gurney," I yelled to the wards-man, who stood frowning at us for pulling into the ambulance bay.

Running inside, he came back out with the gurney I asked for. "We didn't know any help had reached the base yet," he told me as they lifted Dante onto the stretcher.

"It hasn't, I was there when it happened. We're going straight to radiology."

"Shouldn't he be triaged?"

"I've done that. I need to see if there is any shrapnel left in him before we close him up."

Radiology was right next door to emergency, so we bypassed triage and headed straight for the MRI room. Monique was there holding the door open. Her eyes went wide when she saw Milton and Rion, and she disappeared into the booth. Directing the men to get Dante set up, I understood Monique was not going to stand in the same room as them.

"Everyone out!"

"Wait, that's metal in him," Milton argued after Rion and the wards-man left. "You turn that machine on-"

"It's going to rip it right out of him," I nodded, confirming his fear. "It won't be fatal, and he can shift and heal the worst of it immediately after." Pushing him out the door, I walked next door to the booth. "Do it," I ordered Monique as I stepped inside.

She pressed the button to load Dante into the machine. Following me, Milton stared at Monique. "She's one of the strays."

"She is the only person with the knowledge to save your brother at this moment. Shut up and let her do her job," my wolf's voice coming through. Whimpering, I bent over, clutching my abdomen, the agony still demanding my attention.

"Annie," Monique came to me.

"I'm fine, turn the machine on."

19

KNOX

We took the prisoner to Quantum. After five minutes in the room with him angry, I'd felt Anique's pain shatter through the bond. Standing, I'd smashed everything in the room to pieces, the man retreating to the far corner terrified. It had taken a lot longer than usual to get my wolf to give me back control. By then, the prisoner was trembling and crying, sitting in a pool of his own urine by the time I moved close to him.

"My wife was on that base, and I've lost communications with my men there. I'm going to leave now. If you haven't told my man everything you know by the time I get back to base, I will hunt down your family, stake them to the ground, and have rabid dogs rip them apart. If anything has happened to my wife, I will hunt your family down, stake them to the ground, and have rabid dogs rip them apart. You won't have to imagine their screams; I'll film the entire thing for you."

Storming out, I left the door open as I ordered the capture of his two wives and five children, making sure to use their names, so he knew that I was aware of exactly who I was looking for. He'd been squawking by the time Sasha walked in and shut the door.

The helicopter flew low over the base, fires still burning in several piles of rubble that were once buildings. From above, the majority of activity was happening around the demolished holding facility. The bird's eye view didn't improve my mood as Anique's pain continued to roll in like waves. She was alive, at least. That was the only consolation as I frowned at the mess below us. Everywhere there were the lights of emergency vehicles.

"Alpha, you there?" Rion's voice came over comms.

"Where the fuck have you been?"

"We're at the hospital. Dante's bad, Anique and Milton found him, and we rushed him here, he's in surgery."

"Where's Anique?" I'd felt her pain, so I knew she was hurt.

"She's assisting on the surgery," Rion sounded worried. "She saved his life, Alpha."

"Tell him about the stray," I heard Milton in the background.

"Tell me about Anique first. How badly was she hurt?"

Static filled the line, and I thought I'd lost them when Rion came back on. "She's got pain, but she wouldn't tell us what caused it."

"I know what fucking caused it," Milton growled in the background.

"She's assisting in the surgery, but I heard one of the doctors telling her that straight after, he's taking her to get checked. Look, the radiologist here, she's one of the strays we've been looking for."

"Get hold of her; discreetly."

"We'll have to come back for her. Rhiannon just called Milton. Evaline felt Dante get hurt and went into labor. I told them to come to the hospital."

"We do home births for a reason, Rion!"

"The baby is breech!" Rion snapped. "If she doesn't come to the hospital, we'll lose both the baby and mother. They're on their way."

"When it rains, it fucking pours," I muttered, stroking the

bridge of my nose. Huffing, I turned to the pilot. "Take me to the hospital."

Ten minutes later, I was marching in the doors of the hospital. Rion was there waiting. "We're set up in emergency. I used that we are there to identify and assist to get us in. Try not to get us thrown out."

When I growled at Rion, he ignored me and waved to the nurse at the desk who buzzed us back. Milton was inside with a clipboard writing down names and platoons of the men being brought in.

"I didn't think we had this many injured," I admitted, looking at the ten or so men with burns.

"We didn't until the assholes got themselves cornered in the holding facility and blew themselves up," Milton informed me. "These were the ones outside; they are still digging the others out. Three went in to negotiate a surrender."

"You need to tell him," Rion muttered.

Cringing, Milton frowned. "The three inside were White and two of his men."

"Shit, they are good men." I liked White.

"Promise me you won't freak out," Milton demanded, waiting until I nodded. "Anique was at the base to see White. They're married, and she was dropping something off he needed before he flew out for his next mission."

Clenching my jaw, I stared at Milton. Anique was married. She'd gone back to White after I abandoned her and married him. Staring at him, I blinked. Milton swore under his breath, sensing the conflicting turmoil inside me. Taking several deep breaths, I focused on the bit of information I could handle in this environment. "She's been here the entire time?"

"It would appear so," Milton confirmed. "She changed her name when she married and is now Annie White."

"Explains why the hospital denied an Annie Burns working

here," I contemplated. "And at least one other stray is here, so I think we can assume none of them ever left."

"Either we have gotten terrible at finding people," Rion shook his head, "or these girls are very good at hiding in plain sight."

"Annie is the ringleader behind this. I saw her with the other stray. Annie is still their Alphia," Milton murmured.

"Then, we'll use Annie to bring us the others." A nurse walked by us. "Excuse me, can I get an update on Dante Morgan? I'm his lieutenant, and I've just arrived from the base. His wife is about to arrive in labor, and I'd like to be able to put her at ease."

Going over to the phone, the nurse made a call. After a few minutes, she hung up and came back. "They are just finishing up. There were no complications and should be no issues. He'll be taken to recovery in about half an hour, and I've asked for someone to let you know when you can see him."

"Thank you." She dashed away to deal with the wounded as I assessed the room. "Am I the most senior rank here?"

Milton checked his list. "Yes."

"Then I better do my duty and check on everyone, then you can start calling people who need to be called."

For the next twenty minutes, I checked on the men from the base. Most were relatively minor injuries. One was bleeding badly. The nurses were struggling to stabilize him until they could get him into surgery. His prognosis wasn't good, so Milton was calling his family, and I listened to his last request. After watching him be rushed off to the surgical ward, I scrubbed my hands of his blood.

The doors opened and screaming filled the room. "Evaline," Rion announced. We all moved forward. Milton pulled Rhiannon into his arms and hugged her tight. She looked relieved to see he was okay.

"Dante?" Evaline asked me. Walking beside her as they rushed her through to maternity, I took her hand.

"He's going to be fine. I just spoke to the doctors, and he's looking to make a full recovery. You focus on you and the baby; he'll be by your side as soon as he can be." Keeping myself calm, I used my will to soothe her.

Taking a deep breath, Evaline exhaled, and instantly relaxed. "Thank you," she whispered. They wheeled her through the next lot of doors.

"I'm going with her. Let me know when Annie is out, and I'll come to see her. I need to know she's okay." Rhiannon disappeared through the door after her sister, and we all wandered back to our posts.

It took another thirty minutes before a flash of red hair caught my attention. Lifting my tired eyes, I met green eyes that looked just as exhausted. Looking me over, Anique swallowed visibly as she walked towards us. She didn't address me, turning her eyes to Milton instead and giving her words to him.

"Dante's out of surgery," she informed professionally. "I prevented them from giving him a blood transfusion, so he should be able to shift when he regains consciousness and heal entirely." Keeping her voice soft, Anique checked around her. "Probably wait a few days to avoid raising suspicions, though."

Without warning, Milton pulled Anique into a hug. "Thank you for what you did. I know it hurts you to do it, but thank you."

Anique was stiff with tension when he released her. As Milton stepped back, we watched Anique force herself to relax and take another step back from us. "Have you heard from Brett?" Anique's voice was weak asking that question, and I wasn't sure if it was because she was asking it in front of me, or because she feared our response.

"Nothing yet. He hasn't been brought in, so he may be okay." I could tell it was a lie, and by the sharp look Anique gave Milton, she could too.

"Your sister Evaline is in maternity," I cut in. Refusing to look at me, Anique swallowed so hard I worried the sound of my voice was painful for her. "The baby is breech, and they need to do a cesarean. Rhiannon is with her and wanted you to come in as soon as you could."

Anique nodded, the tension as thick as a cinder block as she turned her back on me and walked towards the doors that led to maternity. Halfway there, Anique crumpled on all fours with the most torturous whimper escaping her lips. I was moving toward her, but Rion pulled me back.

A doctor rushed forward and helped her up instead. "Right, time to check you out, Annie. I want an X-ray to see if that silver shard has moved."

The wind got knocked out of me as I watched Anique be helped through the doors to radiology. "Did he just say...?" I pointed after her as I looked at Milton and Rion.

"She recognized the scent of silver in Dante's wounds at the base," Milton started. "She used her wolf to force him to shift..." Despite trying to keep my shit together, I gaped at Milton wide-eyed. "She's that strong that she didn't need to shift, but I think the silver burns her whenever her wolf comes forward."

"That's why I held you back from helping her," Rion confessed. "She's tired and emotional. Her wolf is near the surface, and if you make her angry..."

"I'll cause her immense pain," I nodded, understanding.

Ten minutes later, Anique walked back through the door with the doctor and went to a computer where he pulled up her X-rays. Casually reading the list of names I took off Rion, I moved closer to eavesdrop. "...a fraction of a millimeter, it's probably what's causing you so much pain," the doctor discussed.

"It's moved closer to the artery," Anique assessed her X-rays.

"Yes. I'm sorry, Annie, you're looking twelve months at best if we don't remove it."

"I'm not ready to face that risk yet, Eric."

Eric took her shoulders in his hands. "It's a risk, either way,

Annie. You need to talk to your husband and make the decision about children because if the shrapnel moves any further, we won't have a choice. We need to take that silver out before it nicks the artery, and the potential is the surgery will damage that blood supply and we'll need to perform a full hysterectomy." Eric rubbed Anique's shoulders. "You can't avoid this anymore. Our research hasn't given us the answers you wanted."

The doors flew open as Nathan came running in beside paramedics. "Annie! It's Brett."

Brett was on the gurney, blood everywhere, groaning loudly. Rushing forward, Anique jumped onto the stretcher as they kept moving forward. "Brett? No, no, no," she murmured as she assessed his wounds. "You swore you'd stay safe!" Turning her head, she found her doctor friend. "Eric, scrub in."

My stomach disintegrated, the pain in my chest making it hard to breathe. My heart was racing with anxiety and fear, but I didn't know the source. Lifting my eyes to the tragic scene unfolding before me, to the redhead trying desperately to determine if she'd lose the man she loved, my world came tumbling down.

"You can't come, Annie," Eric told her, sympathy but determination as he faced her tears. Her heart ached like it was my own.

"I'm not leaving him."

"Yes, you are," the doctor signaled Nathan to help get her away.

"Brett!" Anique cried his name like a plea to the Goddess as Nathan wrapped his arm around her waist to pull her free.

Knocking the oxygen mask from his face, Brett reached out to snag Anique's hand, the agony of his wounds on his face, but his grip determined. "Annie, I don't regret one moment," Brett rasped, his eyes begging forgiveness.

Clinging to him, Anique sobbed, "I love you."

All these years, I'd like White, but at this moment, I admired him greatly and understood how he'd won my fierce rogue's heart.

"Go," Eric ordered the paramedics to the surgical ward.

"Take care of her," Brett directed Nathan with death on his tongue.

Watching them go, Anique sobbed in Nathan's arms. As Brett was wheeled through the doors, the heartrate monitor stuttered, then screamed out a solid beep. "No!" Anique tried to run over there, Nathan held her back, but she was fighting him.

Moving forward, Milton with me, we helped Nathan drag Anique screaming from the emergency room. Wrapping Anique in my arms, I tried to use my will to calm her, to soothe her pain and worry. Breaking free, Anique glared at me, knowing what I'd attempted to do. Without loyalty binding us, she didn't have to obey me, and she was strong enough to resist if she genuinely meant it. The look in her grieving eyes told me just how much she felt every word to follow.

"This is your fault! I heard what they said at the base, you brought this here, this was your mess."

"Anique..." I tried to soothe her.

"I've lost him again because of you!" Anique screamed. She tried to shove me, but basically bounced off my shoulders. "It's always you."

"Annie, hey," Nathan pulled her away from me, his voice soothing, his arms around her in gentle restraint. Despite his good intentions, I wanted to tear his arms off. "Knox was doing his job, just like the rest of us. Just like Brett was. The only people to blame are those bastards who blew the place up."

When Anique turned that dangerous glare on Nathan, I was worried she was about to rip his throat out. Instead, tears poured forth, her face fell, and she stepped into his waiting arms, crying her heart out on his chest.

Feeling every single tear like a stab in my heart, I stood there. My mate was in pain, her heart was breaking, and I had to stand there and accept it was for another man. Unable to watch her falling apart, I turned and walked back inside. I'd never realized how much of a mess I'd made of everything the night I rejected her. In freeing her of her loyalty to me, I'd forgotten, Anique had marked me hers, and she had never released me of her.

Feeling her pain, her love for another, it was the Goddess's punishment for my pride.

20

ANIQUE

"Are you ready to go back in?"

Sobbing, I nodded. Nathan moved his body, so just his arm was around my shoulders. Shivering in discomfort, I stepped out of reach as we walked back inside. Half an hour had passed already. Knox was still there, doing his job.

"How about we sit in the waiting room outside the theaters?" Nathan suggested, seeing the way I glared at Knox. He was trying to keep us well apart, which I could understand; the bad blood was evident between us. Still, the waiting area for the surgery unit overlooked the area Knox and his pack had been set up in to do their job.

Having Knox in the same space was beyond hard. I was trying to think about Brett, and my wolf wanted me to crawl on my belly to Knox and beg him to soothe me. The frustration was only making me angrier. Knox's wolf must have needed the same. His eyes kept coming back to me. He'd take a step towards me, then physically stop himself and focus on one of his injured.

By the time Eric came out, my nerves were on edge, along with my anger and frustration. He didn't need to say anything. The way his eyes avoided meeting my own was telling in itself. "No!" I pleaded for him to tell me anything other than what he was going to say.

"I'm sorry, Annie." Eric caught me in his arms as my legs failed me. "There was nothing we could do. Brett's injuries were too extensive." Eric held me upright while I fell apart.

"No, no, you have to save him," I demanded, trying to shove Eric away, to force him to go back in there and save the man I love. "I can't lose him, please!"

"Annie, I'm sorry, Brett is dead."

Those words every doctor had to say, to make you hear it and understand it was final. But, I couldn't, and wouldn't listen to them. With a final push, Eric stepped back from me, tears falling down his own face as I shoved him towards the door.

"Annie, stop." Grabbing me from behind, Nathan pulled me away from Eric.

Fighting off his arms, I pushed Nathan away from me and turned my pleading eyes back to my friend and mentor. "Please!" When Eric shook his head in sadness, I screamed my heartache.

Approaching me, Knox took me in his arms, and for a moment, I let him embrace me, to soothe me. My fists clutched in his shirt as I sobbed against his solid chest. Something shiny caught my attention. Turning my head, I spied the wedding rings on my finger, rings that the man holding me hadn't given me. The pain tore through my insides in a way I'd never felt before. Not the pain from the silver I was all too familiar with, but a ripping agony that reached into my chest cavity and clawed at my fragile heart.

Remembering this was all Knox's fault, I screamed. He'd caused my heartache. His rejection and then bringing those men to the base. I wanted Knox to hurt like I was hurting. I wanted him to feel the pain he caused me. In the middle of emergency, I went crazy and started trying to tear Knox to pieces.

"Annie, stop!" Nathan tried to pull me away. More arms and

cursing as Knox's pack tried to get between us, but I wasn't going down without seeing Knox bleed the way I felt I was hemorrhaging inside. Security waded into the fray, and I spotted the silver of their cuffs as they reached for my wrists. My vision washed to muted hues as I threw the punch that Brett taught me to one face, an elbow to another. They ended up out cold, and my focus went back to Knox.

Through it all, Knox stayed and took my hate. He didn't try and back away or resist me. He stood there and watched my pain, and I made damn sure he felt it. I screamed and clawed and kicked. Knox took it until he couldn't. When my nails dug into his chest, Knox grabbed my wrists, pulled my arms around him, and held me so tight I couldn't breathe. I mean that literally.

"I'm sorry, Anique," Knox murmured against my ear. "He was a good man."

Lifting my face to his, intent on spitting on him, I couldn't. Knox's eyes were glassy with hidden tears, and I knew it was hurting him, too, that he hated what he was about to do. His arms tightened around my chest until the fight left me through a lack of oxygen, my ribs creaking from the constriction, then he held me a little longer. The bastard suffocated me until I passed out.

Sitting in the kitchen watching the sunlight the sky, a cup of coffee in my hands, I heard the shower start. The noise brought me back to the here and now. Picking up the cold coffee, I tipped it down the sink before I brewed a fresh pot.

"Coffee," Mandy purred, coming into the kitchen. Already prepared, I handed her a cup; black, one sugar. "Lifesaver," Mandy inhaled the smell of the coffee, then gulped a mouthful while I poured myself a fresh cup.

"Thanks for staying last night." Taking my seat back at the table, I watched Mandy plop into the other chair.

"Staying wasn't the problem. The bottle of vodka Danielle talked us into was," Mandy groaned and dropped her head on the table. Danielle could drink a sailor under the table. Mandy lifted her head. "You going to be okay today?"

"I've been through worse."

"Don't give me that. This is different in every way."

Not arguing, I took another drink of the coffee.

Mandy finished her cup. "I'm going to head home and get ready. Got anything else you need me to take with me?"

"No, the only thing of mine left is the clothes I need."

Mandy squeezed my hand. "I'm really sorry, Annie. We all know how much you loved him."

My eyes prickled, but I didn't cry. Staring out the window, Brett and I fooling around in the backyard played like a movie behind my eyes. My phone buzzed on the table, pulling me back to reality again. Picking it up, I put it to my ear.

"Annie, it's Nathan. Do you want a lift to the funeral today?"

"That would be nice, thanks, Nathan."

"I'll pick you up at ten then," he informed and hung up.

Messaging Mandy, I let her know I had a lift. It saved her from coming out of their way to get me. Then I stood up and went to the bedroom. Slowly, I unbuttoned Brett's shirt I'd slept in since the attack, his scent still all over it. Changing into my workout gear, I ran my usual track, trying to calm myself through routine and the familiar.

When I got back, I showered and dressed and finished the last bit of packing that I needed to do; Brett's clothes. I'd taken two of his tops that I loved, the rest his team would deal with for me. The house belonged to the base, along with most of the furniture in it. I'd kept the photos of us, the rest of his things Nathan was going to deliver to Brett's parents. I'd never met them, Brett hadn't got along with them, so I'm not sure they even knew I existed.

"Annie," Nathan called from the front door.

Grabbing my cardigan from the bed, I went out to meet him. "Hi, thanks for picking me up."

"It's not a problem, I live two minutes away," Nathan replied, following me to his car. "Have you found a place to stay?"

"I'll stay with Mandy temporarily," I answered as I dropped into the seat.

"What about your place?"

"I have tenants in. I'd have to give notice, but they are good tenants, and I'm not sure I'm staying anyway."

Turning the car around, Nathan headed out of town, his head tilting as his mouth turned down. "You're leaving the hospital?"

"Taking leave, currently," I grumbled. "Forced leave."

"You did knock that security guard out cold. I knew Brett taught you to fight, but that guy wasn't small. I've heard of people finding inhuman strength when in danger, but never grief."

The reminder made me cringe.

"I thought you were going to rip Morgan's heart out of his chest." Nathan glanced warily to the side.

"I'm pretty sure I tried."

"He's going to be here today," Nathan reminded me gently.

"I know." Turning my attention out the window, I closed my eyes.

"He's not to blame, Annie."

"I know." I'd always known that was the case, but the grieving part of me needed someone to blame, someone to hate.

"If you attack him again, we'll throw you in a mental institution," Nathan warned.

"I won't."

Nathan tapped the wheel. "You and Brett, there was always a connection between you two that us boys could never explain. We could see it, clear as day whenever you two were in the same room, but we couldn't explain it. You made us all believe in soul mates."

Biting my lip, I closed my eyes on the tears threatening to spill. Knox was supposed to be my soul mate, but I knew the connection he was talking about. I decided while Knox was my wolf's mate, Brett was the soul mate to my human half. It was the only explanation.

"Every one of us understands, Annie. If you truly are soul mates, you lost a part of you when Brett died. We lost our mate and a good team leader, but you lost half your soul. So, what happened, you tearing at Knox like the she-demon from hell, we get it. We've all seen you this week, checked in, and helped you pack. We know you've returned to our Annie, so no one is going to judge you about what happened that night."

"What happened when I passed out?"

Nathan took a deep breath. "Honestly, we all breathed again. None of us was going to take on Knox after what you'd just done to him, and frankly, we were all grateful to him for being the one to do it." Nathan waited. "All I'm saying is, you can't blame him. If you feel yourself getting worked up, do the girly thing and pass-out or vomit." When I didn't say anything, he let it go.

We arrived at the crematorium with plenty of time to spare. Brett was an atheist, so there would be no church, and he didn't want to rot in a grave. His team, who survived, they lost three men in total, were all there waiting. They were the pallbearers. They all gave me a hug and their condolences, told me how much Brett had loved me, and how they'd be there for me if I needed anything. The girls arrived shortly after and joined our group, who were talking about the clean-up at the base.

I felt him before his scent hit me. Closing my eyes to rein my wolf in, I lifted my gaze to the door to watch Knox enter. He had half his pack with him. Spotting us straight away, Knox locked his eyes with mine, and I had to swallow down my desire to go to him.

When Mandy's breath caught in her throat, I turned to find her staring towards the door. Following her gaze, I saw Rion was looking at Mandy the same way. "Oh god," Mandy murmured when someone walked between them. Grabbing her hand, I waited for her eyes to come to me. "What do I do?"

"Two choices, get to know him or run for the hills before he gets your scent," I advised quietly. Mandy was trembling beside me while Rion informed Knox he'd just found his mate. Rhiannon was with Milton. As soon as she saw me, she made a beeline for me. "Get some air," I directed the girls.

They were out the side door before Rhiannon reached me, Knox and Rion watching where they went. "Annie," Rhiannon wrapped herself around me and held me tight. "I'm so sorry."

"Thank you," I pulled out of her arms before the urge to cry in them took me. "How's Evaline and the baby?"

Rhiannon smiled, wiping the tears away. "Good. They named her Grace."

"It's a good name." With the Olympian's still beside me, I introduced my sister to Brett's friends.

"Where did the girls go?" Rhiannon looked around confused. "I'll introduce Rion to Mandy." When I gripped my sister's hand, her smile dropped. "Or not," she winced, taking her hand back. "You've met my fiancé." Rhiannon took Milton's hand as he joined us.

"Anique." Taking my hand, Milton squeezed it gently. "Ah, Knox doesn't want to upset you again, so he's going to stay in the back."

"Thank you, I appreciate the consideration."

"You saved my brother's life, it's the least we could do."

Shifting my eyes to Knox, I nodded my thanks. He bowed his head slightly then went to find a seat. Leaving his Alpha, Dante came forward and pulled me into a hug. He didn't say anything, just gave me a quick hug and moved away again.

"You made a quick recovery," Nathan appraised Dante as they shook hands.

"I had a good doctor."

They both looked at me. "Yeah, you did," Nathan looked me over in a way that should have made me blush. It didn't.

Noticing it, Dante frowned. "What's the acceptable grieving period for a military widow these days?" Dante asked Nathan quietly, but he knew I could hear.

Nathan scoffed. "You're married, so if you're asking for Morgan, you can tell him he's out of luck. Wives are left to the care of a soldier's company."

Dante raised a brow. "You think you have a better chance than Morgan?"

"Morgan doesn't have a chance," Nathan assured Dante.

Moving over to them, I put my arm through Nathan's. "The hearse just arrived," I informed them. Patting my hand, Nathan excused us from Dante and led me over to the front row of seats. He left me there to go carry the coffin.

Gazing out the window, I made eye contact with Monique. She grabbed Mandy's hand, and they came straight back in, sitting down at my side. "Verdict?" I asked Mandy. I needed this, a distraction from my pain for a moment.

"I was hoping you would tell me. Danielle is saying hell no, Monique is telling me to give him a chance."

"What is your gut telling you?"

"That he has really nice eyes," Mandy swooned a little. Catching herself, Mandy cleared her throat. She looked at me wide-eyed. "Is this what it was like for you?"

"It's different for everyone, I think. Why?"

Mandy shrugged. "I just can't imagine you swooning over a guy's eyes."

"His smell. And his touch. I loved the way they both smelled and how their touch made my past disappear."

Mandy put her hand in mine as the first tear escaped. "You were so happy with him. Do you think you could have that again?" Her eyes drifted towards the back corner where Knox was sitting.

"After what happened, I never thought I'd have it at all. I don't think I could have if I hadn't met Brett and learned not all men are assholes. One of the things he taught me was never to say never."

With her eyes still flitting to the back corner, Mandy bit her lip, her hand trembling in mine. "I'm terrified of returning to pack life and the sexist mentality."

"Do you think I would have sent the others to them if the Valleymorgans were like your family pack?"

Mandy shook her head. "No, and you wouldn't have allowed Rhiannon to go with them."

"She wouldn't have gone." Taking a deep breath, I gave her my honest opinion. "I think you could be happy there, Mandy. You could negotiate your life with them. Morgan was willing to let me keep working, but if you're unsure, speak to Rhiannon. She's been there six months now."

"You give good friend, you know that?" Mandy nudged my shoulder. "You're my best friend, I'd miss you if I went to live with them."

"Don't fret. Knox doesn't allow even a true-mate to live with them until the fourth phase."

"He let Rhiannon," Mandy countered.

"The fourth phase wasn't the issue. Her being a major flight risk was."

Mandy smirked. The most senior military official led the way for the coffin. Nathan and the four survivors of their team carrying Brett. Yes, they cried, and I respected them all more for letting their grief show. My tears were already falling, just knowing my heart was in that coffin. Closer to the surface since the attack on the base, my wolf wanted to howl my grief.

The casket was placed on the conveyor with muted color in my vision. Human's held three color-sensitive receptors, but wolves only have two, so their perception of different hues is significantly reduced. When my wolf was close to the surface, colors were there, but more muted, and I was less able to perceive the different hues.

A fire burned through my abdomen, and I doubled over in pain. The silver made my wolf retreat, leaving me mostly human again. "Annie," Nathan whispered my name as he helped me sit down. Mandy was helping support me as well. Curling over myself, I sobbed from the pain, both in my heart and belly.

Sympathy rolled over me from everyone around me, but the two beside me. Those that knew what that pain was from, their compassion was dosed in worry, and fear for my well-being. I didn't realize Nathan knew until that moment, but his emotions told me he knew what was happening to me, which means Brett had confided in him.

Before I could wonder just how much Nathan knew about me, the turmoil of concern and anger pummeled me from the back of the chapel. Knox had seen my pain and wanted to be the one comforting me. It was killing him to stay away, to stand back and watch not only my heartache but to feel my physical pain. That alone made me focus on pulling myself together.

The Major approached and offered his sympathies. He then took the podium and spoke about the lives lost. Three from the Olympians were taken down in the holding cells, and they lost all of their people in the communications building. Those that hadn't died right away, had escaped only to be assassinated while lying in pain. Even Captain Franks had been murdered.

My eyes went over my shoulder to Dante. He gave a slight bow of the head. He was only here because I'd known how to save him.

How he'd been riddled with silver from a missile attack was something I still wasn't clear on, but I'd done what I could.

What took the longest to accept, was that it wouldn't have mattered if I'd left Dante to die and been there to help Brett. I'd read the report, harassed Eric until he brought it by for me to see. He'd talk me through all the injuries, but I'd known the moment I read the report, there was nothing, even with all my years of medical training, that I could have done to save him.

Had it been Knox? Yes, I could have helped him to shift and begin the healing process, then change back again to accelerate the healing even more. Not with Brett. Not with the man I loved.

Shifting didn't heal significant wounds, but the molecular changes required to shift accelerated healing. So, minor injuries could be treated instantly, the major ones could be prevented from being life-threatening. Due to the energy needed to change, without the aid of another strong wolf, they wouldn't be able to shift and would die. That's how most Alpha's went. Because they were the strongest, and if they were challenged and beaten, the only one strong enough to save them, was usually the one digging their grave for them.

Nathan squeezed my hand as he stood to do the eulogy. It snapped me back to my current reality. Enthralled, I listened to Nathan talk about Brett, how they met as new recruits to the base, both having come from different parts of the country. He shared some funny stories, including how Brett started hurting himself on purpose whenever he knew I was at the hospital on placement, just as a reason to see me.

"I was dating a nurse from the hospital at the time. Brett told me I had to keep dating her just so he would know when Annie was there and what sort of injury he would need," Nathan smiled. "I tell you, things got a bit dicey when Annie was on her obstetrics rotation." Everyone laughed. "That's when Franks ordered Brett to go ask the girl out already. So, Brett being the good soldier he was, stalked Annie for three days before he approached her. He told her she was the love of his life, and could they get married and have babies now."

Smiling sadly, I remembered that day like it was only yesterday.

"Annie told him to get lost, as any sensible girl would," Nathan jested. "So, Brett kissed the poor girl senseless. Victory was his. It took him a few more years to talk her into marriage, and when he did, terrified she'd change her mind, he whisked her off in the dead of night to the Major's house, who just so happens to have the authority to marry. Coupled legally, he had her trapped for life. I'm still cut at him for depriving me of my best man's rights."

While everyone else was still chuckling, Nathan's face fell. "I was the luckiest bastard for having Brett White as my friend. Everyone here who ever went on a mission with him, used his shoulder to prop ourselves up when the girls we loved broke our hearts, knows they were lucky to know such a great man. I'd say Annie was lucky to have his love, and she was, but we all know how in love those two are, were..." Nathan looked at me sadly, "...are. How in love they still are."

Nathan shifted uncomfortably and swiped a tear from his cheek, I'd given up wiping mine.

"We are all a little jealous of what they had." Nathan sniffled and took a breath. "I challenge any person in this room to say they didn't like Brett," Nathan's eyes lifted to the burbling pot of rage I could feel boiling in the back of the room. "There's even a man who coveted what Brett loved most in the world, who still would have fallen on his sword for Brett. That's how good a man Brett White was, and we will forever feel his loss. I guess it's true what they say. Only the good die young."

Tears streamed down my face as my heartache ate me up. I hadn't really been able to cry until now. I'd been angry, tried to deny it all happened, felt like I'd been trapped in an alternate reality. But today, with that box sitting before me, with all his mates mourning him, I had to accept the truth.

Finally, I thought I'd found my home, created my new family, could be happy here until my life ended. I was meant to go first, not Brett. Internally, I cursed and thrashed against the Goddess for taking this happiness from me. After what I'd already endured, at the hands of my pack, at the hands of my true-mate, how could she take the one good thing that ever happened to me?

As the coffin slid into the incinerator, I howled my pain and torment. Not like a wolf, but as a woman, who loved someone wholeheartedly, and unable to contain it, released her grief on the world that stole him from her.

KNOX

"I can't handle this," I whispered to Dante. Getting up, I left. Hearing people talk about my mate loving another man was bad enough. Still, it was nothing compared to the sound of pure agony that escaped Anique's throat as the coffin slid from view. Watching Nathan and Rion's mate restrain her, was like claws gouging troughs of resentment in my spine.

Anique's grief slashed to the core of me. It was either walk out or take Anique and make love to her until I was the only one left in her heart. Only my pack was at the back to see me go, and every one of them could feel my emotions strong enough to understand this wasn't retreat but protecting Anique.

"It shouldn't be like this," I murmured to Dante when he came to stand by me. "Our bond should soothe her by me being in there, it should have muted her heartache for another man."

"Everyone says Brett and Anique were soul mates," Dante suggested casually, but I could feel his words being chosen carefully. "Maybe there is a difference between a soul mate and a true-mate that we have never heard of before?"

My eyes were drawn back towards the door. "We don't have soul mates."

Raising his eyebrows, Dante met my eyes. "I beg to differ. Anique has been through hell, and Brett had seen hell on earth. Can you think of two people who could better understand each other?"

"That's my mate in there crying over another man!"

"That is a woman who has lost everything time and time again, losing the one thing that hasn't hurt her or rejected her. This is not about you. This is about Anique." Turning away, Dante scrubbed his hand through his hair in frustration. "Perhaps the way you rejected her damaged your bond somehow, who knows? All I know is that woman saved my life, and the man she loved, a man I liked and respected, died. I will give you your right to feel slighted, Alpha, but not today, and not without acknowledging that everything wrong between you and your mate is your doing."

Barely restraining my temper, I glared at Dante. He was my beta, the only one who could come close to challenging me physically, which is why he'd followed me out, in case I acted on my feelings. He'd be the only one who could try and dissuade me. It's not that I disagreed with what he said, it was my wolf wanting to throw Anique over our shoulder and steal her away from the world, to mate with her until Brett White was just the name of a guy she once knew.

Dante met my eyes without flinching. "You need to be a big brother to your mate today, not her lover, and you need to leave your anger and resentment at the door." Dante went to walk away, stopped, and about-faced. "Oh, and the Olympians are going to get in your way. Nathan was very clear. They'll give her a mourning period, and then the ones who always envied what Brett had, are going to try and take his place." Dante left me there to stew on that.

Exhaling forcefully, I took ten deep breaths to bring my emotions in check. The chapel started emptying. The wake was being held at the Army Bar on Main Street. Anique walked out with her pack around her like a protective barrier of sexy and black. Yet, the air they gave off was enough to repel anything but passing condolence.

Having composed herself again, Anique held her head high and took the sympathies offered by others like she'd trained for it. It made me wonder if her medical background was coming into play.

As if hearing my thoughts, Anique's head slowly turned to me. Her eyes red from crying, but it didn't detract from her beauty. She'd cried a river already today, and she was still the most spectacular woman I'd ever seen. Always a vivid green, but unlike the fierceness I'd seen a week ago, today they held complete sorrow.

Stepping up beside Anique, Nathan placed his hand in the small of her back and walked her to his car. My hands curled into fists without warning. Closing my eyes, I took another ten deep breaths.

"Morgan," Major Ellis approached.

Another deep breath. "Yes, Sir," I stood straight after years of training.

"It was a hell of a hit we took, especially on home turf."

"How did intelligence miss this?" I'd been asking these questions all week. We all had. The secret stash of silver bullets Franks kept in case it was needed on us had enraged me. When Comms exploded, Dante was halfway out the door. The explosion turned the shells into shrapnel and taken him out. I'd ripped shred's off Ellis when I'd found out. "How did they get together so quickly? And how the hell did they get those weapons here?"

"All excellent questions. You'll have your chance to ask intelligence yourself tomorrow at Quantum," the Major announced. "Report to the base with your team at zero six hundred, and you'll be flown across."

"The information the prisoner gave has been verified?"

"Yes, and we're going to hit those bastards where it hurts. You won't be coming home until the job is done, so make sure the family knows not to expect you home anytime soon." The Major walked away.

Damn it, Milton was getting married in two weeks. Rhiannon would have our heads if we had to reschedule. When I looked around, my pack was making their way to the car park. Anique and the strays were gone. Taking a deep breath, I caught Anique's scent close by me. I froze.

"She loves you too," the female voice came from behind me. "She hates you for the way you treated her, for taking the one faith she had left in our kind and destroying it, but the Goddess made her love you too."

Turning, I took in the brown hair and golden-brown eyes of Rion's mate. "Another Alpha's progeny?" Her head held high because she wasn't weak. Scared, but not soft. Anique's scent surrounded her, and I realized her closeness with Anique went beyond being packmates. "Are you gay?"

The woman smirked. "Not hardly," she watched me sniff the air again. She put her nose to her clothes. "Ah, it's Annie's dress, and I've spent the week with her at night, so she wasn't alone."

If she hadn't washed her hair today, then it could easily explain the confusion. It didn't help that like Anique, this wolf masked her scent. If I didn't know Anique's smell, I wouldn't have even known she was a wolf.

"Which pack was yours? Are you the bride who poisoned her pack on the day of her banquet?" Just who was Rion's mate.

"No," the she-wolf frowned. "I wouldn't be here asking for an honest description of my mate if I was that one?"

"Why?"

"Because she killed her mate that day." She watched my anger at that revelation. "Don't judge her, Alpha, you don't know what her pack did to her, what she endured. Or, maybe, since you know

Annie's truth, you could sympathize." The wolf stepped closer. "Could you imagine undergoing the first phase, finding your true-mate, while he raped your throat, and his best friend raped your ass?"

Swallowing, I took another breath. I was verging on oxygen oversaturation today.

"They wanted her to still be virginal for her mate, you see. So, until her Alpha chose her husband, her pack used to beat and rape all her other orifices. For three years, they did that until she dared to raise her eyes and plead with the asshole buried so far down her throat she couldn't breathe, and wham," she clapped her hands loudly. "That bastard was the true-mate the Goddess put on this earth for her."

Observing the hate in her eyes, the disgust with the males of her own kind, I worried, but then, I also couldn't blame her if these were the experiences these stray, she-wolves suffered.

"She went a little nuts after that. Annie keeps her in check; otherwise, your pack would have been wiped out just for how you treated Annie."

It was a warning, her voice even, but a little deeper and like honey. She had power, not like Anique, but it was there. The way she kept her distance told me she didn't want to be talking to me, but curiosity got the best of her. "What's your story?"

"Nowhere near as exciting, I'm afraid," she paused, hesitating. "I'm Amanda Solace. I came from the Solarflares pack. You can check with them; my pack still lives. I'd prefer you not to mention my name, though."

So, one of the packs destroyed wasn't attached to this group of strays. "You chose to be a stray?"

Biting her lip, Amanda moved back a step. "My family were killed by the current Alpha when I came of age. Because I'm a she-wolf, he gave me a choice, leave or become his mate. We had a few females, so it wasn't a lack of choice. Still, I don't think he thought

I would choose to be a stray, and when I did, he didn't plan to let me leave. I snuck out while they were all drunk from celebrating the murder of my father and my two younger brothers," Amanda snarled.

That explained the disgust. Killing the Alpha's progeny was unwarranted, especially if they were underage. Putting my hands in my pockets, I shifted my stance to be non-threatening. "You waited until the others left to approach me?" The car park was nearly empty now.

Meeting my eyes evenly, Amanda tapped her clutch purse against her leg. "Anique supports your pack, and your stance as a progressive Alpha, despite what happened. I..." Amanda gulped, her first physical indication of fear. "I'm not opposed to meeting my mate, but I'm not inclined to join a pack that I know so little about. I'd like you to tell me about him and about your pack."

Looking around, I indicated a bench. "Shall we sit, and I'll answer all your questions, in exchange I'll ask you to answer two for me."

She didn't move. "Ask your questions first."

These girls didn't hide here this long because they were stupid. "Has Anique been involved in the killings?"

"Of the hunters or the packs?" Amanda's eyes narrowed.

"Both?"

"No, she didn't even know about the hunters, she flipped when she found out," Amanda started walking towards the bench. "Annie isn't a killer. "

Taking a moment to absorb her words and that she wasn't denying her involvement, I sat down, but Amanda stood waiting. "Who hid here first? Who decided hiding your pack in my territory was the way to go?"

Exhaling, Amanda sat at the furthest end of the bench from me. "Annie and I met at university in the city. I don't think she ever planned to settle here, but then Eric was willing to take her research on if she did her placements here. The hospital has a hard time getting quality students. Annie came with a research program relevant to the base, so it was a double win for the hospital."

"So, Anique brought you all here?"

"We followed her, yes. Just like we all went into the health service after meeting her. Annie had been through so much, and she was still so vibrant and optimistic. When she met Brett, and they fell in love, she thought her life would turn around, and she was happy for all her years with him."

The seat creaked under my grip.

Checking where my hands gripped the bench, Amanda considered me. "Sorry, that must be hard for you to hear, but it's important. He's the reason she stayed. He taught us to defend ourselves. He taught Annie to love and trust again, something you nearly destroyed." Amanda shook her head. "Without loving him, she would never have let you near her. You need to accept your mate is badly damaged, and she's terrified of you."

"She's worried I'll be as bad as her pack?"

"That night you completed the phases, Annie wanted to tell you about the silver and her wolf. You took her before she could explain, and she was terrified the entire time she was with you because Annie knew how you would react when you realized she's wasn't rogue by choice."

I'd known Anique had been scared, but not why. She'd wanted to talk first, and I'd rushed ahead. "I regretted my reaction once I cooled down. I tried to find her, but Anique is very good at hiding," I sniffed the air. "I have her scent now, but she can still manage to disappear."

"When Annie vanishes, you'll never find her again," Amanda mourned. Head bowed, she waited a heartbeat. "What's his name?"

Sitting back, I took a breath. "Rion, and he's a good man. Very moral."

"Where are you staying tonight?" Nathan asked as we arrived at the wake.

"Home. I'll leave the keys in the letterbox tomorrow."

"Can we keep in touch, Annie?"

Turning to observe Nathan, I sighed. "I married Brett, not the platoon."

"He ordered me to take care of you, Annie." He placed his hand over mine. "It was his dying wish."

Gritting my teeth, I reefed my hand out from under his. "Don't you dare try and use that to hit on me, or I swear to whatever God there be, I'll rip you to pieces."

Nathan swallowed hard, probably remembering the way I attacked Knox. Growling, I opened the car door. "Annie," halfway through the car park, Nathan grabbed my hand. "He was my best friend; he told me everything. I know what you've been through, and I wouldn't use Brett's memory to seduce you. I really just want to be your friend and be here for you."

Breathing through the pain in my chest, I squeezed his hand.

"Thank you. Let's just get this done with. I've still got a few more things to finish up before I leave tomorrow."

"How long will you be gone?" Nathan took my arm to walk me inside.

"I was given a month's forced leave, but I could be gone longer. We'll see."

"I heard the doctor mention an operation that you need."

"Brett told you about the shrapnel?" Nathan nodded. "It appears I'm running out of time. It's going to be a risky surgery. As a result, I may never be able to have children, and the metal toxins that have leached into my system will kill me anyway within a few years."

"A few years is better than this year, Annie," Nathan lectured. "Have the surgery. We can't lose you yet, or your girls will turn into maneaters and the entire company will be lost." When I smirked, Nathan shook his head. "I'm deadly serious, Annie. Those girls will rip our hearts apart."

"Oh, I'm smiling because you don't know how right you are."

"Especially, Danielle. I considered going there with her once. Clark did, the story he told left me a bit more cautious."

As we walked inside, I frowned. Monique and Danielle were already there, flirting up a storm. We all grieve in our own way, I guess. "Why?"

"Hot, kinky, but Clark said there were moments her eyes changed, and she became almost violent," Nathan revealed, noticing when I cringed. "Sorry, I know she's your friend, but that's the only reason she didn't top our list of suspects for those men being murdered with their dicks ripped off."

My feet froze, eyes wide as I turned to see if Nathan was joking.

Nathan's gaze flared. "Shit, Annie, Brett never told you about them?" Shaking my head stiffly, I couldn't move; if I did, I would start to hyperventilate or look at the girls the wrong way, and they would know. Danielle and I walked a fine line as it was, but this, and hearing how she was during sex. She was partially shifting, potentially ready to kill the men she slept with.

"Damn, I'm sorry. It was a running joke with us that after what happened to you, maybe it was you getting even..."

Swallowing my tongue, I stared at Nathan, horrified that anyone would consider I could do that.

"...then Clark told us about Danielle, and she became our prime suspect." Licking his lips, Nathan observed me. "No one truly thought for a moment that you could do that, Annie, don't fret okay?"

"Have..." I had to clear my throat. "Have there been men go missing locally?"

"Oh, the men in the forest weren't from here," Nathan dismissed my question and started walking us to the bar. "The Hounds were assigned to help the MP's with that investigation, but White said they weren't local. If there have been men going missing locally, I haven't heard."

Exhaling in relief, it didn't stop that worry about Danielle from niggling now. Brett had never trusted her, and he hadn't hidden that from me. Now, I knew why. I can't blame him. I'm sure if Brett knew what I knew about Danielle's past, he would have suggested her as a candidate to the MP's.

"Something wrong, Annie?" Nathan touched my hand on the bar, snapping me to attention.

"Yeah, just thinking about how much family can mess you up."

Dropping his gaze from mine, Nathan softened. "Did Brett ever tell you about his parents?" When I shook my head, Nathan sighed. "Me neither. I actually can't tell you anything about Brett from before the first day we met. The problem with this job, Annie, you get used to keeping things to yourself."

"Maybe you're good at the job because you are the kind of guys who keep your hand close to your chest. I know very little about most of you, except the stories you tell at the barbecues of the situations you guys have been in, both work-related and sex-related."

"Possibly." Shifting his body uncomfortably, Nathan hailed the bartender to order us drinks.

Beer, wine, and spirits flowed freely over the next few hours. There was finger food to keep us all a little more sober, but these guys were going to make a day of it no matter what. By the time Nathan ordered his fifth beer, the bartender had sequestered Nathan's keys and told him to pick his car up tomorrow. I noticed the rack of keys was quite full already.

Looking around, the only people taking it slow were the Valleymorgans and the Major. I knew what that meant. Brett always restricted his intake if he was flying out in the next twenty-four hours.

When I came out of the ladies' room and went to the bar for water, Knox's eyes were on me. Mandy was close by, talking to Rhiannon. It told me she was going to try this true-mate thing on for size. Smiling sadly, I exhaled; I was happy for her, but a little jealous.

Going over to where Knox was sitting with his men, I dropped into the empty chair between Milton and Dante. I think they were all a little surprised.

"You know, if it was the other way around, if this was my wake, the wives would have been falling over themselves to bring Brett dinner all week, making sure he still ate. Because I'm a woman, I get left alone, expected to suck it up and cope, and to know how to feed myself." Glancing around at the unsure faces of Knox's pack, I rolled my eyes. "And I was led to believe you weren't as sexist as the other packs?"

Knox smirked. "Dante, be a gentleman and get the widow something to eat."

"Right away, Alpha." Standing up, Dante touched my shoulder gently as he left. "Milton, get on your feet and help me."

Glancing from Knox to me, Milton abandoned his seat. Suddenly, the lot of them decided to eat. When Mandy's mate started to stand, I pointed my finger at Rion and indicated he stay in his seat. Meeting his eyes, I let my wolf come forward a little, enough to improve my senses, not sufficient to cause me pain, and sniffed in his direction. Rion's eyes were molten chocolate buttons, the true definition of puppy dog eyes. Yeah, I could see why Mandy swooned.

"You be good to her. Respect her, love her, give her the freedom to live her life, cherish her for the wonderful woman she is, and I'll have no reason to ever dismember you." When Rion gave me a dubious look, I raised a brow at him. "Don't think I need claws to do it. Surgical steel can cut you just as effectively." Holding his gaze a moment longer, I then turned all my attention to a smirking Knox.

"Go eat, Rion. Then go introduce yourself to your mate." Knox held my gaze while we listened to Rion's chair scrape the polished cement floor of the club and his shoes walked away. "You have something to say?" Knox slouched a little waiting.

"I'm sorry I lost my temper at the hospital, and for taking my pain out on you. Thank you for taking it."

Raising his beer to his mouth, Knox paused with it in front of his lips. "I deserved it." Putting the bottle to his lips, Knox took a long drink. Once his bottle was on the table, he met my eyes and I knew he was Alpha now. My Alpha. "Your secret is out; you can come to your sister's banquet now."

Pressing my lips together to restrain my initial response, I considered I probably needed to sleep more before talking to Knox. Taking a breath, I let my lips pop open and remained quiet.

"I'm not going to kidnap you, Anique."

"If only you were loyal, I might take your word." Raising a brow, I sat back. "Sadly, that's not the case."

Assessing me, Knox took his own deep breath. "I was shocked and angry. I made a bad call, and I lashed out and hurt you for something that wasn't your fault. It's inexcusable, so I'm not going to try. I can promise you I will spend the rest of my life trying to make it right, Anique."

The truth in his words was in his eyes, forcing me to look away. "You don't understand, it's not just my inability to change." Shifting forward in my seat ready to stand, I focused my eyes on my hands and drink. "I can't give you a child. I wanted to tell you before we completed the phases, so you wouldn't be trapped with a rogue and childless mate. I'm sorry, Knox. I'm never going to be good enough for what you want."

Sitting there in silence, Knox sat watching me. "Shouldn't you be standing and walking away? Because that sounded like a walk away statement." He lifted his beer to his luscious lips. Goddess, I wanted to kiss them so badly, to let him take me and make me forget why my heart was aching today.

When I licked my lips, his pupils dilated, and I closed my eyes in resignation. "Can you look away?"

"Why?"

"I can't leave with you still watching me, not with the way you are looking at me."

Knox leaned his elbows on the table. "Where are you living?"

"Goddess, were you even listening?"

"I've heard more than you think I have, Anique. Where are you living?"

Chest tightening, I swallowed. "With my husband."

Knox took a moment. "He's dead." My eyes flared in a warning. "And, the house wasn't his, so I'll ask again."

"I give the keys back tomorrow morning."

"You are my mate, so you have a home with the Valleymorgans

." Knox shrugged, as if it was a given I'd lose Brett and surrender what was left of my heart to him. "I'd give you the address, but I suspect you know where to find us."

Anxiety restricted my chest, a constrictor of grief and fear, causing me to gasp. "I can't do this right now."

Pausing, Knox considered me and sighed. "I'm flying out tomorrow, and I have no idea when we'll be back. Hopefully, in time for the banquet, or your sister is going to beat you to ripping my throat out." He shook his head. "The bad luck of getting three headstrong bitches to mate into my pack."

"Four," I reminded, and covertly pointed to Mandy.

Knox rolled his eyes. "Great."

Touching my shoulder, Dante slid a plate in front of me. "Henderson's heading over," he warned and put his plate down to sit. "I'm just going to grab another drink. Alpha?"

Knox shook his head. "I've had enough."

Averting my eyes, I waited for Dante to leave. "I'm sorry, Knox."

In my peripheral vision, Knox watched me, eyes fierce and determined to get his way as Nathan slid into the seat beside me. "What's going on?"

"Apologies. I'm going to get something to eat," Knox excused himself. "I'm sorry for what you're going through, Anique. White was a good man, and I'd wish him back in a heartbeat. The base won't be the same without him."

Closing my eyes as Knox walked away, I struggled not to break down crying again. Nathan put his hand on mine. "Anique?"

"It's my birth name." Sliding out of my seat, I kissed Nathan's cheek goodbye. "I've taken all I can, I'm going to head home."

"Want me to call you a taxi?"

"No, I need the walk and the fresh air."

23

KNOX

*L*eaving the car at the park entrance, I walked along the nature reserve until I reached the back of White's house. To think, all this time, Anique was where I'd dropped her back six months ago. How could it not have occurred to me to check if she'd gone back to White?

As I expected, there was a gate into the backyard, which gave Anique easy access to the running track. The one I'd found her on with the strays, to the place I rejected my mate. Letting myself into the yard, I moved to the back door. The kitchen light was on, music was playing, but that was the only sound. Anique was in there; her loneliness surrounded this place like a cloud of despair.

Knocking on the door, I waited a respectable amount of time before I put my knuckles to the obscure glass again. The music was too loud, a polite way of ignoring any unwanted guests, but Anique's ears were keen, and I had no doubt she could hear me. "Let me in, Anique," I willed her with our bond.

The moment she felt me, anger barreled through the house at me like a bullet spiraling free from a gun. Despite the rage, the back door opened slowly. She stood glaring at me in nothing but a man's shirt. Her cherry red hair hung free, her green eyes were glassy, and her pale face blotchy from the tears she'd been crying. Taking her in, I felt sorry for Brett for losing this beautiful beast before me. He could have heaven, I'd take Anique any day. Then again, so would he.

"Did you come here to stare at me?" Anique growled. "Just take a photo and leave."

Hoisting the bag I carried, I refused to take her pain personally. She was grieving, and I was trespassing on that hallowed ground. "I came here to make sure the widow eats because you didn't eat the food Dante gave you."

Aware Anique was ready to slam the door in my face, I swung the bag so she could see the name of the restaurant. She froze. "How did you know?"

"It was White's favorite. I remember him saying his girlfriend basically lived off it when she was working." As soon as I started talking about White, Anique softened and unlocked the screen door to let me in. "It was before I met you, but I figured it was you he was referring too."

Basically, ripping the bag out of my hand, Anique moved to the kitchen table to pull everything out. She assessed the burger choices, picked one she liked, took a Coke and chips, and left the rest for me. Retreating to the far side of the table, she sat down and started eating.

"And they say the way to a man's heart is his stomach," I teased. Closing the door, I took the seat she'd designated me. Not bothering to answer, Anique just ate her burger, tears cascading down her cheeks as she did. "Tell me about him? I know the White everyone else knew, but I dare say, that isn't the man you loved."

Meeting my eyes for a moment, Anique shook her head and continued eating. She was starving, and I had to wonder when was the last time she'd eaten properly? Looking at the bags under her eyes, it was probably on par with the last time she slept.

"I heard you have been forced to take bereavement leave?" I pushed, wanting to hear her voice, to have her talk to me. Six months I'd been craving her; I needed something before I left tomorrow. I needed a connection I could build on when I returned.

Nodding, Anique popped the last bite of her burger in her pouty mouth. Sighing, I opened one of the three leftover burgers for me. I'd brought a variety, unsure what she'd eat. "Have you got a place to go?" Another nod. "Do you need help moving your stuff tomorrow?" A shake of the head as she opened the Coke. Now she was just staying quiet to frustrate me.

"Come home with me, I promise you can still live your life. I'll even give you my car for you to drive. You can have your own room if you're not ready to be with me."

Anique stopped. "Were you not listening? I can't give you-"

"I can't have kids now anyway. With or without you, there will be no progeny, so what difference does it make at this point?!" As if my words were fire upon her skin, Anique cringed. Taking a calming breath, I returned my voice to neutral. "None of that stuff matters. I want my mate."

Studying me, Anique popped a chip in her mouth as she turned her eyes to the window that looked out over the backyard. "He had no expectations of me. Brett let me take things at my pace, he loved me despite my scars, and he smothered my hate and distrust. He loved me, not because I was the Alpha's daughter, or because of strong pedigree progeny, or because he could force me to his will. Brett didn't need a reason to love me other than that I made him smile as soon as we were in the same room."

Eating, I listened. Anique talking, even about him, that's all I needed right now.

"I lost my virginity to him," she continued. "Not the physical one, obviously, but he was the first man I let have me willingly. I was so terrified that night, but he was tender, took his time, made sure I was alright with all of it. I hadn't even told him at that point, but he seemed to know." Anique shook her head. "He always seemed to know what I never said."

Finishing her food, Anique stood up and went across the room to throw it in the bin. When she came back, she came to my side of the table. Moving my arms out of the way, she lifted her leg to straddle my thighs, resting her bum on the edge of the table. When she didn't stop me placing my hands on her bare thighs, I slid them up, lifting the top until I could see that she was naked underneath. Picking up my Coke, Anique took a drink.

Lowering my face, I nuzzled the neat red diamond of pubic hair. Lifting her feet to the arms of my seat, Anique laid herself back on the table. Oral sex was a human thing, but Anique was giving me an opening, and the speech before had been a warning. This needed to be at her pace.

Breathing her in deep, my wolf rumbled in my chest, and I grew hard. Squirming to get comfortable, I wiggled my tongue between her labia, drilling along the channel and back to circle around. Anique whimpered, her hands gripping the edge of the table. It was all the encouragement I needed. Diving in, I kissed her like I wanted to kiss her mouth, used my finger to probe her core, find that spot on the front wall, and stroke her heat into a bonfire.

I made love to her with my mouth until her fingers yanked at my hair, and she pleaded my name. Standing, I pulled my button-down over my head in one movement, the top two buttons ripped off when they would have got stuck at my chin.

Kicking off my shoes, I dropped my pants just as quickly. Goddess, I was hard for her, my balls swollen and tight. Stroking my swollen glands against her sex, I smiled when Anique's ankles wrapped around my waist and pulled me closer.

Shifting my head to her entrance, I placed the palm of my hand to her mound and rubbed in circles. Raising her hands overhead, Anique gripped the other side of the table, rocking side to side, panting for me. I couldn't wait any longer. She had to be mine. The moon delivered her for me, and when I'd lost her, the Goddess guided her back to me. I wouldn't refuse the Goddess's gift again.

Entering her slowly, gently, I enjoyed every bit of her. Anique was begging me to end her torture, but I wouldn't rush this with her. Tomorrow, I would get on a plane to who knows where, and I didn't know when I would get to be with her again. Which made the kitchen the wrong place to do this.

As I settled myself in as deep as I could go, I scooped my hands under her back and lifted her to me. "Knox?" Anique breathed.

Wiping the tears from her face, I caressed her cheek. "Shh. Not the time or place."

Lifting her small handful of breast to my mouth, I sucked on the hard bud. Her head fell back, and her body clenched around me. Carrying her through the house, I found the bedroom and crawled onto the mattress with her.

As soon as her back was flat, I started moving within her. For me, this was heaven. With every thrust, my balls grew tighter, my cock became harder, thicker, the head more sensitive and swollen. Sensations radiated out of my groin and through my body like a current, ebbing, and flowing with every stroke. Building steadily, all the muscles in my body tensing as I climbed for the euphoria, which I knew only Anique could give me. Every moan that passed her lips, her whimpers, and curses, and the way she cried my name, I absorbed it all like it was the nectar of the gods. Inside her, I felt strong and invincible. Her skin on mine was rejuvenating and electrifying all at the same time. I needed more, so much more.

Rolling onto my back, I took Anique with me, so she was lying above me, and scooped her breast into my hungry mouth. Crying out, Anique used her feet to move her body up and down my rod. Every time I sucked her nipples, I felt her sex clench tighter around me, bringing her closer to her release.

As a she-wolf, the climax was reserved only for her true-mate.

I'd never got her there that first night, but I would tonight. I needed to make her only ever want me. There would be no cubs, but there would be bliss.

With her growing tighter, her fingers digging into my shoulders as she moved her body faster, searching for that end, I released her breast and grabbed her hips, helping her. Thrusting up, I slammed her down, going as deep and hard as I could. I needed Anique to know why I was the only man for her. Why she had to come home to me, why we needed each other despite all the reasons she felt we shouldn't.

Anique looked down on me, stardust glowing pupils taking up most of her eyes. Growling, I let my wolf join in, my own vision washed with muted hues. Who needed to see when there was all of this to feel. "Let go," I ordered, feeling her riding the edge. Letting my will wash over her, I thrust up to meet her hips.

"Alpha!" Anique cried out, over, and over again. Her voice reached the pinnacle as her body went tumbling over the edge. For a moment, I got to see the beauty of Anique experiencing her first orgasm. Then I was falling into ecstasy with her. Holding her body tight, I cried out and filled her womb with my first real climax in six months. It was the most prolonged orgasm of my life. Pulse after pulse, painting her inner walls until they were coated, and then some.

Pulling herself free, Anique sat on my hips and let the excess pool on my lower belly. We lay there panting for several minutes, and then we lay there just enjoying each other's heat with nothing in between us for a little while longer. When Anique's breathing evened out, I rolled her gently to the side and let her fall deeper into sleep. She needed to rest. The night was still ahead.

Going to the shower, I cleaned myself up. When I got out, my breath rushed out. In the fog on the mirror was a heart, and the words *I love you* drawn by a man's finger. Brett's last message to Anique, still there a week later. She'd kept his shirt on the entire time we were together. With it scrunched up around her face, Brett's scent would have been there while we made love too.

Rubbing my hands over my face, I desperately wanted to erase the message in the mirror, but I couldn't. As much as I hated it, that message was for Anique, and I couldn't jeopardize her hating me more for petty jealousy. Moving out to the bed, I crawled in behind her and held her tight while I sniffed her neck. Stirring, Anique rolled to face me in the dark. The press of her body to mine made me ready for her again.

"Brett," Anique whispered, still half asleep.

There was no hesitation. Kissing her, I rolled her and sheathed myself in her in one movement. I wouldn't deny her need to be with the man she loves again. He couldn't have her physically, but if it helped her grieve, I would give her whatever she needed.

24

ANIQUE

*D*espite making love intermittently through the night, it was still my best night's sleep in over a week. Waking in his arms before the sun rose, I managed to escape his grasp. "Anique," Knox murmured sleepily, trying to recapture me.

"I need to pee," I soothed him, and dashed for the bathroom. When I came back into the room dressed in my running gear, he was asleep.

Last night was amazing. I should feel guilty, but I'd spent most of my marriage ashamed that my mind always came back to Knox, even when I was in love with Brett. What made things harder was that Knox hadn't complained when I'd called him the wrong name last night.

One of the things I'd loved about Knox when we met was how easygoing he seemed to be. He was considerate and secure in himself that jealousy didn't seem to be a problem. So, this morning, it was harder to leave him behind, especially after the amazing sex last night.

Cleaning up the kitchen, I left Knox a note, then grabbed my bag and headed out the door. Leaving the keys in the letterbox for

Nathan and the team to collect the rest of Brett's stuff, I walked towards the hospital. Before I lost Brett from my life, I'd set something in motion. Maybe, Brett dying was the Goddess's way of punishing me. Either way, if you've paid for the crime, you may as well do it. Knox being away for the next few weeks granted me an easy escape. He couldn't come after me.

Letting myself into Mandy's place with the key she gave me, I made myself a coffee. As I poured the liquid caffeine, Mandy zombied out of her room and dropped into a chair at the table. Smirking, I filled a mug for her and put it in front of her.

She'd drunk half the mug of coffee before she actually realized I was there. "I thought I was coming to get you?"

"I needed to get out." She didn't need to know Knox spent the night, no one did. "Did you speak to Rion?"

"Yes," she nodded, and her eyes lit up. "I've asked to take it slow. Rion asked if that was code for hatching a plan for escape. I kind of like him."

"I'm happy for you, Mandy."

"The rest of the Hounds made sure to introduce themselves to Monique and Danielle, but no one was Monique's match," Mandy sighed. "Danielle got a bit uptight. I expect you'll hear about it."

"You know why?"

"Yeah, I do, but I'm not giving up my chance with my true-mate." We sat there quietly drinking our coffee. "The hounds are going away today," Mandy informed me. She refilled both our cups. "Rion has a fear of planes, so he doesn't go away with them."

"Least you don't have to worry about him coming home in a box."

"Staying on base didn't save Brett." Mandy may as well have slapped me, the way I jolted. "Shit, I'm sorry that was-"

"No, you're right. I'm going to go shower and look at train times." Rising up, I left the room. After the shower, I opened the suitcase of my clothes I'd already sent back with Mandy two days ago and got dressed. Repacking the bag with the clothes I'd need; I placed the rest in one of the boxes of my things.

"Are you sure about this?" Mandy asked leaning on the door frame. "You've never gone this line before."

"Train comes in an hour," I answered, getting my stuff together. "I'll see you in two weeks."

"What if the banquet is delayed?" Mandy asked, following me to the door.

"Then I'll see you when it happens."

"What if-"

"Mandy! We are doing this. The banquet is the only window we will get." I waited to see if Mandy would broach any further argument. When she bowed her head in acceptance, I opened the door and left.

Sitting on the train, I was waiting for the six o'clock departure when my phone rang. Frowning at the unknown number, I answered, unsure.

"Did I say something wrong?" Knox's voice echoed a little, letting me know he was using the hands-free in his car.

"I had an early train to catch."

"Where are you going, Anique?" Knox rumbled unhappily.

"Where are you going when you leave base today, Knox?"

"I actually don't know." When I stayed quiet, Knox sighed. "I need you in my life."

"I need time."

"You have my number now. Call me when you're ready to come home, Anique. Even if you want to date a while. Just call me, okay?"

"Okay."

"Morgan," a voice spoke in his car. "Your team is already at the barracks, and I've been told to tell you to be ready for transport at zero-six-thirty."

"Thanks, Jackson," Knox accelerated through the gates. "Don't vanish on me, Anique."

"Too late for that." Smiling, I hung up the phone and checked my call history. Sure enough, I'd sent a message to Knox around two this morning when I'm pretty sure I was asleep. I should have known. Saving his number in my phone, I put it away. A minute later, a message buzzed.

Knox: *'You're the first and only girl I've ever gone down on. I can still taste you on my tongue'.*

Closing my eyes as muscle memory took control of my body, I bit my lip. Breathing deeply, I swallowed over the moan that wanted to come out.

Anique: *'Brush your teeth.'*

He didn't reply, but deep in my chest, I felt a vibration like when you laugh deep inside. My stomach turned with nerves. I'd forgotten that part of the purge was deepening the bond. Every time we had sex, our connection would tighten; we'd be able to feel each other's emotions more intently and from a greater distance. My phone buzzed again.

Knox: *'Five times last night. I should be able to feel you no matter how far I am from home now.'*

He answered my annoyance.

Anique: *'Great. So, you fucking other women will hurt like a hornets bite in comparison to a bee now?'*

The unhappiness of my response was like an angry spider

running around my stomach.

> **Knox:** *'When you come home, that will never happen again.'*
> **Anique:** *'If you do it to me, I'll do it to you.'*

The reply never came. Putting my phone away as the train pulled away from the station, I huffed. Knox needed to know I wouldn't be a submissive little bitch. I was strong enough to control his beta, that should terrify him. However, while I'm sure it did for a moment, I suspected it just made him want me more.

"A worthy adversary can just as easily be a worthy match for your heart," I muttered to myself.

Pulling out a book, I settled in for the two-hour train ride. The weeks ahead would take a lot of planning, and I needed to run a few experiments first. At the end of the line, I departed into the big city, meandering my way to my university.

Yes, I'd officially finished my residency. With my Doctor of Medicine degree, I didn't have to stay living in Campus any longer, I could apply for work anywhere. But Campus was where home was for me, and where my research and friends were. I'd use this time of forced leave to evaluate my feelings. Could I stay living in Campus without Brett? Until I found where I needed to be, I'd set up camp in the city, and I knew just where that would be.

The apartment building where I arrived later that evening was swanky. The doorman greeted me and asked who I was seeing, then directed me on how to reach the apartment. When I knocked on the polished timber doors, it took everything in me to hold my ground. The door opened, and a pale face with eyes like mine and hair more auburn than red stared back at me surprised. "Anique!" Edward looked me over from head to feet. "When the doorman said my sister, I thought it was going to be Rhi."

"Just me." When Edward continued to stare, I cleared my throat. "Can I come in?"

"Yes, sorry." When Edward moved aside, I wheeled my bag in, placing it to the side. "I have to say you were the last person I expected to see."

"I'm in town for a couple of weeks and thought you might let me stay." Slipping out of my coat, I examined him. There was bruising on his cheek and around his eye. When I touched his injuries gently, his eyes filled with tears. "Dad told you?"

"What they did to Rhi, and what they did to you, yes." Edward shook his head, clearing his emotions. A good Alpha, he might just be yet.

I stepped away. "Do they know that you know?"

"No, I picked a fight with Iain over a redhead. I beat him to a pulp, but he got a few good hits in before I took him out."

"I think the pack might catch on quickly if you start having fatal disputes about random women." Moving away, I took in his apartment, looking over his sunken lounge room.

"Dad said the same thing. I was just making some tea. Have you eaten? I can order pizza."

"Pizza sounds wonderful, so does tea." I followed him through to the kitchen. "How's work?"

Edward lifted a brow at me. Blowing out a breath, he picked up the phone ordering pizza for both of us, then we sat, and he told me about his work while we drank tea. When the pizza arrived, I ate, asking Edward questions about his life. Edward answered. When he asked about me, I quite happily told him all about my work.

Getting up, Edward grabbed us both drinks from the fridge. Sitting down, Edward looked at me for a long moment, then slumped. "What are you doing here, Anique? It's been seven years since we've sat and been this civil to each other. Is this a water under the bridge thing? I know the truth now, so you've forgiven me for my ignorance and come to bury the hatchet?"

"I buried my husband yesterday," I revealed quietly. "I still have research to do and can use the time away."

Edward blinked. "Knox is dead? Someone actually challenged that scary bastard?"

Lifting an eyebrow, I shook my head. "No, Knox is alive. My husband was human, a soldier. If he'd been a wolf, he'd have made a good Alpha, but he wasn't. He was killed in action." When Edward just sat blinking at me, I finished my drink. "So, is there a spare room, or should I go find a hotel?"

"Down the hall, on the right," Edward answered, his brow furrowed. I could tell he was trying to make sense of what I just revealed.

"It's been a long day," I excused, cleaning up the mess while my brother sat stumped at the dining room table. "I'm going to bed. Do you still run in the morning?"

"On the treadmill in the gym downstairs."

"I prefer to run outdoors, so I'll head out to the jogging track."

"Okay," Edward agreed, then his eyes went wide. "Wait, no, that's not a safe place to go." The fear coming off my brother was palpable.

Swallowing, I bowed my head, acknowledging that sudden panic. Dan must use the running track. "Perhaps, around the harbor front then?"

Edward nodded. "Yeah, that should be fine."

"Goodnight, Edward." Collecting my bag, I went to find my room. It was easy to do. His smelled strongly of him, and somewhat like a brothel. Sex, condoms, lubricants, and multiple layers of perfume that made me think he had different lady friends visit throughout the week. Typical single wolf, and with my brother being an Alpha male, entirely expected.

Alpha progeny were always more highly sexed than the lesser wolves. My theory revolved around a higher need to procreate for stronger cubs. Still, humans had their fair share of manwhores, why should wolves be any different?

25

KNOX

'*What are you thinking?*' Dante mind-linked as we looked down at the handful of men with their throats torn out at our feet.

'*They knew we were coming, left the ones who didn't matter, and they've gone and hid.*'

Dante sniffed around the room on one side, I went to the other looking for the most recent scent of our targets. Catching a few reasonably fresh scents, I called for my team to come and get a whiff, and then we followed it until we were outside and on the other side of the compound. Checking none of the four wolves with me were injured, we set out after our targets. Our collars held communicators in them and allowed the rest of my team to track us as we moved.

We'd run a few kilometers before the smell of landmines reached us. The bastards had escaped through a field full of mines. There was no way we were going in.

Pawing the dirt to leave a signal for our team, we split to either side and went around the field, searching out the scents for their exit. We reached the other end, and there was not a whiff of them.

Swapping sides, we went back around. Nope, we definitely hadn't missed their exit. Our team was waiting at the transport when we got back to the far side.

Getting out, Milton opened the back of the SUV's for us, where we melted back into human form. "Mark it," I ordered before removing the collar and pulling my clothes on as I jumped into the back seat. "Edgar and Miles are on all fours with two others. Scout five kilometers around in case someone tries to sneak out the back door."

"Yes, Alpha," the human forms answered. The others yipped.

"Tell command it's in their hands, we'll stay as back up, but this job is for another team." The Hounds didn't do tunnels if we could help it. Too much chance of getting injured. Those who weren't staying got in their seats, and our team casually drove a safe distance away.

Reporting in, Sasha nodded at what was said. "They've got it on satellite. They watched Edgar's team run around the field. There has been no movement in or out of the field, so the base must be under it."

Sitting back, I closed my eyes. Ten days we'd been on their trail. Hopefully, this party ended tonight. I'd pulled Milton off the hunting because getting him killed two days before his bond with Rhiannon was formalized, would probably get me killed. Especially with Rhiannon with cub. Not that it had been announced yet. They would wait until after the banquet because traditionally, that's when the fourth phase took place. However, I smelled the difference in her scent the last few days before we left. I knew what that meant.

If Milton had formally informed me, he would have stayed home on monitoring duty with Rion. He knew that, but he hadn't. Milton wanted revenge for the base and our fallen, just as much as the rest of us had.

After a bloody two weeks, we were finally at the end of the

trail. Closing my eyes, I thought of Anique, like I did whenever I got a moment to myself. The way her body felt, the sound of her voice as she lost control. I couldn't stop thinking about that last night with her.

"They're here," Sasha announced.

Lifting my weary head, I looked at my watch. Two hours. Either they were not far behind us, or they'd been flown in from a nearby base and dropped, vehicles and all. "Any movement?" I asked as the others woke up. The two in front were on shift.

"Zero movements, Alpha," Sasha informed as the hit team SUV pulled up beside us.

"Let's go, say hi." Opening my car door, I stepped out to meet the platoon leader, but I barely resisted a laugh when I saw who it was. "Hex," I greeted as Nathan Henderson stepped toward me. He wasn't smiling and cocky like I'd expected.

"Alpha. This is our show now."

"Here purely for back up."

"Appreciate it. You guys have been having all the fun for weeks. It's about time we got in on it." Henderson turned to assess the field. "You said it's a minefield?"

"There must be a hatch, but we weren't going in to find it."

Henderson watched me a moment. "I need to ask; do you know where Annie went?"

That surprised me. "No," I shuffled. "I'm worried about her."

"Me too," Henderson took something out of his pocket. "When we went to get White's stuff, we found this note on the kitchen table." He handed it to me. Unfolding the piece of paper, I read the flowing script.

*'Losing him changed everything. He was my true north.
I'm sorry. Without him, there is no saving me.'*

My hands shook a little. This note was for me, but I was running late and hadn't seen it.

"Do you know what it means?"

"White was her moral compass," I answered, folding the note. "Without him, she fears her demons will drag her to hell."

"Can you find her?"

"I never expected to see the day one of the Olympians' asked a Hound to track someone for them."

"Even gods need their dogs," Henderson muttered. "I spent a week looking for her. When that girl vanishes, she vanishes. It doesn't help that she came out of vapor as well. I figure, with your knowledge of her family, you'd have more insight."

Tucking the letter into my top pocket, I sighed. "We are called hounds for a reason, Hex."

Considering me, Henderson turned his attention to the field. "They never have just one in."

"I agree. We've scouted around, found one potential exit point. We're happy to go babysit it if you like?"

"Agreed. We'll call you when the party is over," Henderson decided and turned to his team.

Returning to mine, I climbed into the SUV. "Let's go join Edgar. We'll create a perimeter. Anything not one of us, we take it out, human or not."

"Goat?" Sasha asked.

"Definitely, I'm starving."

The Olympian's ordered a drone strike on the field, causing something to blow up and throw fiery debris our way. We roasted goat and watched the fireworks from a distance. Two men appeared out of the back exit. We took them out quietly, then threw a few grenades in the open hatch. That seemed to convince them this wasn't the way out.

The goat was delicious after a week of rations. The stars were muted by the fire in the field, but that was a thing of beauty in itself. It's incredible how perspective works. Even chaos and pain can look beautiful from a distance.

The Olympian's called in to let us know the job was done. We told them there was still some goat if they were hungry. They hadn't been in the desert long enough to find that attractive. We convoyed back to the base, then had a two and a half day's wait after reporting in to ensure the task was complete. When the all-clear came, we were on a Lockheed an hour later and home twenty hours after that. One day before the banquet. Driving home, I had my car to myself, so I called Anique. Apparently, she didn't have voicemail, and the call rang out.

Rhiannon was by the garage waiting when I pulled in. "The others should be right behind me," I told her as I walked up. "Have you heard from Anique?"

"She was in the city," Rhiannon answered quickly, too distracted by waiting for her mate to get home.

"Was?"

"I don't know if she's still there. Edward will be able to tell you when they arrive tonight. He'll know if she's still there or home."

"Home being?" I asked a little frustrated.

Too distracted to even feign her usual annoyance for me asking about her sister, Rhiannon started moving forward as headlights came up the drive. "She was staying with Mandy last we spoke. And no, I don't know where that is. They didn't tell me, so I couldn't tell you. Try getting Rion to lure them out for you. Are you coming to dinner with my parents?"

"I'll try." I'd rather have dinner with her sister.

Evaline came out with little Grace, and a few of the other wives greeted me as they passed. I needed a shower and a run, followed by another shower. Between each activity, I tried calling Anique. The more I tried to contact her, the more irritable and angrier I felt, and yet, I knew that wasn't my emotion.

During the second shower, I zoned in on Anique's emotions, trying to understand if it was just my calling that was upsetting her, but I didn't think it had anything to do with me. In my mind, I caught glimpses of her. Her pupils sparkled with stardust, her smile was insincere, almost malicious, and in her hand, she held a silver blade.

A cold shiver swept through me as I realized how feral and wild Anique seemed in that vision. Glancing down, I took hold of my physical reaction to the idea of Anique going wild. Squeezing a little, I gritted my teeth and stroked my length. My muscles tensed. Wolves didn't masturbate, this is what our women were for. Then again, we didn't do foreplay either and look what one night with Anique had taught me.

Closing my eyes, I thought about that night, imagining being buried in Anique again. My breath came out in a rush, and I pumped my hand hard, thinking of Anique and the sounds she made when she came. I was getting close to climax when my phone started ringing. Peeking through the glass with one eye, I saw Anique's name flashing on my screen. With a smile, I opened the door, reached around, and grabbed it. "I was just thinking about you."

"I know. Stop," Anique panted. "I'm kind of in the middle of something, and you're dragging me into it with you."

"If you were here with me, I wouldn't have to," I countered while I continued stroking. "But, since you're on the phone."

"No, I'm not alone, and since when do Alpha's bat off?"

"Since their mates are nowhere to be found. I've already eaten your-"

"Goddess, Knox! Just go fuck the imitation redhead," Anique snapped and hung up.

There was a moment where I imagined her feral features

moving through darkness and the silver blade slashing. Blood arced from the cut, splashing stone walls and filling the emptiness with the muted cries of a man in pain. Frowning at the phone in my hand, I spoke out loud as I texted her. "What the hell are you doing?" No reply. I tried calling her again, but the phone was turned off.

No longer in the mood for anything but finding Anique, I finished my shower and dressed. In the kitchen, I found Rion on his phone. "...an idea?" Rion asked the phone, hopefully. I watched his face fall. "Oh, I see. I didn't realize she still wasn't coming?"

Fixing myself a cup of coffee, I took a seat at the island.

"What about tonight? I could be there in twenty minutes?" Rion tried again, but I watched a frown creep across his face. "Mandy, can I be straight? I feel like you're giving me the runaround."

With my hearing, I could hear Mandy explaining that her plans had been in place for over a month, and it's just impossible for her to change them. She promised to call him when she got back and ended the conversation. "Blown off?" I asked when Rion threw his phone across the bench.

"Yeah. Apparently, the girls are going away with Anique this weekend to keep her mind off not being able to attend the banquet." Rion frowned at me. "I thought you'd sorted things with Anique?"

"In the process of. She's at least talking to me. I just got blown off by Anique, if that helps?"

"Not really," Rion pouted.

Edgar walked into the room whistling. I dare say he and his mate had just finished consummating his return. Was I jealous? Yeah, a little. "Can I ask you about the bond?" I addressed Edgar.

"Sure."

"If you imagine your mate doing something, does it mean she's doing that thing?"

Considering the ceiling, Edgar shrugged and kept on with

making himself a snack. "Sometimes. Other times it can be representative."

Not really making me feel better, I told Edgar about my vision of Anique. He listened, so did Rion. "She's a doctor, perhaps she's in the middle of surgery?" Rion proposed when I finished.

"With a silver blade and a screaming man?"

"Edgar said it can be representative," Rion countered.

Lifting a brow, I looked at Edgar. "Rion makes a good point," Edgar informed slowly, careful of his word choice. "Perhaps, she is also drunk somewhere, imagining her vengeance on the men who killed White?"

"She didn't sound drunk on the phone. Plus, she's on bereavement leave after attacking me, so the surgery idea is out."

"Alcohol heightens emotions. Our mates see interesting things when we are drinking and thinking about our fantasies. The things Marine has seen of me when I've been drunk," Edgar winked.

"So, your sage advice is to ignore it?" I raised a brow because I dare say some of the things Edgar had done behind his mate's back were covered with the idea of him being drunk. Infidelity could happen, even between mates.

"Unless you find your mate standing over a dead man with a silver blade, try not to overthink it."

Rion waited until Edgar retreated to his hungry mate with his snack. "I'm not an Alpha, but I'm pretty sure Edgar wasn't so easy going about Anique and that vision of yours as he made out."

Having recognized that myself, I turned to consider Rion. "Did Mandy say where they were going with Anique?"

Rion shook his head. "The only thing I know is that they are catching the train now to meet Anique this evening and going from there."

I sighed and stood. "I'm going out."

Rion stood, his head level with my shoulder. "Think Louise

would do both of us? It's been months since I got out, and after meeting my mate, I've been horny as buggery."

Smirking, I pulled out my phone. "I'll see if one of her other girls has an opening."

Rion, like me, preferred to use the services of a low key, high-class brothel for our needs. It saved having one-night stands that got clingy or couldn't handle our roughness. Louise, or as Anique called her, the imitation redhead, was the Madam. She rarely serviced clients anymore, but she made special considerations for me. The fact that she didn't always service her book also meant if I left her sore and unable to walk for the rest of the evening, which I most often did, it didn't affect her income.

Hanging up from Louise as Rion and I walked out the door, I opened the SMS app and started typing. "Important?" Rion asked as he dropped into the passenger seat.

"Just reminding Anique she gave me permission to fuck someone else," I finished typing the message and sent it.

Rion frowned. "Have you asked her permission every other time?"

"No, but after the wake, she made it clear if I made her suffer through it, she'd return the favor. I just want to make it clear she gave permission this time."

Cocking a brow, Rion smirked. "After the wake?" I smiled as I gunned the engine up the drive. "I wondered where you spent the night," Rion chuckled. "The Olympians will chuck a shit if they know you bedded White's widow the night of his funeral."

"Then, don't tell them."

ANIQUE

*K*nox and his damn cock. Glaring at the rain, I cursed. I couldn't focus when he'd dragged me into his masturbation fantasy, and I'd nearly got hurt. Now, I was waiting at the train station for the girls and was stuck watching, hearing, and feeling his fuck fest with the imitation redhead.

When I turned my phone back on, I'd received his messages. Did he really think what I said in anger was going to make me accept suffering through this? To be annoying, I'd started texting him my criticisms.

Anique: *Driving while you're getting off puts my, and every other life on the road, in danger.*

Does she really think anyone believes she's a natural red?

Obviously, you know she's not. I thought sex workers waxed?

Is that the best you can do?

Make her scream, why don't you?

You're not even half as big for her as you get for me.

You know doggy is out with me, right?

You are never taking me on my knees.

Can you actually cum without me?

It was childish, but it made me feel better. If only because I knew the imitation redhead was getting annoyed with his phone buzzing every minute. The car doors opened, and the girls piled into the car quickly to get out of the rain.

"Let's go," Danielle sang into the silence.

"I have to wait for my mate to get his rocks off," I informed them as I typed out another message.

Anique: *I need to drive asshole. Just think of my mouth around your cock and blow already.*

Eyes glazed, I waited. The redhead cursed when his phone buzzed again and turned back to watch Knox read the message. It did the trick. My nails gripped the seat, and I cringed as Knox got himself off on another chick. Then it was over. Exhaling, I started the engine.

"You're texting your mate?" Danielle scowled from the back seat. "Mandy is talking to hers, so I can only assume you'll both join them, probably drag Monique and me along whether we want to or not. Then, because our mate isn't in the pack, they'll parade us around other packs to find our mates. When that doesn't work, I'll be sold to the highest bidder."

Rolling her eyes, Mandy looked at me from the passenger seat. "All the way here."

"Oh, I'm sorry, is my worry for my freedom annoying you?" Danielle snarled.

"No, but your selfishness of only ever thinking about you is," Mandy snapped back. "Shut your mouth, Danielle, I'm sick of hearing it. You were unfortunate that your mate was one of your abusers, but you know what, you didn't have to kill him. Once the phases were completed, he wouldn't have let any of the others touch you. You could have taken out the rest of the pack and started over with just the two of you left. You made your own bed. Stop hating on us for taking what the Goddess gave us."

"You wouldn't let them take us, would you, Annie?" Monique squeaked.

"That's not going to happen, Monique," I replied calmly, driving to the drop off point. "Now, can we discuss tonight?" Silence. "Danielle, are you still good for your part? If you are pissed off and want to just up and leave town, then tell me now. You won't be a good lure if he can smell your violence a mile away."

Danielle took a deep breath. "I'll be fine."

She was confident, that's all I needed to know. I passed back the bag she'd need. "The photo is from four days ago. We'll drop you at the club, and you can take it slow. We are going to need at least four hours, okay?"

"I'll text you when we leave," Danielle assured. "What if he takes me to his place in town?"

"He won't. You're a stray she-wolf." The three of them nodded. Every pack without females would kidnap any she-wolf they could find, stray or otherwise. It's the reason I'd learned to mask my scent and taught the girls to do the same.

"Will this stuff work?" Danielle held up the small vial from the bag.

"I've tested it on four different wolves. It'll work."

Danielle smirked, looking at the liquid like it was a lava lamp. "Who would have thought, something so innocuous could turn a wolf off?"

"It has the same effect on us, so make sure you don't ingest any. You'll want your wolf around when the fun starts."

"He won't feel it?"

"The others didn't, and Dan is no more aware than they were."

Danielle giggled. "Oh my, I'm excited. All the times we've taken down a pack or a hunter, it's never been this thought out or fun."

"Anique has never been at the helm of it before." Mandy looked over her shoulder. "Enjoy it tonight, Danielle, we won't be doing this again. I'm only here for Annie as it is."

Danielle glared at Mandy then turned her attention back to the vial. "Where'd you get this, Annie?"

"I made it."

"And how did you know how to make it?" Danielle was fishing for information I had no intention of ever giving her.

"Lot's of research," I answered vaguely. Pulling over to the side of the road, I pointed to a black Porsche. "That's your ride, Danielle. Let us know immediately if anything goes wrong. Also, let us know if it's going right."

"Where'd you get the ride?" Danielle pointed to the car.

"Leftover from the Venture Pack."

"You stole the Alpha's ride?" Danielle's eyes were bright. "And you what, just left it parked somewhere all this time?"

"I had it in storage. Same with this thing." I tapped the wheel of the Mustang. "If you like the Porsche, you can keep it."

"What?" Mandy and Monique complained. Shrugging, I waited while Danielle dashed smiling through the rain for the waiting car. "You gave that bitch that car?" Mandy asked, exasperated.

"You two have mates waiting. Mates who are going to treat you well. If this stops her planning from killing off the Valleymorgans for this weekend, let her have it."

"She's planning what?" Mandy looked back at Monique. "You know about this?"

Monique nodded. "She's been trying to convince me to help her. We all know if Annie falls to Knox, we'll be sucked in by our link. I know Annie won't abandon us, but Danielle feels like she already has."

Sitting forward with a huff, Mandy looked at me sideways as we drove towards the Beachrunners. "Wait, when did Monique meet her true-mate?" She asked, finally catching what I'd said about both of them having mates.

"Oh, I haven't yet," Monique answered, "but I've suspected who it is for some time, and Annie has too."

"Why?"

"Because of the draw between Monique and I." I took a breath. "Which brings me to the other half of the plan." Filling the girls in, I finished up as I turned down the driveway to the packhouse. Turning off long before the house came into view, we made our way slowly down the old overgrown track. I'd cleared it out this week to be able to get the car through. Admittedly, this car wasn't the best for this terrain, but it got us there without too much complaint.

We piled out of the car and into the cottage that changed my life. Taking a deep breath, I instantly regretted it. Decaying corpses really stank. Mandy and Monique both cringed as they followed me inside. "Hopefully, his wolf senses are offline before he gets in here, or that smell is going to be alarm bells for him," Mandy decided.

Opening the bag, I handed the girls the carefully sealed silver daggers coated in wolfsbane. "Here, get used to the weight. I've got thyme for the smell in here." Moving to the dark corner where the three bodies of Dan's friends lay crumpled, I shoved handfuls of fresh thyme in their mouths and the gaping wounds the blade had caused. They were the ones who were in the room at the start. The ones who beat me and held me for each other to violate.

Once I finished with them, I moved to where Mandy was standing over the last one I'd finished with before I came to pick them up. His wounds were worse than the others. Squatting down beside his pale face, I remembered him laughing as he held me for Dan, how he'd joked about me having another hole for use, and then shoved his cock in my mouth.

Gripping his jaw, I shoved thyme into his mouth, pushing it right towards the back despite his keening. "Come on, scream for me," I purred sarcastically. Putting my hand out to Monique, she handed me the massive jelly dildo from the table of supplies. Easing it into his mouth, I jammed it down his throat. His eyes went wide as he tried to breathe in, and the thyme got lodged in his windpipe.

Scowling with disgust, Mandy kicked him every place she could see him bleeding. Watching him suffocate, I stayed quiet. The wolfsbane that tainted his bloodstream was killing him anyway, but his suffering had gone on long enough.

"That's it, Bitch. Choke on my dick," I murmured sweetly. Mandy continued to kick him between his legs. Watching the light fade from his eyes, I straightened. "Payback is a bitch. Literally."

Waiting until I ensured he was dead, I removed the dildo and put it aside, then the girls helped drag him over to the pile of his dead pack mates.

"Are we ready?" Mandy asked.

Snapping back from staring at the men who'd ruined me, my eyes came to Mandy; I was so tired. "Yeah."

"Annie." Mandy took my hand to hold me back a second. "None of us would think less of you if you decided to stop it here. That's already a lot of blood on your hands."

"Danielle would," Monique reminded us honestly. "I think you are strong just standing here; I feel like every part of me is out of place here."

"Violence and hate leave a mark," I explained before I met Mandy's concerned eyes. "I can never come back to this place psychologically. With Brett taken from me, Knox's rejection, I need to take the ghosts of my past out now, if I'm ever to have peace. You know that."

Squeezing my hand, Mandy retrieved the silver dagger I'd given her. Unwrapping the coated blade, she nodded. "Then let's go slay."

Walking through the rain-shrouded night to the packhouse, we didn't talk, choosing to keep our focus on the task. Entering through the kitchen door, we didn't even hesitate. The wolf making himself a snack was surprised, and he fell to the ground choking on his own blood from the stab through his throat.

We moved quietly, only stopping for one stab per wolf as we crossed their paths. The pack wasn't large, only fifteen wolves, not including my immediate family. We were finished in less than thirty minutes, the first wolf in the kitchen already dead from the wolfsbane in his system.

Over the week, I'd trialed these blades on the first three wolves I'd lured to the cottage. I knew the concentration we needed for quick kills. Of course, the wolfsbane diluted with every kill, which is why there were three of us.

There were only ten wolves in the packhouse tonight; the ones who all used me later. The initial five deserved more than a quick pain-filled death. Four dead in four days. Tonight, the ringleader had a special place in hell waiting for him.

\\\\

My phone buzzed as we dragged the last body out of the packhouse. "Danielle has dosed his drink and is getting ready to leave," I informed the girls. They nodded and kept preparing the pyre. Yes, it was pouring rain, but with the right fuel, that wouldn't matter. The bonfire went up without issue.

We arrived back at the cottage just as Danielle messaged to say she was heading our way. After moving the car out of sight, I went into the cabin to wait with the girls. "His phone buzzed," Mandy showed me the newly deceased wolf's phone and the message from Dan. "Old habits die hard."

"Reply back, 'we'll be there.'" Barely containing a growl, I looked over to the dark corner. It was the truth, after all.

Thirty minutes later, we heard the car pull up outside. Dan had Danielle drive because her car left abandoned would draw attention. "This is your place?" Danielle asked, sounding unimpressed.

"Not my permanent place, no, just a cottage that belongs to the family. It hasn't been used for a while, but it will give us privacy tonight." Shutting and bolting the door, Dan flicked the switch for the lamp by the bed.

"Smells like it," Danielle crinkled her nose as she walked towards the bed. She turned to face him, the psychotic Danielle now alight in her eyes. "What's it been, seven years?"

Tilting his head to think about it, Dan nodded before he caught himself. Pausing, he glared at Danielle. "How did you know that?"

"Because I told her," I whispered behind him.

Jumping, Dan turned, his eyes were wide like I was a ghost. Stepping in behind him, Mandy wrapped the silver chain around his throat before he could react. It burned his flesh as he struggled against Mandy. As Monique joined in restraining him, I stepped forward and sliced across his abdomen with the silver blade. The one with the lowest dose of wolfsbane I'd used on his best friend. Yelling in pain, Dan reached for his wolf, his eyes opening wide when it was nowhere to be found.

"Sucks to be defenseless, doesn't it?" Kneeing him in the family jewels, I smiled when Dan went down, but he still tried to grab the knife from me. Shifting, Danielle pounced, mauling his right arm, even though I'd turned my body and moved the knife free from him before punching him in the face with the hilt of the blade. Dan fell to the floor, screaming.

"Danielle," I called her off. She backed away but stayed in fur.

Grabbing Dan's wrists, Mandy quickly shackled them, then threw the chain over the heavy beam, with the towel we'd set there for the chain to slide freely. Grabbing the chair and the heavy-duty carabiner, I stood ready. Using their combined weight and strength to heave Dan up, Mandy and Monique left him dangling above the ground. I clipped the carabiner in place to hold him just as Dan kicked for the chair I was standing on.

Surging forward, Danielle mauled his leg. Crying out, Dan drew his other leg back to kick her in the head. Dropping into a crouch, I arched my arm for force and drove the silver blade into his raised leg. Dan screamed again while Danielle moved away, cautiously. Jumping down, I kicked the chair away and pulled the dagger free from his leg.

"You won't get away with this, Anique. The rest of the pack are on their way," Dan panted in pain.

Grinning, I grabbed his shirt and turned him to face the dark corner. Grabbing the torch, Mandy turned it on. Dan's breath sucked in as the light fell on the dead and mutilated corpses of his friends.

Letting him go, I stepped away. "They're all dead, Dan. Every man who touched me without my permission. You condemned an entire pack that night. All these years, I've been waiting until my sisters were free of here, until my family was away, leaving you all ready for hell's open arms."

Taking the pair of scissors, Mandy cut Dan's shirt off, while Monique removed his pants. Danielle shifted back into human form, now utterly naked. Even in his current condition, growing weaker from the little exposure to wolfsbane, Dan reacted to Danielle's nudity. Snapping on a pair of gloves, Danielle collected the dildo from the bench, then dipped it into the jar of specially formulated lubricant I'd made, just for Dan. Liquid silver nitrate.

While Dan was hard, I stood up, grabbed hold of his dick, and put the silver blade to the underside. While I engraved the letters A and B into his erection, Dan screamed like a woman. Stepping away, I went over to the preparation bench to put the blade down. Mandy and Monique followed me over, leaving Dan to pant and wheeze where he hung.

"Do you want to do the honors?" Danielle asked, holding up the dildo.

"I'm never touching him again unless it's with this," I explained, holding up the blade.

Grinning, Danielle made her way over to Dan. "Did you know my pack raped me? For two years, nearly every day, I was sodomized. It is unforgivable for anyone to rape a woman. To strip them of their power, to violate them, to convince them they deserved it, or asked for it, or that it is your right to use their body for your pleasure."

"Do you think it's Dan she sees or her mate?" Monique whispered to me.

"Rape is unforgivable. To take a woman's or child's innocence with such violence and selfishness should be punished worse than murder because it murders their soul." Danielle's smile turned sinister. "There is something even more humiliating in sodomy. Absolute debasement. There is no explaining how any of these things truly affect the soul. Only those who have experienced it, who have paid the toll, will know, will be able to look you in the eye and without words, tell you they understand."

"Her mate," Mandy and I whispered to Monique in unison.

"My pack, bastards that they were, never touched me until I shifted. You are a monster worse than any of them. You took a frightened child on the verge of womanhood, and you killed her." Danielle got in Dan's face. "I've seen her medical file. Do you know how many times they had to resuscitate her?"

Dan shook his head, but there was no regret, no ounce of apology in his eyes for what he did. The side of Danielle's mouth twitched as she held the dildo aloft. "Tonight, I'm going to use this on you, the same amount of times they had to bring her back to life."

With his eyes wide as saucers, Dan started shaking his head.

"Anique is going to slice you with the dagger, for every blood transfusion she received. And then, finally," Danielle smiled, closed her eyes, and breathed in as if we'd entered a chocolatier. "Ah, but why spoil the surprise? Shall we start?"

"You're fucking mad, the lot of you," Dan raged as Danielle walked around behind him.

"I wonder what made us that way?" Danielle scolded and slapped his ass with the dildo. Dan's eyes went wide as the silver nitrate burned his skin, causing him to scream again. Danielle didn't give him a chance to draw breath. Placing the tip at his sphincter, she jammed it in. Even I cringed.

It was nearing dawn when the torture was drawing to an end. As Danielle promised. She'd sodomized him four times during the night. One for every time my heart stopped. Dan now sported more than ten slashes across his body, back, and front, equaling all my transfusions.

Danielle was still buzzing, but the rest of us were wearing down. I'd been torturing for five days now; it's not something I'd ever planned to do with my life or someone I thought I could be. Initially, the plan had just been to kill them all quickly. When Brett died, something in me called out for blood and violence, and Danielle served this idea up to me on a cold dish of revenge.

"It's time for you two to go," I told Mandy and Monique. Picking up my car keys, I put them in Mandy's hands. "Go to the banquet, introduce Monique to my family," I directed quietly, so Danielle wouldn't overhear before I turned to Monique. "It's time."

Stepping forward, Monique took my hand. "Annie, I'm scared."

"Don't be, he's a good man."

Monique shook her head. "No, I…" Monique dropped her voice to the quietest whisper, so even I could barely hear it. "Danielle has her own plan."

I knew. I'd known from the moment she challenged me and lost that she'd find a way to do it again. Patting Monique's hand, I kissed her on the forehead. With one last hug, Monique walked out the door. Giving me a big hug, Mandy followed her. Taking a deep breath, I steadied my emotions, rebolted the door, and went back to the bench.

Picking up the hollow cylindrical pole as Danielle came over, I held it out to her. "It's time for the finale." Grinning, Danielle coated the cylinder in the silver nitrate lube, then went back to Dan and shoved it where nothing was going to shine again. Coming back, Danielle picked up the strand of barbed wire. Giving me a wink, she went back to Dan.

"Do you know, in prison, they used to do this to pedophiles," Danielle announced. "Don't even get me started on what I think of protecting those sick fucks." Her sweet smile returned as she held the wire up for Dan. He was dying quickly, only an hour or two left now. "One barb for every man you let rape Anique. That's fifteen."

Dan lifted his eyes to me. "Anique, don't let her do this, please?"

Pulling up a chair, I sat down, folding my arms. I had to watch and had to hear. It was my doing and my revenge. While I was happy to let Danielle do the work with this one - I'd done enough with the others - I put this in motion, so I had to see it out. However, cutting them up was my limit. This sort of stuff was Danielle's bag of fun.

Inserting the wire up the center of the hollow pipe, Danielle then pulled the tube out and threw it aside. Dan cried out as his bowel contracted around the barbs. "Fifteen rapists, led by you. You didn't just steal a girl's innocence, you stole her wolf from her and made her a pathetic human," Danielle snarled, her eyes flashing. She was basically alone with me now, and I knew, once Dan was dead, she would turn on the Alphia she deemed unworthy.

When Danielle yanked the first barb free, Dan wailed. That was the unique thing about the human bowel; it doesn't like to let go. As Danielle pulled barb after barb free, Dan's colon came with it.

27

KNOX

"What about surrogacy?" I spoke out loud to myself as I typed the text to Anique on the phone. "We could harvest your eggs now and have Rhi carry them for us later." There was no reply. To say I was worried about Anique was an understatement. I'd been seeing nothing but pain and violence in the visions of her for days. There was a ball of dread building in my stomach.

"Alpha," Rion knocked at my office door.

"Enter."

"I just heard from Mandy. She's decided to come to the banquet tonight, and she's bringing a friend," Rion grinned.

"You think the friend is Anique?"

"Mandy told me the friend will need to sit with Rhiannon's parents." Rion looked so positive and overjoyed.

For a moment, I allowed myself to be happy at the prospect, but then terrible pain ripped through my middle, and violent anger gouged at my lungs. Toppling out of my chair, I fell to the floor. Rion rushed to my side. "Alpha?"

"Anique," I panted, the pain burning. Is this what it felt like every time her wolf was in control. "It's Anique's pain. Her wolf is trying to take over." The pain was so severe, I wanted to vomit. "Goddess, is this what it does to her? Is this what I did to her that night before I rejected her?"

Dante and Milton came running into the room. "What happened?"

"He's feeling Anique's pain as she tries to shift," Rion answered.

"This is a first," Dante frowned.

"The bond has been strengthened," Rion informed them but left it at that.

Digging my nails into the floor, my wolf crashed against my insides, demanding to go to its pained mate. He thrashed and clawed at me with every new wave of pain, throwing me to the side and hurling me across the room. If I didn't control it, my wolf would take off after her. Without knowing where she was, I could wind up anywhere. He broke through my resolve just enough to throw my head back and howl.

Exposed to their Alpha, the three of my pack dropped straight into their wolf form and joined my howl of worry for my mate. The pain lasted, maybe two minutes, and then it retreated, enough that it left me anyway. Lying on the floor of my office, I cringed as my vision washed with Anique panting in agony on the floor opposite me. Her eyes were locked on the face of a dying wolf, a wolf I recognized.

This is what you wanted,' Anique scowled. There was someone else, a shadow of someone I wasn't seeing, who those words were for. Then, there was smoke, and Anique was surrounded by fire. Her eyes finally locked onto mine. *'Knox,'* she sobbed in pain still, her hand reaching out to me.

"Get up! Get out!" I yelled my will at her. Snapping back to reality like a bungee cord in recoil, I came back to my surroundings. Dante, Milton, and Rion were just regaining their human form as I found my feet. My claws had left gouge marks in the floor, and my breath was still ragged. "Phone Mandy. I want confirmation that my mate is safe," I snarled. "Now!" I snapped at Rion when he wasn't dialing fast enough.

Rion put the phone to his ear. "Mandy, it's Rion. Can you call me back immediately." Rion hung up. "I got her voice mail."

Grabbing my own phone, I tried to ring Anique. It rang out. "Get Rhi to try ringing her," I directed Milton. He ran from the room.

"What did you see?" Dante dared to ask.

"Anique, crippled by pain on the floor, surrounded by smoke and fire. The wolf who ruined her lay dying beside her, and I swear there was someone else there, another female, who caused it all."

Milton came back into the room, shook his head, then Rhiannon followed him in. "Why are you feeling her pain?"

"She's my mate."

"That's never mattered before now. How many times has she been in pain since Brett died, did you feel her agony then?"

"Yes," I admitted. It wasn't as severe, but I'd felt enough of it.

"What about the night you rejected her?" Rhiannon scolded.

"Stop living in the past, Rhi. We were newly mated then. I'm worried about your sister, that she might be with Dan."

"That will never happen." Her face sobered as she looked at her toes and fidgeted. "If you saw him through her eyes while she was trying to hold back her wolf, then you saw in her mind. She blames him for her condition. She likes to imagine him lying in pools of his own blood, suffering. When she's in pain, that fantasy is what tethers her to reality, stops the pain from driving her insane."

"She's told you this before?" I asked gently.

Averting her face, Rhiannon nodded, and her hands went to her womb protectively. "The pain, it's something she's had a long time, Alpha. You'll need to learn to cope with it like she has. It's not going away." Rhiannon lifted her eyes to mine, guilt causing her agony. "I'm sorry." Turning on her heel, she ran out of the room.

Milton looked at me, unsure. "Go, soothe your mate." He bowed his head and left.

A second later, Rion's phone rang. "Mandy," he answered, throwing it on the loudspeaker. "Is Anique with you?"

There was silence for a moment. "No, why, has something happened?"

"Her mate sensed her in a lot of pain."

"But not dying?" Mandy was way too eager.

We all could hear it. When the eyes in the room turned to me, I shook my head. "No," Rion confirmed. "He saw her surrounded by fire and crippled with her pain. He's worried."

Again, a moment of silence. "She's camping, the fire might be the campfire."

Snarling under my breath, I hit the mute button. "That was a blatant lie." Having heard it himself, Rion nodded.

Another phone rang, and another female answered. "Annie, what's happened?"

"That's the radiologist," Rion informed me, recognizing her voice.

"But, you're okay?" The girl asked relieved. "Does that mean?"

"Danielle challenged Annie," Mandy announced, aware we were listening. "I can explain at the banquet in a few hours." The call disconnected.

In the silence that followed, I stared at the phone; we all did. "Did she just tell us a rogue, who can't even shift, just survived a challenge against an Alpha's progeny who can?" Rion checked.

Dante seemed to recover first. "That, I can actually believe."

Picking up my phone, I messaged Anique. She was on the phone to Monique, which meant she should get the message immediately.

Rion put his phone away. "I guess we should go get ready for the banquet then."

When I nodded, he left. Dante stayed a moment. "She forced me to shift. She's your perfect mate, rogue, or no."

Focused on my phone, I took my seat. "I already know."

"She's dying." Dante swept his hand through his hair. "I could feel it. She risked her life to save me, and she knew it. When she forced her will on me, she exposed her vulnerability. Every time she nearly shifts, it steals more of what time she has left. The closer to a full shift she comes, the more time she loses."

"The doctor at the hospital, he gave her a year after she saved you."

"If she just did the same again," Dante began, but then he stopped. "Your time left with your mate could be very limited. May I suggest, after tonight, you take leave, you find her, and you love her for the time she has left?"

"I'll take it under advisement."

Leaving it there, Dante went to get ready for the banquet. Sitting back in my chair, I fidgeted with my phone. How much time had I stolen from Anique the night we finished the phases? When I tried to force her to shift?

My phone buzzed, surprising me.

Anique: *You can't save me. Let me go. Please.*
Knox: *Come home. Let me try.*

No response. Frustrated, I stood and went to my room to get ready for the banquet. I was walking out of the front door when Dante stopped me. "Where are you going?"

"I need to see someone. I'll see you at the banquet."

Driving to Dempsey hospital in Campus, I headed into reception. The admin person smiled brightly at me. "Can I help you?"

"Yes, I work at the base. I was here after the attack and spoke to a doctor. I only recall his name as Eric, but he performed the surgery for removing shrapnel."

The receptionist phoned the surgery unit to get the doctor's name. She told me I could find Doctor Eric Solomon in orthopedics. I made my way there and got an appreciative smile from the nurse staffing the desk. She paged the doctor for me and asked me if I'd like to catch dinner tonight. I explained I had my sister's wedding.

"Can I help you?" Eric Solomon approached me slowly.

"I'm hoping so. I'm worried about a friend of mine, Annie White."

"I haven't seen Annie since her husband died," Eric deflected, a slight twitch in his eye.

"I need to know how we can save her?"

"I can't discuss this with you," Eric dismissed and turned his back on me.

"She's gotten worse." Eric stopped walking. "At the funeral, she nearly collapsed with the pain. Just tonight, her life was put in danger because the pain crippled her."

The doctor turned to look at me. "How do you know that?" He moved towards me and lowered his voice. "I recognize you. You're the man Annie attacked, the one she blamed, the one who held her so tight she passed out. How do you know about Annie?"

Meeting his eyes, I recognized jealousy flashing in them. "Annie and I are close. I know everything about her, except how to save her."

Licking his lips, Eric bowed his head. "I need coffee. I just finished pinning a cadet's legs back together after he shattered both of them by stuffing up an abseil."

"That's a medical discharge."

"Let the kid recover before you kill his hopes, soldier. Hope heals faster than disheartenment." Leading the way to the staff lounge, Eric started making a coffee in the pod machine. "I was a resident when I met Annie. She was such a mess by the time those bastards finished with her that I honestly didn't think she'd make it."

Picking up the coffee, Eric handed it to me while he made another. Taking it, I sat down.

"I mentored her through medical school, not that she needed any academic support. But when she had to choose her research project, I offered to be her supervisor."

"The effects of blood transfusions?"

Eyebrows high, Eric lifted his head. "That was my project. Annie came here to work with me on ways to remove embedded shrapnel. There are a lot of soldiers with shrapnel in their bodies that are considered too dangerous to remove. However, our bodies are living and breathing, constantly changing over time. That shrapnel can be a living time bomb."

"As it is for Annie."

"I can't talk to you about Annie's case. However, I can tell you about one of my transfusion research projects who also happens to be in Annie's shrapnel study. The patient was an adolescent female when she first joined the program and had a sliver of silver embedded near a major artery. She should have had years before it became fatal," Eric shook his head.

"Seven years ago, the prognosis was that the only immediate risk was if she fell pregnant. Carrying a baby could have shifted the shrapnel and killed her, so the patient wasn't too worried. After the incident that left her with embedded shrapnel, the girl was not considering sex or children for it to be a concern. But she grew up, recovered to an extent, met a man she could trust and fell in love. On recent scans, that sliver has moved a lot just in the past year, and now it's too close. The girl has gone through a lot, but will now need surgery sooner, rather than later."

"Will the surgery be dangerous?" I asked.

"Yes." Eric studied the coffee in his cup. "When she first became sexually active, I advised this patient to store her eggs, so children could be an option later, but she wouldn't do it. I thought her husband would have brought her around, but I don't think she ever presented those options."

"Is it still an option?"

Eric's eyes flashed. Suspicion and distrust. Sighing, Eric looked away. "If she wouldn't do it with the man she loved-"

"Let's say he wasn't compatible genetically," I informed him, causing Eric to frown at me. "Recessive gene issue or something like that. But she meets someone new who is compatible, is it still an option?"

Eric looked surprised. "Well, if the patient wanted to, yes, there could be a chance we could freeze her eggs, and then perform the surgery. If the worst happens, she can use the eggs with a surrogate. If the surgery goes well, she could possibly have children without issue. Not for a few years, mind, but it could happen."

"Why hasn't she had the surgery yet? She loved her husband, why didn't she do this to have a lifetime with him?"

Pain racing across his features, Eric scrubbed his head. "The blood transfusion. There is no way we could perform the surgery without a transfusion. She had a bad reaction the last time. It scares her."

Intrigued, I sat forward. "What was the reaction?"

Exhaling hard, Eric relaxed a little. "This I can discuss openly as I've written papers on it that you could find and read anyway. Annie was the basis for my study. After the multiple transfusions to save her life, Annie swung into a deep depression. At one stage, she told me she felt like she'd lost part of herself. When I told her that it was usual for rape victims, she informed me that's not what she meant. Annie explained to me that she had always had this, inner strength, certain preferences for things. Having other people's blood in her muted that until she couldn't feel it anymore."

"That could have still been psychological," I argued.

"That's what I said, but Annie was determined it was the blood. She discussed food preferences, started keeping a diary. After every transfusion, her preferences changed, and so did her way of coping with what happened to her. I had months studying Annie. Her personality actually changed with every transfusion. Then, by the time she was able to leave, I started to meet the real Annie."

"She became your test subject."

"Annie happily gave me all the notes she kept through the two months she was in the hospital. I applied to research it further, and Campus offered to fund it. That's what brought me here."

"If I can convince Annie that this surgery is worth trying? How long are we looking?" I asked, checking the time.

Pressing his lips together, Eric considered me. "For us to harvest the eggs of a woman, it takes about a month, depending on her cycle, the surgery should be a few days after."

"I'll talk to her." Standing up, I offered him my hand. "Thank you for talking to me about your research."

"I'd appreciate it if you could keep this between us, I can lose my medical license. I only told you about my research because I can see you care deeply for her," Eric farewelled.

Leaving for the banquet, I really wanted to go find Anique, but I needed Mandy to tell me how to do that.

28

ANIQUE

"*E*verything's ready," I informed Danielle.

Turning from the preparation bench, she walked over with two bottles of water, handing me one. "You okay?" Danielle hadn't redressed, a clear sign she wasn't finished.

"Yes." Opening the water, I lifted it to my lips.

Danielle looked over to the corner. "I have to say, Annie, I didn't think you had it in you." Turning back to me, she looked down at the now half-empty bottle. Her smile grew. "Thanks for letting me have the fun with this one." Watching me lift the bottle to my lips again, Danielle turned to Dan, where he hanged from the ceiling and fondled what was left of his mauled genitals. Half dead, Dan still screamed bloody murder.

"You seem very practiced at tearing a man up."

"Don't be like that, Annie. I assure you they all deserve it. I never played at home, so relax."

Shaking my head, I put the lid back on the empty bottle. "I'm not getting into it with you. This is the last time any of us will do this. You keep going, you do it against the Lunas."

"You'll hang me out to dry?"

"You are already the prime suspect for the hunters you dumped behind the base."

Tensing, Danielle swallowed. "What do you mean?"

"The MP's who are investigating know about your sexual proclivities. The only reason they gave you the benefit of the doubt is our friendship and my relationship with Brett." I met her eyes. "That connection is gone now. It won't protect you any longer."

Narrowing her eyes, Danielle scowled while her nostrils flared. "I don't need your protection. You're going to hand us over to the Valleymorgans . Monique and I are better off without you."

"Monique won't be going with you, Danielle. She's going to meet her mate tonight, so you are going to end up alone."

"Monique doesn't even know her mate."

"She's never met him, no, but we've both suspected who it is for a few years now."

"And you've waited until now to act on that suspicion?"

"I waited until Monique was ready, and it was safe."

"And what about me, Annie? What are your plans for me?"

"That's where you are confused, Danielle. I've never made plans for any of you. I've let you live your life how you needed. You all chose to follow me, but I never offered or demanded anything from you." I met Danielle's eyes. "Now that I know how you've been living your life, I don't want you in mine." Turning my back, I started to leave.

"Do you think you are above reproach?" Danielle snapped. "Look around you, Annie. Look at the blood on your hands. Look at the lives you've taken."

Refusing to look back, I spoke to my shoulder. "The difference being, I didn't enjoy this."

"You should've been the one person who understood me, Annie. These monsters did worse to you than was done to me."

Feet stopping, I sighed before turning around." What about the men who went home with you for some fun only to be torn apart?"

Raising my voice only a little, I stepped towards her. "There is always a line, Danielle. The difference is where that line lies for each of us. Take the Porsche and go. Go live the life you want. Get away from Campus before you run afoul of the Valleymorgans ." Turning, I walked away. The snarl only gave me a moment's notice, and I reacted automatically.

Spinning as I dropped to the ground, I caught Danielle's jaws in my hands as she went for my throat. Kicking my legs up into her abdomen, I sent her flying over my head, her momentum carrying her into the door. The wood splintered under the impact and exploded outwards, sending Danielle tumbling out into the midday sun.

Before she came bounding back through the door, I was back up on my feet. When she went for my throat again, I caught her jaws, her weight slamming me back onto the floor, her claws tearing at my chest. My wolf came forward in defense, the silver burned, but the rage at being challenged by someone unworthy, of the betrayal, pushed through the pain.

My hands changed, fingers lengthening, causing me to scream. Pressing claws into Danielle's jaw, I yanked to the side. The flesh around her jaw ripped open to expose the bone. Toppling to the side, Danielle whimpered in pain. Her Amber eyes wide on my half-shifted hands, her shock and surprise passing through me.

In the next moment, as I rose to my feet, I felt her confusion and the memory of me drinking the water. "Oh, you thought you were clever, not giving all the inhibitor to Dan, thinking you could use it on me, right?" I raged. "Did you actually see the water pass my lips?"

Snarling, Danielle came for me again. The next few minutes were full of snarls and screams of pain on both our parts. To defend us, my wolf breached the barrier, raging at the silver in my blood, which imprisoned her. I wasn't able to handle much more; just letting my wolf forward was torture. Seeing my last chance, I stuck my fingers into Danielle's mutilated jaw, she whimpered and pulled away. Going with her, I slashed my claws at her throat. Danielle screamed, her wolf limping back and collapsing to the ground.

Collapsing in agony, I whimpered. "I'm sorry, Danielle, I never wanted this. This is what you wanted."

Shifting back to her human form gave her enough healing to get to her feet again. Standing, Danielle aimed a kick at my abdomen. The pain already too much, I screamed. Her jaw was still mangled, but Danielle's eyes declared her hatred. Her body was covered in wounds from my claws. Bloody and torn up, she shuffled her way to the prep bench.

There were no words of victory as Danielle lit a match and threw it onto the pile of bodies in the corner. The kerosene ignited instantly, and the fire started to spread through the cabin. Grabbing her clothes, Danielle began to shuffle for the door. Gritting my teeth, I forced myself to my feet, grabbed up one of the silver daggers laced with wolfsbane, and launched myself at her.

My abdomen chose that minute to seize, burn, and cramp. Missing, I fell on the ground hard, crying out in agony. Turning around, Danielle snarled and launched a kick at my chest. Pushing through the pain, I blocked her kick and stabbed her in the calf at the same time. Howling, she stumbled back from me, falling out the door. I let her go. Dropping the dagger, I watched the flames grow, the pain still tearing through my insides.

Pale green eyes floated before me, worry and fear flooding me from another source. "Knox," I sobbed, the adrenaline leaving my system and the pain leaving me crippled.

'Get up! Get out!' He didn't just press his will on me, Knox threw it at me like a grenade.

Coming to on the grass out the front of the burning cottage, I lay there, wheezing and coughing from the smoke. My wolf was gone, but the pain was still there.

Sucking up my strength, I forced myself to my feet. Halfway to the Porsche, I found Danielle. She was sprawled on the ground, her Amber eyes vacant with her death. Tears washed down my face as I closed her eyelids. "May the Goddess grant you happiness in your next life." It hurt. Not just my physical pain, but to have killed someone I'd once considered a friend. It didn't matter how it came about, just that it was my hand that snuffed her life out.

Collecting the keys to the Porsche from Danielle's hand, I then grabbed the bag I'd stashed with my belongings beneath some ferns. Starting the Porsche, I drove away. The fire would probably spread to the surrounding bush, so I didn't want to be here if it did.

Once I was back on the road proper, I called Monique. "Annie, what's happened?"

"Danielle challenged me. Well, challenge may be too honorable a word for what she did, but I'll give respect to the dead."

"But you're okay?"

"I'm still breathing."

"Does that mean…?"

"I'm sorry, Monique. Danielle's dead." Gritting my teeth at the pain still searing my abdomen, I concentrated on staying on the road.

"I understand, Annie. I don't think any of us would have been safe in the end," Monique replied, surprising me with her insight. "What will you do now?"

"I'm going to be uncontactable for a while. Let my family know I love them."

Monique sobbed on the other end of the line. "We'll miss you."

Aiming to get as close to Campus as manageable, I drove for as long as I could. When I could barely stay conscious, I pulled off the road into a rest spot. Stopping in a parking bay, I turned off the ignition and all but passed out in the car. When my phone buzzed, I managed to look at the message.

Knox: *I need to know you're alright. Please call me.*

Tears ran down my cheek. He could never forgive me now. Not after I'd taken part in the torture and mutilation of an entire pack. All of them deserved it, so I shouldn't feel bad for it. Mostly, I didn't.

Knox: *Come home. Let me try.*

My home was with Brett. Knox was part of my soul, but Brett was the one I loved. I should have stayed in the cabin and let Danielle kill me, then I could have been done with the pain, and back with the man who I loved. Placing my medi-alert card on my lap, I dropped my phone to the side and closed my eyes.

"Miss?" I heard a man call, followed by tapping on a window. "Miss, are you alright? My name is officer..."

Pain ripped through my core, welcoming me back to the waking world. Reaching forward, I opened my door. The police officer pulled it the rest of the way open. "Miss, are you hurt?"

"I need a hospital," I gritted as I handed him my medi-alert card. The pain was too much, I fell out of the car into the policeman's arms. Staring at the cream leather seats of the Porsche, the policeman swore. Following his gaze, I saw the pool of blood I'd been sitting in. Closing my eyes as the pain ripped through me again, I considered, maybe I was going to Brett after all.

"...**Wish** the true-mates healthy cubs, and welcome Rhiannon, officially, to the Valleymorgans ," I finished the traditional banquet speech. Everyone cheered. "And now, the feast."

Rhiannon and Milton decided to be traditional and hunted the deer, which would be served tonight. Since it was a small gathering, with only our pack and Rhiannon's parents and brother, we'd hired a function center in Campus. We provided the caterers with the venison for the meals.

While the new couple made the rounds serving, I took my seat at the table with Rhiannon's parents, Edward, and Monique, Edward's true-mate. The first phase hit them when they were introduced twenty minutes ago, and they now sat whispering, getting to know each other.

"Monique told Edward Anique sent her tonight knowing they were mates," Stirling murmured. "It's a pity she didn't come herself."

"If my guess is right, Anique is not at her healthiest tonight?" Stirling turned concerned eyes to me. "Did you know Anique is an

Alphia?" Stirling shook his head, but I saw a flicker in his eye, the question confirming his suspicions. "She formed her own pack of stray she-wolves in this very town. Monique, Mandy," I pointed out the two present, "and a third, Danielle. They've been together since Anique went to college, and have hidden in my territory undetected until I met Anique."

Stirling's Adam's apple bobbed.

"Danielle suffered a similar fate to Anique at her own pack." The sting of that new knowledge flaring Stirling's wolf to life, changing his pupils to stardust while I watched. "She underwent the first phase with her true-mate while he and another packmate raped her."

"That would have been horrific," Stirling growled, turning his gaze to the cutlery in front of him as his irises changed to be more wolf than man.

"Indeed. Apparently, it definitely distorted the bitch's psychological stability. She murdered her entire pack, true-mate included, at her banquet. My understanding is that she has been behind the annihilation of at least two other packs since then." Everyone at the table had stopped to listen. Monique looked very uncomfortable.

"And you haven't done anything about her?" Stirling asked, concerned.

"She's remained elusive. In fact, until Rion underwent the first phase with Mandy, Anique's pack had managed to escape our detection repeatedly."

Smirking, Monique hid her face. Edward noticed, and his brows drew together. Anique's brother didn't impress me the first time I met him, but at that moment, I saw the intelligence he held. In an instant, he realized his mate was not only a flight risk but possibly involved in the fate of those murdered packs.

"Danielle hasn't taken well to the rest of her pack meeting their true-mates and challenged her Alphia today." Stirling sucked in a breath, but I held up my hand. "Anique defeated her, but at great cost to her health. I'm concerned for her, and for my mate. Unfortunately, Anique is like a leaf in the breeze. Very hard to get a hold of, and even harder to locate."

"What about her pack?" Edward asked. "They could find her easily if they are a true pack."

All eyes turned to Monique. Her shoulders rolled forward under the attention of three Alphas, then she shook her head. "Annie never shifted. We never learned her true scent."

Like a shot to the head, I understood why I'd never been able to track her. Our wolf scents were different from our human forms, the pheromones different. That's how we located our pack mates. Now, it was clear why the phases finished with the mating, in not only skin form but also our wolves. It wasn't about the domination of the female or her acknowledgment of submission. The mating was gaining each other's pure scent, inhaling each other's pheromones, so one could never be truly lost from the other.

"No, but you took a call from her immediately after," I countered. "You know where she is."

"I don't. Annie sent us away. When we spoke to her, she told us she would be uncontactable, and that we should tell her family she loves them."

Ire rose within. Anique was meant to come home to me. "You've known Anique for a long time, you must have some idea how to find her?" The table was quiet as we watched Monique chew her lip. After a moment, Mandy walked over to the table, placed her hands on Monique's shoulders, and Monique relaxed.

"You have to understand, Monique is very loyal. Anique protected Monique, saved her from being abducted by the Venture Pack." The Venture pack was one of the first packs wiped out that we'd attributed to the Lunas. Assessing them, I tilted my head. Anique's family was here, I wasn't going to reveal these girls were a pack of vengeful bitches, not when one was about to marry into the pack.

"Mandy, will you dance with me?" I requested, walking around and offering my hand. She would be one of mine soon enough; best she learn loyalty to a new Alpha now.

When Mandy took my hand, I led her to join others from our pack already dancing. "Is this where you tell me that since I will be joining your pack soon, I should start showing you some loyalty?" Mandy raised a brow as we started to dance.

"This is where I ask if your pack wiped out the Venture Pack to help Monique?" I queried instead. Mushing her lips together, Mandy shook her head. Meeting her eyes, I used my bond with her Alphia and willed her to talk.

"We weren't a pack back then. I didn't meet Annie until after," Mandy rushed. Her face fell when she got to that point. With a deep breath she sighed. "You can't hate her for this, I'm surprised it wasn't revealed during the second phase."

"The Goddess was pretty intent on me knowing every minute of what ruined my mate, not on any sins she committed since."

Mandy nodded. "When Monique first escaped her pack, she was captured by the Ventures. They didn't rape her or anything, but we're going to force mate her. Around the same time, they found Annie." My spine stiffened. "Annie was in her first year of Medical school. They took her, and the Alpha made the mistake of trying to force Annie to his will. Annie threw it right back at him, dominated him in her will alone, and saved herself."

"How? Her will would have stopped the moment she turned her back."

"You have to understand, after what happened to Annie, she hated wolves, and she would have chosen death over letting that happen to her again. Preferably, their death. So, she made the Alpha stab himself in the neck with a silver blade he had on display in the cabinet," Mandy exhaled. "He liked collecting silver blades."

"How did she escape the pack?"

"They were already dead. The Ventures were only a small pack of five and newly formed. Annie made the Alpha kill his pack members before he killed himself."

Jaw working, I stared at Mandy. "You said Anique wasn't a killer," I reminded her of her words outside of White's funeral.

"She's not. Not a cold-blooded one anyway, not like Danielle." Mandy seemed to struggle. "Back then, what she did, she did to survive. She freed Monique, and they both drove back to town. Annie gave Monique a few tips on surviving and went her own way. I met Annie a month later. By then, Annie had created a way to hide her scent and seem human to any wolf she came across. I liked her, liked her drive, so I became her friend."

"And she wasn't involved in the other three packs?"

Mandy shook her head aggressively. "No, that was Danielle. She killed her own pack, then she met Monique. Monique explained how Annie wiped out the Ventures, and they took out another pack together, that's when they came to find Anique. Danielle wanted her own pack, but she didn't realize Annie would be the Alphia, nor that she wouldn't approve of killing. Even when we took out Monique's pack, Annie only approved of it because she found out about the hunters and that it exposed us to you."

"She needed to remove a threat to the safety of her pack," I nodded, understanding.

"She didn't take part in it though, or the planning. She doesn't like violence. She used to fight her wolf's violent desires. Brett helped her. Well, actually, he dampened her blood rage completely," Mandy mourned. Her eyes lifted to mine. "You would have as well, you know, if you hadn't have released her from loyalty to you. She was so terrified of you, but her belief in true-mates was the last part of her wolf she held on to. You took that from her."

My stomach twisted in knots.

Mandy shook her head. "I know Brett was human, but he was an Alpha, and a decent alpha if ever I did meet one. He was worthy of Annie."

"And I'm not?" I asked. Mandy stayed quiet. "With White gone, and her loyalty to me nonexistent, only Annie can control her wolf and her blood rage now. That's what you are trying to tell me?"

Mandy looked pained. "Something snapped in Annie when you rejected her. You brought her wolf closer to the surface than she'd ever been before. Then White died, and her wolf has been trying to be released ever since. Danielle took advantage of that and attacked Annie when she thought she would be weak. I heard the pain in Annie's voice. Having to kill Danielle, losing Brett and you, I don't think she has the will to fight her wolf anymore."

"But the silver..."

"If the wolf pushes through, she'll die." Mandy closed her eyes, and the tears she'd been holding back ran free.

Pain ripped through my abdomen, not real pain like earlier, but the memory of pain. Tensing as Anique's scream filled my head, I watched in my mind as Anique fell into the arms of a policeman, her seat pooled with blood. "Anique is dying," I muttered, more to myself than anyone else. "I need to find her."

Everyone was looking at us. That's when I realized I'd voiced Anique's pain. Starting for the exit, I growled when Mandy followed and grabbed my arm. Turning with a snarl, I struggled to hold back my wolf coming to the surface.

"Listen!" Mandy waited to ensure she had my full attention. "Annie has a Medi-alert. If anything happens to her, if she's found by paramedics or police, they'll call Campus hospital and notify Eric Solomon. If she is here, she'll be rushed to him, if she's far, they'll fly him to her."

"Because she is his research project?"

Mandy nodded slowly. When I went to leave again, Mandy

gripped my arm tighter. "Blood," she murmured. "She'll need blood. Annie discovered all wolves are the same blood type."

"AB positive, I know," my entire pack was the same. "Universal takers, but no one but us can take our blood."

"The Goddess's way of preventing cross-contamination between her children," Mandy confirmed. "Don't let them give her human blood."

Understanding, I nodded and turned. "Dante!"

"Alpha?" Dante was beside me as I walked out.

"I need you and your wife to follow us to the hospital. Anique is going to need blood, have Rion bring his mate too."

"We'll be right behind you," Dante assured.

As I sped towards the hospital, I called Eric Solomon. It took only a few minutes to reach him from the switchboard. "Mr. Morgan, you said it was important?"

"Anique is hurt and hopefully on her way to you. I'll be there in five minutes. She's going to need blood, but you aren't going to give her any unless it's mine or her family."

"Mr. Morgan-"

"No arguments. Trust me when I tell you, if you want Annie to live, she can only have her own blood type. Consider it part of your research," I directed as I sped into the hospital car park.

"Okay, Mr. Morgan, I'll play this game, but there are procedures."

"I'm aware. Be ready to blood type me when I get inside. Anique's family won't be too far behind." Grabbing my phone as I pulled into a park, I jumped out of the car.

"I've just been notified Annie is twenty minutes out. Come straight to emergency. I'll be waiting for you."

Hanging up, I typed instructions to Dante as I entered the hospital. As I approached the emergency desk, Solomon approached from the side. "Mr. Morgan," he called me to join him and opened the door. "I'll need you to sign forms that consent to be part of my research," he explained as he handed me some paperwork. "You can fill them in while we get your blood."

"That's fine, but you can't give our blood to any others. It will give them a bad reaction, so you need to destroy it after Annie doesn't need it any longer."

Solomon eyed me. "Something I should know?"

"I think you already suspect."

Solomon smirked. "There's a reason my research was brought to Campus, Mr. Morgan. I'll agree to your terms."

I handed him the forms back. "Put it in writing."

Solomon took the forms while I was led into a room where a nurse was waiting, setting up empty blood bags. "These are emergency supplies for a surgery about to take place," Solomon informed the nurse. "The patient has a rare blood type, and so her kin is coming in to donate. We need the typing done stat."

"What about screening the blood?" The nurse asked, surprised.

"Yes, for the civilians, the men are from the base and are screened regularly, so we can use their blood without."

"I was screened three weeks ago, my results should be on record already," I informed. The nurse took the military ID I handed her to pull up results on the computer. Slipping off my suit jacket, I rolled up the sleeve of my dress shirt. Solomon gave me the paperwork with the alteration I'd requested. "I have to scrub in."

"Doctor Solomon, I'll need to wait outside once you have my blood. Let me know as soon as there is something to know."

"Why?" Eric asked, his forehead creasing.

"Remember what Anique was like when she lost her husband?" Solomon nodded sadly. "I'll be ten times worse if she dies." The nurse must have been on duty that night because she took three significant steps back from me.

Closing his eyes, Solomon nodded. "I'll have a nurse keep you updated throughout. Give Nurse Jones your number to call you.

Wait in the restaurant across the road. Annie always said the food there calmed her down and kept her alive."

As Solomon walked out, the nurse warily stuck the needle in to start taking my blood. Closing my eyes, I prayed to the Goddess. "Hold on, Anique. Just hold on."

In hindsight, I should have gone outside straight away, not waited outside the room with Rion and Mandy while Evaline gave blood.

"...hemorrhaging internally. We've given her Gelofusine, but she'd lost a fair bit of blood before we got there. Her vitals are low, and HCG levels indicate she was at least two weeks pregnant, but this is more than a miscarriage..."

Staring at Anique's unconscious form as she was wheeled past us, I reacted as if I'd been punched in the solar plexus and left winded, unable to draw breath. Over all the commotion, I could hear Anique's heartbeat, the slowest thud, thud, barely doing its job. Fist's clenched, I closed my eyes. "Live," I willed. "Live, and I will love you like no other."

Anique's heart jolted. "That's it, Annie," the paramedic encouraged when he saw Anique's vitals spike. "Fight to be here. It's worth it. Sometimes it sucks, I know, but that's life. It's hard work, but the good times make it worth it. Smiles and laughs with those we love most, make it worth it. So, you fight."

The doors to surgery one closed, cutting off his encouragement, but Anique could hear him, his words brought her a mix of happiness and grief. She also felt my presence, and that had a similar effect.

"Did he say Annie was pregnant?" Mandy asked astounded, looking back to me.

"Yes," my own grief settling like a stone in my stomach.

"When did that happen?" Mandy asked wide-eyed.

Staring at Mandy, I glanced at Rion, then handed him my car keys as I turned on my heel. "I'll be across the road, until I'm not."

KNOX

*S*taring at the fallen tree, I saw flashes of a redhead running through the forest with three wolves. Stepping closer to the fallen log, I sniffed along the ground for anything. No, her, I was looking for her in the only place I held her. My memory.

Sweeping back the fronds, I found her, sitting by the edge of the pond, watching the fish swim. She almost looked like a cat, the way her head tilted as she watched the fish. *'I don't want a mate. I don't care what the Goddess says, I won't submit to you.'*

Chasing after her, catching her quickly because of the strappy heels she wore. *'You kill people. You enjoy what you do, torturing, and killing.'* Shivering, she backed up another step, lifting her eyes to the sky and cried. *'What did I do to offend her so badly? First him, now you.'*

At the fallen tree, I turned her under my arm, caught her waist in my hands, and kissed her. Pulling her closer to me, I stepped her back against the log. She moaned when I deepened the kiss, rubbed her body against mine.

Cuffing the back of her neck, I kissed her harder, with more need. Skimming up her thigh, lifting her dress to touch her naked flesh. Flinching away a little at my touch, her fingers grab hold of my shirt as if she might sink into the ground if she let go. *'Wait, we need to talk.'*

Determined that I wasn't leaving here until she was mine in every way, I kissed her hard. Just as the head of me touched the silk of her, she sank her canines into my shoulder. My eyes went wide at the pain and pleasure her marking me as hers caused me. Fisting her beautiful hair, I used it to pull her mouth free and lifted her head, so I could access her mouth. Her eyes blinked, coming clear for a moment, long enough for her to cry out for me to stop, anguish choking her pleasure.

Pushing my hips forward, I surged into her. It wasn't just our bodies, but our souls were merging with every thrust of my body into hers.

'What happens now?'

Whimpering, I sunk to the ground, nosing the dirt where she'd abandoned her knickers in her haste to get away from me. I'd promised to protect her, vowed to ensure she was never hurt again, and now I knew how much pain I'd caused her that night. How much shorter her life became because of my actions.

Catching a noise to my right, I lifted my head, keeping low. A rusty colored wolf ran along the track. The bitch was beautiful, her fur so sleek it almost shined with the moonlight. Slowing as she approached the fallen tree, she looked hesitantly between the log and the path ahead. As her indecision grew, I rose out of my hiding space and moved slowly toward her. She stepped back, but she didn't run.

'Stay?'

Tilting her head, she watched me.

'I hurt my mate, and I let her go. She only suffered more heartache. I should have never let her go. I should have asked her to stay sooner.'

There was a flash of a woman clawing at me, screaming in

grief, her emerald eyes crying as she tried to rip my heart out. My heart lurched in my chest.

'I felt her die today,' I admitted, recounting that moment as I sat in the restaurant. I'd been out of my skin and running through the forest two minutes later. *'I couldn't bear the pain. Stay with me, till the pain goes away?'*

The she-wolf stepped towards me, tentatively, with her head slightly lower. She rubbed her face against mine and whispered with remorse. *'Pain is life. If you can feel it, you don't belong here.'*

Licking across my snout, she trotted off towards the path.

'I don't feel it when you're here.'

She froze. My heart thudded hard. Was it my heart? It felt like my heart.

"Alpha!" I heard Dante calling in the distance.

'Stay!'

She looked back at me with the saddest green eyes. Those eyes matched the other pair I'd been hunting, matched the ones that belonged to my heart. Another jolt, heart thudding wildly.

"Alpha!" Dante still called in the distance.

Checking in the direction of his voice for a moment, when I looked back, I was alone.

'No!' Lifting my head, I howled in grief. I didn't want to be alone.

When my cries stopped, my heart pumping wildly, light flitted through the trees. Moonlight. Her light. Giving chase, I was desperate to feel her light upon me one more time. Desperate for one more look from her emerald eyes, one more word from her luscious mouth, and one more touch from her moonlit skin.

My heartbeat was growing stronger.

'Stay!'

I chased the light, all my focus on it, determined not to lose it.

'Stay!' I willed it.

Racing hard to catch it.

'Stay. Stay. Stay.'

Leaping into a clearing, I caught it, bathed in the light.

'Stay!'

The light submitted, and I howled victory. The light filled me, merged into me, faded from sight, but I still felt it's warmth inside me.

Thud, thud, thud, thud, thud.

Even, steady, heartbeats.

"Alpha," Dante called my attention to where he stood next to me.

Flowing into human form, I collected my clothes from the ground where the light had led me. "I know. She's fighting."

Breathing out with relief, Dante nodded. "Her heart stopped, they were just about to pronounce, then something brought her back."

Smiling to myself, I thought about the wolf in the forest. "Her wolf wants to live. Come on." Running back to the hospital, I kept telling her to live. I needed to stay close. I needed Anique to feel she wasn't alone, her wolf to feel it's mate willing her through this. An hour later, I was sitting in the waiting room trying to be patient, focusing on nurturing the light I could feel inside me.

"Morgan?"

Lifting my head, I sucked in a breath. "Henderson. You heard about Anique?"

Nodding, he took the seat next to me. "Anything?"

"She's fighting to be here."

"Well, that's something, at least," Nathan exhaled. We sat in silence for a minute. "I don't want to be rude, Morgan, but why are you here?"

Giving him a side glance, I pointed to Evaline sitting across the hall with Dante. "We were at Milton and Rhiannon's wedding. Anique didn't show, then we got the call. She's a rare blood type, so we all came to donate," I explained, grateful my suit covered my arms so he couldn't see that my arm was healed already.

"You and Annie are the same blood type?"

"Yes, why?"

Henderson frowned. "Brett was AB positive too."

I froze. "You sure about that?"

"Yeah, it's in his records. He said that's how he knew Annie was the woman for him."

Sitting straight, I assessed Henderson. "Did you get his stuff back to his family?"

"Yeah, I wasn't really welcomed, and they weren't too concerned about his death. Apparently, he was a bastard child. Father made out like his mother had been the hired help or something. Anyway, as I said, he wasn't too interested until he caught a whiff of Annie's perfume, then he wanted to know everything. Who she was, where she was, how she was connected to Brett. Henderson shook his head. "Wasn't going to let me leave until he knew where to find her."

My fists were clenched until they were white. "What did you tell them?"

"Said she left town and headed for the city. I told him she didn't want to stay if her soul mate wasn't here anymore," Henderson growled. "I think the bastard was planning on hunting her down, don't know why."

I did. If my suspicions were correct, I knew exactly why. "Do you happen to remember where he lived?"

Henderson gave me the address, but I didn't have to look it up. It was six hours flight from here, but the Whitetails were a very well-known pack in our community. They lived like overlords of their territory and treated humans who worked for them as slaves. Scrubbing my face in my hands, I stood up. "Excuse me. I need a coffee, you want one?"

"Yeah, thanks."

Tapping Rion on the shoulder as I headed for the kitchen, I gestured he and Dante follow. Once we were in the kitchen, I turned to face them." Brett White was the bastard halfbreed of the Whitetail's Alpha. I'm guessing, when he hadn't shifted by his teenage years, they kicked him out."

"Are you sure?" Dante questioned. "I didn't think we could get human's pregnant?"

"It's rare," Rion confirmed. "Only females of the rarest blood type can carry to term, and many used to die in childbirth if the baby's blood got into their blood supply. Point-six percent of the human population is compatible with us."

"Mandy said White was Alpha material, I think she was right. I think White was everything an Alpha was minus the wolf." We stood there while the percolator filled the silence. "Damn, I knew I respected him for a reason."

"He respected you too, but he would never have been on par with you," Dante objected.

"He was as far as Anique was concerned."

"No, she chose you over him too, right up until you rejected her," Dante challenged.

"So, if White was raised wolf, he would have known about us?" Rion considered. "He tried to apply to be a Hound, remember?"

"If I knew he was a halfbreed, I would have let him."

"He was probably worried if he told you, you'd reject him like his family did," Dante dismissed. "God, he must have hated you when you took Anique from him. He would have known why he lost her."

"Yeah, and I'm pretty sure the reason he didn't punch my teeth in was that she came back to him," I agreed.

The coffee machine finished, and I grabbed two of the coffees. "The Whitetails are looking for Anique, they think she's a stray, we need to let them know that's not the case."

"I'll take care of it," Dante volunteered. Nodding thanks, I took

Henderson his coffee. We sat there quietly, drinking for another half hour.

"She was pregnant," Henderson frowned. "Did she know?"

"Doubt it," my stomach turned. As if I hadn't done enough to Anique. "Doesn't matter now."

"It will matter to her. Brett said she didn't want kids, but to find out you're carrying your dead husbands-"

"We're not telling her unless she needs to know, Henderson," I snapped. "She's already lost enough. She doesn't need more to grieve."

Henderson rocked back, swallowed, and bowed his head. I couldn't correct him about who's baby it was, not without hurting Anique. The truth is, had we not been bonded, it could have been his. He was the same blood type, a half breed. They could have started a family together.

"She's a doctor, Morgan. The first thing she is going to do is to read her chart. She'll know."

Glaring at the surgical doors, I willed someone to come through them and give me an update. "Then we will help her through it when she is ready. Let's get her through this first."

The doors opened; Eric Solomon stepped through looking exhausted as he dragged the scrub cap from his head. "Mr. Morgan..." Standing up, I walked over to him, everyone else standing but not getting close. When Henderson tried to move closer, Dante got in his way and shook his head in warning.

"We've stopped the bleeding. The shrapnel pierced the artery, but not to the point where we couldn't save it. Annie lost a lot of blood before she was brought in, and the miscarriage only added to the trauma."

Letting Solomon get his thoughts in line, I waited. Slowly, a smile of relief spread across his face. "She made me fight to keep her here, but she's here, and unless a complication pops up, she'll have a few years in her yet."

Trembling, I was scared to exhale and relax.

"The metal poisoning is still an issue," Solomon cut in. "Once we got the shrapnel out, her bleeding slowed dramatically. As we gave her your transfusion, her heartbeat became stronger, so I expect your theory was correct."

Hearing what he said, I tipped my head. "You didn't give her my blood first?"

Solomon shook his head. "I tried her sister's blood first, hoping the closer genetic connection may help. Then it was what we grabbed, which happened to be the last taken. We'd just set up the line for your blood when her heart stopped. I was so busy fighting to keep her here, I didn't think about it. When her heart kicked back in, I realized half the bag of your blood was in her system. Her vitals really picked up from there, so whatever is in your blood, did the job."

Closing my eyes, I took a deep breath. "When can I see her?"

Wringing his scrub cap in his hands, Solomon stepped from foot to foot. "She's in the intensive care unit, only immediate family can visit her there. I'm sorry."

"Evaline and Dante," I called. They came forward. "Dr. Solomon is going to take you to see Anique." As Evaline came beside me, I touched her trembling arm. "She's going to be fine." Evaline broke down in tears. She'd held it together so well until that moment.

"I'll call Milton, and let the rest of the family know," Rion offered. "Then, I'll take Mandy home."

"Mandy should go in." I looked to Solomon to see if he would object, he didn't. Striding over, Mandy gave me a tight hug. "Call me if she needs me," I murmured. Nodding, swiping her own tears, Mandy took Evaline's hand, and they followed Solomon and Dante through the doors. Rion went to make the call.

"What was the prognosis?" Henderson asked.

"She'll live," I sighed, sinking back into my chair.

"They won't let you in?"

"Family only."

Henderson looked at his watch. "Army club is still open."

Glancing at him, I stood up. "So, is the wedding reception, and the booze is free."

"That an invitation?"

"Yeah, just be warned, our lot party hard." With Henderson in tow, I walked out to find Rion, hoping he had my keys.

"I'll drive, Alpha," Rion decided.

Not in the mood to argue, I let it go. When we got to the banquet, I let Anique's family know that their daughter and sister was alive, and, for the first time in eight years, silver-free. Then Henderson and I took full advantage of the open bar.

31

KNOX

$\mathcal{M}$y head hurt, so I'd hate to think how Henderson was feeling this morning. Groaning, I checked my phone. Rion messaged to let me know Anique still hadn't woken up and to give me the latest update from her medical team.

Taking a long shower, I tried to scrub the fuzz from my head before making my way to the kitchen only to find Anique's father and brother were there. "Morning, Knox," Stirling greeted.

Wincing a little, I poured a cup of coffee before sitting down to join them." Heading up to see Anique?"

"Edward is going to go this morning. I'm going to go home and check on things, then come back tonight."

Reading the uneasy way Stirling was sitting, and Edward's tenseness, I lifted a brow. "Something the matter?"

"My pack, I can't feel them, and no one is answering the house phone or their mobiles."

Glancing at Edward, I read the energy off him as anger and something unusual. Vindication. "That sounds highly suspect, Stirling. I don't think it's a good idea for you to go alone." Losing contact with your pack was usually a sign of changed loyalty. The pack had turned on you and sworn allegiance to a new alpha in your place. If that had happened to Stirling, the new Alpha would challenge him when he got home. Knowing how despicable some of his pack were, I couldn't see them challenging him honorably if they could surprise him.

"My wife will stay at the hospital with Edward." He suspected he was going home to his death. "No one is expecting me home until tomorrow. I'd told them I was taking the opportunity to secure a few connections with other packs for us to meet their bitches. So, it will surprise them for me to come back early this morning." Stirling was trying to get the upper hand. He stood, shook my hand, and went to collect his things.

"I offered to go with him, but he didn't want me getting caught up in things," Edward explained. "I've met my mate. He thinks I'd be better off taking her and setting up a new pack, then being killed and subjecting Monique to those wolves."

"I agree." Finishing my coffee, I stood up. "I'll give you a lift to the hospital. Your mother can come with Rhiannon and Milton later." Evaline came home with Dante late last night to be with her cub. Rion had stayed at the hospital with Mandy.

When we arrived at the hospital, I was informed I could see Anique. Walking into intensive care, all I could smell was suffering and death. Anique, thankfully, didn't stink like death, but the pain was there. Sitting by her bedside, I took her hand in mine. She groaned in her sleep. Smiling, I rubbed my face across her knuckles. "It must have been hard," Edward murmured across his sister, "to meet your mate and find her already married."

"You know about Brett?"

"She came to me when he died. Told me she was married to a human."

"Halfbreed. He was Alpha progeny, and he was a good and decent man."

Brows rocketing into his hairline, Edward sat back." You knew him?"

"Before we loved the same woman, we were friends."

Edward blew out a breath. "Did Anique know he was one of us?"

"I'd known him for over ten years, and I didn't know he was one of us until he died. If he'd been born with a wolf, he could have survived. Anique could have forced his change and helped him heal."

Edward swallowed. "Will you complete the phases now?"

Glancing at Edward, I rubbed my lips together. Honesty was needed, but not in a way that tortured Anique. "We completed the phases already. Her grief in losing the man she loved opened the door for me. I took advantage of it. It's why I felt her pain at the banquet. It's why she ran away."

"It's not why she ran away, at least, it wasn't to run away from you," Edward countered.

"The graduation was a lie, Edward. She graduated when she finished studying, not because she finished her residency."

"I know," Edward watched his sister's face. "I knew that was a lie when she came to stay with me. I know my sister, Knox, and I know Anique was in the city with a purpose. By the extensive research she was doing and the smell of silver on her clothes when she came home, it was a purpose that was related to her injuries. At a guess."

Relief washed through me. I'd been so sure Anique's leaving was despair for what happened between us. Knowing that wasn't the case, well, it made my wolf happier.

Stepping through the curtain, Solomon picked up Anique's chart. "Anything?" He asked. Looking back to Anique, I shook my head. Walking over to the monitor, Solomon hit a few buttons on the screen. "See this? This is Annie when she's sleeping." He pressed another button. "This is what it looks like when she's awake. She's awake right now, but too weak to let us know it."

Picking up Anique's hand, I kissed her knuckles; Solomon watched but didn't say anything. "So, she'll hear what we are saying?" Edward asked.

"Yes, though she may not remember it as real when she finally wakes fully."

Edward kissed her forehead. "Thank you for sending Monique to meet me, and for protecting her. I know that's why you sent her away, in case you didn't win. She's beautiful, thank you for finally bringing her into my life."

When Edward stepped away, Solomon put the chart down. "I need to check her wounds. I'll get you both to wait outside until I'm done."

Rubbing my cheek against hers, I put my mouth to her ear. "I love you. When you are ready, I'm going to take you home, and we are going to let your wolf go for her first run. I met her last night, she's ready, Anique." Her hand gripped mine which made me smile. "It won't hurt now. You watch, after what you've been through, it will be a breeze." When her hand relaxed, I looked at Solomon. "She squeezed my hand."

"Good. Annie might wake before I finish my shift then." He indicated I leave, but when I tried to step away, Anique gripped my hand. Solomon saw it. "Okay, Annie, he can stay, but you try to claw his heart out again, and I'll shackle you to the bed."

Her hand relaxed, and I got the flutter of laughter beneath my ribs. "She thought that was funny."

Solomon looked to where I was rubbing my chest. "You two are connected?" I nodded without answering. "That's how you knew she was in pain and getting worse. Did Brett know about you two?"

"Yes." Anique's fingers twitched. "It's okay, Anique, I'll explain later. You just need to focus on waking up and giving me a smile."

Though I didn't catch the words that went with it, I felt her sarcasm. It made me chuckle. Solomon, slightly perplexed by what he was witnessing, pulled the screen entirely, then folded back Anique's bedsheets and lifted her gown.

It wasn't the horrendous gaping wound I was fearing. Anique's abdomen was bloated, but there were three insignificant cuts, one three times bigger than the others. Still, it was already pink and puckering in the stitches.

"She's healing quickly," Solomon told me. "I would expect to see this three days out from her surgery, not the next day." With his eyebrows drawn low, Solomon pressed down slightly in areas around her abdomen.

When he pressed near an old scar, I suddenly felt achy and queasy. "That hurt and made her want to vomit."

"It's where the silver was embedded."

"What's that beneath the tattoo?" She would lose that as soon as she shifted the first time.

"The guy who did this to her carved his initials in her when he was done, then left her for dead," Solomon growled, but it was nothing to my growl. I'd seen that part but had forgotten that specific detail as I tried to make sense of every other image flashing through my head at the time.

Covering her up, Solomon looked at the monitor. "She's sleeping again."

"Is this normal?"

"In my experience, the faster healers tend to shut down to put all their energy into healing," Solomon lowered his voice. "You've proven brain activity for me, now it's just allowing her body and mind to be ready." Solomon slid the screen back and continued on his rounds. Edward stepped in with a look on his face.

"Your dad?"

"He's safely home and under no threat that he can tell," Edward informed me. "He wants you and your team to come up."

"He's inviting my pack to your packhouse?" Despite having let Stirling and Edward come to mine, I was a more powerful wolf with a bigger pack. We could annihilate them, and they knew it.

"That's the thing," Edward whispered. "The pack isn't there. They've all been killed."

Tensing, I felt a flutter of anxiety in my chest. My eyes went to the monitor. Anique was still asleep, but I swear that was her reaction. Nodding to Edward, I sent a message to Dante to bring the team except Rion and Milton.

As I walked out, Solomon was coming back and giving a young nurse instruction. "You're leaving?"

"Something's come up, I've been called in." Writing my number on a piece of paper, I handed it to him. "If she wakes, please call me. I'm hoping to make it back before she wakes, but if I don't-"

"I'll let her know you were here," Solomon nodded, placing the paper neatly in his coat pocket.

Waiting in the car park for my team, Edward seemed calm, almost excited. "You're happy they are dead?"

"They raped and brutalized two of my sisters," Edward replied. "Not a pack I want to be Alpha of. I'm happy to start again."

"You know there is a chance your mate was involved in this. It doesn't worry you?"

"Do you think Anique is a cold-blooded killer?"

Remembering all the flashes of men screaming in pain that I'd witnessed this week; I assessed her emotions during them. "Cold-blooded? No. She wouldn't enjoy it."

Edward nodded. "I feel the same about Monique. She told me last night, what she's done, she did it to protect herself."

When Dante pulled up, Rhiannon and Evaline got out of the car with their mother and little Grace. "They are going to stay with Anique until we get back," Dante murmured quietly.

"Edward is coming with us," I informed them.

Rhiannon glared at her brother as he hopped in the car, then walked her mother inside. Milton walked up to me. "Why am I not coming?"

"You built a good rapport with Anique when the base was attacked. I need someone here who she trusts until I get back."

"Translation?"

"She wakes up, make sure she doesn't disappear on me again," I ordered.

"If her will could shift Dante, she's stronger than me," Milton reminded me quietly.

"And with the silver out, probably even stronger," I hazarded. "You, however, are stronger than both her sisters and mated to one who has a lot of sway with Anique. Convince your mate that my mate needs to stay put."

Lowering his eyes, Milton nodded then marched inside without a word. I knew I was asking him to risk his wife's ire, but that was my mate in there, and I needed to know she was somewhere safe. Dante drove, heading to the Beachrunners packhouse.

"You think this will be the same as the Barrows?" Dante asked.

"If it's who I think it is, yes," I answered simply. "Where are the others?"

"Waiting at the rest stop twenty minutes north of campus," Dante informed.

We drove in relative quiet until we pulled into the rest stop. Edward whistled in the back. "Nice Porsche. Now, who would leave a car like that abandoned here? Lucky it's not stripped."

While observing the car, something sparked in my memory. "That's a lot of mud on it," Dante pointed out.

"Pull up," I told him. He did, and I stepped out, ignoring the other car and marching straight to the Porsche. The driver's seat was stained with blood, and there was a police sticker on it, marking it waiting to be towed to the impound lot. Putting my fingers in my mouth, I whistled. My team was beside me in an instant.

"Alpha?"

"Anique was in this car, it's where they found her," I pointed to the blood. When I tried the door handle, I found it locked. "I want to see what's in the boot. I can smell another she-wolf in this car."

Stepping forward, Edgar sniffed. "It's weak but smells like one of the bitches who killed those men in Campus."

Taking out his phone, Edward opened an app I'd never seen before. Placing his phone by the car handle, he pressed the red button. A dial started turning, numbers coming up on the screen. A second later, the blinkers flashed, and the door unlocked.

"Should I ask?" Opening the door, I popped the bonnet because Porsche engines were in the back, and the luggage compartment was under the hood. Catching a whiff of a wolf's scent beneath the metallic saturation of Anique's blood, my hackles rose.

"Electrical engineering was my major with a minor in computers. I work for an auto electrical company now," Edward informed us, as if that should explain why he had an app that could hack car security systems. "We specialize in developing the security systems in cars, so we tend to be able to override them as well."

"And you have an app for that?" Sasha asked.

"There's an app for everything," Edward smirked.

Opening the bonnet, I pulled out the bag in it. "This isn't Anique's, her's was in the back seat." On top was a file which had a photo of Dan and an address. Beside it was a small mostly empty vial. Pulling the stopper, I took a whiff. "That's not wolfsbane," I stated, handing it to Edgar to confirm.

The rest of the bag was just clothes. Putting everything back in the bag, I handed it to Sasha. "When we get home, I want to know what was in that vial." Moving to the passenger door, I called Edward over. "Use your nose."

He did, his eyes widening. "There is no way Anique would hop in the same car as Dan willingly."

Grabbing Anique's bag, I circled my finger in the air. "Lock it up. Let's go."

"What are you thinking, Alpha?" Dante asked after several quiet kilometers on the road.

"Either Anique sent one of her wolves to take out Dan, or the other bitch conspired with Dan to get Anique."

"Mandy did say Danielle challenged her," Dante offered.

"Let's wait until we see what's waiting for us before we speculate," Edgar advised. "There are too many possibilities, and the only facts we know is that a bitch and wolf were in that car before Anique drove it here. She possibly stole the car to get away."

Edgar was right; we couldn't jump to conclusions. "Sasha, run the plates, I want to know who the registration of the car belongs too."

Opening his phone, Sasha started typing a message. It took thirty minutes for him to get a reply. "Rion says the car is Anique's. She's owned it nearly six years now."

"What?" Edward looked skeptical. "She owns that car but catches the train everywhere?"

"Edward has a valid point, she even caught the train to my wedding," Dante agreed.

"She had just finished a seventy-hour shift. She probably caught the train to be safe and get some sleep," I challenged.

"Check the owner's history," Edward told Sasha. "If dad bought the car for Anique, I'm going to be having a word. He told me he only bought her the house, just like he did me. I'll be shitty if she got a Porsche."

We waited for Rion to respond. "Car previously was registered to-" Sasha stared at the screen. "That can't be right. It used to belong to Michael Venture."

"The Alpha of the Venture pack?" Dante frowned.

"Didn't Mandy say Anique saved Monique from the Venture pack?" Edward asked quietly in the back.

"Yes. The Ventures found and took Monique and Anique seven years ago. Anique killed the Alpha to escape. She must have escaped in his car and kept it."

'He liked to collect silver blades,' Mandy's voice rang in my head, the same time the image of Anique with a silver blade flashed through my consciousness. I didn't voice my concerns, though.

"The spoils of war," Edgar chuckled, then the car returned to quiet.

When we arrived at the Beachrunners, Edward guided us down the forest drive. "Where does that track lead?" I asked, seeing the visible signs of recent traffic down a muddy path.

"The cottage. No one has been down there since-" voice cutting off with a snarl, Edward didn't finish. He didn't need to say it.

Stirling was waiting out the front when we pulled up. He didn't stand up, just sat on the front step, and waved us in. The smell of blood was evident the moment you stepped inside. There were splashes of it everywhere. Whatever happened here had been brutal, but fast to overcome a pack of wolves.

"Where are the bodies?" Edgar asked.

"Follow me." Stepping back inside, Stirling led us out through the kitchen. In the clearing behind the house, was the still-smoldering remnants of a bonfire. Drag marks and blood were pointing to it. As we got closer, the smell of charred flesh was unmistakable, and Edward recoiled in disgust. My team had smelled it enough times before.

"Whatever the accelerant was, it was effective considering that storm last night." Considering the sky, then the fire, Dante eventually looked at me. "You have that look on your face."

"What look?"

"The look that says you don't think this is the worst of it."

"The worst thing about that look is he is usually right," Sasha bemoaned.

"Stirling, you were here until the day before the wedding, right?" I asked.

"Yes."

"Edward said the cottage hadn't been used since Anique's attack? So, why was the track to it freshly used?"

Both Edward and Stirling turned to look in a particular direction. That's where I started walking, everyone falling in around me. The cottage was further away from the house than I expected. "No wonder it made the perfect place to rape and torture," I muttered. "No one comes here unless they are going to use it, do they?"

"No," Stirling confessed.

"This is why we send ours on a honeymoon. Having a cottage that's never checked gives your enemy a base of operations they can attack from," I schooled.

We were walking for a good half an hour before the smell hit me. It wasn't just the burned flesh, but the scent of bitches and silver. A clearing opened around the remains of the cottage, effectively just a pile of charred rubble, which made it easy to see the she-wolf lying dead on the far side.

Standing over the body of the bitch, I remembered seeing her at White's funeral. "This must be Danielle," I decided. "Edgar?"

Edgar had his gloves on. He rolled her, and we studied her injuries. Most weren't severe, even the cut on her leg wouldn't have been fatal, but it didn't look like it had started healing either.

Sniffing all her wounds, Edgar recoiled from the leg. "Silver blade covered in a strong concentration of Wolfsbane." Standing up, he looked back at the cottage. "She was able to walk out of that. I'd say she thought she defeated Anique, torched the place, and dropped out here from the poison."

"Tainted meat, the animals won't eat it. Burn the body, bury what's left." Turning away, I walked back to the cottage where the others were picking through the mess. "Dante?"

"We've got four skulls over in this corner, another center of the cottage," he pointed out the remains they'd uncovered. He walked me over to the other side and pointed.

Crouching down, I studied the disfigured blades among the ashes. "Silver blades tainted with Wolfsbane."

'He liked to collect silver blades.'

Standing up, I looked at Stirling. "I believe our conversation about how to deal with this issue is now invalid. I think you will find this was Dan and his four mates who raped and beat your youngest."

"That doesn't mean that Anique did this," Stirling mourned. "She may have been lured here by that other bitch."

"Possibly," I acceded, my eyes falling to Edward, who was pointedly staying quiet. "Or, your daughter saw her sister's banquet as an opportunity to clean house."

"You said this has been happening for years, and Anique hadn't been involved," Stirling debated. He didn't want to believe Anique was capable of this.

"Never this clean, never this organized," I assessed.

"Never this deadly," Dante added, studying the knives. "It was always a sloppy messy affair before this. The only other clean massacre was-" Dante didn't say it, but when I met his eyes, I knew what he was thinking because I was already feeling it.

"I think it's clear what happened here, Stirling," I turned, my mind made up. "Mandy said Anique beat Danielle, she didn't say she killed her. Obviously, this bitch left, Dan found her and brought her here planning to do to her what he did to Anique. However, he picked the wrong she-wolf to abuse this time, and after she finished killing this lot, she went to the packhouse and killed them. When she came back here to start the fire, one of the wolves, who lay dying, cut her with one of these blades. She died before she could escape."

Stirling studied me for a moment. It wasn't just his daughter we were protecting, but his future daughter-in-law. He gave a solid nod. "Then best we clean up the house before your mother gets back, Edward. Thank you for coming, Knox."

"My men will take care of the remnants, bury them respectfully," I assured. Behind me, Dante snickered where he could see my fingers crossed behind my back. Stirling's lips twitched a little letting me know he got the sarcasm.

Waiting until his father was out of earshot, Edward shook my hand. "I told you, I know my sister, she would only kill to protect. Now, it was safe for me to meet my mate." With a wink, he walked away.

"What did he mean by that?" Sasha inquired.

"It means he knew why Anique went to the city." Moving to where Edgar was burying the remains of the five who desecrated my mate, I stood over the grave, placed my feet, and unzipped my fly.

"Which was?" Sasha pushed.

Urinating on the skulls of the dead, I literally pissed in their eyes. "To give Monique a safe home."

"She's saved her twice now," Dante said, joining in my respect for these wolves.

"And Monique knows it," I nodded, finishing up.

One by one, my men all let the worth of those five bastards be known. Then Edgar, who had returned by driving one of the cars down the track, stacked it with kindling, added some kerosene, and placed Danielle's body in it.

"She looks like a bitch that's into kink," Edgar chuckled as he stood back up. Unzipping, he relieved himself into her mouth. "Yeah, this bitch is such a golden showers chick."

"Edgar, really?"

"She tried to kill your mate, Alpha. Just showing my respect for my new Luna," Edgar answered cheekily. Zipping up, Edgar lit a match and tossed it into the pit. Flames erupted and engulfed the body. "We'll stay and finish the burial when it's over. You should go back to your mate." Edgar pointed to the track. "Take the road, it's faster."

Nodding, I turned, taking the path to get back to the packhouse and our other car. Dante and Sasha following along. "Be glad the body is already burning," Dante murmured. "He might have wanted to kink that bitch another way."

Snarling in disgust, I didn't deny it. Edgar was one of those odd buggers. He was a good man, loyal to his pack, but he didn't mind doing the dirty work. He'd been my father's enforcer, and some of the stories he'd told me... let's just say, I wouldn't put what Dante suggested passed Edgar. "His poor wife."

Sasha and Dante laughed, understanding immediately.

32

ANIQUE

It felt like I'd been doing tequila shots for a week straight. After trying a few times to open my eyes, I successfully managed to crack the seal of darkness. The room was blurry, my mouth was dry, and there was no mistaking the sound of the hospital. When I opened my mouth to ask what the hell happened, the flashes of the policeman catching me, the blood and the pain, Danielle and the wall of flames started.

Something cold touched my lips. "Drink." Closing my lips around the straw, I sucked the ice water. I was grateful for the person holding that straw to my mouth.

"Anything?" Eric asked. "Oh, she's awake."

Releasing the straw, I forced my eyes open towards the sound of Eric's voice. "What happened?" I rasped.

Touching my shoulder, Eric explained. He told me the silver shrapnel was removed, and they managed to save the artery without too much damage. "Did I need blood?" I still remembered too well the horrible feeling of loss the last time human blood was in me. Strangely, I wasn't feeling that this time.

"Yes. You received four different transfusions, but on advice from a specialist in your area, we only gave you other AB positive blood," Eric explained.

"Specialist?" Eric looked to my other side. Knox stood holding the cup of ice water. He wasn't smiling, just watching me. "Your blood?"

"And Evaline, Dante, and Mandy. We all donated so you would have the best possible chance of surviving," Knox clarified humbly.

"How do you feel?" Eric asked.

"Disoriented, like I've drunk a bottle of tequila plus the worm, but I feel like me. More so than I have since-" Flashes of mutilated bodies and Dan.

Watching me, Knox took my hand in his. "You're here, that's what matters."

Seeing Eric writing on my chart, I put my hand out for it. "Not yet, Annie. We need to discuss some things, but I want to wait until your head clears to do that. We can get you out of intensive care in the morning. Tomorrow, we can talk things through."

Eric took my chart with him, so I couldn't steal it later. Sighing, I looked at Knox. "How long have you been here?"

"Just covering the shift change. Your sisters left about an hour ago, Mandy is coming down when her shift finishes."

"I dreamed about you."

"I dreamed about you too."

"You begged me to stay."

Knox kissed my hand. "I had that dream too." The silence stretched between us. "I need to tell you something. White, he was one of us." Frowning, I shook my head. "Halfbreed, very rare, and he didn't develop a wolf. His pack cast him out, but he was the Alpha's bastard, and he knew about us."

Mortified, I stared blankly as my world unraveled. "Then, I could have saved him, I could have-"

Knox placed his hand gently on my shoulder. "You can't force a man to shift if he hasn't got a wolf, Anique. You know that. It would have been the equivalent of me trying to force you to shift while the silver disabled you. You couldn't have saved him, none of us could." He was gentle and reassuring, but the ache was still in me.

"I needed to tell you because when Henderson took White's stuff to his father, they caught your scent and wanted to know where to find you," Knox kept his voice calm. "Dante has called the Whitetails and informed them that while you were married to White, you met your true-mate in the Valleymorgans and belong to us now. We've agreed to let them meet Caprice, to see if she fits their pack."

"But the Whitetails are-" Horrified at the thought of such a pack seeking me out, being responsible for bringing Brett into the world and raising him.

"They are good to their own kind, Anique. They don't mistreat their women. White was raised by them, and they raised him well, he just couldn't stay when he failed to take a wolf," Knox reassured.

"Because he was more human, so they would have treated him as below them," I nodded understanding. Knox squeezed my hand. Mandy stepped into the space. Seeing me awake, she hugged me tightly and I whimpered a little in her grasp. Knox stood up to leave, but I gripped his hand. "Can you stay?"

"I'll come back. I need to eat and the food here is unforgivable. There's a burger place across the road that's to die for." Knox winked. The bastard knew that was my favorite place to eat and was teasing me.

"If you don't bring me their double bacon and smoked cheeseburger, you'll die alright. I'm starving," I whined.

"I don't know if you're allowed to eat yet," Knox replied, worried.

"Has it been twenty-four hours?" Knox nodded. "I can eat. Bring me a burger, or I'll walk over there in my hospital gown to get one myself."

Smirking, Knox rubbed his top lip and left. Mandy sat beside me on the bed. "He's barely left your side," she murmured. "You died, and he couldn't handle that, but he came back when you did." Sighing, I put my hand in hers. "They found the bodies," her voice dropped lower. "Your father called Knox up to investigate. He knows."

My hand tensed in hers, then relaxed. I was exhausted yet energized. "How far are you and Rion?"

"The second phase, he knows my secrets now, and I know his," Mandy cuddled in beside me. "It didn't seem to bother him."

"Knox would have prepared him."

Mandy put her head against mine. "You were pregnant, but you lost the baby." Swallowing, I closed my eyes. "When did you two manage that?"

Holding the tears in, I squeezed her hand and switched into doctor mode. "Go find my chart for me?"

Coming back two minutes later, Mandy handed it to me and took the chair. Reading it for several minutes, I eventually sighed and gave it back to her. Lifting her brow, Mandy tucked it beside her." What's the prognosis, Doc? Good or bad?"

"I should be able to shift now."

"But?"

"The metal poisoning is still there, and there will be scar tissue from the surgery, which could prevent a family."

"Does that upset you?"

"No, but I understand now what I was feeling from Knox. He lost his child too."

"Not everyone knows it's his. The humans think it belonged to your husband, so they are wrapping you in cotton wool." Rising out of the chair, Mandy squeezed my hand, then took the chart back out. When she came back, we just lay there holding hands and watching the television until Knox returned. "I might head off," Mandy squeezed my hand. "I have a date with Rion."

Letting her go, I assessed my ability to sit up. Placing my burger on the table, Knox helped me sit up. "Are you in pain?"

"A little uncomfortable, but I don't feel too bad."

"My blood has made you heal faster. Once your body gets its blood supply back, with the silver gone, you should start healing like the rest of us."

Eating my burger, I felt so much better by the time it was done. "Real food makes a difference," Knox advised, taking his time with his own meal. "Do you remember what you did?"

"Some," I confessed.

"I know why you did it. If it had been purely revenge, I might feel differently, but I realize now, every time you've taken a life, you did it to protect your pack. Considering what I do for a living, I can't be angry about that. No Alpha could."

Waiting on saying anything because there was a big but coming, I bit my lip. Yet, Knox never voiced it. He sat there thinking deeply about how he wanted to word what troubled him, and at the same time, I don't think he truly wanted to know. So, I let us lapse into silence, and eventually, I fell back to sleep. Knox was sitting there, holding my hand, his eyes closed and breathing steady as if the simple touch of my hand was peaceful to him. Then again, his hand in mine was much the same.

An ache bloomed in my chest, telling me I didn't have the right to feel this way. Brett only died three weeks ago, I should want his hand in mine, and I did, but it wasn't the same as this calm. Knox still held my hand when I was moved to general the next morning. He only left my side when Eric came by for rounds and to examine my wounds. It was at this point Eric told me the news. When I didn't burst into tears, he patted my hand and left, but the guilt of what I'd done, sleeping with Knox the night of Brett's funeral, it ate at me.

When Knox came back in, he took my hand and met my eyes.

"In your time, Anique. I'll wait." With his hand in mine, I fell asleep crying.

The curtains slid back, and I opened my eyes to see Nathan coming to my other side. He saw Knox's hand in mine, and instantly his eyes became hostile. "I loved him. So, much it hurts to breathe without him," I pleaded for him to understand.

Nathan looked to Knox and away again.

"It doesn't take the pain away; it just makes it bearable." At the accusation in his eyes, I shook my head, tears falling down my cheek. "I'm not ready for that." I lifted my eyes to the roof. "I'm not ready for this."

Nathan looked to Knox for an explanation. "They told her," Knox murmured from beside me.

Face softening, Nathan placed the flowers he carried on the table and took my free hand. We sat like that quietly until the next lot of rounds. The nurse kindly suggested the boys go get some dinner while I have my first shower in a few days.

Walking was easy. Since I was managing, the nurse left me alone. Cleaning up, I grabbed my gear and left. I didn't want to be in that bed anymore. I hadn't been discharged, and I knew Eric would spew chips, but I had to get outside, to breathe fresh air, to run.

Walking to the bushland behind the hospital, I dumped my gear beneath some bushes and felt the change come over me. It was supposed to hurt the first time, but after years of the silver burn whenever my wolf came forward, the shift washed over me like a wave of relief.

My humanity melted away, my senses and thoughts were overtaken by my wolf. Sheer ecstasy raced through our veins at finally being free to roam. Racing through the darkening forest, we enjoyed taking fur form. Dashing deep into the woods, we hunted our first prey and ate, then ran more. At this point, I wasn't in control, and I didn't want to be.

My wolf had waited a long time to be in her fur form and run. So now that she was free, that's what she did. Running away from the hospital, away from Campus, and away from my skin.

My wolf wasn't being selfish, she wasn't demanding her time after too many years trapped in my skin. She was doing what was best for both of us. She wanted her mate, but she understood, I was grieving for the man I'd loved for six years. He'd been one of us. An alpha. If I'd never met my mate, Brett would have been strong enough for us. My wolf had loved him too until Knox came along, so she understood my loss.

The wolf wanted her mate, wanted us both to be happy again, so she gave me time. As the days washed into nights, as our focus was solely on hunting to survive and exploring our new surroundings, I lost track of time. We lost track of home. Soon, she started pushing at me, wanting something from me, but I couldn't tell what it was. Floating in my isolation, I enjoyed the stars at night and the sun by day.

A crushing sadness filled my insides, a longing for something lost, but not gone. Something that was in easy reach, that she could feel, but I wasn't understanding. The wolf tried to encourage me to seek it out, but I couldn't understand what it was anymore. Helpless with my inability to understand, the wolf lifted her snout to the moon and howled.

She sang a song of yearning, and then she cried for help.

33

KNOX

---

*D*espair with a side of guilt. That's what waited behind the curtain where Anique was only an hour before. "Where is she?" Henderson asked the nurse. The nurse checked in the shower, then the ward. Opening the cupboard, I found her clothes and wallet gone.

"She's left," I informed Henderson. An ache I associated with not knowing where Anique was, if she was safe, burst to life inside me. It wasn't new, I'd caused this pain to start with and lived with it for months until I found her again.

"Wait," Henderson stopped me when I turned to leave. "Did she go home?"

"Does she have a home?"

Shaking his head, Nathan swiped his hand across his brow. "Let me get the guys, you get yours, we can search together."

That wouldn't work. "You look around her old haunts, you'll know them better than me. I'll contact Mandy and see if she knows anywhere, and I'll try her family up north."

"Okay, let me know if you find her."

Once I was away from Henderson, I called Dante to organize

the boys. Walking into the nature reserve, I started trying to find Anique's scent. It had changed since the operation, all our different types of blood circulating inside her. With my blood and smell the most dominant, I was getting turned around by my own scent. Frustrated, I stopped.

"Alpha," Dante arrived with the others an hour later, "Any luck?"

"Her scent is being masked by my own. I've searched between here and the hospital, but I'm getting lost in my own smell. I need someone else to track her until we find where she shifted."

"You're sure she went wolf?" Dante queried.

"Eight years unable to," I reminded him, "how long do you think your wolf would wait once you could?"

Dante turned to Milton. "You track towards the base, Rion, backtrack to the hospital, Sasha, you go that way. Howl when you find her bitch scent." Shifting, they took off. Dante waited until we were alone to talk. "What are you feeling?"

"She wanted time. Her wolf is giving her what she needs."

"You're worried about how long?" Dante shifted uncomfortably.

"There is a reason we always supervise the first five changes."

"She's strong and intelligent, Alpha," Dante tried to allay.

"She's emotional and unsure of herself, which is more worrying." We started walking through the woods. "I need to find her."

We walked for a good twenty minutes before the howl went up. Dante and I ran through the trees to reach the place where Milton was sniffing. He pointed behind him at Anique's clothes, then lifted branches of a bush and pulled the rest of her gear out from beneath it. "She's gone wolf," Milton confirmed. "If you smell her clothes, you'll get her scent and be able to track her."

When I breathed her in, my wolf enjoyed the scent of his mate, and then I started undressing. "Give her stuff to Dante, get a radio collar, and follow me at a distance. Once we find her, signal Rion to come and get us."

"Yes, Alpha," Milton nodded, handing off Anique's gear and running back to where the car would be. I gave Dante my phone as I started to undress.

"What if work calls?" Dante queried.

"I'm not coming back until Anique comes with me, so you'll have to tell them I'm taking leave."

"I'll submit a leave request when I get back," Dante informed.

Letting the change wash over me, I caught Anique's scent, and then I was gone. It wasn't a matter of just running after her because I needed to follow the smell, so my following after her was much slower than her just running off into the forest. More than two hours behind her already, she only got further away with every passing minute.

It took a good two hours of following her scent before I realized in which direction I was heading. Shifting back to skin form, I walked to the end of the bluff and smiled down on the ValleyMorgan packhouse in Paw Valley. Taking a seat, I waited there for Milton to catch up. He did in under half an hour and shifted. "Home?" He asked, eyebrows jumping high.

"It would make sense," I informed him, proud of Anique for her survival instinct. "She lived here how long, and we never encountered her. She scouted us out, possibly scouted our entire territory, keeping enough distance not to alert us to her presence."

"Do you think she went to the house?"

"No," I turned my eyes north. "Remember when the Infinity pack disappeared, and we took over the territory?" Milton nodded. "There was a cave not far from our border."

"And you think that's where Anique has gone?"

"I think her wolf took her somewhere safe to grieve, but within close proximity to us, so when she was ready, she wouldn't have far to go."

Mouth dropping open, Milton swore under his breath. "Well, she didn't hide in our territory five years by being stupid."

Getting up, I indicated he press the talk button on the radio collar he wore. Touching it, Milton waited for Rion to answer. "You found her?"

"We have an idea of where to find her. Tell everyone the old Infinity territory is off-limits for now. Milton will mark the border, so everyone knows where to stop."

"Will pass it along, Alpha." The comms disconnected.

"Mark the old border, then head back to the packhouse. Pack a camp bag for me and include communication. I'm going to set up camp just inside our border and wait until Anique is ready to come to me."

Shifting, Milton dashed off to perform his task. Flowing back to fur, I hunted down my bitch. It took another few hours to find her, but when I did, I kept my distance, lowered myself to the ground, and watched as she frolicked and played. Enjoying seeing her happy, I reached out to Anique, but she wasn't anywhere near in control. The joy was the wolf's alone, but even she held grief at her core. My concern for Anique only grew when I realized she had no comprehension of what her wolf was doing.

Eyeing where I lay watching her, the she-wolf paused her play. Lifting the side of her lip, she twitched it in a warning. She didn't mind me being here, just as long as I kept my distance, and we didn't force the issue. As dawn threatened the sky, the she-wolf sought sleep within the cave. Leaving my scent for her to follow, I headed back to my territory.

Milton found me just on dawn with a camp pack. Shifting, I dressed in the warm clothes he'd brought. "Is she okay?"

"She's given her wolf free reign."

Milton paused with his eyes full of sympathy.

"I can bring her back from this. I just have to wait until the bitch is ready to help me."

"And if she doesn't want to help?"

"She would have chased me off," I relaxed. "She knows I'm her mate. The she-wolf is giving Anique what she needs, and enjoying her first chance to play, but she'll want to be with me just as much. Our bond will play in my favor."

"So, your plan is...?"

"To let her know I understand, and that I'm willing to wait," I assured. "And I'm going to do that close enough for her to feel me but give her enough distance that she'll also miss me."

"How long do you think?"

"I'm hoping only a few days. Any longer and luring Anique to change is going to be difficult."

Milton handed me a satellite phone. "Call if you need anything."

Taking the phone, I went about setting up camp. "You know where to find me if anything needs dealing with."

My pack knew this was my issue. I was the Alpha, and Anique was a strong Alphia. If she lost her human self to her wolf, she could be impossible to bring back. Despite the odds, I was hoping our bond and Anique's determination to survive, would be enough to draw her back when the time was right. I just had to bide my time.

Three days later, I approached again, I couldn't stay back and watch any longer. Trotting towards my mate casually in fur form, I shouldered the playful wolf. Lifting her nuzzle, she licked me, then showed the deference expected. We greeted each other as mates, but she didn't offer herself to me. Our wolves were just like the animal versions, so the females only mated in fur during their heat. In skin form, they didn't have to be in heat to conceive, but the chances were almost a hundred percent if it was during a bitch's heat.

Anique's wolf and my wolf discussed Anique's absence. When I called to Anique, I got nothing. The only thing giving me hope was that her wolf could still feel her; otherwise, I would have had to mourn my mate.

While we communicated, her wolf tried to encourage Anique

to pay attention, to recognize me, and to recognize herself. That's when we realized the problem. Anique had forgotten her skin form. She wasn't aware that she wasn't in her natural state.

The she-wolf asked for time to coax her back, to visit places that should spark her memory. Hesitant to allow her to go alone, I acceded when the she-wolf insisted it was better that way. Showing her where to find me, I let her go.

During this time, Dante filled me in on what was happening at home. Leaving the boundary, I went home to attend to my duties as Alpha. Two days later, I was making my way back to the campsite when I heard my mate sing a song of mourning to the moon. Panic filled me. Had she lost Anique completely?

It was too much to bear, the idea of losing her again. I shouldn't have let her go off alone. The only places to remind Anique of her human-self would evoke memories of Brett, of the thing Anique was trying to forget. Perhaps, the reminder drove her beyond saving. Picking up my pace, grief already suffusing my heart, I raced to my mate. Then she cried for help.

Stopping, I sniffed the air and caught the whiff of two male wolves who weren't Valleymorgans . Throwing my head back, I howled silently for my pack. The collar at my neck vibrated with the alert I sent. Then I was racing to the aid of my mate.

There was no need to hunt her, I knew if she returned to where she came. Slowing as I approached the campsite, I scouted the scene. A wolf, strong, but not an Alpha, was facing off with my she-wolf. They circled each other keeping each other insight, but my mate wasn't fooled, she knew there were two. She'd circle only part of the way, then quickly dash in another direction and circle that way. She made it look like she was trying for the other wolf's throat, but I knew Anique was strategic.

Taking note of the wolf's behavior, I circled around to the area to which Anique refused to turn her back. Sure enough, that's where the other wolf was crawling forward to try and pounce from. The attacking wolf was attempting to maneuver Anique towards him, and both were getting frustrated by her unusual attack pattern. Sneaking forward, I prepared my footing, then launched.

The wolf was too focused on Anique and didn't even hear me. When I landed beside him, he jumped, lifting his head. Snatching his throat, I pinned him back down on the ground and growled menacingly. Easily stronger than this wolf, I held him down until he knew it too. He submitted with nothing more than a whimper. His pack mate, distracted by my attack, took his eyes off Anique for a moment. The she-wolf didn't hesitate. Lunging forward, she grabbed her attacker's throat in her teeth and started shaking her head vigorously.

'He's not a rabbit,' I laughed watching her.

Forcing her opponent to the ground, she raked her claws through the fur of his chest. Blood splattered the ground. Clenching her jaw a moment longer, she released him and moved away. Watching as the she-wolf circled the wounded wolf, I was unsure if she was going to attack again.

Turning my focus to the wolf at my feet, I threw my will at him. *'Shift!'*

Shivering violently, the wolf vibrated into his skin form. He was a small man, but there was cunning in his eyes, telling me his rank in the pack was achieved through his intelligence, not strength. I snarled at him.

"I get it," he spluttered. "I'm not stupid."

Stepping back as my pack ran into the clearing, I left this one for my men to deal with. Anique's wolf was lying on the ground watching the man in his skin form with her head tilted. Gazing at the wolf she'd maimed, Anique slowly lifted herself from the earth and approached him.

'Alpha?' Dante worried.

'Let her do what she needs to do.'

We all watched as the she-wolf prodded the injured wolf. When he whimpered at her, she looked to the one in skin form then back to him. Even I could see what she wanted. The wolf whined but didn't comply. Poking him with her paw this time, Anique waited, getting impatient. Studying her, I saw a flash of awareness and felt hope.

'Milton, shift in full view of Anique, and tell the wolf to shift now.'

Padding into the circle, Milton gained my she-wolfs attention. Barking once, he threatened her not to go for his sausage, then flowed from fur to skin. Head flipping to the side, Anique sat back on her hindquarters.

"She's shocked," Milton surmised as he turned a smile to me. "She just licked her lips looking at my dick, Alpha." When I growled, Milton laughed and went to the man leaning against the tree. "Tell your packmate to shift now, or we kill you both."

34

ANIQUE

It was the adrenalin that brought me out of my free existence. A surge of anger and fear so strong, I couldn't ignore it. Opening my eyes, I saw the world through muted colors. This confused me; I remembered the world as brighter.

A wolf was approaching me slowly, showing his teeth in a threatening manner. Snarking back, I surprised myself because that wasn't the thought I'd had. That's when I realized I wasn't in control, that another consciousness was running the show. Spying something as the unwelcome wolf circled me, I tapped the sentience on the figurative shoulder. *'There's another one.'*

Immediately, we lunged towards the wolf before us, changing direction at the last second, so we could reach the other side, putting us far away from the second wolf. The consciousness brushed mine, a flurry of pictures in my mind. A bigger wolf, *a friend, a lover,* and the assurance he was coming.

The wolf lunged at me. We dodged and circled. Then we realized he was moving us towards the hidden wolf. We jumped him this time. This dance continued a few more rounds of the campsite.

'Campsite? Is this my campsite?'

A negative response and then images of that bigger wolf again, *friend, lover,* and the assurance he was coming to help. Almost as soon as the pictures finished, we heard a wolf whimper and caught a glimpse of that bigger wolf taking down the hidden one.

The wolf before us was distracted. Leaping at him, we snarled, grabbing his throat and taking him down. He tensed beneath us, ready to try something, but we jumped our body free, keeping our jaws tight. Pushing for control of my body, I raked my claws down his torso.

Whimpering, the wolf dropped limp. Squeezing his throat in warning, he whined, and we backed away. Checking on the bigger wolf, *friend, lover* - oh the images she gave me for that one, but he wasn't an animal in those, well, not the fur kind - he demanded the other wolf shift.

Trembling violently on the ground, the wolf almost vibrated into a man. Legs going out from beneath me, I gaped. The wolf was a man. He wasn't a pure animal. Flashes of other men shifting before me spun through my consciousness, females too, some attacking, some running with me. Fascinated, I looked to the wolf we'd taken down. *'Can he shift too?'*

Confirmation came from the other consciousness.

Wandering over, we sniffed him. *'Make him change.'* We poked him; he whimpered but stayed in his fur.

One of the wolves who came with our friend padded into the center of the campsite. Images flashed in my mind of him in skin form, of a rather large penis, and a do not bite sign pasted over it. Grimacing in disgust, I huffed, which made him laugh. Then he shifted.

I was excited - not by his only slightly over imagined sausage - but wondering if I could do that. Images of a female with cherry-red hair and green eyes flashed like mad in my head. Getting a headache, I groaned. The flurry of images stopped on one of a blond woman shifting to wolf form and trying to attack me.

As a woman, I stopped her and demanded she shift, forcing her back to skin. The images went wild again, sights and smell filtering in, and then there was a wolf lying hurt in a battlefield. Gazing across the clearing, I recognized him, standing right by the strong one, *friend, lover, Alpha*... And I'd forced the injured wolf to skin form.

The consciousness brushed against me like a pet wanting pats, but the intention was clear. Moving forward to the wolf I'd just maimed, I stood over him. He hesitated with my being there. Focusing on how I made the others shift, I forced my will on this wolf. Howling in pain, the wolf tensed then exploded into human form, wet serum splashing over everything around him, including me. Jumping back, I started shaking to try and get the muck off me. I didn't like it; I didn't want his muck on me.

Vicious memories of being held down, of other men forcing their muck on me, flashed in my head. Whimpering, I tried harder to get it off. Suddenly, a bottle of water was being poured over me, washing the muck off my fur. Glaring up at the man who joked about his sausage, I whimpered.

"There you go, Anique. I know how you Alpha's don't like to get your paws dirty," he teased. Growling, I snapped at his dangling sausage. He jumped away laughing, not even worried I intended to bite him. "Now, now, your sister would be distraught if you did that. This big bastard is why Rhi fell in love with me, you know."

Growling, I shook the water off me, splashing him.

"Really?!" he groaned.

A wolf barked, getting my attention. The Alpha stepped forward, making sure I was watching, then he shifted, fluid-like, and seamlessly. One minute he was on all fours as a wolf, the next, he was standing before me as a man. His cock was bigger. "Grab a set of pants from my bag, Milton, then throw me mine."

'*Knox*,' his name came to me. Watching me, he smiled. He caught his pants and put them on. Whining, I was a little disappointed at him covering up his beauty. Knox laughed, so did Milton.

"Should have shifted and stood naked before her days ago, Alpha," Milton teased. "Apparently, your cock really made an impression."

Ignoring his packmate, Knox squatted to be at eye level with me. "Your turn, Anique." Tilting my head, I stared at him. "Annie? Would you prefer Annie?"

That name flicked a switch, my headache growing as years of memories crammed into that name. *Brett*. Oh, Goddess! Brett. It was all coming back now. Meeting the man I would love and marry, and then watching him die.

Knox. Memories were there for him too. Good, bad, the kitchen table, the bedroom, and the hospital when I tried to kill him because I lost Brett. The bathroom mirror.

'I love you.'

Whimpering, I dropped to the ground, hiding my nuzzle in my paws.

"I know you miss him, Annie. We all do," Knox soothed. "No one expects you to get over him. You never will. He was my friend, he had you, my true-mate, and I never challenged him for you. I don't expect you to stop loving him or forget him. I do expect you to remember how to live, to remember being you, to be Dr. Annie White, and save lives in his memory."

Turning one ear to his words, I cringed as more memories crammed in my already crowded head.

"I hope you can love me one day, as much as you loved him," Knox continued, "but I will never ask you to forget him."

The consciousness brushed across me again, urging me to go to Knox, to be with him as the feisty redheaded doctor she portrayed. I would have laughed at the impression my wolf had of me. Fierce and determined, strong and capable, good and kind. Lifting my snout, I watched Knox.

"Milton, hand me that shirt," Knox pointed to his rucksack. Throwing the shirt to his Alpha, Milton stepped back. This time, when Knox spoke, he spoke with an authority that even I had to obey. "It's time to come home, Annie. It's time to live again."

He held out a hand towards me and images of my sisters shifting, of Mandy, Danielle, and Monique flowing into their wolves played in my mind. Pressing up from my crouch, I imagined flowing gracefully into the redheaded woman I saw in the mirror. Reaching out my paw to Knox, I surged upwards, feeling like I was standing in the water at the beach and wave after wave was passing over me. My hand connected with Knox's, and he stood with me as those waves raised me up.

Knox smiled, eyes glassy with pride and relief as he looked over me. My hand in his was delicate and pale. "Knox," I breathed his name, a shiver passing through my body, "I'm really cold."

Laughing, Knox pulled me against him, hugging me tight and letting me steal his body heat. "Don't ever run away like that again, Annie. I thought I lost you for good. It broke my heart. I never want to feel like that again."

His despair was mildew in the air, but his relief at holding me again was burning it away. Through our bond, there was an understanding for the pain in my heart because by losing me, he understood what I felt for Brett. Knox knew no one could ever cure him of me, so no one should expect to cure me of the man I'd loved with all my heart, even my true-mate.

Slipping the shirt over my head, Knox held me tighter still. He didn't try to kiss me, though, I could feel the desire to kiss every inch of me just in sheer relief. "Please, come home?" Knox hushed against my ear, his hand finger combing my hair.

"Lead the way," I whispered, calming his anxiety that I would still reject him. "I'm desperate for a hot shower." Just to press my point, I shivered in his arms.

Stepping away, Knox went to another bag. The other wolves and Milton had distanced themselves, giving us space and privacy. The two intruders had been moved to the far side of the clearing, well away from me. Opening the bag, Knox pulled out a pile of clothes, shoes and all, handing them to me. "Get dressed, your sisters will be relieved to see you."

Tears running down my face still from the onslaught of emotions, I took the clothes and started dressing while Knox packed up the campsite. "What about them?" I asked, pointing to the stray wolves.

"They belong to Brett's birth pack. The ones who threw him out and wanted nothing to do with him until he died and left a bitch widowed," Knox informed me. "What would you do with them?"

Glaring at the wolves, I knew what I wanted to do to them for dismissing Brett and then hunting me. Sighing, I closed my eyes. When I opened them again, I looked at Knox. "It is your call, Alpha. I just want a shower and a warm bed." Stepping closer to him, I fisted the shirt and jacket he'd put on and lowered my voice. "A warm chest to rest my head on, and strong arms to hold me, so I know I'm safe."

Knox was happy, I could feel it, but hesitant just the same. Hugging me for a second, he kissed my forehead. "I can do that. Let's go." Taking my hand, Knox made a gesture with his other hand to Milton. I didn't understand, but I was confident, by the grim nod Milton gave Knox, that it ordered the trespasser's fate.

Eyes forward, Knox led me into the forest and into the ValleyMorgan territory, holding my hand the entire way.

We walked quietly, my anxiety growing the closer we got to his packhouse. Eventually, Knox stopped and looked at me. "What is it?"

"Every time I've been in a packhouse since I was sixteen, bad things have happened to me."

Knox frowned, anger flaring on the knowledge of my past. "That will never happen in my pack, Annie. That will never happen to you again." He touched my shoulder. "You bear my mark. Every wolf, no matter how weak, will know I will tear them limb from limb if they ever harm you."

My hand drifted to my shoulder, brushing across his mark, I turned my eyes away. "He must have known. He was one of us but just didn't have a wolf. He must have known all along what happened."

Taking my hand from my shoulder, Knox kissed the palm of it. "White loved you too much to care, Annie. He knew why you left him. White also knew I mistreated you because of your disability, which Brett could empathize with because he'd been rejected by his family for the same reason. He also knew the moment anything happened between you, I'd be here for you. Brett knew how much I regretted my mistake with you, and he could sympathize with that too." Enfolding my hand, Knox led me forward again until the packhouse was in sight.

For several minutes, we stopped and looked up at it, then Knox looked down at his shoulder and me. "Are you ready?"

"No."

"Your sisters call it home, and they are happy here. It could be like it was before it all went bad. You will have your family. Mandy will move here in a matter of months, and you will be free to live your life as you please. Just as long as you always come home to me."

He was right; my family and friends were here. Taking a deep breath, I could already envision having the family life here again. "I might get anxious around your wolves."

Knox bowed his head. "None of them will do anything against your will." He put his mouth to my ear with a smile. "None of them could if they wanted to. You are stronger than any of my men. If you could force your will on Dante, you are strong enough to rule them all."

"All but one."

"You wouldn't love me if I was weak, Annie."

He was right. Squeezing my hand, Knox took a step forward. "One step at a time. Just focus on that shower and bed for now. Tomorrow morning, we can deal with the rest."

Taking one step, then another, Knox led me to the door and opened it to the next chapter of my life. I just had to step through.

35

KNOX

She looked like an angel. Exhausted, Anique fell into my bed after the shower and hadn't stirred in hours. Holding her, I combed my fingers through her wet hair, her regular breaths blowing across my chest, wet from her drool. Drooling or not, she was still an angel in my arms, in my bed. An ease that had been missing since the moment I met her settled within my bones. Anique was where she belonged, and the restless bind between our souls was finally at peace.

Unable to sleep, my mind energized by her presence, I looked at the clock. We hadn't partaken in the purge yet, and as I held her, thoughts of sating myself with her for days on end did nothing to wind me down.

As if sensing my thoughts, which she probably did subconsciously, Anique rolled away from me. I chose not to feel rejected; she was exhausted from her first shift taking nearly a week. Cubs were barely able to stand after their first shift of only an hour. Kissing her temple, I got up to find a clean shirt.

"Alpha, is she okay?" Rhiannon asked when I walked into the kitchen.

"Exhausted, but perfectly fine, Rhi," I soothed. "Actually, she's the healthiest she's been in eight years, now that she is silver free."

Rhiannon brightened. "Goddess, it would be great if you got her with cub right away, then all three of us could raise our cubs together."

"Rhi, we aren't sure that's even an option. Between the miscarriage, the hemorrhage, and the surgery, we don't know what permanent damage was done."

Rhiannon looked crestfallen. Reaching out, I touched her cheek tenderly. "Let's just let that go for now. We need to focus on giving her a reason to stay here with us and teaching her how to shift between forms."

"Hands off my mate, Alpha," Milton teased as he came into the kitchen. Despite the tease, I removed my hand as Milton wrapped himself around his mate, smothering her in his scent. Wolves were so protective of their mates. Add cubs into the mix, and teasing or not, he had given me warning.

"I need to call Henderson and tell him we found Anique. There are also a few more things I need to address that I've let slide this week. Rhi, would you mind sitting in my room and staying with her in case she wakes? I need someone she trusts to be there when she wakes."

Milton growled at the idea of his mate being in my room. Rhi rolled her eyes. "She's my sister. I'll leave the door open if that makes you feel better." Milton wasn't happy, but as much as I wasn't messing with a wolf's pregnant mate, no one messed with a pregnant she-wolf. Our term for she-wolves didn't become an insult for human women by accident.

Making my way to my office, I dialed Henderson's number. "We found Annie."

"Is she okay?"

"Yes. Anique took time to grieve. She's staying with her sisters now." The other teams all knew we lived close to one another, but they didn't realize we were all in the one lodge.

"She needs to go back to the hospital," Henderson informed me. "Annie was never signed out. Her doctor had conniptions when she disappeared."

"I'll call him."

Henderson sighed. "Do you think she'll see me?"

"I'll ask," I wasn't making any promises. "Anique really loved White. You could be convinced they were soul mates."

"Hard to compete with, isn't it?" Henderson mourned.

"The trick is not to. Every relationship is different. You don't try and compare, you build a new one based on what you have together, not what someone else had with them."

"You're going after her, aren't you?"

"Anique was always meant to be mine, Henderson."

"The arranged marriage thing? But, you rejected her."

"I reacted badly to her past."

"The gang rape?"

"Once I'd had a moment to process it, I knew I'd stuffed up. I told Anique that."

"She won't forgive you."

"Probably not, but all Anique has right now is her faith, and that means accepting me for who I am, and that I make mistakes." Nathan was quiet. "I'll treat her right, Henderson. Anique's survived hell; she deserves happiness, but since the man who gave her that is waiting for her in the afterlife, I'll do my best to fill the space."

"White always liked you. When I used to bitch about your methods, he used to tell me that you were an honorable man, but we all have our demons to play with." Nathan groaned as if he was standing up after sitting for a long time. "She wouldn't see Brett straight after a mission. He hated it. He'd come home worked up, needing to vent, and Annie wouldn't come near him. They did once; Brett got rough, and Annie took gouges out of him because she couldn't handle it. Brett told me Annie was the most beautiful soul ever put on this earth, but those bastards dragged her into hell and tore her up. He said even Angels could be demons when they fall."

"He knew from experience. White grew up with his demons all around him,"

"You know his family?"

"I know of them. The Whites are in our community, but we don't deal with them."

"Explains so much about Brett, why he never talked about his past."

Inhaling, I looked out the window. "When the demons pull you apart, if you can survive and escape, you don't look back. You keep an eye on the shadows, but you don't look back. No one wants to live through that again."

"I can empathize," Nathan sighed. "I'd like to see Annie if she'll see me."

"I'll ask."

"Thanks for calling. I'll see you at the base."

Putting my phone down, I kept my eyes on the window. Anique couldn't look back. I needed to make this place different to the hell she escaped, and that meant coming out of the shadows myself. I also needed to get my head around Anique loving someone else.

I'd never been in love. Growing up, I'd been too focused on my training, and later, on being a good Alpha. Falling in love outside of a mating was never a consideration. My father taught me the only woman I should ever hope to possess was my true-mate.

Our elders taught respect for women, to treat them well, and if they give you a night in their bed, to appreciate it. It was my father who took me to the brothel first. He told me, as Alpha, my lusts would be higher, but I should spend that energy on women whose job it was to take my passion, and never force it on a she-wolf who was not my mate.

As an Alpha male, we tended to attract women who would want more, too, so not getting involved with humans was important. For that reason, I appreciated escorts. They provided an invaluable service to a man like me.

Now, I had my true-mate, but she loved another. There was no jealousy that Anique had been with White. After what happened to her, I dare say she would never have let me near her if White hadn't have taught her not all of us were pricks. I was, however, envious of her feelings for him.

Opening up my computer, I got stuck into the work I'd let slide while I'd been away. After two hours of getting bills and other business sorted, I closed my computer and made my way back to my bedroom. The room was empty. Taking a deep breath, I followed Anique's scent out to the kitchen.

Eating and laughing with her sisters, Anique held baby Grace in her arms. Entering the room quietly, I enjoyed watching her smile and interact with the baby. A hollow pooled in my stomach the moment I thought that could be our cub one day. Anique's smile flinched, and I knew she had felt my moment of disappointment, and that she knew I was there watching.

"I think I've hogged her enough," Anique excused, handing the cub back to Evaline.

"Are you and Knox going to try?" Evaline asked gently. "He's great with the cubs."

Hesitating answering, Anique's eyes flashed to where I remained cloaked in the shadows. "It's probably best not to get our hopes up. I'm content with being an aunt and taking babysitting duty on my nights off."

"Nights off?" Rhiannon frowned.

"I'm going to keep working. I worked too long and hard to be a doctor, so I'm not going to stop now," Anique fired up. "Dante wouldn't be alive today if it wasn't for my work. Perhaps one day, it could be Milton or Knox who needs me at the hospital doing my job. Just because I'm mated, that isn't going to stop."

Evaline and Rhiannon weren't sure how to respond. Stepping out of the shadow of the door, I gained their attention. "Of course, you will still work. Your sisters can also work if they choose. I believe it benefits you to have that modicum of independence."

Anique rewarded me with a smile. Rhiannon and Evaline barely stopped their mouths from falling open. "So, if Grace decides to go to university and study, you will allow that?" Evaline tested.

"She'll need to stay living at home, but I won't object to her furthering her education or working. Until she is mated, it isn't safe for a she-wolf to spend nights away from the packhouse. Anique can testify to that." Anique wasn't happy to agree, but she couldn't deny she had been taken by a pack while at university.

Smirking, Rhiannon stood. "Come on, Evaline, you can help pick out decorations for the nursery."

While they left, I started the espresso machine. "Coffee?"

"I won't say no to another," Anique smiled, bringing over her empty mug.

"Are you hungry?" When she brushed against me, I closed my eyes to keep my control.

"Famished," Anique murmured from my other side.

She wasn't talking about food, but I wanted to keep control until she knew for sure. "Well, the fridge is always well-stocked. Help yourself."

"Knox," Anique breathed my name, "do we need to discuss this?"

"I'd like to know what you want."

Anique moved her lips closer to my ear. "If you can bear me as I am, stubborn, independent, and barren. Then I want you." Her teeth nipped my ear lobe.

Patience be damned. Growling, I captured Anique's mouth

with mine ferociously. Our hands tugged, pulling at each other's clothes desperate to be free of them. Lifting Anique to the bench, I didn't care about my own rule about sex in shared rooms and caught her breasts in my hands.

Anique moaned beautifully as I sucked and caressed her breasts, tugging on her nipples, flicking and sucking them as I worked my way between her legs. Pulling my head up, Anique captured my mouth with hers as I nudged my weeping cock between her lower lips. "No one else, Knox. I can't bear another having you ever again."

"I am entirely yours." As I pressed into her, I knew no one else was ever going to feel as good as Anique, so there was no point being with anyone else. Having felt Anique's sex drive while she was with White, I knew we were very compatible, so there was no need for me to go anywhere else but to the arms of my mate.

Thrusting into her desperately, needing to feel her so thoroughly, I drove as deep as I could, and then I pounded her pale body into the kitchen bench. Anique was crying out my name as her body tightened around me. At that moment, I had never felt more alive than with Anique laid out across the stone counter, naked and calling my name, and when she came…

The kitchen door opened, and Milton stopped, took in what was happening, and immediately turned, pushing whoever was behind him back out of the room. Smiling, I dragged my eyes across the beauty of my world before me and cried out her name in praise.

Gazing with half shuttered eyes at me, Anique chuckled. "We probably should have gone to your room."

Pulling her up to me, I wrapped her in my arms. "Probably. The common rooms are not meant to be used this way. I'm going to owe the kitty a hell of a tax."

"Kitty?"

Wiping the hair back from her face, I smiled. "We fine members for breaking the rules like not cleaning up after themselves, or eating food ordered for another," I explained as I helped her down from the bench to dress. "Once a month, the money from the kitty can go towards something for the common rooms. The coffee machine was purchased after Evaline kept drinking all of Milton's chocolate milk for a week. She was craving it, but she didn't order her own, so she was fined. Lesson learned."

Anique grinned. "Should I ask what the fine for sex on the kitchen bench is?"

"Sex in any of the common rooms is an instant grand," I grimaced. "Sex on food preparation spaces, five thousand."

Anique blinked at me. "You're paying that, right?"

Drawing her to me, I laughed. "It was worth doing it all again." As I kissed her slowly, my body reacted. The purge wasn't going to be denied any longer. "Get something to eat, and let's go to my room before I end up being fined enough to renovate the entire kitchen."

Opening the fridge, Anique looked back at me with a grin. "What is the fine for eating someone else's food?"

"Hundred on the first offense," I informed her, pouring our coffees.

Taking the chocolate mud cake labeled with Evaline's name out of the fridge, Anique shrugged. "Worth it."

36

ANIQUE

---

*S*itting in the cafe, I stared at the wooden box. Observing me, Nathan sighed and looked away. "You look well."

"Is that a bad thing?"

"No, it's been over a month. I just meant, compared to the last time I saw you."

"I was recovering from nearly bleeding out and surgery, in a hospital gown, in a hospital bed." I raised a brow. "No one looks good like that."

"No, I guess they don't." Nathan waited a heartbeat while the waitress put our coffees down. "So, Knox?"

Raising an eyebrow, I sipped my coffee.

"You disappeared; he took a month's leave..." Nathan pursued.

"Did he? I didn't see him until two weeks ago when I called him for help."

"Help?"

Shaking my head, I forgot for a moment that Nathan wasn't one of us. "Some guys who wouldn't take no for an answer."

Nathan shifted uncomfortably. "Knox told me you came back to live with your sisters."

"He brought me back to them." We sat drinking our coffee quietly. "Did you hear Rion and Mandy are engaged?"

"Jesus, you lot like to keep it close to home," Nathan muttered.

"My brother and Monique met at Milton's wedding to my sister, and now they are also dating."

"Next, you'll tell me Danielle is marrying Sasha?"

Slumping back in my chair, I bit my lip, my eyes itched as memories flashed in my mind.

"Annie?" Nathan looked appalled. "Is Danielle getting married?"

Shaking my head, I swiped a tear from my eye. "No, she um... she got herself killed, Nathan. She picked up a guy and..."

Reaching across the table, Nathan touched my hand. "What happened, Annie?"

Pulling away slowly, I shook my head." I think you were right about her and those men. I didn't know. I should have." Swiping at the tears, I remembered her trying to kill me. "She picked someone better than her this time."

Mouth hanging open, Nathan looked away before he forced it closed. "I told Brett it was her, but none of us knew why she was like that."

My breath caught in my throat. "What happened to me, it happened to Danielle too," I explained awkwardly. "Continuously, for two years. Not as violent, not as young, but that sort of violation, it fucks you up when it happens even once. For it to be done repeatedly..."

Staring at the table, Nathan frowned. "Mandy and Monique?"

"Mandy wasn't raped, but her parents and family were killed in front of her. Monique was abused at home, then abducted by a group of men, but she was saved before they-" my voice cut out.

Nathan covered his face with his hands. "Jesus, we always think we can pick you girls," he dragged his hands down, "but none of us would have picked you, Annie, if Brett hadn't explained."

My eyes went back to the box. "Brett was the only reason I

turned out as I did, you know. Meeting him, even that first time, it saved me. He pulled me above the surface of my fear and hate. Danielle didn't have a Brett, and my arm couldn't reach the depths she had sunk too after so long."

"She most likely would have pulled you under anyway," Nathan huffed. "That's the sort of bitch she was."

That is what Danielle had tried to do, and she had with Mandy and Monique to some extent. My hand reached out and caressed the wood of the box. It felt so cold. "He's gone now, but he's always going to be in my heart."

"I'm not going to hate you for moving on, Annie," Nathan put his hand over mine on the box. "Brett wouldn't want you to stop living either, not when you fought so hard to live. Not when you have the chance to be loved."

Licking my lips, I took my hand away. "Have you started recruiting to replace your lost team members?"

"Not yet. We have some potentials training with us, but we haven't offered anyone a permanent posting. It's too soon for us too." Standing, Nathan bent down and kissed my cheek. "Good luck, Annie. If Morgan ever makes you cry, just tell me, and the Olympians will kick his ass." It made me smile. "I'm sorry I sprung this on you. If you need help, just let me know."

"I'll see you at the hospital."

Laughing, Nathan shook his head." Don't curse me, Annie."

"I meant when you visit the poor academy students, that you train."

With a wink, Nathan left the coffee shop. Gazing at the box, I sighed, that ache in my chest demanding my attention. Picking it up, I made my way to Eric's rooms. His receptionist greeted me, and I took a seat to wait.

When Eric walked out to call me in and saw me carrying the box, he freaked. "Jesus, Annie, you had pretty intensive abdominal surgery a month ago, what are you doing lugging this around?" He took it off me.

"Be careful with that, it's my husband."

Studying the box, Eric walked into his office and placed Brett's ashes on his desk, his eyes full of emotion. "Get up on the bed."

"I'm fine."

"Bed, Annie."

"Eric, I..."

"Bed!"

With a huff, I kicked off my shoes and climbed up on the bed and lay down. Looking over my file, Eric then came over and lifted my top, pushing my skirt down low and feeling around my tummy. "Any pain?"

"Not in general."

"But some?"

"During intercourse. Not enough to distract from things, but afterward, I'm getting bad cramps."

"Annie, you should not be having sex already, you know this."

"Eric, I'm not normal, you know this," I mimicked his tone.

"I'm not a gynecologist, you should see Blake; he assisted in the surgery."

"Not yet. If I go now, he will be wondering what miracle was performed for me to not even have any scars."

"True," Eric agreed, still palpating my tummy. "It took me a lot of scotches to accept coming across you, Annie." Stepping back, Eric washed his hands and then walked to his desk. Fixing my clothes, I followed him over.

Eric was writing on an X-ray form as I sat. "I want a scan of your abdomen to ensure I got all the silver and to check the state of everything," Eric explained. "We will do an ultrasound, internal and external..."

I groaned miserably; things guys never had to endure.

"...and I want an MRI." Eric slipped the request across the desk to me. "You come back to me with the scans. If I see anything concerning, you go see Blake. I'll come up with some bullshit about a miracle cream, and you neglect to mention you've been banging a soldier's brains out."

I raised a brow. "Soldier?"

"You have a type, Annie," Eric grouched. "And the two who stuck by your bed at the hospital were pretty obvious about how they felt for you. If I didn't know how much you loved Brett, I might have been convinced you were screwing around."

Frowning at the accusation, I shook my head. "Knox and I dated when Brett and I broke up for a while. He's been there for me."

Eric looked at me through his brow. "Figured that would be the case." He sat back. "Get the scans done today if you can. I'll ring Blake to discuss the surgery and prognosis once we have the results."

"My month forced leave is up," I braved reminding him.

"Scans first. We can discuss your return to work right after you explain your disappearing act from the hospital."

"I was healing too fast, Eric. I couldn't stay there."

"Try again."

Bowing my head, I averted my gaze. "I couldn't stay there. I needed to escape all the grief boiling over inside me. I had to get away from here until I could cope."

"Thank you!" Opening his drawer, Eric pulled out a card. "Make an appointment. I'll have the referral waiting when you return."

"A psychologist?"

"You've been through a lot, Annie, and I don't just mean this last month and a half." Standing up, Eric walked to the door. "You want back into the fellowship program, then you'll need to speak to Victoria and get an all-clear to return to work."

"I'd rather quit," I sulked.

"Suck it up, Annie. You need to get it out." Eric looked at his desk. "Leave Brett here with me, to ensure you come back."

With a glare at Eric - he was lucky that I admired him as a doctor and friend - I left his office and went about organizing the scans. While I waited for those, I made an appointment with Victoria, the psychologist.

My phone vibrated against my hip while I was sitting in the radiology waiting room. "You promised to give me the morning," I murmured.

"I did," Knox agreed. "I didn't count on you sneaking out while I slept, though."

"You looked peaceful, and I was worried if I didn't, you wouldn't let me out of bed again for another four hours."

"Sore?" Knox chuckled.

"What do you think?" I huffed, but I couldn't help the smirk pulling at my lips. Deliciously sore would be more accurate.

"Are you finished yet? It is twelve-o-one, so officially, the morning is over."

"I'm waiting to have some scans done, then I need to go back and see Eric for the results."

"Is he worried?"

"Not yet. Truthfully, it was stupid of me to start having sex again so soon."

"The purge waits for no one, Annie," Knox sighed. "Want me to come and get you?"

"I'll be a while yet."

"I can be there with you. I want to be there for you."

"By the time you get here, I'll be in, and you'll be left waiting outside for me."

"Actually, I'm at the base, so I could be with you in ten."

"The base? I thought you were on leave?"

"I am, but I was asked to consult on something, and I had a test scheduled."

"Fit for duty?"

"Yep. Don't worry, I showered. I'll be there in seven minutes."

"You don't even know where I am."

Knox chuckled. "Annie, close your eyes."

With a deep exhalation, I did as he requested.

"Imagine me. Wonder what I am doing right now."

Taking a deep breath, I asked myself where Knox was. In my mind, I saw him driving down the main road of Campus, just passing the traffic lights on Marlborough Road.

"Where am I?"

"Main street, you just passed Marlborough."

Even from here, I could feel Knox smiling. "I'll be there in three minutes." He hung up as he pulled into the car park. Putting my phone away, I smirked to myself. A minute later, Knox walked through the door and came to sit by me. The moment he took my hand in his, I relaxed.

"Can we talk?" Knox began.

It had to happen. We'd spent the last two weeks as slaves to the purge. Now that it was done, what had been delayed, needed to be said.

Exhaling, I tried to word this correctly. "I know you won't agree, Knox, but I'm not ready. I'm still married to Brett in my heart, no matter what my body thinks, and you don't deserve that. What I need is time apart while I deal with this, and while I get my life back on track."

"I know, and I accept that, but even with my mark, it's too dangerous for you to be traveling to foreign countries." Knox squeezed my hand. "Doctors without borders is out, I'm sorry."

Pressing my lips together, I knew he was right. What happened in the forest near his pack showed me that. On top of that, I was still learning to shift on my own. We hadn't spent much time on that yet, so I needed to be with others when I tried. But, I needed time and space.

"I have a compromise. I've been asked to go to the training base and fill in as an instructor for six months. They were willing to fly me back in every weekend, but perhaps, I just go for a few months straight out, then start coming back on weekends when you are ready."

"You'd leave your pack for me?" Sure that my mouth was gaping open, I stared at Knox bewildered.

"No, and you are going to have to take care of them while I'm away."

"You want me to play Alpha?"

"You did run your own pack successfully, Annie."

"One of them turned out to be a murdering psychopath."

"I've already vetted this pack, so don't worry about that. Though, watch Edgar, he has humanity issues."

Staring ahead as the gravity of what Knox was offering seeped in, I frowned. "Six months will be a long time for both of us."

"I know, but I will try if you will. I figure after two months, I'll come home on weekends, and we can date. Get to know each other, perhaps, you might fall in love with me?"

"And you with me?"

"Oh, that happened already, Annie." Knox squeezed my hand. "I was in love with you a long time ago."

Tears filled my eyes. Could I be so lucky as to find first Brett, and now Knox? I didn't want him to leave; being in his arms felt too good. I also knew what we had couldn't become what it should be until I'd dealt with losing Brett. Until I could think of my husband and not feel like my heart was bleeding. Knox knew it too, and he was giving me what I needed for both of us.

Knox going would be beneficial for both of us. Being an instructor usually led to promotion, so independent of us, this was good for Knox, and I knew it had always been his plan. It would also make him a better Alpha, learning to instruct, rather than just order. A quiet smile settled on my lips. I didn't doubt for a second that when he came home, we would begin as we should have. "When do you leave?"

"Four days from today. I'll run you through the business side of the pack over the next few days. We'll set you up in your own bedroom, so when I do start coming home, you don't feel pressured."

Swallowing my fear, I lifted my eyes to his. "I don't know how I will go around the males in the pack without you there."

"From what I heard, you could handle parties with the Olympians."

"Brett was always there."

We fell into silence. "If it gets too much, Mandy still has her place. Though, I think immersion in a pack lifestyle, being with your sisters and friend, is what you need, Annie. You've bonded with Dante, he will keep the others in line. If you get scared, crawl into my bed. My scent will still be there, and I'm not going to complain if I come home and can smell you in my bed."

"Oh, God, I'm going to have to feel you masturbate again."

Smirking, Knox took my hand in his. "If it's the only way I can be with you, Annie, I'm going to take it. Six months is a long time to wait."

"You won't be tempted to call the redhead?" I worried at my lip.

"After the last two weeks? Not a chance. I'd rather imagine being with you than hurt you again. You're it for me, no matter how long it takes."

The silence fell between us, and I gripped his hand. "I'll try."

Knox kissed the top of my head, the disappointment of leaving already heavy in the air. "I'll tell the pack tonight."

He stayed with me through the scans, which made the Sonographer uncomfortable during the internal, especially when Knox started growling deep in his chest. Afterward, Knox walked with me back to Eric's office and waited with me.

"Okay, Annie," Eric called as he came out from another patient.

Seeing Knox, Eric tensed his jaw. His eyes weren't happy when Knox followed me into the office.

Sitting down at his computer, Eric brought up the scan results, reading the report before looking at the scans themselves. Frowning, Eric picked up the phone and dialed a number. "Blake, it's Eric. Can you look at some scans for me and give me your opinion?" Eric then gave the gynecologist the access code.

Glancing to me, Knox reached out and took my hand in his, giving it a gentle squeeze. Eric's eyes tracked it, but his attention was drawn back to the screen as he nodded his head, listening to the specialist for that part of my body.

"That's what I thought, but I wanted to get a second opinion before I explained," Eric answered. "Yeah, it is." There were a few more hmm's and nods before he thanked Blake and hung up. Eric swiped his hand through his hair.

"No kids," I understood his bad-news face. Knox's hand tightened in mine.

"I'm sorry, Annie. Everything looks good from the surgery, very little scar tissue. Still, the silver was in your system for such a long time that it caused massive organ damage, which hasn't healed like the rest of you. Blake is guesstimating a ten percent chance of falling pregnant, a one percent chance of carrying through the first trimester."

Bowing my head, I exhaled. I'd accepted my chance of having a family years ago. Beside me, Knox cleared his throat. "Can I ask...why didn't you remove the shrapnel years ago?"

"The shrapnel was embedded in Annie's pelvis, close to major arteries and nerve supplies. Medical procedures seven years ago could have caused her to bleed out or for major nerve damage to destroy her career as a doctor," Eric explained. "Annie worked her ass off and overcame so much to become a doctor, I wasn't willing to take that away from her. Now, we have robotic-assisted surgeries. It makes the sort of surgery we performed on Annie more accurate and less deadly."

"Well, on the bonus side, you don't have to worry about me applying for maternity leave, and I get to really enjoy being an aunt on my days off. Is there anything else?"

Eric nodded. "The silver poisoning is still an issue. I can't guarantee that you will live a long life, Annie, I'm sorry."

None of this was anything new. My organs were damaged from the poison, even being able to shift wasn't going to heal that overnight.

"You should probably practice safe sex," Eric continued, and Knox scoffed. "But I can't see any reason for the cramping after sex, unless it's, umm… because your partner is, umm," Eric frowned, looking over Knox.

"Huge?" I offered, trying to resist the smirk. Knox grinned.

"And aggressive," Eric finished.

"No, it's just huge," Knox dismissed casually, his eyes twinkling with his ego.

Scowling at Knox, Eric looked to me. "He's not aggressive. He's thorough, but in control. With what I've been through, I couldn't handle violent sex." Eyes slightly more full than usual, Eric double blinked. Knox just sat there with an eat-shit smile. I wanted to kiss him and smack him down at the same time.

"Well," Eric cleared his throat. "Maybe dial it back a notch when you are thrusting. Your body will get used to it, but deep and hard with a sizable object is always going to leave you cramping afterward."

Lifting an eyebrow, I turned to Knox. "Did the redhead used to cope?"

He shrugged. "She would have to take a day off afterward, so probably not."

"I'm seriously not sitting here giving sex advice for oversized cocks," Eric grumbled.

Understanding Eric was referring to the man, not his appendage, I chuckled. "Okay, we'll get going then." Standing up to leave, I went to collect the box.

"Let your friend carry your husband," Eric scolded. "Healed or not, you are still recovering."

For the first time, Knox looked at the box. "Is that White's ashes?"

"Nathan gave them to me. Brett wanted to have them dispersed in the forest."

Taking the box from the table, Knox bowed his head. "I know the perfect place." Glaring at him, I dared him to suggest the bog. "All my ancestor's ashes are thrown from the clifftop near the cascade down the rock face," Knox explained. "The wind spreads them throughout the woods."

Tears welling in my eyes, I smiled. I knew the place he was referring too.

Two days later, I stood near the cascades with Knox, his pack, and the Olympians. Waiting for a strong gust, I released the lid on the box. Stepping back to Knox's side, I watched the wind collect Brett's ashes from the urn and free him to the forest below.

"Thank you for honoring him this way."

"He was one of us," Knox acknowledged. "Had I known; I would have let him join the hounds. He was a good man and a good soldier. I would have given him a home." Cuddling into his side, I said my final goodbye. We wouldn't kiss or do anything more than this. We were here for Brett.

"Life isn't always what you imagined. Bad shit happens. Brett taught me it's what you do after that makes the difference between existing and living," I informed Knox. "I may not have a long life, but I'm determined to live my life to the fullest."

"That's good," Knox murmured as the last of Brett's ashes floated away, "because I'm determined to live my life with you."

"Okay, everything accounted for?" Eric asked. The nurses did their counts and cleared us. "Annie, close the boy up."

A smile pulled at the side of my mouth, hidden by the surgical mask, but you get used to watching people's eyes when you can't see their faces.

"You still think of him every time you suture, don't you?" Louisa, the anesthetics nurse, queried.

"Every time!" I remembered Brett's eyes smiling up at me as I sutured his brow. The first stitches I ever sewed. I never cried anymore. My memories of Brett were happy ones, so when I thought of him, I only allowed that emotion.

"When you finish up, you can go tell whoever his trainer was how it went, Annie." Eric was standing back, letting me do it all. It was my first solo surgery. Still under supervision, and Eric was instructing, but I'd done all the work.

"How do they decide which official has to sit out there?" One of the nurses asked.

"Whoever was running the class is responsible. Whenever Brett ran a course, if one of his kids got hurt, he had to come straight after he finished teaching. Then, he had to revisit his risk assessment and determine if the accident was avoidable by changing something, or if the kid just did something stupid."

"How often was the instructor at fault?" Louisa chuckled.

"Nowhere near as often as the student. The problem is when they are learning things like abseiling and parachuting, or weaponry, you already have a high risk. All you need is one kid not listening to instructions correctly, and you can have a fatality on your hands. The trainers take it hard when one of their students get hurt too."

Tying off the last suture, I stepped away from the leg. Stepping forward, Eric observed my work. "Okay, Annie. Go inform whoever is waiting, and then you're done for the day."

"Got plans this weekend, Annie?" Louisa asked as I started degowning.

"Mandy's wedding," I answered as I smiled at Eric. "I'll see you there?"

"I wouldn't miss it," Eric grinned.

Washing up, I headed out to the waiting room. Nathan sat drinking coffee. When he saw me, he stood up. "Annie, it's been months."

Four to be exact. "I guess you trained the parachuting class today?"

Nathan scrubbed the back of his head. "Yeah, how bad is it?"

"Not as bad as it looked. I've reduced the fracture and repaired the lacerated tendon. Six weeks on crutches, physio, and he'll be fine to try his luck jumping out of planes again in about three to six months."

"Oh, that's great. When I saw the laceration and all the blood, I was worried that would be a medical discharge." Nathan pulled me into a hug. "Thanks, Annie. Can I see him?"

Gently extracting myself from his arms, I took a massive step back. "He'll be in post-op right now. I'll have a nurse come and get you once he's in recovery."

Blinking at the way I'd pulled away, Nathan backed up. "Sorry, Annie, I forget you don't like hugs." He looked me over. "You look good, Annie. Really good. Are you happy?"

Hesitating, I searched for the right words. "I'm a lot healthier since the surgery."

"That's not what I asked," Nathan muttered. "I heard you moved in with Knox?"

"I've been house-sitting for him while he's away training," I answered honestly. "Knox's weekends at home, I've been staying up with Mandy, helping her prepare for the wedding and pack ready to move in with Rion."

Tilting his head, Nathan assessed me. "Annie, I'm not going to be angry if you're seeing another man. I know you and Knox are dating again; I saw you having dinner a month ago."

Biting my lip, I looked at my toes. "I don't want you to think that I've just forgotten about Brett. I haven't. I couldn't if I tried. There is too much to remind me of him daily." Taking a deep breath, I lifted my eyes to meet Nathan's. Sympathy shined down upon me. "I am seeing Knox, and yes, while we are taking things slow, I live with him now. I feel safe in his house, and I have a family again. I expect once Knox returns home permanently, our relationship will become more."

Nathan exhaled hard. "Good. I know you are fiercely independent, Annie. I still feel better, and the team feels better, knowing that someone is taking care of you and helping you move on."

"Are you okay, Nathan? He was your best friend."

"Like you, I have daily reminders, and like you, I have a hot blonde pediatric nurse helping me move on," Nathan smirked. He gave me a wink. "I'll let you get back to work."

Chuckling, I headed for the change room so I could get out of my scrubs and into human clothes. "Annie, someone's in the tea room waiting to see you," one of the nurses called as I walked past the nurse's station. With a sigh, I went into the tea room. My feet stopped when Knox sat at the table, talking to Eric. They both looked up.

"Here she is now," Eric smiled. "I'm going to head home. I'll see you both at the banquet tomorrow night. I'm excited that it's going to be a traditional wedding for your kind. I'm intrigued by what it will be like?"

"Have you been to human weddings?" Knox chuckled. "It's like that with fewer speeches, more food, and the dancing gets a little nuts."

Eric laughed. "Sounds like my sister's wedding. It should be fun." Eric walked out.

Knox stood up to face me. My eyes were scanning his broad shoulders, his neck to his square jaw with its five o'clock shadow, across his cheekbones to rest on his pale green eyes. I adored his eyes. "I thought you weren't back until tomorrow morning?"

"There was a transport coming across this afternoon. I figured I'd get it and meet you here for a lift home. Since you have my car."

"Hmm, about the car. I've grown attached."

"I'm taking my car back when I'm home, Annie. Don't come between a guy and his Aston."

"You could have my Porsche," I offered.

Sauntering closer, Knox lowered his mouth to my ear. "Porsches are penis extensions. We both know I don't need a Porsche to make a girl happy, Annie." I closed my eyes at the reminder of how well Knox could get me happy. Shifting, Knox brushed against my hip. "Besides, we discussed on my visit home last month about you selling the cars you stole from the Venture Alpha. I'm more than happy to take you car shopping when I'm home next month."

Swallowing, I turned my face to meet his eyes, the heat in his suffusing my body. "Can I buy an Aston?"

"Can you afford an Aston?"

"Probably not," I sighed. "But an Alpha should treat his pack with the same luxuries he treats himself."

Knox turned his body, so it pressed mine into the table. "We are not officially mated, Annie. You marry me officially, and I'll get you any damn car you want as a wedding present."

My hands smoothed over his shirt. "But we are fully mated?"

"Actually," Knox stepped back. "That's one of the things I want to talk to you about. Shall we head home so we can speak in private?"

Taking a breath, I huffed. "Let me get changed." Moving out to the locker room, I changed back into my clothes for the drive home. Collecting Knox on the way out, we made our way to the car park. "Have you changed your mind?" I asked when I sank into the car.

"No." Pressing the start button, Knox shifted the car into reverse. "I need you to tell me about this." Taking a small vial out of his pocket, Knox handed it to me.

Blinking rapidly, I stared at the bottle, my mouth opening and closing for several seconds. "How did you get this?"

"I found it in your Porsche before the police impounded it," Knox explained. "I thought it was going to be wolfsbane, but it is something different. I've had it analyzed, but no one can tell me what it does. But I think you know."

"Why?" I tried to appear innocent.

"Because I'm your mate, and I can smell you on that bottle. Confide in me, please?"

Closing my eyes, I took a deep breath. "Its Rogues Venom. At least, that's what I called it. It turns someone's wolf off, leaves them… human, until the effects, wear off."

"You synthesized it?"

"Yes."

"How?"

"Eric's research into the effect of blood transfusions along with my understanding of wolf physiology," I explained. "This is all I made if you're worried."

Knox shifted gears. "When Mandy and Rion went through the second phase, he saw things that equally fascinated and disturbed him. While he didn't tell me most of it, he did warn me you were quite the experimental chemist."

"Everything I made was for one purpose. I have no intention of doing that ever again," I defended. "You and your pack have nothing to fear from me unless you hurt me."

"That's not what this is about, Annie," Knox dismissed.

"Then why are we even talking about this?"

"Because you have no loyalty to me, and I need that to change before this goes any further." Blinking at him, my mouth fell open. Inhaling, Knox reached out to take my hand in his. "I'm loyal to you, Annie, but you have no required loyalty to me as your Alpha. That is my fault; I own the responsibility, which also means it is up to me to fix it before we can move forward."

"What are you suggesting?"

"I re-mark you. You've already undergone the bond virus, so your body should react instantly, and you shouldn't suffer the side effects of the first infection. I mark you, and the loyalty to your Alpha repairs, then we set a date for our banquet."

Breath coming shallow, I stared at our entwined hands. "It would reset the purge."

"I'm home for the summer break, Annie," Knox explained. "That gives us two weeks to sort this out."

"Can I think about it?"

"Of course! Dante tells me you've regularly been shifting?"

"I've been changing daily, but Dante won't let me leave the packhouse without one of the males with me," I grouched.

"Initially, he said it was so they didn't lose me to my wolf again, now he says it's to make sure I don't get taken. I thought you spoke to Brett's father?"

"I did, Alpha to Alpha. I explained that while you were married to Brett, you met your true-mate, that we have now mated, and you are unavailable," Knox explained. "That doesn't mean other packs won't come sniffing around, Annie, and it doesn't mean it is safe for you to run around by yourself. Every female in the house can only run with a male escort. That's for your protection, not a restriction."

We let that fall between us. After a few minutes, Knox cleared his throat. "We don't typically need to shift daily. Are you struggling to control your wolf, or is there something else?"

"Oh, no, it's not her pushing through," I confessed, fidgeting with Knox's hand. "I've been hoping the regular shifting will help push the toxins from my body faster, to reverse the cellular damage caused by the longterm silver poisoning."

Knox's brows furrowed. "You're shifting to heal? Do you think it's working?"

"Well, I have reason to believe I can undo the damage, yes. Remember how there was a particular mark caused by silver in my flesh that I couldn't get rid of because it healed before I shifted?" Knox growled as an answer. He hated Dan's initials in me, more so since the tattoo had vanished after my first change. "I reopened the wound, literally cut the scar tissue away, and shifted. Now, there is no mark. That part of my skin is smooth and unblemished," I celebrated.

Pulling off the road, Knox hit the brakes, a snarl filling the car with his rage. "You sliced yourself up? How did I not feel that?"

Cringing away from Knox's anger a little, I chewed my lip. "Well, I enlisted help from Monique. She's still working at the hospital. She and Mandy gave me nitrous oxide, laughing gas," I clarified, seeing Knox's worry. "Mandy cut the scar tissue away for me, and then they took me out to the woods, and we shifted. So, I didn't have any pain, they supervised me through the shift, and Mandy insisted I change straight back to prevent any issues."

Knox just sat there, blinking at me. I couldn't tell if he wanted to hit something or yell at me for what we did. I didn't care; I wasn't spending the rest of my life with that bastard buried in my flesh. Lifting my summer dress to my hip, I pulled the knickers down on the side. "See?"

Licking his lips, Knox reached out and brushed his thumb over the smooth and flawless skin above my womb. "I want you to have the scans done again. It's been five months since the silver came out. Let's see if daily shifting has helped."

My teeth snapped shut. I'd felt Knox's disappointment when Eric gave us the news last time. The last thing I wanted was for either of us to get our hopes up and have them destroyed again. Lifting those pale jade eyes to mine, Knox firmed his fingers around my hip. With a flex of his arm, Knox pulled me across the seat until our breath mingled.

"I mark you; we purge, then you get the scans redone," Knox murmured. "If there is no change, you stop exhausting yourself and wolf by shifting daily, and we accept your diagnosis and set a date."

"And if there is an improvement?" I worried. The shot of hope fired through Knox, but he instantly tamed it.

"The answer to that is all going to depend on what level of improvement there is," Knox replied. The way he said it sounded professional, medically termed. Squinting, I peered at Knox, wondering what he and Eric discussed before I arrived. "I'm not going to hope, Annie. I'm going to love you no matter the outcome. We can discuss our options once we know the prognosis."

"You ass! You went to the hospital to discuss the change with Eric first. You knew!"

"Do you think I can't feel your exhaustion from the regular shifts?" Knox lifted a cheeky brow. "Or perhaps you think I can't feel that small spark of hope in you after every shift. The power of that hope erupting every time you hold Grace in your arms, or see Rhi's belly swollen with cub?" Knox caressed my nose with his. "I've felt it, Annie. I wanted Eric to tell me it's a prospect before I asked, just in case that spark was just wishful thinking. I want you to be happy, and if there is anything I can do to make that happen, I will do it. If Eric tells us you've healed and you're able to conceive, I will take leave and keep you in bed until my cub grows in your womb. If that's what you want, Annie, I will do everything I can to give it to you."

My eyes were threatening to spill over with tears. "Do you know what I want right now?" I asked him as I released my seat belt. Sucking in a breath, Knox watched as I slipped my knickers down my legs. "I want to fuck the sexiest guy I know in his impressive Aston Martin."

Smirking, Knox reached to the side to move his seat back and lay it down. "As my Alphia wishes."

Straddling Knox's lap, I pressed my mouth to his. We hadn't been intimate since he left for training. We'd enjoyed mutual masturbation, but even when he started coming home after two months, for one weekend a month, we'd only dated and talked. Now, I couldn't resist him. The idea of having cubs with Knox made me hot and horny. Okay, maybe I'd been randy as a minx for months, but the baby talk took my restraint and threw it out the window.

"You know," I panted against Knox's mouth. "If the scans come back good, an Aston Martin will be an impractical car for a family."

Knox unzipped his fly. "For you, yes. I won't be taking cubs to base with me." Gripping my hips, Knox rubbed my naked sex forward over his hardness.

"I won't be taking them to the hospital with me either," I gasped at the friction.

Clenching my hips in his grip, Knox pulled back from my lips. His lust gazed eyes peered up at me. "We need to talk this through more."

"Agreed," I swallowed as he nudged at my entrance. "Not now."

"Annie," Knox captured my face in one of his hands. "Are you due for your heat?"

That question stopped me as I considered how randy I was, how much the talk of cubs was driving me wild. "Shit!" I went to move away, Knox's hands held me in place. "Knox, I don't want another miscarriage."

"I know. There are condoms in the glove box," Knox murmured. Watching each other a moment, I was about to ask why he kept condoms in the glove box, but then the imitation redhead came to mind, and I decided not to query it. Hurriedly locating the pack, I pulled one out and put it in place. Knox groaned as my hands rolled over him.

"If your heat is coming, we'll change the plan," Knox decided as I fed him into my entrance. "Scans first. Then I'll mark you, and we'll purge whatever emotions come from it."

"Knox," I breathed as he sunk deep. "Stop talking practicalities and start talking dirty."

Grinning like a demon, Knox captured my face in his hands. "I want you to know how special you are to me, Annie. I've never fucked a woman in my car. Only you get this privilege."

Meeting his eyes, I kissed him deeply. Slipping his hands under my skirt to grab my naked hips, Knox pulled me down on him and started fucking me hard and fast.

Whimpering as my body climbed for a quick release, I gripped his shoulders hard, holding on for sanity, my breath rasping in the confined space. "Knox, I want something."

"Anything."

"If Eric says yes to cubs, I want to mate traditionally."

Swelling inside me, Knox tightened his grip. "In fur form?"

"Yes," I panted, walking the edge.

A broad grin broke across Knox's face seconds before his head fell back, and his eyes squeezed shut. "Goddess, yes!"

His body jerking inside me caused my body to seize and stars to explode in my vision.

"Welcome to the Valleymorgans , Mandy," I greeted Mandy after the bride and groom served the food.

"Are you a huggable Alpha?" Mandy squeaked. She was all giddy and happy. Rion and Mandy had chosen to go full traditional, and Rion marked her with the third phase in front of everyone. The fever hadn't hit them yet, but by that time, everyone would be drunk, and Mandy and Rion would be driving off to their honeymoon to instigate the fourth phase and start the purge.

"I can't see how a hug could hurt."

Jumping forward, Mandy gave me a tight hug. She was firm and soft and smelled of lemon drops. A low growl sounded from behind me, Mandy and I snapped apart in surprise, and Mandy took two more retreating steps fearfully. At the same time, I turned to appraise my jealous mate.

Blinking wide eyes behind me, Anique stood with her hand on her chest. "Sorry. She didn't like another female touching her mate," Anique explained. "I didn't even know I could do that."

Pressing my lips together to stop from laughing, I tugged

Anique closer to me. When I let my eyes go to Mandy, she was watching Anique with confusion. Glancing down, I smirked at Anique rubbing her cheek across my chest. "It's normal when a she-wolf is approaching her heat to become overly protective of her mate," I explained. "Rion will be the same about you once you mate; heat or no heat, Mandy."

Mouth turning up in a wicked grin, Mandy gave me a coy look. "I'll be worse. All those other bitches can keep their skanky hands off my man," Mandy chirped. It made me laugh. "Do you mind if I steal Annie for a second?"

"Just as long as you return her." Kissing Anique's upturned face, I let her step away. "I'm going to go talk to your brother and Monique. He owes you a dowry."

Anique frowned. "Dowry?"

"Monique was a Lunas pack member, and you were the Alphia. Therefore, you receive the dowry for the bitch he took." Anique didn't look convinced, so I lowered my voice. "It is tradition, Anique."

"Oh, well, as Alphia of the Lunas pack, you owe me the dowry for the bitch you took as your mate and Rion's," Anique sassed, backing away. "Plus, I'm going to charge a dishonor fee. It should come to the cost of that beautiful car of yours." Turning, Anique took Mandy's hand, the two of them walking away laughing like schoolgirls at Anique's joke.

Considering Anique's retreating form, I let her feelings circulate through me. Damn it! She wasn't joking. With a sigh and a small smile at my mate's intelligence, I went over to greet her brother. "Edward; Monique," I bowed my head, keeping my hands to myself, just in case Anique was watching.

"Knox, you look happy. I gather dating my sister is working out?"

"Yes, the calls have been helpful, allowing us to get to know each other better," I confirmed. "We are forging a bond of friendship with the distance, and one of deep attraction in each other's company." In my months away, we'd talked on the phone regularly. Initially, to discuss the pack and Anique double checking things, but then I'd ask about her day, and the conversations grew from there.

"I'm pretty sure the attraction was already there and mutual," Monique chuckled. "That's what made it harder for Annie. Losing the man she loved, and wanting you when she should have been wanting him. It tore her up," Monique mourned.

Edward looked hurt by that revelation. "Monique, why don't you go join the girls. Make sure they are free for our banquet date." Smiling up at Edward, Monique kissed his cheek before going off to join her pack mates.

"Are you okay, Edward?" I asked, concerned by his sudden misery.

"Anique has been through a lot," Edward replied glumly. "When the second phase hit, I didn't just see Monique, but I saw my sister saving her from another pack. She was so strong and fierce, and yet, there was a fragility to her I never thought to see in my sister." Edward bowed his head. "I fucked up, Knox. I should have gone to the hospital to see her, even when she told dad not to bring me. I believed Dan when he said he loved Anique. I thought he would make her happy, and she was just stubborn and independent. Dad never told me what happened, just that Anique got hurt."

"Did you ask Annie why she didn't want to see you?" I worried. That didn't sound like Anique, pushing her family away.

Edward nodded his head sadly. "When she came to the city. She told me having her father in the room was torture for her. Just the smell of a male wolf made her want to vomit repeatedly and scream. Every time dad went to see her, she vomited for hours after. She knew she couldn't handle having dad and me there at the same time." Edward looked tormented. "I failed my baby sister. What if I fail my mate?"

"Your pack is dead, Edward. There is little chance of that."

"Monique still wants to work. What if a stray finds her, or another pack?" Edward shook his head. "How can you let Anique leave the house, knowing what she's already endured?"

Shifting uncomfortably, I swallowed down my wolf's growl. "To be honest. Telling your sister that I want her to give up the career she loves scares me. I've seen her at her worst, she's terrifying. At the same time, I want to give Annie everything her heart desires. For fuck's sake, I spent the day secretly shopping for a high-end car for her. So, the idea of taking a job she loves away from her makes my insides twist in a way that is discouraging," I admitted. "I think, once you are fully mated, the idea of making Monique give up her independence will be a bad taste on your tongue too. Try to remember; they've survived without male wolves out there in the real world for over eight years. Of any bitch walking the streets, our mates are the safest."

Fidgeting as if unsettled, Edward eyed the girls laughing across the room. "Her Alpha force mated her. Held her down while her brother raped her. I saw it through her eyes, and it nearly broke me," Edward revealed. "And all I could think about was that was only one. What Annie went through was ten times worse, and I tried to make her come home and marry the wolf who did that to her."

"Edward," I clenched the drink in my hand a little too tight. "Did you want me to beat the shit out of you? Is that what you are looking for here?"

Edward blinked. "No, I, just thought maybe out of anyone, you would understand."

Placing my hand on his shoulder, I gripped it hard, allowing him to feel the anger I held about this topic. "You will find no more absolution here than Rhiannon did for the part she played in harming my mate," I confessed. "What Rhi did, she did out of love for her sister. You acted out of loyalty to your pack. Ignorant as you were, Annie doesn't hold a grudge against either of you about it. I've experienced her emotions being near you, Edward. She's happy that you can be near each other again. Annie wants to leave the past behind her and focus on the future; I suggest you find a way to do the same." Giving his shoulder one last good squeeze, I waited for Edward to wince before I stepped back. "Now, we have business to discuss."

Edward rubbed his shoulder with a grimace. "Business?"

"Your mate belonged to the Lunas pack. As such, there is a dowry to be paid."

Edward smirked. "You're going to make me pay through the nose, aren't you?"

"She is an Alpha's progeny."

"And, since the payment goes to Anique, I make amends for my ignorance with a financial settlement."

Leaning towards Edward, I shadowed him in my prestige as an Alpha far superior to him. "Nothing can ever make up for the lack of support and insight you gave that situation, Edward. You'll pay for the bitch. Bring up your ineptness as an Alpha in my presence again, and I'll take you outside and take a pound of flesh instead."

Mouth falling open, Edward quickly snapped it shut and lowered his gaze. "Of course, forgive me."

While I understood Edward wanted to make amends, forgiveness was not a currency I exchanged quickly. Stepping back, I went to turn away but stopped. "There is one thing I want to know. She-wolves are responsible for the cubs in the house. Your sister was a child. Why didn't your mother know she was missing earlier?"

Inhaling through his nose, Edward rolled his shoulders back. "Evaline had to spend two weeks at the university campus doing her practical sessions for her coursework each year. Our mother went with her so they could go shopping and have some time away from the packhouse. Father and I were working, Rhi was at university every day, and no one thought to wonder why we hadn't seen Annie for days on end." Edward lifted his eyes, tears glistening within, but not falling. "My father has never forgiven himself for not making sure she was tucked safely into bed each night."

My heart pounded in my chest, the tightness in my shoulders from restraint, pumping my blood faster. "It seems your entire family carries a modicum of guilt for the part you all played."

A hand slipped over my forearm and down to interlace with my fingers. The tenseness of my muscles eased at the feel of my mate's skin on mine. "Everything okay here?" Anique asked carefully. When neither Edward or I answered her, Anique tugged my hand. "I was going to ask Eric to dance with me, but I realized, for the sake of Eric's ongoing wellbeing, that I should ask you instead."

Smiling into Anique's beautiful emerald eyes, I stepped with her and instantly was pulled free from my darkness. "I'd love to dance. Edward, we can talk later." Leading Anique to the dance floor, I pulled her into my arms. Stepping into the music, I smiled down at my mate as Anique softened her body to let me lead her. "Thank you."

"I think it should be Edward thanking me," Anique scoffed. "What on earth were you talking about to get so worked up?"

Lowering my face, I kissed her forehead. Anique sighed in understanding. We moved around the floor quietly for a few moments. My eyes moved to Anique's mentor and boss, chatting animatedly with Mandy and Rion about the banquet. "Did you speak to Eric?"

"He's booked me in to see him on Monday morning. I'll have the scans done, and we can talk about the results." Exhaling, Anique rested her cheek against my cheek. "He didn't seem hopeful."

"He doesn't understand our physiology well enough, yet. His

studies have been in your blood before you could shift. Your body chemistry will have changed since then." We moved in a circle. "Did you know he was aware of you?"

"I knew he suspected I wasn't like other people," Anique revealed. "I didn't know the government knew and was funding his research to differentiate how different."

"That worries you?" I squeezed her suddenly cold hand.

"What if they find a way to make the serum I created? If they turn our wolves off?" Anique considered. "What if they can do the opposite and give a human a wolf? With half-breeds like Brett out there, they may try experimenting on them first, see if they can bring a wolf out in a dormant genome." Anique lifted her worried eyes to meet mine. "Why are you smiling?"

"Because you are cute when you go all science nerd," I chuckled. "If you are worried, why don't you find a way to counter the inoculation you made? Create something which can undo it."

Anique considered me. "I'd have to find out how long the Rogue's venom lasted. The only test subjects I had are dead. You don't exactly want me testing it on our pack. What if it's permanent?"

I kept dancing, working through the problem in my head. "There are always strays that need dealing with, Annie. If we captured them instead of killing them, we could test the venom on them first. See how long it takes them to come back to their wolf."

"And if they don't?" Anique worried.

"Then we let them go, I guess. I'm not one for killing humans."

Tensing in my arms, Anique lifted suspicious eyes to me. "I've seen your secrets, Knox. Don't lie to me," she threatened.

Observing my mates ire, I rubbed my lips together. "What you saw was me doing my job. I go up against the worst kind of humans out there, Annie. People who blow up innocents, who drive trucks through Christmas carol gatherings, who murder and rape innocent women and children. My job is to hunt down evil creatures. Sometimes to find viler beings, at times to seek and destroy. You heal the body; I cleanse the earth of putrid waste. That's just what I do."

Anique looked torn. I felt the niggle of disgust and understanding, hatred and retribution, and the determined sense of duty overcoming ethics. She understood the need to clean out the rubbish, she didn't enjoy it, but she understood. That's not what worried her right now. The doubt crawling up my spine like a spider in the night wasn't that I killed. Blowing out my breath, I held her closer. "I take no pleasure from doing that to another being, Annie. I do what needs to be done to keep innocents safe. As my father did before me, and his father, and his father, have all done."

When Anique rubbed her cheek across my chest, my insides unclenched, muscles eased, and a feeling of belonging surged through me. "Where are your parents?" Anique sighed. "I remember Evaline mentioning the old Alpha dying young, but never anything about your mother."

Sorrow filled me. It had been decades, but I still felt my parent's loss like it was yesterday. "My father was killed in combat. My mother died of a broken heart within six months of him. I was nineteen when I took the Alpha position in our pack. One of my uncles challenged me for it. I won. He left and became Alpha of the neighboring territory, the Infinity pack." Anique gave the smallest flinch. "He and the handful of wolves who went with him were wiped out five years ago in much the same way as your father's pack was destroyed. Neat and organized." Lowering my eyes, I met her cautious face. "Since they didn't have any females, I can only gather, they found a female stray that was able to overpower them."

"If you want to ask, then ask, Knox. Mates shouldn't have secrets between them."

"Did you annihilate the infinity pack, Annie?"

Rising up on her toes, Anique kissed my lips lightly. "Take me home, Knox. It's a story you'll want to hear in private." Without missing a beat, Anique swung herself under my arm and led us off the dance floor. We bid everyone goodnight and headed outside. Approaching the car, Anique put her hand out. "You've had a bit to drink tonight, I think it's best if I drive."

While I didn't like handing over my keys, I did because of the sense of determination coming from my beautiful mate. Taking the passenger seat, I waited as Anique drove us out to the mountain pass that would take us into Paw Valley. Flashes of green foliage flitted outside the window, the lights on the stereo and dashboard reflecting off the glass, blackness all around us.

"I like to go hiking," Anique broke through the song playing on the radio. "When I first started coming here, I hiked all around these mountains, finding territory lines and learning them. I kept clear of any of the packhouses, and only ever moved around the borders. It might surprise you how many packs fail to monitor their borders more than once a month. The day I met your uncle was on your territory border, with his entire pack. I believe you were away with the hounds at the time. Your uncle had discovered you were gone, and he was going to attack your pack and take the unmated females who lived there. One of those was China, a female stray I directed to you only a week beforehand. The Infinity pack were scouting when I came across them. Overhearing their plans, I quickly made my own. That night, while they camped by the cave and prepared for their late-night attack, they met the Goddess at the point of one of my silver blades. Your females slept through the night unharmed and none the wiser."

Watching Anique shift gear to turn the tight hairpin on the mountain road, I studied her. "Did you keep hiking my territory border after you took up with Brett?"

"I was always drawn to Paw Valley, Knox. I tried to convince myself it was the desire to be part of a pack again or to keep an eye on a potential threat," Anique revealed. "Subconsciously, I probably knew it was my mate, just as I always suspected the draw between Monique and me."

"I regularly was induced to run the lines over the years," I confessed. "I never understood this random need to go running into the forest. I suspect, had I given in to the urge, we might have met sooner."

Anique was quiet as she shifted gears to turn the car as the road folded back on itself again. She wasn't upset, she was calm, almost at peace with her sins and her past. Reaching over, I put my hand on her thigh as she drove. As my finger drew up the inside of her leg, Anique released a small gasp of air from her lips. Just a few inches of touch, but Anique's body sank a little in the seat, and her legs parted just a bit.

"Do you know your cycle?" I asked, wondering if she had days or hours until her heat would drive us mad with lust.

"I should have four more days," Anique admitted. "Please tell me you are not due to fly out again at that time?"

"I'm with the teaching unit right now. Base can't call me up. I'm home for two weeks." I rubbed that finger over that spot again. As soon as we got home, I was taking her to bed.

"Brett and Nathan completed their training qualifications," Anique stated. She was trying to distract, talking about something that didn't make her blood itch along her sternum, tightening her breasts, clenching her insides with longing. "Will you teach at the academy once you finish?"

"That's the idea. We haven't had a hound training at the academy since my father died. With some of our cubs reaching their adolescence, we need one of us there ready for them to come through. Once I've finished the training, I'm going to nominate Dante for the training and Milton after him. That way, if something happens to me, we will have a hound in place to train our young wolves as they come through."

"Nothing is going to happen to you anytime soon," Anique murmured.

"It's the nature of the job, Annie," I soothed. "You know that."

Her eyes glistened in the reflection of the dash light. "I've already lost one husband, Knox, and no one will even tell me how that shit happened. It would be cruel of the Goddess to take you too."

My heart fell into my stomach. The GPS tracking chip buried in our prisoner's skin had led his people straight to us. That they'd had people set up on our soil wasn't expected. The intelligence community suspected there was an imminent threat to safety, but not what. Luckily for them, that threat was diverted to our base when we took one of the militant's critical assets, prisoner.

The attack on the base was intended for a civilian population. Still, that information was never going to be made public. People wanted to sleep at night, knowing they are safe. Making the risk of a terrorist attack general knowledge wasn't going to encourage sweet dreams. "You know I will share any of my secrets with you, Annie," I confided. "But I can't tell you the secrets of my work, much like your Hippocratic oath binds you to doctor-patient confidentiality."

Turning into the driveway, Anique cut through the night to the warm lights of the packhouse. "There are ways around confidentiality clauses, Knox," Anique challenged, she pulled into the garage and turned off the ignition. "After all, you managed to get around it to discuss my condition with my boss?"

"We didn't discuss you as a person. We discussed one of his research patients. No names or identifying factors exchanged," I debated.

Smirking, Anique opened the car door. "So, remove the identifying factors, Knox. Hypothetically, how does intelligence miss a planned attack on a military compound?"

Climbing out of the car, I walked around to meet her at the

hood. "Hypothetically, they don't. But they wouldn't be able to expect an attack planned for location A, changed to position C. Especially without any leading causes." Watching her face fall, I took her hand and pulled her in close. Lifting her pale, delicate fingers to my lips, I kissed each one of her knuckles. "I'd suggest we go for a run, but I think your wolf needs a night off." Caressing her delicate wrist, I pressed my lips into her palm. "Come to bed with me?"

Anique stepped in until she was pressed against me, and I could feel the anxiety in her desire. "The entire length of my marriage, I wanted you while I loved him. Now, I love you and miss him. Even before I lost Brett, loving you hurt my soul."

When I caressed her cheek, Anique tilted her head to present her neck out of instinct. "I will fix that, Annie. As soon as we get home from Eric's on Monday, I will mark you and heal the damage done to our bond."

Anique's emerald eyes glistened. Stepping past me, still holding my hand, Anique led me to my bedroom.

ANIQUE

*W*armth, comfort, belonging. Unlike four months ago, the guilt of being in another man's arms was fading. Four months ago, my heart belonged to Brett. He remained but dating Knox the past two months had given him purchase on my heart too. So, here in his arms, in his bed, felt right, finally.

Lifting my head from his bare chest to watch him sleep, I could feel his happiness radiating through me in pulses. It'd been the same when we started talking on the phone. Initially, anxious on both ends, his joy washed over me when the conversations became comfortable, and more a call between friends. The masturbation, preempted by a text message to make sure it wouldn't intrude on what I was doing, was hot.

Knox usually tried to hold out for late at night or very early morning, and his recall of our time going through the purge was clear enough for me to see it too. Honestly, I'd initiated mutual masturbation on a few occasions. What I hadn't told Knox, was that I crawled into his bed, surrounded myself in his scent, to add to the moment for me.

Climaxing by my touch had been weird and unexpected, but it

turns out, a she-wolf can climax by herself if she's thinking about her mate. It was good to know, moving forward. If I needed to give Knox the cold shoulder for something, I didn't need to go without.

Taking my wrist from his chest, Knox slid it down the sculpted definition of his torso. His sparse body hair up his midline tickled the palm of my hand, thickening into a forest of softness just before his manhood. Wrapping my hand around the thick girth of him, Knox groaned as air escaped his lips in a rush. With soft lips across his smooth chest, I lifted my body over him, thighs wide to straddle his breadth, and a gasp of my own as he entered me.

Knox opened his eyes, pale jade and glassy with desire, pulsing with love and adoration. Removing my hand from his length, I slid onto heaven. Unable to keep quiet, my voice escaped me with my rushed breaths, Knox's large hands holding me steady. Warm lips lapped at the tip of my breasts, sucking and flicking my nips with his tongue, the electrifying current pulsing weighted pleasure to my womb.

My nails dug into the bedhead, looking for purchase on something that could keep me from falling apart into a million pieces of bliss, but it didn't save me. Tilting his hips, Knox sucked my nipple, and I shattered into oblivion. Praising the Goddess, worshipping Knox, and thanking the stars as my muscles became paralyzed, I fell, weightless.

Rolling us, Knox rose above me, a ship on the sea of my ecstasy. "In or out?" He asked, eyes piercing, and breath harsh.

"In," I panted. Was it a stupid call I'd live to regret? Perhaps. But as Knox thrust forward, as he pierced deep into my body and soul, it was the only answer to give. Knox filled me, encompassed me, stilled the spinning world, and narrowed my focus to him. Nails clawed four red lines marking the way he drove me out of myself, only for those lines to be replicated and multiplied across his back.

Delving as deep as he could go, Knox circled his hips, searched out that place that made me sing, and then he built the melody, joined in the chorus, and made it a duet of passion and love felt through every inch of flesh and bone. Staying embedded, making sure my body knew this was home now, Knox kissed me until our breathing was sensible again.

"What was that thought about touching yourself and denying me?" Knox whispered cheekily. His lips nipped down my neck, then back-tracking to my chin. Our eyes met, our mouths followed, our bodies reacted, and I was pulled back together only to be shattered by the hammer of euphoria.

The kitchen bench was cold under my hands, the stone still grasping the stillness of night before the ding of the day overwhelmed it. My womb cramped, and I rubbed at it and cringed a little. Damn, Knox left a long-term impression.

"Are you okay? Is it the silver? Something else?" Rhiannon worried, rushing across the kitchen like a running duck, to get to my side.

"I'm fine, just cramping."

"Cramping?" Rhiannon frowned. "And why do you stink of my Alpha?"

My lips pressed together as the corners lifted. "Our Alpha, Rhi. He's the Alpha of our pack." I took a sip of my coffee. "And I stink of him because he's my mate."

Rhi frowned, then her brows jumped, and her mouth fell open momentarily before it pulled together with a smile. "Oh! I didn't realize the talking and dating had finally led to that point."

"Just yesterday. I'm due for my heat this week, and resisting Knox would have driven us both insane. Plus, four months have passed."

"And it's not like you didn't spend two weeks purging on each other previously," Rhi finished. With a wink, she opened the fridge.

"Don't stress, Annie. You don't have to justify jumping your mate to me. I banged Milton eight ways from Sunday before we even started the phases, on multiple occasions."

My cheeks heated a little, just the same.

"I'm impressed you've held out this long," Rhi praised, taking a glass of milk and plate of cookies to the table.

"It's felt wrong up until now. Please tell me you are not eating that for breakfast?" Before she could answer, I raided the fridge and started cooking.

"So, you feel okay to move on from Brett now?" Rhiannon asked gently.

"It doesn't feel like I'm betraying him anymore. I still think about him, and I miss him, but knowing he understands about true-mates, I get the sense he would support me moving on with Knox. He liked and respected Knox. Brett was angry when I left him, but not as much as most men would have been. I don't think the anger was towards me but towards himself. Like he still harbored self-hatred for not having a wolf." Remembering Brett, I stared at the oats I was stirring. "Is it weird that now that I know, I can look back at things that happened between us, hear the words he said to me, and see everything in another perspective?"

"No," Rhiannon agreed. "I do the same. Every time I met Brett, he inhaled my scent just like pack members do to each other. It didn't even occur to me that a human shouldn't do that. It probably was just a habit he got into as a kid and never shook off."

After cleaning up, I carried the two bowls of porridge over and put one in front of Rhiannon. "I added brown sugar and cinnamon to make it just as appetizing as the cookies, but healthier." Smirking, Rhiannon started eating. "You didn't talk to Edward last night?"

Rhiannon's spoon popped from her mouth, and her eyes drilled into me.

"Want to tell me what is going on between you two?" I asked carefully.

Rhiannon took a deep breath. "When I told dad what happened to us, I told him everything. Our old Alpha told his heir. When Edward heard you miscarried after Brett died, he blamed me. He said it was my fault you ended up rogue, that I'd killed two of your cubs now and how dare I stand there, expecting to start my own family when you might never be able to."

Rhiannon said it without emotion, cold, distant, detached. Not even a tear in her eyes. Struggling to keep the realization of what she just admitted from showing, I stared at my bowl of oats. Rhiannon was due in a matter of weeks. Any upset could cause issues, so I needed to keep my emotions to myself. As it so happened, I also needed to get the hell out of here.

Taking a breath, I stood up and moved around to sit next to her. When I put my arm around her and hugged her, Rhiannon flinched. Holding her tighter, I made sure she knew I wouldn't be letting her go. "I have never blamed you for anything that happened to me, Rhi. Never. Dan and those bastards did this to both of us. We were never at fault."

A hiccup, and then Rhiannon started crying. "But, if I had told our Alpha what they did to me, you would have been protected. It would never have happened."

"Dan would have found a way, Rhi, don't doubt that for a second. Mum being out of the packhouse, just gave him the opportunity." Twisting in her seat, Rhiannon cuddled into me. Anxiety slithered up my spine. Concentrating for a moment, I felt Knox and another wolf near, luring my eyes to a shadow by the door.

Sniffing the air, Milton reeked of anger and anxiety, and Knox was right there beside him. When I frowned at them both, Knox placed a sure hand on Milton's shoulder and moved him back out the door, leaving us alone. "We took our vengeance on the ones who hurt us, Rhi. There is no one left to blame. Stop punishing yourself for something that was out of your control."

Sobbing into my shoulder a few more minutes, Rhiannon slowly got her breathing under control and then pulled away, swiping at her face. Locating the tissues, I brought the box over to her.

"You know, Mum doesn't talk to you because she feels just as guilty as Dad," Rhiannon sniffled.

"She didn't exactly rush back to the hospital, Rhi. She didn't care before that all went down. Edward and Evaline were her favorites, that's always been the case."

"Blah, little miss perfect Evaline," Rhiannon scoffed and rolled her eyes. "The perfect she-wolf."

We'd received numerous lectures growing up where Evaline was the poster girl we were meant to look up to. "She has been the model example of how a mating should take place," I allowed.

"You should have heard mum when she sniffed out I was already pregnant at the banquet," Rhiannon complained. "Evaline at least waited till the purge like a good she-wolf should mate with her husband," Rhiannon mimicked our mother flawlessly. "Boring! What if Dante had a small cock? Then she wouldn't be crowing about how her mate is perfect compared to ours. Her husband didn't hesitate in taking the phases. Her mate met her and abided by custom without a minute's hesitation or regret."

Swallowing, I shrugged. "I'm sure Dante has what it takes to make her happy, but I've seen all our mates naked. Dante has English sausage, but Milton's packing German sausage." I winked.

Rhiannon burst out laughing. She knew Milton had told me not to eat his sausage when he shifted in front of me. Sobering, Rhiannon, met my eyes. "I am sorry that what happened will stop prevent you from being able to provide your mate with progeny, Annie. I was only trying to protect you."

Placing my hand over hers, I tried to ignore the ants crawling between my shoulder blades, but they were faster now, and there were a lot more of them. Shifting my shoulder blades back and down, I tried to escape the unease. "The Goddess wills as she wanes and waxes, Rhi. Who am I to question the path she set before me?" Rising, I cleaned up my bowl from breakfast. "Eat your porridge. I'm going to go for a walk."

"Annie," Rhiannon called after me. "Was it Edward or Knox who told you?"

Realizing Knox knew, my throat worked over the pain of swallowing. "Neither betrayed your trust to me. No one told me. No one needed to." Rhiannon's eyes went wide as I pushed through the kitchen door and headed straight for the stairs outside. My skin was itching, and my vision was changing to muted colors.

"Annie." Knox caught my shoulder, but he didn't try to pull me back or close to him. His voice stern enough to stop my feet; his concern palpable. "I understand the need to escape, but you don't have the best track record for staying present when you shift to escape your reality."

"You could come with me, keep me grounded?"

"With your heat coming on, my wolf wouldn't be able to resist yours," Knox objected. "And I want to mark you before we mate that way."

Stepping into him, I lifted my eyes to him, daring him. "Do it. Mark me now, and then let's shed our skin and run."

Large warm fingers caressed my cheek, sweeping away the salty debris of my emotions. "When you say that without anger clouding your judgment, I will happily concede. For today, let the person walking calm waters lead you free of the emotional storm you are hiding."

Gritting my teeth, I shoved him. "You knew and didn't tell me. How did you know if I didn't? How did you know what she did to me?"

Tilting his head, Knox studied me. "Milton confided in me after the second phase. He wasn't sure if he could go through with the mating after he saw the truth of your disability."

Breathing was hard, and my blood was pooling as half-moons in my palms, where I had held my rage in until I could get away from Rhiannon. I blinked through the tears, blurring my vision. "I need to get away from her for a few hours," I pleaded. "An Alphia is the dominant female; their emotions can affect the other she-wolves in the pack. Rhiannon still has a month to go, so I can't be near her like this. I don't want the guilt of causing her to lose a cub plaguing my conscience. Look what it's done to Rhi."

Stepping closer, Knox wrapped his arms around me. "I'll get us a room at a hotel for tonight. Would that work?" Nodding against his chest, I clung to him for saving. "Okay, let's go pack our bags," Knox urged. He held me a few more seconds, then walked us inside and to my room.

"What the hell!?" Knox stared at my bedroom horrified. Wading into the mess of my bedroom, I started shoving stuff in a bag. "Annie, how is your room this messy? Did someone search it for something?"

Frowning, I looked at the piles of books and discarded clothing that I would pick up when I washed next. "No."

"How would you know?" When I just blinked at him, Knox pointed to the discarded clothes. "Don't you have a laundry basket?"

"Usually, I'm so tired coming home to bed, I just strip as I walk in and fall into bed," I explained. "I don't exactly have free time to run around and clean up. I'm still working ten to twelve-hour shifts at the hospital, and when I get home, I have to do your job here. I sleep and read in here, that's it."

Knox looked around himself. "When we start sharing a room, this can't happen, Annie. I like everything neat and tidy."

"Then hire a maid. I don't have the time to clean up the house, Knox. I work for a living." Turning my back on his, I kept packing.

"Annie, if you put your clothes in a laundry hamper, you wouldn't need to clean up after yourself. You just don't make a mess to start with."

Glaring at Knox, I refused to even have this argument right now. Wasn't I angry enough? Was this really the best time to discuss my inner sloth? When Knox met my eyes, jade green pressure pushed me back a step, insistence that I keep my room tidy bearing down on me like the weight of the world on Atlas's shoulders. Gasping, not used to another's will dominating mine, I licked my lips and lowered my eyes, turning my head from the force pushing down on me. The ground shifted, sucking me beneath, trying to pull me away from the looming shadow that was growing to encompass the room, dwarfing me, smothering me. Shoulders rolling forward, I whimpered. The pressure backed off.

When Knox touched my chin, I jumped out of my skin, his body so warm against my coldness. "Shh, Annie, I never push a wolf to break. It would be pointless and mean." Wrapping his arms around me, Knox cooed to me until I relaxed into him, rubbing my face against his chest, whimpering noises escaping from my throat. "You're like a cub scolded for the first time. Did your father never Alpha you?"

Clinging to Knox's shirt, I shook my head. For some reason, it made Knox chuckle. "I always thought I'd end up mated to a spoilt Alpha's progeny. You had me convinced I'd been wrong, but I wasn't. You were daddy's little girl, weren't you?"

"Yes, but I never got in trouble because I behaved. I was the perfect she-wolf until I couldn't be."

Knox held me tighter. "You're a powerful wolf, Annie. You would have rebelled eventually and failed to bow down to an Alpha less than you. The Goddess willed you to me for a reason, Annie. A female needs a stronger male to-"

"Protect her from enemies and herself, and to support her

when she asks for help," I finished for him, lifting my tear-streaked face to meet his eyes.

"Your father taught you Alpha King Lincoln's words?"

"Edward used to read it to me when I was a cub, to help me sleep," I breathed.

Knox's lips turned up at the side. "Then Edward just gained a little more respect and prestige in my eyes." Knox guided me to the bed. "Let's get out of here."

Nodding, I scanned the mess of my room. "You go pack. I'll just do a quick tidy up."

The side of Knox's mouth lifted as he kissed my forehead and left me to obey his will. I guess if he was going to assert dominance for anything, cleaning up after myself wasn't that bad.

⸙

"Annie," Eric called from the staff room door. With Christmas only a week away, no surgeries were scheduled. For the next few weeks, it was emergency surgery, if needed, and patient rounds. "Is Knox still around?" Knox had come to my early morning appointment and to get all the tests done. We'd had to wait for the blood tests, so I'd gone back to work.

Closing my eyes, I concentrated and smiled when I found where Knox was. "He's just across the road getting me lunch. Did you want a burger?" Picking up my phone, I texted Knox with Eric's order. Eric, like me, never turned down the burgers across the road.

"A. That's just creepy that you can track each other like that. B. I'd love lunch. C. Can you teach me that trick if I ever get married? With the rate of infidelity in this industry, it'd be a handy thing to do," Eric considered.

"Humans have the technology to stalk your partner. Buy her a set of earrings or necklace with inbuilt GPS. Or, you could just try trust."

"Do you and Knox trust each other?" Eric challenged.

"Knox and I are two halves of a whole. If he has sex with another woman, I feel it. It's horrible, like being repeatedly bitten by wasps. Hell, he can't even have a tug without me feeling it. Any high emotions, we share." Cringing, I rubbed my stomach. "Like anxiety. I feel it like a snake slithering around my belly."

Eric squinted. "Did you have that with Brett?"

Shaking my head, I dropped my shoulders. "No, but we had trust, love, and sincerity."

Eric shifted. "Sorry, I keep bringing him up. That's unfair with you trying to move on."

"Brett was a major part of my life for a long time, Eric. I didn't give him up, and I'm never going to stop thinking about him. Knox monopolized my thoughts from the moment we met, that won't change either." Lips twinging in a sympathetic smile, Eric walked around the table while I finished my coffee.

"Did you want to discuss the results here or in your office?" I asked.

"You're a patient, so office," Eric sighed. "But we can eat lunch out here first." He took the seat opposite me.

"Have you seen the results?"

"I have, and I've already spoken to Blake about them too."

My phone buzzed. Glancing at the message, I smiled. "Knox says you can't tell me anything until he gets here, and he's in the elevator."

Shaking his head, Eric smirked. "Still trippy the way you two do that, but I'm getting used to it. I'll make myself a coffee."

"I'm going to be away for two weeks as of tonight," I informed. "I hope that's not an issue?"

Eric considered me as he prepped the coffee machine. "Do your kind celebrate Christmas?"

My lips lifted. "No, but we do celebrate the solstice. That's not why I need the time. Knox and I are going to cement our connection, and that requires two weeks of isolation afterward."

"Is that code for eloping and honeymoon?"

Swaying my head to one side, I bit my lip as I thought about it. "If we are comparing to human mating rituals, then yes."

Eric lifted his brows. "Wow, can you tell me how your mating ritual works?"

At his request, I lifted a brow. "Well, there is the seeing, which is when we meet and recognize each other as future mates. The knowing is when you share your biggest secrets with each other. You get to know each other as if you had known each other from birth. This phase is effectively the engagement of our ritual. Usually, the marking happens at the banquet."

"That's when Rion bit Mandy, right?" Eric queried. Mandy and Rion had gone full traditional and performed the marking before their packs. I'd never seen Mandy look so happy as when Rion slid his incisors into her.

"That's it, and the mating usually takes two weeks after," I finished.

Eric sat back down with his coffee. "Why aren't you and Knox doing the banquet?"

"Because I fucked up the ritual back when we first met," Knox answered, standing by the door. Coming into the staff room, he stopped by the seat next to me, placing the food on the table. "Annie and I have already completed the stages, but I messed it up, so we have to do it all again."

Taking his hand in mine, I allowed the great warmth of him to smother my small hand. The bees buzzing around my brain slowly flew away as Knox's anger at his actions cooled. The truth was, I was glad Knox rejected me. His actions meant I spent the last six months of Brett's life in happiness. The idea that Brett would have been miserable for the months leading up to his death didn't sit right with me. It made a difference, remembering his smiles and laughter.

Peering down at me, Knox squeezed my hand a touch, enough to let me know he was aware where my mind had gone. Meeting his pale green gaze, I stared into the starlight pupils of his wolf's jealousy, and lifted my lips to one side, mouth closed. A sad smile. Turning my eyes down, I tilted my head, and my fingers caressed the place Knox's teeth had marked me, the place he would mark me again.

Hand loosening, Knox blew out a breath as his pupils returned to black, then he placed a kiss to his claim on my neck and took his seat. While Knox put our meals in front of us, I found Eric watching, brows furrowed, but he didn't verbalize his curiosity or his concern.

For the next twenty minutes, we ate and talked about Eric's research, and Mandy's banquet, then Eric stood and went to his office. Exhaling, I got up and cleaned up just to distract and postpone a little longer. Then, with nothing left to use as an excuse to delay, Knox and I walked hand in hand towards Eric's door.

"Annie," Knox murmured and held me back a step. "No matter what the tests show, I love you, and I will spend the rest of my life loving you."

Eyes itching with emotion, I pressed a chaste kiss to his lips and led Knox into Eric's office. Sitting on the opposite side of his desk, we replicated our visit four months prior. The only difference, Brett wasn't here with us this time. My eyes drifted to the spot his ashes had occupied during that visit.

"Let's start with the scans," Eric announced. "No scarring remains whatsoever. Everything seems normal, and in fact, your ovaries are currently preparing to release an egg." Eric turned the screen so I could see the small follicle cysts competing to produce an ovum.

"What's this?" I pointed to an opaque part of my ovary.

"That's the silver poisoning." Pressing a button, Eric brought up my scans from four months ago to show them next to the most recent. "And it's shrinking, Annie. It's still in your organ tissue, but your body is very quickly filtering it out, renewing the cells affected, and returning you to full health."

Turning the screen away, Eric used his mouse to click through options. "Now, your blood tests pretty much support what we can see in the scans. The metal toxicity in your blood has more than halved in the last four months. Your life expectancy has more than doubled. In fact, only a few more milligrams and the level in your blood won't even be considered toxic any longer, by human standards anyway."

Knox and I sat there holding hands. His hope was growing with every word out of Eric's mouth, mirroring my hesitant expectations. Taking a deep breath, I dared to ask the question we were both wanting to be answered. "So, if I were to fall pregnant in the next two weeks?" I held that breath, ready for the blow that would kill this growing idea of my future with Knox.

Eric looked at us, then down at his notes. "I called Blake and asked him that same question. Not necessarily the time frame, but I posed the possibility." Eric lifted his eyes to mine. "Blake feels you currently have a seventy-five percent chance of conceiving, but only a forty percent chance of carrying to term."

My shoulders dropped, and despite having tried to bury the hope, and to shield myself from it, my eyes filled.

"But, given your current rate of healing, Blake thinks in another six months, you could have the same statistics as any other healthy twenty-eight-year-old." Eric closed my file. "Another six months would also see you finish your first fellowship year, Annie. If I were to give you any advice this minute, it would be that the future looks good for you starting a family. Don't rush into it now. Give your body the time to heal thoroughly, finish your fellowship, and then start your family."

Turning my glassy eyes to Knox, I didn't need to ask what he thought. His expectations were set like cement already. Knox was determined that Eric spoke gospel, and it was already filtering through our bond, infecting me, and telling me how it was going to be. "So, eighteen months?"

Knox met my gaze with surety. "That should be fine." Wiping away a tear that escaped my eye, Knox soothed me with that touch. "Your health and happiness first, Annie. The Goddess waxes and wanes as she will."

EPILOGUE

Knox

———

One Year Later

"Rion," I greeted as the hounds, and I made our way into Comms to report. Rion was grinning like a maniac.

"Alpha, Mandy is with cub," Rion murmured to me, voice giddy and excited.

"I thought she wanted to wait?" The she-wolves had gone into heat the week before we flew out, all of them now conforming to Anique's cycle. I expected Mandy wouldn't be the only pregnant female when we got back. With all the women on the same schedule, the last week we were home had been a rut fest. The only time any mated wolf left their room was for food. The unmated wolves had spent a lot of time out of the house, spending time with human women, or visiting the brothel.

"Mandy did," Rion confirmed. "She wanted to be with cub the same time as Anique, but the heat took us."

He meant they got caught up and forgot to use protection. "Happens to us all, Rion. Congratulations." Giving him a wink before walking forward to report in, I smirked. At least I didn't need to replace Rion in the field for the time Mandy was with cub. If Rhiannon or Evaline were pregnant again, it wouldn't impact. They only stayed close to home for the first cub and when their mate was approaching her due date. I would be the only one needing base duties if Anique conceived, and she wasn't ready yet.

Physically, she was. The silver poisoning was all but gone in her scans two months ago, and her body was that of the average she-wolf her age. We were free to start trying for cubs, but Anique wanted to wait until she finished her fellowship. That wasn't to say the heat didn't catch us on occasion over the last year; we'd even mated in fur once or twice, but luckily, my seed hadn't taken.

Every second I was absent from her, I missed Anique. If we were in the same room, I needed to be touching her. Not smothering, but I liked to have my hand on her leg, or our feet interlaced, just some form of a physical connection. These days, I never relaxed in her absence.

The team had showered and changed and were heading to the cars when I came out from reporting. "See you at home, Alpha?" Dante checked.

"Rion, is Annie working this afternoon?" I asked, checking if I needed to go to the hospital first. I could have felt where she was, but having found her elbow-deep in blood during surgery a few times, I preferred to know she wasn't working before I sensed her. My wolf did not like seeing his mate covered in blood.

"She finished up two hours ago, Alpha," Rion conveyed. "She went home to rest before she meets her family for dinner."

Closing my eyes, I sensed my mate running through the forest. "Resting my ass," I grumbled.

Rion shrugged. "Mandy said it was a rough day at work. There was a massive car accident on the freeway, and the victims transported to Dempsey, so Annie spent all day in surgery. Mandy told me they were going for a run to burn off the adrenalin."

"She's exhausted. She should be sleeping." Gritting my teeth, I took a breath. "Best I go shower and get home, so I can drive her up the mountain again."

"Because you're not exhausted?" Dante challenged.

"I caught some zees on the plane home." Waving them off, I started towards the barracks for a quick wash and change. Driving home separately from the unit was my time out. While I loved my pack and my team, I also liked my solitude. Before I jumped in the car, I concentrated on Anique and felt her stretching after her run. She was calmer but frustrated.

By the time I pulled into the driveway, the sun was setting. Checking the clock, I'd have time for a quick debrief on the pack and to change before heading back to town for dinner with Anique's family. As I walked in, Evaline was chasing Grace, who was running, toddler style now. Rhiannon's first cub, Emmanuel, was in Evaline's arms, knees red from crawling.

Catching Grace in my arms, I threw her into the air. She giggled and then wrapped her little arms around my neck. "Knock, knock," she laughed, trying to say my name.

"He's Alpha, Gracie," Evaline schooled. "Alpha Knox." Evaline put her arms out for her cub. Handing her back, I greeted Emmanuel. He looked just like Milton at the same age; we'd compared photos to prove it.

As I leaned in, I caught a whiff of Evaline's scent and smiled. "Congratulations, Evaline. Grace will have a sibling in a matter of months."

Cheeks flaming, Evaline looked away coyly. "And cousins. In fact, the house will be overrun with babies in six months. All the mated females conceived on their last heat. Even Edgar is going to be a father again."

For a moment, I got excited. "All the mated females?" Six females with cub at once was enough to make me want to spend another six months training, but not if a particular she-wolf was expecting.

Evaline's face fell. "Well, all but one." Evaline watched my smile dim. "I'm sorry, Alpha. I should be more careful of my words and not generalize. It was cruel for me to do so." Quickly bowing her head in deference, Evaline moved the cubs out of the room. Dante greeted her in the doorway, and I watched her whisper to him before kissing him and moving on.

Dante moved forward carefully. "Alpha?"

"Do you think it's me, Dante?" I asked quietly. "Maybe the Goddess has made me sterile as punishment for rejecting my mate so cruelly. Perhaps, it's why she mated us?"

Dante shook his head. "No, I don't. Not for your reasons, but I believe the Goddess knows Annie has suffered enough. The Goddess mated you because Annie deserves happiness. If Annie desires cubs, I think the Goddess will bless her with them."

Bowing my head, I hoped Dante was right, but look at what the Goddess had already subjected my Annie too. "I should go get ready for this dinner and check-in with the Alphia on the state of my pack," I excused. Stepping aside, Dante watched me go with concern. "Congratulations on the news," I added as I reached the hall.

"Thank you, Alpha."

Making my way to my bedroom, I found Anique laying half on the bed. She was dressed ready to go, her eyes closed, hands over her flat abdomen. Did a little spark inside me die out at the awareness her womb held no life? Yes.

Taking a deep breath, the scents of forest and earth, summer humidity, night-blooming Jasmine, herbs, aniseed, and musk hit me. Pausing, I sniffed the air, pulling more of Anique's scent into me. She still tried to hide her smell; her body wash, and her body cream the homemade mixtures she used to mask the wolf in her from others. But, not from me, not from her true-mate. Now, I could find her no matter where she went.

Sitting down on the bed beside her, I took one of her hands in mine. "I thought, perhaps, I should visit the doctor. Have my sperm tested?" Her frustration and annoyance were a buzzsaw in my head the moment I stepped into the room.

Opening her eyes, Anique lifted onto her elbows. "Why?"

"We weren't exactly careful, Annie. Every other mated female in this house is with cub. You've been tested. We know it's not you. That only leaves me as the issue."

Tilting her head, Anique studied me quietly for a moment. Reaching out, she grabbed my shirt, pulling me across to meet her lips. "Firstly, that's not how you greet your wife after being away for three weeks," she sassed. "Secondly, there is nothing wrong with your sperm. Alphas are the most fertile wolves in a pack. They provide the most progeny, they have the sex drive of a minx, and they should always greet their mates by showing them just how much they missed them."

"You weren't exactly waiting at the door for me as the other she-wolves do for their mates."

Anique smiled. "That's because I'm an Alphia. I don't wait anxiously by the door for my mate's return. I wait in our bed so he can show me how much he missed me.

Lips tilting up, I pressed my mouth to hers, pinching, kissing, showing her I missed her. Pulling Anique into my arms, I rolled onto my back. Our mouths were slow, languorous, firm. Anique's small delicate hands touched the skin of my waist, slid up my torso, across my chest, around to my shoulder blades, forcing my arms up as my shirt lifted over my head.

The delicate material of her dress scrunched in my fists as I pulled it up to her waist, then her smooth pale ass fit in the palm of my hands. Using the tip of my fingers, I slid the material of her scanties into the gully, so I could hold those cheeks bare.

Two loud thumps on our bedroom door jolted us. "Alpha, the rest of us are heading to Campus for dinner," Dante called.

"We'll be right behind you," I called back breathlessly. Anique's soft lips were moving to my neck to let me speak, her fingers making quick work of my belt and fly. "I'm just getting changed now."

Chuckling, Dante walked away. Stepping off the bed, Anique yanked my jeans to the floor, leaving them caught around my boots and ankles. Mesmerized as she shimmied out of her scanties, I swallowed all the spit in my mouth as she straddled my hips. "I've missed you, Knox," Anique breathed in my ear.

Turning my face, I caught the pulse point on her neck with my lips. "I love you, Annie. I miss you too much for words to say." In my peripheral, I watched the corner of Anique's mouth turn up. It opened, and her breath rushed out as she slid over me, taking me deep within her steadily.

Falling back on the bed, I moaned at the wonderful feeling of being connected with my mate. We were whole again, two halves melding into one. How was I ever fool enough to give this up? Rocking over me, Annie gripped my shoulders to add strength to her grind, her mouth marking across my neck, chest, and jaw. Her lips were pulling up further with every lustful sound echoing from my chest.

Holding her hips in my palms, I added to the pressure, thighs clenching to thrust up and meet her, driving deeper. When Annie sat up, her nails raked my chest, head hanging back, mouth open, and moaning my name, I couldn't hold back any longer. As her body gripped mine, I could barely keep my eyes open to watch her shatter into pieces above me, the best thing in the world to witness.

Falling to my chest, breathing laboriously, Annie smiled, her eyes mirroring my happiness. When our breathing was calm and our bodies slowly remembering how to move, I lifted and kissed the top of her head. Taking a deep breath, I frowned at the strangeness of her scent. "Did you change your mixture?" I asked, breathing deep to try and identify the new fragrance.

Laughing, Anique lifted sparkling eyes to meet mine. "You did," she stated plainly. Sitting up, Annie continued to smile at my bewildered state. Taking my hand, she placed it on her abdomen. "I wanted to be the one to tell you. I wanted it to be my surprise for you."

Eyes wide enough for my eyeballs to escape the socket, my mouth fell open. "A cub?" Biting her lip on the excitement radiating out of me, Anique nodded. Flipping her onto her back, I withdrew so I could lower my mouth and kiss a hundred kisses over her tummy. The Goddess had blessed me with the perfect mate, and now she would bless us with a family. Dante could have his ideal she-wolf, Anique was perfect for me. She kept me grounded, netted my ego to stop it getting too big, and taught me to value the Goddess's gifts for more than just what I thought they were. I'd never been happier in my life.

Hesitating, I met her eyes. "But, the fellowship?"

Smoothing her thumb across my brow tenderly, Anique watched me, radiant in joyful bliss. "I will finish a month before our cub is due. Everything is going to be fine," Anique soothed. "Just promise you will always come home to me, and I will be happy."

We both knew that I couldn't promise her with surety. White had already failed that promise before, and I wasn't about to make her suffer another broken promise. "I will do everything in my power, Annie. You are my home. Whenever I am able, I will be with you."

Anique smiled, her lips finding mine as she kissed me deeply, happiness and acceptance wrapping around me and holding me to her. "Can we announce it tonight at dinner?" I asked. "It will make Stirling happy."

"I was hoping to do so," Anique agreed. "You should know. Dad is standing down. Since the pack is no more, and Edward is expecting a cub of his own, dad decided Edward should be Alpha."

Caressing her face, I stepped away. "Then, I will greet your brother as a fellow Alpha tonight and make a treaty with him for future sniff sessions when his cubs have come of age."

Taking my hand in hers before I could walk away, Anique held me with her eyes. "If we have a girl, I want her raised as more than a wife and future breeder. I want the world to be her oyster and nothing to be impossible for her."

Hesitating to promise that freedom, I licked my lips. "I would give all our cubs the world, Annie. But it is full of danger and too much freedom can be a mistake. I will do what I can to see that every dream she has is achievable. That's all I can promise."

Giving me a half-smile, Anique let my hand go. "It's a start."

My lips twitched at the playfulness of her voice. She wasn't angry, but she planned to work on me. Her determination to give our daughter's the world was admirable. For sure, I would enjoy every negotiation we made to its fullest extent. Anique's eyes glinted, naughty desires slithering around my hips. Laughing, I recognized I wasn't the only one imagining just how our debates would go.

Placing my hands on either side of her on the bed, I dropped a peck to her nose. "You're perfect for me, Annie. I'll never give you up now that I know how flawlessly we meld."

Her soft hand smoothed over my chest and up my neck, her thumb caressing the place she claimed me as hers. "I know." She kissed my lips once. "You should get ready. If you stay naked much longer, we won't make it to dinner at all."

Tempted by the thought, I growled as I removed myself and found my control. The team was home for a few days, so I had plenty of time to play later. After showering again, I dressed while

Anique pinned up her russet locks. "I thought you were going to cut your hair?"

Now that she was shifting, the long hair was an issue in fur. Wrapping a lock around her finger, Anique sighed. "I can't do it. I like my hair long. And, it's not like I'll be slipping my skin for the next six months."

Wrapping my fingers into the length, I pulled my mate into my arms. "Good! I love you just the way you are."

BOUNDARY

Vera Cana has given her life to escape her abusive ex. She's earned her freedom and has the scars to prove it. Now, she's starting a new life. Purchasing a cottage in a lush forest, she's ready to live out her days in peace. The goddess has other plans.

If Vera thought by hiding out in her little cottage she could avoid any more packs and their alphas, she was wrong. When her new neighbor knocks on her door, the draw to him is magnetic, but the scars of her past are a barrier higher than the boundary fence between their properties. Dale's presence causes a heady mix of calm and excitement, which only adds to the potency of his patient, but determined personality. Vera is about to learn a lot about the way packs work, and she's going to discover how strong she can be.

Nothing takes more inner strength than learning how to trust someone with your heart.

Chapter 1

The cottage was perfect. From the moment I paid the settlement fee until I arrived this morning to pick up the keys, I worried it was a con. But it was even prettier than in the pictures. Now, I had to hope the inside wasn't derelict.

A gaudy yellow high-end sports car pulled up beside me, and a man in a designer suit stepped out. After checking his styled blond hair in the mirror of his car, he walked to me. "Good morning, are you Ms. Cana's daughter?"

Raising a brow at the assumption, I folded my arms across my chest. "No. I am Miss Cana."

Brows jumping, the man's eyes widened as he looked me over. "Really? I was expecting an older woman to want a cottage like this."

At twenty-eight, I wasn't too young to own my own home. "Yes, my name is Vera Cana, and I purchased the cottage." For the first time in years, I didn't have to force my smile. Not that this egotistical man caused it. The cottage and the keys to it that this man was holding gifted me this joy.

Grinning, his eyes traveled over me a second time. It wasn't lecherous, there was nothing to see. My long sleeved teal boat neck top covered my breasts, and the loose black slacks went all the way to my ballet flats. Since I couldn't be bothered straightening it today, my mahogany wavy hair was up in a bun. I wore no makeup, so my skin was my natural alabaster, something my ex didn't find attractive.

That was my look now, neat, put together, but as unattractive to the opposite sex as I could be. Danny Ready perused my appearance, then frowned and returned his eyes to my fake muddy brown ones. My eyes were actually a vivid green; a feature men tended to pay attention too. To be unremarkable, the eyes needed to stay hidden.

"Well, it's nice to finally meet you. I'm Danny Ready. Your real estate agent's representative here since they don't have an office down this way." Danny held up the keys. "Here are the keys to your new home, Miss Cana. Should we look inside to make sure it's what you purchased?"

Taking the keys, I met his eyes again. "Is it furnished still?"

"Yes, of course, that was part of the sale contract. Mr. Ways son only removed personal effects and memorabilia. Even the crockery and cutlery remain in case you wanted that."

Grateful, I smiled. I'd spent the vast majority of my savings on the purchase of the land, and I didn't want to have to buy anything to move in.

"Excellent, well, I can take it from here, Mr. Ready. Thank you." Turning my back on him, I moved to collect my bag from my second hand, but immaculate coupe.

"Would you like me to help you with your things?"

When Mr. Ready followed me to my car, I huffed. Forcing my well-rehearsed smile, I turned back. "No, I only have my overnight bag. The rest of my belongings will follow." Lie.

"Oh. Well, very well then." Danny handed me his business card. "If you need anything, or have any questions, don't hesitate to call."

With a nod, I accepted his card then turned my back on him again. Frowning in the reflection of my car window, Danny turned away. Collecting my handbag from the passenger seat of my car, I closed and locked the door as I moved to the boot.

Revving his sports car, Danny Ready drove back up the long drive. The cottage was on the grounds of a historic manor house and used to belong to the owner's loyal butler. The bungalow and land gifted to him by the owner for his service.

Danny had told me the butler served two generations of the family before he died at age eighty-three. His son left for college as a teen and never returned, and the wife passed thirty years ago. The son listed it for sale without even offering the estate owner the chance to repurchase it.

The listing went live at the same moment I was looking for a perfect out of the way place, and I'd bought it within the hour. The owner of the manor house hadn't been happy the cottage sold. His lawyer emailed me a few weeks ago and tried to reverse the sale.

This caused a two-week delay in taking possession. Our lawyers examined the deeds and determined that, yes, I now owned the cottage. There was nothing Mr. Hern could do about the sale. The extra expense it cost me in legal fees obliterated the rest of my savings, but at least the cottage was mine.

Grabbing the overnight case and the two bags of food I'd bought on the way here, I looked out over the cottage. The deeds gave me the bungalow, the acre of cleared land around it, and the driveway. The forest surrounding my allotment belonged to the manor house. The real estate agent told me the woods were full of deer and rabbit, and the previous owner had been free to use it.

Of course, that was before the owner tried to steal the cottage back from me. He would likely have me charged with trespass if he caught me wandering the woods around his home now. Then again, Mr. Hearn lived and worked in the city, three hours away from here and only came home on the weekends. So, there might be some room for movement.

Unlocking the front door of the cottage, I stepped inside. My smile bloomed. The place was perfect. A simplistic single story with a well-orchestrated floor plan. The long, wide hall displayed art and landscape photographs.

There were two large bedrooms to either side of the entrance hall, each with a walk-in closet and bathroom. Walking into the master bedroom, I deposited the suitcase containing my only belongings. Then headed off to find the kitchen to put my groceries away.

The open living area in the rear of the cottage contained the kitchen and lounge. The floor to ceiling glass windows overlooked the yard, the forest, and the veranda off of the living area. The cottage was beautiful, and everything I needed.

After a few minutes of unpacking, I spent the rest of the afternoon getting acquainted with my new home.

Opening my laptop, I connected it out to the internet. The technicians came out earlier this week to set the cottage up with high-speed internet. It was another costly venture, but since it provided my income, it's what I needed more than clothes.

Making myself a small salad for dinner, I toasted my new home and life with a small glass of wine. After supper, I showered and changed into the only pair of pajamas I owned; a little black singlet and short set. Wrapping my long black dressing gown around me, I walked out onto the back deck to overlook the yard.

The lights around the perimeter of the yard were aglow, though I hadn't switched them on. There was a path of lights leading into the forest from the yard. Assessing their direction, I decided it led to the main house. More than likely created to enable the butler to get home in the dark.

Feeling brave, since it was the middle of the week, I stepped off the back porch and wandered along the path. The trees were dense, and the smell of wood and earth suffused my senses.

An animal noise made me stop. Peering to my left, I spied a small pond and a doe drinking from it. Moving off the path towards it, I kept low and quiet. Having never seen a live deer before, I was curious how tame the animals were here.

The doe lifted her head to watch me approach. "It's okay, I'm not going to hurt you. I'll stay on this side of the pond. I just want to watch you."

The doe hesitated but allowed me to come closer. When I reached this side of the pond, I squatted to watch it, tucking my robe around my legs so it wouldn't get in the dirt. The doe and I sat staring at each other, my smile growing.

Then the doe cocked her head, eyes widened with fright, and she darted off into the forest. Standing surprised, I wondered what startled her. Turning my attention to where the doe spooked, it took me a moment to see the golden eyes reflecting the moonlight in the dark.

Swallowing the lump of fear in my throat, I took a step back as the snout of the dog became clearer. "Nice puppy." My voice trembled like my legs as adrenaline coursed through my veins.

The dog snarled, it's lip lifting to show enormous canines. Backing up, I exhaled hard when I rammed straight into a tree. Cringing with the pain that burst through my already injured side, I prayed that this was a dog from the main house. "Okay, not a puppy. Nice doggy?"

The animal lifted itself from the foliage and stepped into the clear, allowing me to see it. It lowered its large head and snarled again as it evened its weight on its paws. Knowing that maneuver from the discovery channel, I tried to plot my retreat while keeping an eye on the dog.

The animal was huge, and it took me another moment to

realize, it wasn't a domestic dog breed I'd ever seen before. "Oh, god. Not a nice doggy then."

Bolting through the forest towards the cottage, I used the lights of the path off to my left to guide me. The snarling and snapping of foliage let me know the dog was chasing me through the scrub, gaining on me.

Making the clearing, I tripped on a cable I hadn't seen before. Falling to the ground with a yelp, I caught myself on my hands. Refusing to take the time to feel the cut across my shin from the cable, or the fact breathing hurt, I rolled over. Sprawled on the ground, I stared at the angry dog as it slowed and crossed the boundary of my land.

It snarled at me again, stalking closer. Whimpering, I cringed back as it lunged for me. Snatching my dressing gown, the dog tried to drag me back to the forest. Clinging to the ground, I dug my fingers in to try and prevent it pulling me to my death.

When material started ripping, I realized it gave me an opportunity. Letting go of the ground, I yanked the tie on the robe and shrugged out of it. Sobbing as I backed away, I crawled further into the yard toward the cottage. My ankle was on fire, so trying to stand and take my weight would only disable me.

Growling, the dog swung his head, throwing my gown to the side before he lunged forward. Throwing my arms up to protect me, I prepared for the worst. Nothing happened.

The dog was standing above me, his breathing angry, but it didn't bite me. Opening my eyes, I dared a peek. Standing astride my legs, it was staring at my body, then lowering his snout to my exposed abdomen, the dog sniffed.

Whimpering when he poked the freshly healed wound in my side, I cringed. The stitches only came out last week. He nuzzled the bruising across my abdomen, causing me to sob louder.

Stepping back, the dog nuzzled the dark bruises across my thighs. Lifting its head, the dog frowned at me, tilting his head in question. Biting my lip on the fear inside me, I found the sudden pity in the beast's eyes disturbing. Waiting, he barked at me before poking my bruised thigh.

"You're not the first beast to attack me." Trembling, I pulled myself out from under him and glared into his eyes. I swear they'd changed. Not so gold anymore, not so animal.

The dog backed up a step, then another. Turning to consider the forest, it then glared back at me. With an undercurrent of growl, it snapped towards me.

Jumping, I whimpered, nodding my head. "Stay out of the forest. I get it."

With another growl, the dog turned and leaped over the cable I'd not seen, and back into the forest. Sobbing as the night became quiet around me again, I collapsed and bawled into my forearm.

I'd survived years of abuse and risked death to earn my freedom. To near die at the jaws of a wild animal on my first night of freedom was too much. Fate could be cruel.

Keep Reading

ALSO BY EBONY OLSON

Dark Urban Fantasy / Paranormal Romance

Standalones

Of Shadow and Light

Boundary

Halos (September 2020)

Hierarch Series

(Radish Fiction Exclusive)

Succumb

Numinous

Masked

Exodus (Coming 2020/21)

Raven's Wing Trilogy

(Radish Fiction Exclusive)

Phased